'I need to  **prepared to** **any further** **need to kno** **as Luka said**

'You'll do whate

The spitfire he had known was returning, and Sophie jabbed a finger into his chest as if to make her point.

'Whatever. It. Takes—'

'No,' he interrupted calmly.

Despite the cool façade she attempted, he knew that she was as Sicilian as the volcanic soil they were from, and as he watched her struggle to hold in her temper he didn't suppress his triumphant smile. She was just as volatile and passionate as he remembered. Those traits in Sophie were everything he both loved and loathed.

'After what you did…after what you said about me in court…'

'Lose the drama, Sophie.' His voice was completely calm. 'I accept that I have a moral debt to you, given all that has happened, but even with several years' interest added I do *not* owe you that much. I will agree to be your fake fiancé, but never your fake husband. Know that now, or get out.'

He hoped for the latter. *Get out of my life, my head, my heart. Just get out!*

Instead Sophie must have accepted his terms, for she sat down again.

It was time to talk business.

Playboys of Sicily

Taming Italy's most notorious men!

Tycoon Luka might agree to be ex-flame Sophie's
fake fiancé…but at what cost?

Sicilian's Shock Proposal
Available July 2015

Bella hasn't seen millionaire Matteo since *that* night.
He's as irresistible as ever, but will he still want her
after he discovers her secret?

His Sicilian Cinderella
Available August 2015

You won't want to miss this sizzlingly dramatic
new duet from *USA TODAY* bestselling author
Carol Marinelli—available only from
Mills & Boon® Modern™ Romance!

SICILIAN'S
SHOCK PROPOSAL

BY
CAROL MARINELLI

Published in Great Britain 2015
by Mills & Boon, an imprint of Harlequin (UK) Limited,
Eton House, 18-24 Paradise Road, Richmond, Surrey, TW9 1SR

© 2015 Carol Marinelli

ISBN: 978-0-263-25070-1

Printed and bound in Spain
by CPI, Barcelona

Carol Marinelli is a Taurus, with Taurus rising, yet she still thinks she's a secret Gemini. Originally from England, she now lives in Australia and is a single mother of three. Apart from her children, writing romance and the friendships forged along the way are her passion. She chooses to believe in a happy-ever-after for all, and strives for that in her writing.

Books by Carol Marinelli

Mills & Boon® Modern™ Romance

The Playboy of Puerto Banus
Playing the Dutiful Wife
Heart of the Desert
Innocent Secretary...Accidentally Pregnant

The Chatsfield

Princess's Secret Baby

Alpha Heroes Meet Their Match

The Only Woman to Defy Him
More Precious than a Crown
Protecting the Desert Princess

Empire of the Sands

Banished to the Harem
Beholden to the Throne

The Secrets of Xanos

A Shameful Consequence
An Indecent Proposition

**Visit the author profile page at
millsandboon.co.uk for more titles**

PROLOGUE

'A WOMAN WHO says she's your fiancée is in Reception, asking to see you.'

Luka Cavaliere looked up from his computer and saw the wry smile on his PA's face.

'I thought I'd heard it all until now,' said Tara.

Women would try anything to get an audience with Luka, but to have someone pretending to be his fiancée was a first. Tara knew from bitter experience that the woman in Reception was lying—the only thing that Luka ever fully committed to was work.

She certainly wasn't expecting his response.

'Tell Reception that she can come up,' he said in his rich Italian voice.

'Sorry?'

Luka didn't respond to Tara's question. Instead, he got back to the work he was doing on his computer. Certainly he did not need to repeat himself to his PA, nor explain things to her.

'Luka?' Still Tara hovered at the door, unable to believe that he knew who this woman was—he hadn't even asked for her name.

'Do you want a second warning?' Luka checked. 'I have already told you that I should not have to give out my instructions twice.'

'No, you want to *give* me a second warning so that soon you can fire me.' Tara's voice was thick with tears. 'You want me gone...?'

Of course he did.

'It's because we made love, isn't it?' she simpered.

He could correct her but he chose not to. Luka didn't make love—he had sex.

Often.

His wealth attracted shallow women, but his dark good looks and skills in the bedroom did not lead to the fleeting encounters that he preferred. Always they wanted more than he was prepared to give. He knew that he should never have got involved with his latest PA, especially when he'd just trained her up to be useful.

'I'm not going to get into a discussion,' Luka said. 'Send her up.'

'But you never said that you were engaged. You never even gave a hint that there was anyone else—'

Bored now, Luka thought. 'Take as long as you like for lunch,' he interrupted. Yes, he wanted her gone. 'Actually, you can take the rest of the day off.'

Tara let out a hopeless sob and then turned and rather loudly left the office.

The slam of the door made Luka's eyes shut for a brief moment.

It had nothing to do with his PA's brief outburst, or the noise from the door—it was what would happen in the coming moments that he was bracing himself for.

There had *always* been someone else.

And now she was here.

He stood up from his desk and moved to the window and looked down below to the London street. It was the middle of summer—not that he usually noticed. His life was spent in air-conditioned comfort and he dressed in the same dark suits whatever the month.

It was ironic, Luka thought, that he and Sophie, after all these years, should meet in London—the place of their far younger dreams.

Until recently he had always assumed that if they did come face to face again it would be in Roma, perhaps on one of his regular visits there. Or even back in Bordo Del Cielo—the coastal town on Sicily's west coast where had grown up. He had only returned once, for his father's funeral last year, but he had been wondering whether he might go back one final time if Sophie's father decided he wanted to be buried there.

Luka still hadn't made up his mind if, when that day came, he would attend the funeral.

He knew that that day was coming soon.

And that, he also knew, was the reason that Sophie was here.

His hand reached into his jacket and he took out not a photo, not a memory; instead, it was a brutal reminder as to why they could never be.

He stared at the thin gold chain that wrapped around his long fingers and then he looked at the simple gold cross that lay in his palm. Yes, he would go to her father's funeral, for this necklace belonged in that grave.

It took only a few moments for Sophie to make her way from the foyer to his suite yet it felt like for ever as he awaited her arrival, but then came the knock at the door that he recognised from yesteryear.

How much easier might his life have been had he not answered the door that long-ago day? Perhaps, Luka thought, he should not respond to it now.

He pocketed the necklace and cleared his throat.

'Come in.' He managed a deep summons but, as the door opened, he did not turn around.

'Your assistant asked me to pass on the message that she's just resigned. Apparently I'm the final straw.'

The sound of her voice, though a touch stilted and measured, still held, for Luka, the same caress.

For a man who feared little, he was nervous to turn around.

Luka rather hoped that the years that had passed since they'd last met had not treated her kindly—he fleetingly hoped that a nice little drug habit might have aged her terribly, or that she was pregnant with triplets perhaps...anything that might douse the eternal flame.

He turned and found out that time had indeed been cruel, to him at least, for perfection greeted his navy eyes.

Sophie Durante stood before him again.

She was wearing a simple dress in the palest ivory that showed her curvaceous figure. Her glossy, long black hair was worn neatly up in a French roll when he remembered it spilling over naked shoulders.

Her neutral-coloured high-heeled shoes enhanced her toned olive legs.

He forced his gaze up but only made it as far as her mouth. Her full lips were pressed tightly together when he remembered them once laughing and smiling. Then he remembered them somewhere else, which was a rather inconvenient image to have sprung to mind, so he forced himself to meet those dark brown eyes again.

She was just as beautiful as he remembered and, just as they had at their parting, her eyes showed she abhorred him.

Luka stared back with mutual loathing.

'Sophie.' He gave her a curt nod.

He did not know how he should greet her—shake her hand, or kiss both cheeks perhaps?

Instead, he gestured for her to take a seat.

She did so; placing her designer bag by the seat, she neatly crossed her legs at the ankles.

'You look well,' Luka said, and hoped she might miss that he then cleared his throat—for those first delicate traces of her scent had now reached him and his mind was firing taunting glimpses of memory.

'I am well,' she responded, and gave him a tight smile. 'I am very busy, of course.'

'Are you working?' Luka asked. 'Did you ever get to work on the ships?'

'No.' Sophie shook her head. 'I am an events planner.'

'Really?' He didn't even attempt to hide his surprise. 'You were always running late for everything.'

He glanced at the ring on her finger—a ruby stone set in Italian gold. It was very old-fashioned and far from what he would have chosen for her. 'I have terrible taste in rings, it would seem,' Luka said.

'Don't!' she warned abruptly. 'You will never insult me again.'

He looked up and into the eyes of the only woman he had ever made love to as she asked him a question.

'Aren't you going to ask why I am here?'

'I presume you're about to tell me.' Luka shrugged. He knew damn well why she was here but he'd make her say it just for the pleasure of watching her squirm.

'My father may be released from prison this Friday on compassionate grounds.'

'I know that.'

'How?'

'I do occasionally glance at the news.' Luka's sarcasm didn't garner a response, though his voice was kinder when he asked her a question. 'How is he doing?'

'Don't pretend that you care.'

'And don't *dare* assume that I don't!' he snapped, and he watched her rapid blink as he continued speaking.

Seeing her, he had been momentarily sideswiped but now he took back control and made a vow never to lose his control with her again.

'But, then, that's you all over, Sophie. Your mind was always made up even before the jury had been chosen. I'll ask you again. How is your father?'

'He is fading, he is a little confused at times.'

'I'm sorry to hear that.'

'Isn't that what prison does to an innocent man?'

Luka stared back and for now said nothing.

Paulo was not as innocent as Sophie made out.

'Not that a Cavaliere would know about prison,' she added.

'I spent six months in prison awaiting trial, two of them in solitary,' Luka pointed out. 'Or were you referring to my father being found not guilty?'

'I have no wish to discuss that man.' She couldn't, Luka noted, even bring herself to say his father's name. How much worse would this conversation be if she knew the truth? he wondered. He could almost feel the heat from the necklace in his pocket. He was actually tempted to toss it across the desk to her, to end them once and for all.

'Just what are you doing here, Sophie? I thought we ended our engagement a long time ago.'

'Firstly, I don't want you to think, for even a moment, that I am here for any romantic reasons.'

'Good, because it would be an extremely wasted journey if that were the case.'

'However,' she continued, 'my father believes that you upheld your promise. He thinks we got engaged and that we now live together in Rome.'

'Why would Paulo think that?'

'It was kinder to lie and let him think that you upheld your commitment to me. I never thought he would be let out and now that he might be I need to keep up the pretence. I told him that the terrible things you said in court about me were in an attempt to protect him.'

'They were,' Luka responded. 'I said what I did in the hope of protecting him, or rather protecting you. You simply refused to see it from my side.' He looked at her for a very long moment and found he could not stand even having her in the same room so he shook his head. 'It wouldn't work.'

'It *has* to work,' Sophie said. 'You owe me.'

'I do.' Luka did not concede with those words. He knew she spoke the truth. 'But apart from the fact that neither of us can abide being in the same room together, I do have a life. I might be seeing someone…'

'I don't care if this upends your life for a while. This is going to happen, Luka. You might sit a rich man in your posh London office and live a jet-set lifestyle but you are *from* Bordo Del Cielo, you cannot escape from that. You might go through women like tissues but the fact remains we were promised to each other from childhood and where we come from that means something.' Luka let out a tense breath as she asked again. 'Will you help my father die in peace?'

'You want me to move in with you and pretend that we live together?'

'No, I read that you have an apartment in Rome… we will use that.'

'Why not yours?'

'I share with my friend Bella. You might remember her...'

Luka bit back a sarcastic response. From what he had heard, a *lot* of men might remember Bella!

'She runs a business from our home.'

As she spoke, he noted that Sophie ignored his slight sardonic smile, even though she must know what it insinuated.

'It would not be fair to disrupt Bella and it would look odd for us, as a couple, to be sharing a home with her.'

'And would this loving couple be sharing a bed?' He voiced the obvious question but she did not answer directly.

'It would look strange for us to sleep apart.'

'Would there be sex?' he asked, wishing a blush would rise on her cheeks, for Sophie to give some indication that this hurt like hell for her also, but she stared back coolly as she delivered her response.

'I would think not,' she said. 'Since that evening, given what happened, I have a phobia...'

Luka's eyes widened. Was Sophie saying that there had been no one since him? There was a small rush of giddy relief that he quickly doused but she hadn't finished speaking. 'But if that is what it will take for you to agree, then, yes, there can be sex.'

'I thought Bella was the whore.'

'We can all be whores,' Sophie responded with spite, and Luka looked at the beautiful yet hostile stranger whose innocence he had taken, never to return. 'So, yes, if sex is to be part of the deal—'

'No, thanks,' Luka interrupted. 'I don't need charity sex and, anyway, martyrs don't turn me on—it's extremely willing participants that do.' He watched the slight swallow in her neck and he knew, he just knew she was remembering how good they had been so he cruelly walked her down memory lane and, as he did so, he reinforced a truth. 'Surely you know how much I like a woman who instigates things.'

He'd thought she'd blush as he pointed out how she had been the one who had practically begged him to make love to her yet, rather than blush, Sophie surprised him with a shrug and a smile.

'Well, there will be no sex for us, then, because I won't be instigating anything. Are you going to do this, Luka?'

'I'd like some time to think about it.'

'My father doesn't have time.'

'Leave me your business card, Sophie, I'll call you when I've made up my mind.'

He watched as she went into her bag and for the first time appeared flustered. 'I don't have any with me.'

'Give me your number.'

'I will contact you.' Sophie stood and went to leave but at the last moment changed her mind. 'You owe me this, Luka, we were promised to each other. You took my virginity.'

He could only admire her for, unlike most women, she spoke of their time together without misty recall. In fact, she reduced it to cold fact.

Almost.

'Took?' he checked. 'What an odd choice of word. You see, from my recollection…' Now a blush spread from her neck and rose to her cheeks. He came around the desk and stood in front of her, and she backed up to the desk. 'Are you going to jump up, Sophie…or do your prefer a kitchen bench to an office desk?'

Now she was struggling to keep her cool.

'Why didn't I marry you?' He played devil's advocate. 'You being such a good Sicilian girl…'

'I told my father that it was my dream for him to walk me down the aisle. I told him—'

'Stop there,' Luka interrupted. 'I need to think about what I'm prepared to agree to but before we go any further there is something that you need to know.' They were face to face as he said it. 'I will *never* marry you.'

'You'll do whatever it takes.' The spitfire he had known was returning and she jabbed a finger into his chest to make her point. 'Whatever. It. Takes.'

'No,' he calmly interrupted. Despite the cool facade she had attempted, he knew that she was as Sicilian as the volcanic soil they were from, and as he watched her struggle to hold in her temper, he didn't suppress his slight triumphant smile. She was just as volatile and passionate as he remembered. Those traits in Sophie were everything he both loved and loathed.

'After what you did, after what you said about me in court…'

'Lose the drama, Sophie,' His voice was completely calm. 'I accept that I have a moral debt to you, given all that happened, but, even with several years' interest added, I do not owe you that much. I will agree to be your fake fiancé, but never your fake husband. Know that now, or get the hell out.'

He hoped for the latter. Get the hell out of my life, my head, my heart.

Just get out!

Instead, Sophie must have accepted his terms for she sat back down.

It was time to talk business.

Finally, together, they would face the mistakes of their past.

CHAPTER ONE

'HAPPY BIRTHDAY FOR TOMORROW!'

Sophie smiled as Bella went into her bag and bought out a neatly wrapped package.

'Can I open it now?' Sophie asked. She already knew what it was—a dress for her engagement party next week. Even though they worked as chambermaids, Bella was a talented dressmaker and Sophie had spent the last few weeks having sheets of paper pinned to her. She couldn't wait to see the real thing. Bella had kept it a complete surprise and Sophie didn't even know what colour the dress was.

'Don't open it here.' Bella shook her head. 'Wait till you get home. You don't want to get sand on it.'

Though tired from the shifts as chambermaids at the Brezza Oceana hotel, just as they always did they had come to their secret cove. It wasn't really a secret cove but it was tucked behind jagged cliffs and could not be seen from the hotel. The tourists didn't really know about it as the small beach was accessible by a path that the locals of Bordo Del Cielo kept to themselves. When the hotel had first been built, much to the locals' disgust, it was here that Sophie and Bella would come after school. Now, even though they worked together most days, still the tradition remained.

Here, where no one might overhear them, they came and sat, their legs dangling in the azure water, chatting about their hopes and dreams and voicing some of their fears...

Not all of their fears, though.

Bordo Del Cielo was a town of secrets and some things were too dangerous for even the closest of friends to discuss.

'Now I can get on with making my own dress,' Bella said.

'What is yours like?'

'Grey,' Bella replied. 'Very simple, very sophisticated. Maybe then Matteo might notice me...'

Sophie laughed. Matteo was Luka's best friend and had been Bella's crush for years, but he had never given her so much as a glance.

'You must be getting excited,' Bella said, and Sophie was about to smile and nod.

In fact, she did so.

'Of course I am,' she said, but her smile, the one she had worn so determinedly whenever her upcoming engagement was discussed, suddenly wavered and rare tears started to fill her expressive brown eyes.

'Sophie?' Bella checked when she saw that her friend was struggling. 'Tell me.'

'I can't.'

'Are you worried about...?' Bella hesitated. 'Sleeping with him? I know he might expect you to once you are engaged but you could tell Luka that you are a good girl and want to wait for your wedding night.'

Sophie actually managed a small laugh. 'That's the only part I'm not worried about.'

It was the truth.

Oh, she hadn't seen Luka in years but she had grown

up nursing a crush on him. Luka's widowed father was rich; Malvolio owned the hotel and most of the businesses and homes in town. Those Malvolio didn't own he took payments from for their protection. When Luka's mother had died, instead of struggling to raise his child, in the way Sophie's father had, Malvolio had sent Luka away. He had attended boarding school on the mainland but, every summer when he'd returned, to Sophie he'd looked more beautiful. She had no doubt that the years he had spent in London wouldn't have dimmed that.

'I'm actually looking forward to seeing Luka again.'

'Remember how you cried when he left?'

'I was fourteen then,' Sophie said. 'Tomorrow I'll be nineteen…'

'Do you remember when you tried to kiss him?' Bella laughed and Sophie cringed in recall.

'He told me I was too young. I guess he would have been twenty then.' She smiled at the embarrassing memory of Luka dropping her from his lap. 'He told me to wait.'

'And you have.'

'He hasn't, though,' Sophie said, her voice bitter. Luka's reputation was as undeniable as the waves that pulled at their calves. 'He didn't back then, he was already screwing around.'

'Does it make you angry?'

'Yes, but more…' She felt a familiar burn rise in her chest—little bubbles of jealousy at the thought of Luka with other women that did not ease when they popped, for it felt like shards of glass were being released in her throat. 'I want what he has had.'

'You want to date other men?'

'No, I want my freedom,' Sophie said. 'I want to have

experiences and chase my own dreams. I've spent my life taking care of my father's home, cooking his meals, doing his washing. I don't know if I want to be someone's wife yet. I want to work on the cruise liners…' She looked out to the sparkling ocean. Travelling, sailing on the seas had always been her dream. 'I wouldn't mind making beds for a living if I could do it on a ship. It's like you with your dressmaking…'

'That's just a dream, though,' Bella said.

'Perhaps not. Your application might be accepted. You might be off to Milan soon.'

'I got rejected,' Bella said. 'My drawings weren't enough for them and I'll never be able to afford models and photographers for a decent portfolio.' Bella shrugged her shoulders as she both tried and failed to convince Sophie that not getting in to study fashion design in Milan didn't hurt like hell. 'I could never have gone anyway. I need my wage to pay the rent. Malvolio would give my mother hell if…' Bella's voice trailed off and she shook her head.

Yes, there were things that should never be discussed, but with her engagement now less than a week away Sophie could no longer keep her fears in. 'I don't want to be pulled even closer into Malvolio's life. I don't think Luka is anything like his father but—'

'Shh,' Bella said, and even though they had the cove to themselves she looked over both shoulders just to make sure. 'Don't speak like that.'

'Why not?' Sophie pushed. 'We're just friends talking.'

Bella said nothing.

'I don't want to get married.'

There—Sophie had said it.

'I'll be barely nineteen. There are so many things

I want to do before I settle down. I don't know if I want to…'

'You don't know if you want to live with Luka in a beautiful home and be taken care of?' Bella's response was one of anger. 'You don't know if you want to be rich and pampered?' Bella was starting to shout. 'Well, I'd take it if I were you and count yourself lucky—after your engagement party Malvolio has told me to stay back. I'll be working the bar. This time next week I won't be making beds at the hotel, I'll be…' Bella broke down then and Sophie held her own tears in check. 'Like mother, like daughter,' Bella sobbed. 'I am not ashamed of my mother, she did what she had to to survive, but I don't want that for me.'

'Then don't do it!' Sophie shook her head furiously. 'You are to tell him no!'

'Do you think for a moment that he'd listen?'

'You don't have to jump to his rules. He can't make you do anything that you don't want to.' Sophie was insistent. She loathed the way everyone jumped at Malvolio's command, her own father included. 'If you can't say no to Malvolio then I shall for you.'

'Just leave it,' Bella pleaded.

'No, I will not leave it. When Luka gets here on Wednesday I'll try speaking with him…'

'It won't do anything.' Bella shook her head and stood. 'I need to get back…'

They walked down the little pathway together and Bella apologised for her outburst. 'I didn't mean to be cross with you. I understand that it should be your choice if you marry.'

'We should both have choices,' Sophie said.

They didn't, though.

Everyone considered Sophie lucky—that, because

of her father's connections to Malvolio, she would marry Luka.

There had been no discussion with the future bride.

They came out of the trees and onto the hilly street and walked past the hotel Brezza Oceana, where Sophie and Luka's engagement party would be held.

'Are you taking your Pill?' Bella asked, because they had taken the bus two weeks ago to a neighboring town so that Sophie could get contraception without the local doctor knowing.

'Every day.'

'I'd better get some,' Bella said, and Sophie's heart twisted at the resignation in her friend's voice.

'Bella—'

'I have to go.'

'Will I see you tonight at church?'

'Of course.' Bella attempted a smile. 'I want to know if you like your dress.'

They parted ways and Sophie was almost home when she remembered she was supposed to have stopped for bread, so she turned and raced back to the deli.

As she walked in, the conversation stopped abruptly, just as it often did these days.

Sophie did her best to ignore the strange tension and when it was her turn she smiled at Teresa, the owner, and ordered the olives and cheese she had chosen, as well as a large pane Siciliano, which was surely the nicest bread in the world, and then took out her purse to pay.

'*Gratuitamente.*' Teresa told Sophie there would be no charge.

'*Scusi?*' Sophie frowned and then blushed. She was being let off paying because she was marrying Malvoio's son, Sophie decided. Well, she wanted no part in that sort of thing and angrily she took out some money, placed it on the counter and then walked out.

'You're late,' Paulo said, when Sophie let herself into their home and walked through to the kitchen, where her father was sitting reading his paper at the table. 'You would be late for your own funeral.'

'Bella and I got talking,' Sophie said.

'What do you have there?'

'Just some bread and olives…' Sophie answered, and then realised that he was referring to the parcel she was carrying, but before she explained what it was she asked her father a question. 'Father, when I went to pay, Teresa said there was no charge. Why would she say that?'

'I don't know.' Paulo shrugged. 'Perhaps she was being nice. After all, you are there every day.'

'No.' Sophie refused to be fobbed off. 'It was uncomfortable when I walked in—everyone stopped talking. I think it might have something to do with my getting engaged to Luka.'

'What is in the parcel?' Her father changed the subject and Sophie let out a tense breath as she set down the food and pulled out some plates.

'Bella gave me my birthday present a day early. It's my dress for my engagement. I'm going to try it on when I have had my shower. Father…' As she cut up the loaf Sophie did her best to sound casual. 'You remember you said I could have my mother's jewellery when I got engaged?'

'I said that you could have it when you got married.'

'No!' Sophie corrected. 'You told me years ago that I could have it when Luka and I got engaged. Can I have them now, please? I want to see how my dress looks with everything.'

'Sophie I've just sat down…'

'Then I will fetch them if you tell me where they are.'

Her father let out a sigh of relief as the phone rang and, though not prepared to get her mother's jewellery, he happily headed out to answer the phone.

He was always making excuses. For years Sophie had been asking for her mother's necklace and earrings and always he came up with different reason why she couldn't have them yet.

'Father...' she started as he came back into the kitchen.

'Not now, Sophie. Malvolio has called a meeting.'

'But it's Sunday,' Sophie said.

'He said that there is something important that needs to be discussed.'

'Well, surely it can wait till Monday?'

'Enough, Sophie,' her father snapped. 'It is not for me to question him.'

'Why not?' Sophie challenged. She was sick and tired of her father being Malvolio's puppet. 'What is this *meeting* about? Or is it just an excuse to sit in the bar for the evening?'

Surprisingly, her father laughed. 'You sound just like your mother.'

Everyone said the same. Rosa had had fire apparently, not that Sophie could remember her as she had died when Sophie was two.

'Here,' Paulo said, and handed her a small pouch. 'These are her jewels.'

Sophie let out a small gasp and then looked at her father and saw that he was sweating and a little grey.

'This means so much.'

'I know,' Paulo said, his voice shaken. 'There are only her earrings.'

'I thought there was a necklace...' In all the photos

Rosa wore a simple gold cross but she could hear the emotion in her father's voice when he told her that he didn't have it.

'It was a very fine chain. I believe that it came off in the accident. Even after all these years I still look for it in the bushes when I take my walk in the morning. I wanted you to have it. I'm so sorry that I cannot give that to you.'

'Is that why you haven't let me have them?' Sophie asked. 'Father, I just wanted something…anything of hers…' She looked at the fine gold hoops, that had a small diamond in each, with tears in her eyes. 'And now I have her earrings. Thank you so much.'

'I have to go to my meeting,' Paulo said, and Sophie pressed her lips together. She didn't want to fight, especially not when he had just given her something so precious, but her father looked terrible and she really did want him to rest. 'I'll try and get back for dinner.'

Sophie simply could not hold her tongue. 'If Malvolio lets you.'

She saw her father's eyes shut for a brief moment before he turned and headed for the door.

Sophie knew it might be kinder to apologise and that she was maybe making things harder for her father by admitting her truth but she didn't like his involvement with Malvolio.

'Father, I don't know if I am ready to get engaged…' She held her breath as her father's shoulders stiffened.

'It is normal to be nervous,' her father said, but did not turn around. 'Sophie, I have to go.'

'Father, please, can we talk…?'

But the door had already closed.

Sophie walked around the small home and picked up a picture of her mother. She could see the similarities there—they had the same long black hair, the same dark brown eyes and full lips. Oh, Sophie wished she was here, just for a moment. She missed having a mother to give her advice so badly.

'I am so confused,' Sophie admitted to the photo of Rosa. A part of her dreaded being married, yet there was another part of her that longed to see Luka again, the man who had always filled her dreams. She had always looked up to him, had always nursed a crush on him, and she wanted her first kiss to belong to them and to be made love to by Luka.

What would Luka want, though?

She blushed in embarrassment at the thought of him returning and being forced to marry her.

No doubt he was dreading next weekend and returning to uphold his father's commitment for him to marry poor little Sophie Durante.

Was that the hold Malvolio had over her father? Sophie wondered.

Well, she didn't need charity and she would tell her father that.

She put down the photo, took her parcel upstairs and finally opened it.

The dress was exquisite. It was in the softest chiffon and the colour was a very pale coral. Sophie badly wanted to try it on but she had a very quick shower and washed her hair and then combed it before picking up the dress.

She slipped it over her head and looked in the mirror.

Sophie found she was holding her breath. All those hours standing as Bella had pinned sheets of paper had been worth it for this moment.

The dress was amazing. It was scooped low at the front and showed Sophie's cleavage. Of course, it would

need a bra but even without it was somehow both elegant and sexy. It came in at the waist and then fell in
layers, emphasising her curves when usually Sophie
did what she could to downplay them.

Yes, she knew she should take it off but instead she
put on her mother's earrings and found the lip glaze
she had bought.

Working at the hotel, Sophie was used to seeing
beautiful women but this afternoon, for the first time
in her life, she felt like one.

Now she blushed for different reasons when she
imagined facing Luka.

She wanted him to see her grown up.

Briefly she imagined his mouth on hers but a loud
knocking on the door snapped her out of her daydream.

It sounded urgent and Sophie ran through the house
but she smiled when she opened the door and saw that
it was just Pino on his bike.

He was twelve years old and everyone used him as
a messenger.

'Malvolio wants you to go to his home,' Pino said in
a self-important voice.

'Malvolio.' Sophie frowned. She had never been to
Malvolio's home. 'Why? What does he want?'

'I was just told to give you the message,' Pino said,
balancing on his bike. 'He said that it is important and
that you're to go there now.'

Sophie went and got Pino some money and thanked
him but her heart was racing.

Why would Malvolio ask her to go to his home?

She had assumed that he and her father were meeting at the hotel bar.

Sophie thought of her father's grey complexion and

the sweat on his face and was suddenly worried that he might have been taken ill.

She slipped on some sandals and ran up the hill towards Malvolio's spectacular home, which overlooked not just the ocean but the entire town. Once there she took a breath and then knocked on the door. She didn't want to be there but he had summoned her after all.

No one ever said no to Malvolio.

CHAPTER TWO

'Why don't you ask Sophie to come over?'

Luka let out a tense breath at his father's suggestion. Against his father's wishes he had been in London for the last six years, at first studying but now he was now starting to make a name for himself.

He had offered some financial advice to a boutique hotel, but when unable to pay him to implement the changes Luka had offered to work for them for a stake in the hotel.

It had been a gamble. For a year he had worked for nothing by day and earned money by working in a bar at night.

Now, though, the hotel was starting to flourish and Luka owned ten percent of a thriving business.

Luka had his start.

He could have it all here, he knew that.

His father was one of the wealthiest men in Sicily, and he should be stepping in now. His father thought he was back to settle down and start taking over his empire, but instead Luka was choosing to step out for good.

His time away had opened his eyes. With an increasing awareness of his father's corrupt ways he had chosen to stay away and had made only the occasional trip home to Sicily.

Deliberately he hadn't seen or spoken to Sophie in that time.

And in that time an awful lot had changed.

'It might be nice to spend some time with her before the engagement party,' Malvolio pushed. 'Angela will be at church all day and I know that there is a bible meeting this evening she wants to attend,' he said, referring to their maid. 'I'll go out and give you two some time—'

'There isn't going to be an engagement party,' Luka said, and met the eyes of his father—a man who he did not even recognise, for Luka had come to understand that he had never really known his father at all. 'Because there isn't going to be an engagement. I'm not marrying Sophie Durante.'

'But the two of you have been promised to each other since childhood.'

'That was your promise, not mine,' Luka said. 'You chose my future wife, the same way you have chosen for me to follow in the family business. I'm here to tell you that I am going to be returning to London. I'm not going to live and work here.'

'You can't do that to Paulo, to Sophie.'

'Don't pretend you care about them,' Luka said, and watched his father start to breathe harder as he realised the challenge he was facing.

'I won't let you do it to me,' Malvolio said. 'You will not shame the Cavaliere name.'

Luka jaw gritted. His father had no shame. His father took from the poor, from the sick, his father ruled the people of Bordo Del Cielo with an iron fist—*there* was the real shame.

'I will speak with Sophie's father and explain that I will not have a bride chosen for me. The same way that

I will not have my career, nor the place on this planet where I live, dictated to me.'

'You will destroy Sophie's reputation.'

'I am not discussing this,' Luka said. 'I am telling you that I shall speak with Paulo about my decision and then, if he will allow me to, I will talk to Sophie myself.'

'You are not returning to London, you will work with me. After all I have done for you—'

'Don't!' Luka said. 'Don't say that you did all this for me when I never asked for any of it.'

'But you took,' Malvolio said. 'You have lived in the best home and I gave you the very best education. I have a business waiting for you to take over. I will not let you walk out on that.'

'Let me?' Luka checked. 'It's not for you to choose how I live. I don't need your permission for anything.' He went to walk off but his father stopped him in the way he knew best.

Luka, at twenty-four, could have halted the punch that was coming to him but he did not. His father sent him crashing back into the wall and there was a gush of warm blood down his face. Not that it would stop Malvolio.

His only son, his only child was now turning his back on everything Malvolio had worked for and Luka had known that it would come to this.

Too often, growing up, it had.

As his head hit the wall his father thumped him in the stomach and as Luka doubled over Malvolio's fist came into his ribs, but all it did was reaffirm to Luka that his decision to leave for good was the right one.

While he did not hit his father, Luka pulled himself back to his feet and faced him. 'Clever men fight with their minds,' Luka said, as Malvolio raised his fist again. 'Whereas you instil fear…' He shrugged his father off. 'But not in me. The next punch you deliver will be returned,' he warned—and he meant it.

'You will marry her.'

Luka might not have fought back but anger raged through his veins. He loathed his father's assumptions and the way he dictated his life, and he told him so.

'I live in London,' he shouted. 'I date models now, glamorous, sophisticated women, not some peasant that you have chosen for me.'

'I have to go to a meeting,' Malvolio hissed. 'We will speak of this when I return.'

Luka said nothing, standing bruised and bleeding and a bit breathless as his father picked up his car keys and stormed out.

He headed up to his old bedroom and stripped off his shirt then went into his bathroom and examined the damage.

There was bruising to his ribcage and on his shoulder where it had met the wall. An old gash above his eyes had opened up and probably needed stitching.

Not now, though.

For now he would patch himself up and then head to the airport. He might call Matteo and ask if he wanted to meet for a drink but they would meet at the airport.

He was done with Bordo Del Cielo.

Sophie.

As he splashed cold water on his face he thought of her.

Yes, this would be hell for her, Luka knew that and it didn't sit right with him. Perhaps before he left for good he should go and speak with Paulo and maybe Sophie too.

He pressed his bloodied shirt over his eye and went

into his suitcase to find a fresh one. He hadn't unpacked. Luka hadn't even been back home for an hour before the argument had started.

He heard a knock at the door but ignored it.

Angela could get it, but then he remembered that she was at church.

There was another knock but more loudly this time, and Luka headed down the stairs and opened the door.

The breath that had just returned after his father had knocked it out of him stilled inside Luka now.

His voice, when it finally came, was low and curious, and even though he said but one word there was a slight huskiness.

'Sophie?'

He was struggling to meet her eyes. In the argument that had just taken place, as he had attempted to wrestle back his life from his father's control, things had been said about Sophie.

Things she did not deserve.

It had been said in the heat of the moment. Vile words in a vile row and Luka could taste bitterness along with blood in his mouth.

Now, though, as finally he looked at her, there was a pleasant silence. No other thoughts other than this moment.

Her eyes were the same, yet more knowing. Her mouth was full and she was wearing a little make-up.

Her hair was thicker and longer.

And her body—he could not help but briefly look down. The skinny teenager he remembered had left and in her place stood a very beautiful woman.

One whose heart he was about to break.

CHAPTER THREE

'LUKA?' SOPHIE FROWNED. 'I didn't think you were getting here till Wednesday.'

'There was a change of plan.'

'What happened?' Sophie asked.

'I decided to fly home earlier—'

'I meant to your face.'

'It's just a cut,' Luka said. 'An old cut that opened up.'

'The bruises are new,' Sophie pointed out, and he gave a pale smile.

'My father,' he admitted.

Sophie didn't really know what to say to that so she cleared her throat and got back to the reason she was standing at the door.

'I just had a message from Pino. Your father said I was to come here. That it was important.'

'I can guess why,' Luka said. No doubt his father had thought that one look at Sophie and he would change his mind. Well, he wasn't that shallow. He saw her frown as he explained things a little better. 'I think my father wanted us to be alone.'

'Oh.'

'You know how manipulative he can be,' Luka said.

She didn't answer. Everyone might think that of Malvolio but no one would ever dare to say it.

'Come in, Sophie.' He held open the door and after a moment's hesitation she stepped inside. 'We need to talk.' She followed him through to the kitchen, her eyes taking in his back and wide shoulders, and she felt very small and not in a nice way.

He was so glossy, so sophisticated, he was everything that she wasn't.

Of course he wouldn't want her.

And now, from the little he had said, and the way he couldn't quite meet her eyes, Sophie guessed she was about to be told that.

Yes, she had her doubts about the engagement—yes, she wasn't sure if she wanted to get married—but it felt very different from being told to your face that you weren't wanted.

'I just need to sort out this cut,' Luka said. 'Take a seat.'

She didn't.

'I don't know where Angela keeps the first-aid kit,' Luka continued as he went through the cupboards. 'Here it is.' Sophie watched as he pulled out a small first-aid kit and even smiled as his long fingers tried to open a sticking plaster while holding the shirt over his eye.

'It needs more than a plaster,' Sophie said. 'You need a doctor to stitch it.'

'I'll get it sutured tomorrow if it needs it,' Luka said. 'In London.'

He looked up and caught her eye but she didn't respond to his opening.

She'd damn well make him say it, Sophie decided.

'I'll do it,' Sophie said, because it really was a nasty cut. She took out the scissors then cut the sticking plaster into thin strips onto the kitchen bench, and as she did so Luka spoke.

'You look well.'

Sophie gave a wry smile. At least he had got to see her in her beautiful dress, she thought with slight relish. She knew she looked her very best and it was a rather nice thing to know when you were about to be dumped.

Let him think she ran around on a Sunday in coral chiffon with lip gloss and jewellery...

And no underwear, Sophie remembered, as she jumped up onto the kitchen bench and quickly put her dress between her thighs.

'Come here,' Sophie said, now that she had set up for the small procedure.

'I don't want to get blood on your dress.'

It didn't matter now if her dress was ruined, Sophie knew. This was the only time that he'd be seeing her in it. 'Oh, this old thing.' She shrugged. 'Don't worry about it.'

Luka went over to where she sat and stood as Sophie concentrated on closing the cut.

'Why were you two fighting?'

'We weren't fighting,' Luka said. 'He was taking out his temper on me. I chose not to hit him back. This one last time.'

'I hate how he treats you,' Sophie said, and her hand paused over the cut as she deliberated with herself whether or not to continue. 'How he treats everyone.'

She thought of Bella and if there was any good that could come out of this then she'd damn well find it.

'Bella's mother is sick,' Sophie said. 'She can't work and now he wants Bella to start doing shifts at the hotel bar.' She assumed, given that his eyes refused to meet hers, that he knew what that meant. 'Can you speak with him for me?'

'Sophie, before we discuss Bella I need to speak first with you.'

'I get that you do,' she said, 'but I would like to speak about this first'. Sophie persisted because she knew she might lose her temper about five minutes from now. Yes, she didn't want to be forced into a marriage but, no, she didn't want to be left here either.

It wasn't just her pride that was going to hurt when he ended things—now that he was back her heart remembered him.

Standing before her was the man she had cried herself to sleep over when he had left last time.

It had been a childish crush, a schoolgirl's dream, a teenage fantasy, Sophie's head knew that but, having him back, feeling him close, her heart was racing again and her body wanted to taste first-hand her forbidden dreams. Yes, soon that Sicilian temper might get the best of her, so she would speak with him now, about the things that possibly could be sorted, while there was relative calm.

Relative, for her legs ached to wrap around him and the tongue that went over her lips now was inadvertently preparing herself for him. 'Bella doesn't want to work in the bar.'

She could sense his discomfort and guessed that it had little to do with the pain from the cut, more the subject matter.

'I'll speak to him,' Luka offered, 'but first I need to speak with you. I was going to go and see Paulo—'

'Luka…' Her hand was on his cheek and she wanted to halt him, wanted to kiss him, to make love and then deal with the rest.

Please, don't say it, she wanted to beg.

Not yet, not until I have finally tasted you.

'Luka, I know this is difficult but…'

She was right. Luka was not looking forward to this conversation one bit. He wondered how best he could tell her his reasoning without destroying her belief in her father.

It was also difficult for other reasons.

Yes, Malvolio was a manipulative bastard and Luka knew that he wasn't shallow enough to change his mind just because Sophie looked sensational. Still, it was rather hard to stand there at eye level with the ripe swell of her breasts, with the warm, musky scent of her reaching into him and then to look into eyes that, Luka realised, knew him.

Perhaps their fathers had chosen more wisely than he had given them credit for, because the ache in his groin and the surprising pleasure of talking to her had momentarily upended his plans.

He had to go through with it, Luka knew.

He had to deny the attraction, the want that was there between them.

Her pupils were large with lust, and he was sure that so too were his as they stared back to her. How the hell did you tell someone it was over when you were hard for them? When you knew, just knew, that with one slip of your hand those gorgeous thighs would part?

He needed to tell her they were over now, right now, before he gave in to the kiss they both wanted, and so he spoke on. 'My father was angry because I told him I wouldn't be coming back to Bordo Del Cielo and instead I would be living permanently in London. I told him I wanted no part of his life. I said that I won't have him choose where I live, how I work—'

'Don't I get a say in where we live?' Sophie said, refusing to make this easy for him.

She wanted to slap him.

Now that he was here, she wanted not just her dreams of freedom and working on the ships, she wanted him too.

Luka, who had swum in the river with her, Luka, who had told her the night he'd left her aching to be kissed by him that she must wait. He had been twenty years old when he had prised her off his lap and she had clung to him like glue.

She wanted the kiss that he had promised her then.

Instead, she finished closing his wound and then put a large plaster over the top as she spoke. 'My father will be upset. He always thought that I would live close to him and that our children would grow up in Bordo Del Cielo.'

Don't do this, she wanted to warn, though she knew that he was right to.

'In my time away, I've come to understand things.' Luka ran a tongue over tense lips as he reminded himself that he was going to do this without criticising her father. 'The way my father conducts business, the way my mother used to turn a blind eye to terrible deeds...' She looked at that beautiful mouth in his unshaven jaw and he confirmed her darkest thoughts. Malvolio was pure evil. 'I don't want any part of it,' Luka said.

'I don't like the hold he has on my father,' Sophie admitted. 'I don't think my father...' She couldn't bring herself to say it but she tried. 'I think some of my father's dealings are also wrong.'

'That's his choice,' Luka said. 'And I am making my own. I don't think that a promise our fathers made on our behalf should be something we feel we have to adhere to. I think we should be able to date and fall in love with whoever we choose.'

'And have you been dating?' Sophie asked, and Luka said nothing. 'Because if you have then it doesn't seem very fair when I have kept myself for you. I haven't so much as kissed another man, even though I have wanted to.' That was a lie, she'd never want another man. She had only ever wanted him. 'I have been to dances and parties and nothing, *nothing* has ever happened.'

Luka remained silent and Sophie assumed then that he was serious about someone.

'Is *she* insisting we break up?' The jealousy in her voice was not faked. Sophie's skin prickled at the thought of him with another woman.

'There is no *one* she,' Luka said. 'I have not been serious about any one person in particular, but...'

'You have been dating?'

'Yes.'

'You've kissed, made love...' all the things she had guessed he would be doing, all the things she had wanted Luka to do with her '...while all the time you were promised to me.'

Her hand came up then and he would have accepted a slap to the cheek but, hell, he'd just got the wound closed so he caught her wrist.

'You still have good reflexes,' Sophie said, because she had watched him play sport, catch a fork, grab her arm before she fell...

Luka frowned at the light tone to her voice and turned his attention from the wrist he was still holding and then saw that she was smiling.

'Sophie?'

'Perhaps I am not best pleased that you have been

having fun while I keep myself pure for you, but maybe
I am a little relieved too…'

He had never expected this reaction but, then, Luka
remembered, she had always surprised him. Sophie
had always made him either smile or want to tear his
hair out in frustration. He'd never known what to expect from her.

'I thought—'

'You thought that I would cry and plead and say that
you have shamed me. Well, I guess that in the eyes of
everyone here you will have shamed me, but I don't
care what they all think. I am nineteen tomorrow, Luka,
and I want a life. I want more fun than I could have as
your wife.'

'Were you ever going to tell me this?'

'I was.' Sophie smiled. 'But after we had made love.
I went and got the Pill…'

'What, did you think I'd be more open to suggestion then?'

'That had crossed my mind.' She smiled again.

'You're really okay with it?' Luka frowned because
this reaction had been far from the one he had been
expecting.

'Of course,' she said, and then her voice dropped.
'Apart from one thing.'

Yes, she always surprised him.

'You still owe me that kiss.'

'Sophie, you don't end a relationship with a kiss.'

'Why not?' she said. 'I want you to be my first kiss.'

'Sophie—'

'It has to be you,' Sophie said, because quite simply
it had to be. She sat on the kitchen bench and her hands
went up and linked loosely behind his neck.

'Remember the party, the night you left for London?'

'Of course I remember.'

'Did you want to kiss me then?'

'No,' Luka said. Then she had been a girl, a teary teenager, now there was no doubt that a woman sat before him—and one who knew what she wanted.

'Do you want to kiss me now?' Sophie asked.

He answered with his lips. She felt the soft weight of his mouth and though she did not want to marry Luka, it did not mean she did not find him beautiful. Every kiss that Sophie had ever missed out on was made up for by this.

He held her face and his mouth was gentle. The last seconds of her lip glaze ensured their soft passage and his kiss was exactly as it should be, better even than anticipated. A soft tasting that had her hands move to his chest as they had ached to do on sight.

In her dreams he had crushed her mouth and his tongue had fiercely parted her lips, but in reality he had no need to for her mouth readily opened to his and mutually their kiss deepened.

Her palms pressed to his naked chest and as his tongue slipped in she slid her hands, loving the feeling of strength beneath the skin. His breathing was harsher as her hands moved over his flat, mahogany nipples and then it was Sophie who took his face in her hands.

She felt he was going to halt their kiss so her tongue pleaded for him not to. She wanted this just as he did.

She wanted his hand that was now stroking at her breast through the fabric of her dress and as her nipple thickened to the touch of his thumb he let out a small moan that sent a vibration to her core. He stepped in closer and her legs parted to enable him to. One hand still toyed with her breast while the other slid up the outside of her smooth thigh, but when he encountered her naked bottom he stilled and pulled his mouth back a little.

'Do you always run around with no underwear on?'

'You'll never know.' Sophie smiled and Luka returned it but when she went to kiss him he moved his mouth back and she ached because he had halted. 'Please, Luka…'

'You said a kiss.'

'*We* want more than a kiss.'

She was so certain in that moment that she could speak for them both.

'I'm not ending things *and* taking your virginity,' Luka said. 'You've already got enough reasons to call me a bastard.'

'Then don't give me another one,' Sophie warned. 'I cried every night for a month when you left but I'm not going to cry this time. You've had all my tears, Luka. I just want a part of what was promised to me.'

'Which part?'

'This part.'

His eyes closed as her hand found him and she ran her fingers over his length. Lightly at first but then she pressed her fingers in a little.

She had never been shy around Luka.

She had never been shy.

She watched as he closed her eyes and felt the bliss as he grew to her touch. The ache in her groin grew too and so Sophie wriggled provocatively closer to the only man she had ever wanted.

She met his ear and kissed it as he pulled her in firmly.

'I want you to be my first.' She stated her wishes. 'It has to be you, Luka… It was *always* going to be you.'

CHAPTER FOUR

GONE WAS THE girl he had tipped from his knee all those years ago. Gone was the teary teenager. Instead of pleading, instead of crying, now she seduced.

Now she removed her hand from where it was teasing him and stopped the dance with her tongue on his ear so that she could watch his eyes open.

With a smile, in one lithe easy motion, she pulled off her dress and naked she sat before him, watching his eyes roam the lushness of her breasts.

'This part,' Sophie said again, and with her legs balanced on his hips she unzipped and freed him.

He was beautiful. His skin was soft and dark and together they watched her explore him till Luka could take it no more. He was there at her entrance and Sophie was guiding him in, her jaw tensing as he stretched her but the rest of her was loose and willing.

'Not here,' Luka said, even though it was contrary to his action, for he was inching just a little more inside her tight space.

'Yes, here,' Sophie urged.

They wanted each other's mouths yet the top of their heads were locked, watching as if from the edge of paradise as he inched in a little further. Bordo Del Cielo meant the edge of heaven and that was exactly where both of them were as he stretched her.

'Not here,' Luka warned again, despite her frantic pleas for him to continue. 'I'm taking you to my bed.'

He tried to zip up but with the protest of her kisses and the scent and oil of her on his fingers further turning him on it was like trying to reset a jack-in-the-box. He gave in and just kicked off his pants and got back to kissing her as he lifted her from the kitchen bench. With her legs coiled around him they kissed all the way up the stairs.

'Here,' Sophie said, when they were halfway up and he halted just to taste her deeper. He almost relented but then reminded himself of a part of the need for getting to his bedroom.

'I've got condoms in my case.'

'I told you we don't need them.'

They just made it to the bedroom and he dropped her onto the bed but, unlike the last time when he'd had had to peel her from him, now, loose-limbed, she let herself fall—because this time Sophie knew that in a moment he'd join her.

'I told you I've already gone on the Pill,' she said, watching the delicious sight of him kneeling and trying to open up his case.

'It's for protection.'

'I've never needed protection from you.'

Innocent, Luka thought, but only to a point. Her words were more seductive than any he had ever heard. Nothing would usually halt him—sheathing was, to Luka, second nature. Not with Sophie, though, because he wanted the naked bliss of them together. Later he would scold her, and warn her not to trust another with such a choice. She was right, though; she needed no protection from him.

'I know what I want, Luka.'

He came over to the bed where she lay and like a panther he crawled with stealth that had her writhing until he was with her, and she would never forget his smile.

'I'm going to talk to you later.'

'You're going to make love to me now, though.' Sophie smiled back.

'Are you nervous?'

'I've never been nervous with you.'

It was true. Around him she was not nervous. How could she be scared? Sophie briefly pondered when the mouth that made her shiver returned to hers.

They kissed naked and long and then he left her mouth and blazed a hot, wet trail down her neck and then to her breasts, where he licked the warm skin, avoiding her aching nipples till her hands guided his head. It was Sophie who moaned as his mouth captured her and sucked deeply, not once, not twice, but over and over till she twitched and writhed. How could she be nervous when her body just came alive to him?

She loved how he gave the same attention to the other breast and yet she was almost pleading for him to stop because he had lifted just a fraction of the lid and she was greedy for the treasure he would bring.

Luka knew it.

He knelt up for a moment and looked down at her.

Her mouth was swollen from his kisses, her breasts were wet and her nipples erect, and there was a small purple bruise on her perfect skin that his mouth had made.

'Luka...' Sophie liked the warmth of his eyes and

the affection of his gaze yet she was on fire. He was intimately stroking himself against her as he had downstairs, but there was no holding back as there had been then—this was just a moment of pure decadent indulgence.

She felt like his instrument, tuned purely for him to play to perfection, and he did. She looked down and this time watched him disappear further in.

'It might hurt,' Luka said.

'It had better.'

He laughed and toppled onto her. His weight was half on her and yet not enough; she liked the feeling of being lost beneath him—how the sight of the ocean from his window no longer existed, how the bark of a dog in the distance receded, how it was late in the afternoon and she welcomed the light just to see his closed eyes as he kissed her. Sophie's friends had needed wine, or long dances, some had demanded the promises of a love that would never die before this.

All Sophie needed was Luka, for this was just how it was supposed to be.

Luka was torn. He wanted to taste her breasts again, he wanted to kiss and make moist every inch of her skin, he wanted the musk of her sex on his tongue, not just his fingers. Badly he wanted her to come to his mouth, but he was as impatient to be inside as Sophie was to be taken.

Later, he told himself.

There would be time for that later.

Like a chip to his skull, somewhere he refuted that, because they ended today, this was it.

Yet there, in that second, Luka knew he would take her again, that this was not the end.

And, yes, he could feel her impatience. Her hips kept

lifting, her mouth was more demanding and then there was almost anger as he removed his kiss.

'Luka.' She was breathless.

'Now!' Luka said, that one word taking such effort to deliver.

'Yes, now,' she said, but then she saw his slow, teasing smile.

'I mean *now* is when you can get anything you want from a man.' He was referring to her earlier innocent thinking. 'Not after...'

'I'll remember that for the future.'

She did not understand the flare of possession in his eyes as she spoke of others, but she didn't have time to dwell on it for he took her then. Luka seared into her and swallowed her sob with his mouth.

It hurt, far more than she had expected it to, far better than she had ever dared dream. He filled her and stretched her and, when she thought she knew what it was to be his lover, still further he went tearing at virgin flesh and then stilling as her body fought to acclimatise to him.

She forgot how to breathe until he gathered her right into him and hooked his arm beneath the small of her back.

'Luka...' Sophie didn't even know what she wanted or what it was she was trying to say, but as he started to move any pain was forgotten because with each thrust he made her more his. His mouth was by her ear now, and he spoke as he did in her dreams. 'I won't hurt you...' he said, when she now knew that he would.

The pain of being taken by him was receding. It was the pain of being left by him that was now starting to make itself known.

She wished that her body didn't love him so completely. She wished that he would take her deeper, harder, faster, rather than deliver, as he was now, the slow torture of his love, because that was exactly what this felt like.

As her legs coiled around him, even as she urged him on, Sophie was frantically trying to hold back.

How do I let you leave? she wanted to sob as her orgasm gathered.

'Luka…' She said it again as she started to come and the intensity scared her.

'Let it happen…' Luka said, and his rapid thrust gave her no choice but to do as his body commanded.

Inwardly he beat her to match his rhythm but it wasn't that that had her toppling over the edge, it was Luka, and the feel of his shoulders tense beneath her hands. It was the last look at the world without fully having the other, this strange brink they both found themselves on. Luka was in that beat before coming, past the point of no return when he felt her pulse to him and he just unleashed. Nothing could ever top this, he knew. Her intimate pulses beckoned and he gave in to the tight, soft warmth of her endless caress.

For Sophie it was the sensation of falling but not a gentle one.

Every bump, every sob, every fear seemed enacted in slow motion. She wanted to curl up in protection but his hands held down her arms. She hoped for a moment of clarity but he was pounding her senses again. Kissing her hard as his climax receded and then thrusting again, giving up the very last of himself as she lay there, knowing she had nothing left to give.

She had been taken.

CHAPTER FIVE

'So that's what it feels like,' Sophie said.

'Not usually.'

They were lying in his bed and watching the evening sun over the ocean.

Sophie's head was resting on his chest and she watched a cruise liner glint in the distance.

'Not *usually*?' she checked.

'Truth?' he asked, and she nodded. 'There is usually a knot of disquiet.' He took her hand and he placed it just beneath where his ribs joined, and he pushed her fingers in. 'Just there.'

'Why?'

'I don't know,' he admitted.

He moved his hand to the same place on her. 'Do you have it?'

'No,' Sophie admitted. 'No knots, no disquiet.'

She knew what he meant, though, as she tried to imagine a moment where the man lying there wasn't Luka.

It felt written in her DNA that this time belonged to him.

'You really want to work on them?' Luka asked, and they must have both been looking at the same thing because he voiced her thoughts.

'No, I really want to be a guest on one of them.' Sophie smiled. 'But for now working on one would be wonderful.'

'What would your father say?' Luka asked.

'What *will* my father say?' Sophie corrected, because it was going to happen, she was determined, but she answered his question. 'I don't know how he's going to react,' she said, listening to the thud of Luka's heart as he stroked her hair. So much had changed now. 'I guess people will understand that I might want to get away after the shame of you dumping me.' She laughed and dug him in the ribs but then she was serious. 'I don't know how my father will be about it but I don't think I can factor that in when I make my choice... I don't know if I want to stay here in Bordo Del Cielo, Luka. There is too much past...'

They were the same, Luka realised.

'I think my father is up to no good,' Sophie admitted. 'I love him yet I want to get away from him. I want no part in that type of life.'

During his last years at school Luka had started to question the way things worked here and he had fought hard to go to university in England. There, his eyes had been fully opened as to his father's ways and from that distance he had decided to stay away.

Sophie had worked it out from here, Luka thought.

Or was starting to.

'My father doesn't work, he sits in a bar most of the day and into the night. What are these meetings he says that he has to go to?' She looked up from his chest and instead of giving her an answer or avoiding the subject he offered the unexpected.

'Come to London with me,' Luka said.

'With you?'

'You could apply to the cruise liners from there. I

could help you to get on your feet. I am a part owner of a hotel, you could work there till you get your dream job...'

Sophie lay there, thinking about it. She wasn't surprised that he part owned a hotel—Malvolio would have seen to it that his son was looked after.

'I have a flat,' Luka said. 'You could stay with me for a while.'

'Stay with you?' Sophie blinked. 'I don't know if that would work out...'

'Why not?'

'Luka, while I accept this is a one-off, I really don't want to be there if you bring another woman home...'

It angered her that he laughed and Sophie climbed from the bed. 'I'm going to have a shower and then I have to go to church...' She stopped talking when she saw the sheets that bore the evidence of what had just taken place. 'Oh.'

'I'll sort it all out,' Luka said. 'I'm not going to leave them for Angela. Go and have your shower...'

As Sophie did so she thought about what Luka had suggested and she thought too about her cross response.

It was true.

She somehow had to hold in her jealousy at the thought of him with someone else. She'd agreed to break things off, a part of her had even been happy about it and certainly she had been relieved...

That had been before they'd made love, though.

How could once with Luka ever be enough?

He had taken her, left her exhausted and sated.

Now, though, even the recent memory was bringing her back to sensual life. She soaped her tender breasts and saw the bruise that his mouth had made. Her sex was hot and swollen and as Sophie soaped the last traces of him away she wanted him again.

She walked out with a towel around her to the sight of a naked Luka changing the sheets. Now from a relative distance she could admire his naked beauty. He was tall and lean and she could see the muscles on his thighs as he bent to rather haphazardly tuck in the sheet. His shaft, though soft against his leg, lifted a little from the movement and she wanted to take the sheet from his hand and get back to bed.

'Is that the first bed you have ever made?' Sophie teased, trying to keep things light.

'It is the first bed I have ever made in Bordo Del Cielo,' Luka answered. He looked to where she stood and wondered if what he had to offer would be enough. She thought him rich and, in London, he wasn't.

Yet.

'Sophie, I have a small flat in London…' Luka would explain it all to her later, he decided. He would go into detail about how he had removed himself completely from his father, that his ways were honest. But he wasn't going to do that here, and anyway there was something else that needed to be addressed before they got to family stuff. Today was about them, about the possibility of a future away from Bordo Del Cielo. 'What you said before about me bringing another woman home if we lived in London, I would not do that to you. In the same way I wouldn't like it if you were staying with me and saw anyone else…'

'I don't understand what you are saying.'

'I'm saying that I don't want it to be over between us. Maybe I don't want to commit to marriage, or getting engaged just yet, it is far too soon for that, but we can date,' Luka said. 'Once we get to London we can go out and get to know each other away from our families. We can do things our way, without all the pressure and expectations.'

Sophie could feel the goose-bumps on her bare arms as she realised that Luka wasn't just offering her a way out of Bordo Del Cielo but a way out *with* him.

'Can I still apply to work on the cruise liners if we are going out with each other?'

'Sophie,' Luka said. 'Tomorrow you are nineteen, of course you must follow your dreams and do the work you want to.' He threw a sheet at her. 'For now, though, you can help me do this…'

Sophie took the sheet and started making her side of the bed. 'Does anything smell better than a sheet dried in the sun?' Sophie asked, because at the hotel it was all starch and bleach.

'One thing does,' Luka said, and he beckoned her to cross the bed. Unabashed, wanting the same as him, she climbed over to him, kneeling up as he stood. 'You do.'

'And you,' Sophie said.

They kissed a slow, long kiss that she wanted to go on for ever but it was Luka who halted things—the sky was turning orange, he could hear the bell in the distance, summoning everyone to church. He had no intention of going himself but he knew that Sophie would be expected to be there so he pulled back. 'I'll go and get your dress. You said you needed to be at church.'

'Soon,' Sophie said.

'You'll be late,' Luka said.

'I'm always late.'

'When we're in London, we can spend the whole day…' He didn't finish. Her towel was slipping and Sophie let it fall. His lovely erection was nudging her stomach as they kissed some more.

'I want to kiss you there,' Sophie said, and now, when she lowered her head, Luka didn't remind her that there was somewhere else she needed to be.

She kissed down his stomach until his erection was too tempting at her cheek to ignore. He held the base as she tasted him first with her tongue then kissed him along his thick shaft and then Luka removed his hands.

Sophie felt giddy as she ran her lips over the salty tip.

Together they would go to London; they would get to know each other's bodies.

The world was theirs.

'Like this?' Sophie asked, and then parted her lips and took him a little way in.

'Like that,' Luka agreed. This, for Luka, was more intimate than sex. More private. He would prefer to give rather than take but he went with it now. His hands were in her hair and she felt the building pressure. 'Deeper,' Luka said, and she obliged, taking him in as far as she could as her tongue swirled on his shaft.

His powerful thighs started to buck a little, his hand coiled her hair into a long ponytail and Sophie loved the traction—the tightness to her scalp gave her delicious direction but then cruelly she stopped.

'Now?' Sophie said, hovering over him, and then she looked up and smiled as he swore. 'Is now a good time to get my own way?'

'Why the hell did I tell you that?' Luka both laughed and groaned. 'What is it that you want?'

'Can Bella come too?' Sophie asked. 'Just till we get on our feet?'

'Sophie…' Luka tried to come up with a reason why she couldn't but, what he hell, he knew Bella and Sophie had been friends for ever and it might make it easier for

Sophie to settle in. 'Sure,' Luka said. 'Bella can come too. Now, get back to work.'

Laughing, happy, she did so. Her hands moved and held his taut buttocks. He let her hair fall and what went on behind the black curtain was a private tasting. Sophie rested on her heels, her sex on fire as Luka didn't try for gentle. She loved his passion, how he told her exactly what he wanted—which was simply more of the same. It was hot work and then he swore again, and it was right to swear because things could never be the same as he swelled in her throat, she pulled her head back and caught him first on her tongue, tasting and swallowing him down, more turned on than she thought possible. But then she realised he hadn't finished, and the sound of him gently swearing as he came over her lips and into her hair had her close to climax.

'Tonight...' Luka scooped her up to him, told her he would wash himself out of her hair, right now in the shower, and then, 'I shall go and speak to your father tonight.'

Not yet, though. He saw her so flushed and aroused and ready that he pushed her back on the bed. Too giddy to stand, he knelt on the floor. She would take a minute. Luka knew. She was almost there. He could see her wet, sore and swollen, her clitoris erect, and God help him but he never wanted them to get out of bed.

Sophie watched, shocked and laughing, as he pulled her to his mouth, and she lay there longing for the building pressure in her to release to his lips. She would later wish she could somehow hold that moment, for it was a time that belonged only to them. A time of pure happiness. A moment without shame, where the future was bright, where dreams were coming true, but then a crashing noise doused her in panic.

There was the sound of footsteps running up the stairs.

A lot of them.

Her first thought was that Malvolio had come home, though there was too much noise for it to be only him, but then the police shouted out that they were being raided.

Luka threw a sheet over her. The bedroom door splintered and as it was kicked open he lay over her as gruff voices told them not to move.

'Non muovetevi!'

Sophie closed her eyes in terror as Luka was hauled from the bed to the floor where he was cuffed.

'Stay still,' Luka warned her. 'Just stay calm.' Then he shouted to them to fetch her clothes but all they gave her was one of Luka's shirts.

'Not in church this evening?' The lewd comment only added to her embarrassment and terror as Sophie attempted to cover herself.

'Say nothing,' Luka warned her. His voice was the only calm in the room but then it changed as they pulled Sophie's hands behind her back and put on cuffs. 'Why are you cuffing her?'

'I don't know what's happening…' Sophie said, and then she looked at Luka, met his eyes and in that moment she did know.

This was about their fathers.

'Say nothing,' Luka said. 'I'll get you a lawyer.'

It had all been perfect and now she had been plunged into a hell that burned ever hotter. Sophie was unceremoniously marched to a car. The entire congregation of the church, it seemed, had come out and were watching from the other side of the road. It was mortifying. The only saving grace was Bella, shouting to her friend,

'I'll get some clothes and bring them.' She was already running down the hill towards Sophie's home.

There was no time to thank Bella. Instead, Sophie's head was pushed down as she got into a police car, but it didn't come close to the loving way Luka's hand had, only moments ago, guided her head.

'Poutana...' She heard the whispers—some even said it loudly. The people she had grown up with had all turned on her in one night and very soon she would start to understand why.

'I suggest you *don't* take your boyfriend's advice and that you do speak,' Sophie was told as the car started to drive off

Sophie said nothing. She trusted Luka to sort this out and she knew that she'd done nothing wrong. She rested her head against the window and lifted her hands to her tousled hair, feeling her mother's earring, then moved her fingers to her other ear.

It was gone.

'My earring,' she started, and then stopped. She would speak with Luka later. It had to be in his bedroom, or maybe on the path as she had been led out.

She looked down at the car floor, wondering if she had lost it when she'd been pushed in.

'So where's your father tonight?' she was asked, but Sophie refused to answer. She had given up looking for her earring and was now back to staring unseeingly out of the window,

'There's Luka's father,' the officer said, and Sophie started to breathe faster as she saw Malvolio being led by the police from the hotel. 'I wonder where Paulo is,' the policeman said. 'Let's take the scenic route.' But instead of the beach road they were heading now towards the hotel and into a small side street, the same street that

Sophie had walked down just a few hours ago. Now, though, it was filled with firefighters and the deli was alight with flames.

'You were in there this afternoon, weren't you?' the officer checked, and there was no point denying it so Sophie nodded.

'Your father went and visited them this morning,' the officer said. 'For the third time.'

It was then, Sophie knew, time for her to start talking.

CHAPTER SIX

'SOPHIE DURANTE.'

Sophie stood as her name was called.

It had taken six long months to get to the trial.

After the arrests she had been released without charge the next morning but her father, Luka and Malvolio had all been charged with various offences.

The last six months she had spent living with Bella and her mother because, even from prison, Malvolio still ruled Bordo Del Cielo. Her father's house had been signed over to him to pay for Paulo's lawyer.

Sophie had been allowed a few short, monitored visits with her father.

She would have preferred to have seen Luka.

It was a terrible thing to admit perhaps, but at every visit she had ached for just a glimpse of him and she could no longer look her father in the eye.

'You will hear many things in the trial,' Paulo had said. 'Some of the things will be true, but most are lies...'

Sophie simply didn't know what to believe.

Trinkets and jewellery had been found in their home. Souvenirs, the police called them, for they had all belonged to victims.

Sophie knew they had not been in her home, she'd cleaned it after all. But she also knew that her father,

though perhaps not a killer, had not been entirely innocent either and it hurt like hell to know that.

'Malvolio would send me to warn people—it doesn't
mean that I hurt them…' Paulo attempted to explain.

'You went, though,' Sophie shot back. 'You terrified
them just by passing on the warnings. Why would you
say yes to him?'

'Sophie, please—'

'No!' She would not simply ignore the facts. 'You
chose to say yes to him and, please, never say that you
did it for me. He kept us poor.'

'You have Luka.'

Sophie let out an incredulous laugh. 'Don't tell me
you said yes to him just for that. I'd have had Luka with
or without your help.'

She was confident of that.

Almost.

She couldn't wait for the trial to be over, to go with
him to London…to take up those tentative dreams and
to run with them.

Sophie looked at her father. He looked so grey and
gaunt and she knew she had to win the battle to forgive him and stand by him, for she was the only family that he had.

'After the trial you can get away from Bordo Del
Cielo and start over again,' Sophie said.

'I'm not leaving your mother.'

'She's been dead for seventeen years! Father, I am
going to be leaving. I'm going to move to London with
Luka. I just want to get away from here and all the
people who have judged me.' She ran a nervous tongue
over her lips for there was one thing she felt her father
ought to hear first from her. 'You will hear things in
court about me too, father. Things that you won't like.

That afternoon, when the raids happened, Luka and I…
we were together.'

'Sophie, you and Luka were practically engaged.
You have nothing to be ashamed about. Walk into
that court and give your evidence with your head held
high.'

How, though?

As her father was led back to the cells Sophie asked,
as she always did, if she could visit Luka.

He had no one. His mother had died years ago and
his father was locked away.

'Non ci sono visitatori ammessi.'

Again she was told that no visitors were allowed
and then she found out that Luka had been placed in
solitary.

'Malvolio too?' Sophie challenged. 'Of course not.'
She answered her own question.

Luka wasn't a security risk, Luka wouldn't contaminate the trial, that would be Malvolio.

'He rules even in here,' Sophie called out as she left
on the eve of the trial.

She took the bus back to Bordo Del Cielo and walked
down the street.

Teresa's café was all boarded up and the locals
shunned her. If it weren't for Bella and her mother. she
would have had nowhere to go.

If it weren't for Luka, she wouldn't even be here, a
still small voice told her.

She was so cross with her father that there was a
temptation to simply take the next flight and leave him
to his fate, given all he had done.

But Luka…

He was the reason she was here.

Sophie halted at Giovanni's the jewellers when she

saw him at the window, adding a new stand to the wares. 'Anything?' she asked when he caught her eye, because she was still hoping against hope that her earring might have been found and handed in.

Giovanni shook his head and disappeared back into the shop, leaving Sophie standing there.

No one wanted to be seen talking with her.

She peered in and looked at the new offerings in the window. There was a huge emerald-cut diamond set on the prettiest rose gold band and she couldn't help but let her imagination take flight.

She wanted that ring on her finger.

Or rather she wanted the engagement that had never taken place.

Walking back to Bella's, she tasted the salty sea air and thought of Luka alone and locked away.

He had no one.

Well, he did, he had her, but there was no way to let him know, apart from to do as her father said and to walk into the trial with her head held high. She would not be ashamed about what had taken place between her and Luka that afternoon.

She was here only for him.

Sophie tried.

Throughout the trial, as a witness she had not been admitted to the courtroom, but today she was being called to give evidence and, though dreading it, though embarrassed at the thought of some of the salacious details of that day being examined, though scared for her father, what had sustained her was that today she would see Luka.

And she did.

Walking into the courtroom to take the stand, finally

she saw him. Those navy eyes met hers and he gave her a small encouraging smile. He looked thinner, leaner and sharper. The scar above his eye had had little medical attention for it had healed badly and even from the witness stand she could see it purple and raised. His hair was cut far too short and Sophie could see the anger that simmered beneath the surface, though not towards her, for his eyes were kind when they met hers.

She awaited the barrage of questions and let out a breath of relief when the rather embarrassing moments of the police raid were skimmed over.

'You knew that Teresa was upset with you that day when you went into the deli?'

'I did?'

'And you asked your father why she might be upset?'

'I just mentioned it in passing when I got home.' Sophie swallowed, her cheeks going a little bit pink as they made it sound as if she had been questioning her father. 'I thought it was to do with my upcoming engagement, that because Malvolio would be my father-in-law...'

'Just answer the question.'

Sophie frowned, as she did on many occasions over a very long day of questioning. Malvolio and Luka had the same lawyer, her father had a different one, yet even he wasn't asking the pertinent questions.

'The souvenirs that the police say they found in my home...' Sophie attempted, for when she had been arrested, over and over the police had spoken about trinkets that had belonged to the deceased or come from buildings that had been destroyed. She wanted to explain they had never been in her home. That she had kept the house and would have known if such things were there.

'We'll get to that later,' her father's lawyer said, yet he did not.

Sophie left the witness stand and now that she had given her evidence she was allowed to watch as the accused were cross-examined.

Malvolio went to the witness stand a sinner but the questions were so gentle and so geared for him that he left the stand looking like a saint and walked away with an arrogant smile.

She sat bewildered as her father took the stand. He seemed weak and confused. Sophie once stood and shouted as his own lawyer misled him but Bella pulled her down.

'Quiet, or you will be asked to leave.'

'It's not fair, though,' Sophie said.

None of it was fair.

Yes, her father admitted, a second visit from him meant there would be trouble if bills were not paid.

A third visit was the final warning.

'I had no choice but to do as Malvolio said.'

It was, Sophie knew, a poor defence.

And then it was Luka.

In a dark suit and tie, his skin was pale from months of being locked inside. He wrenched his arm from a guard who led him, still as defiant, still as silent as he had been on the day of his arrest.

He would not lie to save his father.

Luka refused to lie.

It was not in him to lie and he wanted no part of his father's life so he had decided that he would speak the truth.

The truth could not hurt him.

Or so he thought.

He looked out and nodded to his close friend Matteo, who had been there every day to support him, and then he looked at Sophie. He tried to let her know with his eyes that he had this under control.

But ten minutes into his testimony he started to glimpse his father's game.

'Did your concerns about Paulo's dealings play any part in your decision to not go ahead with your engagement to his daughter Sophie Durante?'

There was a gasp around the courtroom and Sophie stared ahead as Bella took her hand.

'Sophie and I had decided to make our own arrangements for the future,' Luka answered in a clear voice.

'We'll get back to that but first can you answer the question? Did you have concerns about Paulo's dealings?'

'I had never really given Paulo much thought,' Luka answered, though his voice was not quite so clear as he delivered his response.

'Did Sophie tell you that she had concerns about her father's activities?'

His already pale face bleached and he looked into Sophie's eyes briefly. He had sworn to tell the truth but he could not have Sophie's own words be the reason for Paulo being put away.

'No, she did not.' For her, Luka lied under oath.

'So what you did discuss that day?'

'I really can't remember,' Luka answered.

'Because you were busy in the bedroom?' His lawyer was working more for Malvolio, Luka knew it now. Luka didn't have anything to hide so the lawyer would work to secure his father's freedom by throwing Paulo under the bus.

'I'm confused,' the lawyer continued. 'On the afternoon in question you said to your father that you were going to end things with Sophie, yes?'

'Yes,' Luka answered. 'However—'

'Malvolio was upset,' the lawyer broke in. 'In fact, you got into a fight when you spoke poorly about the woman he had chosen with care for you. You said that you did not want to marry a peasant of his choice. Correct?'

Sophie closed her eyes and then forced them open as Luka was forced to admit that, yes, that had been what he had said.

'I was trying to separate myself from my father—' He didn't get to finish.

'You told your father that you preferred the more glamorous, sophisticated women in London to Sophie. Now do you see the reason for my confusion? Sophie Durante came to your home…'

'My father sent for Sophie so that he could move the souvenirs to Paulo's,' Luka said. He could see what had happened now. Six months locked up, two of them spent in solitary, had given him a lot of time to think. His father hadn't been hoping to get Sophie and him together, Luka was sure of that now. Malvolio must have been tipped off about the raids and would have wanted the souvenirs out of his home and in Paulo's.

Only no one wanted to hear his truth.

'Sophie Durante heard that you were about to renege on your promise to marry her. She turned up at your home on a Sunday afternoon to dissuade you and you ended up in bed that same afternoon, or rather you had sex in the kitchen.'

'No.'

'You are saying nothing happened in the kitchen?' the lawyer checked.

'As I have said, I had had a fight with my father, Sophie was sorting out the cut above my eye…'

'Oh, I see—you were bleeding so profusely that she was left with no choice but to take off her dress to stem the bleed…?' the lawyer asked, and Sophie sat burning with shame, completely humiliated as the courtroom laughed.

'My father had suggested that Sophie come over before I told him that I did not want to get engaged. He wanted her out of Paulo's house so that he could move—'

'Did Sophie Durante want to be out of that house too?' the lawyer interrupted. 'Was Sophie concerned that her father was engaged in criminal activity? Did she tell you she wanted to get away from him?'

Luka broke into a cold sweat, he could feel it trickle down his back. He was doing everything he could to stay calm, to somehow give his version of events, but there was no right answer.

His father had a brilliant lawyer, so too did he, and he was, Luka could now see, being used to discredit Paulo.

If he answered yes to the question then he put Paulo away for life.

'No.'

'You are under oath,' the lawyer reminded him.

'No, she did not say that.' Luka's voice was clear as he decided that bedroom talk had no place in the courtroom.

'You did tell your father, though, that you were not going to go ahead with the engagement?'

'Yes.'

'And you told Sophie the same. Yes or no?'

'Yes.'

'Luka.' The lawyer really was the smiling assassin

as he looked at his youngest client, whose father was paying the hefty bill. 'How can you expect the court to believe that there was no conversation—?'

'We were *otherwise* engaged.'

'*After* you had ended things?'

'Yes.'

'Nothing was said about her father?'

Luka did what he had to.

'There really was little conversation.'

'It makes no sense.'

The lawyer was about to pounce again but Luka got there first and turned to the judge and shrugged his shoulders. 'I think that Sophie might have been trying to get me to change my mind about ending things by trying to seduce me so I took what was on offer.' He looked out towards the jury and then back to the judge as he shamed her. 'Am I on trial for my libido?'

The laughter that went around the courtroom ended the testimony.

But as Luka left the stand she did not look at him.

Luka knew that he might have saved her father from conviction by his own daughter's words.

But it might just have killed the two of them.

CHAPTER SEVEN

SOPHIE, EVEN DAYS LATER, could not bring herself to look at Luka as the defendants stood to hear their fate.

'He didn't mean it.' Over and over Bella said this to Sophie, who had held in her formidable temper since Luka had said those words. 'The lawyer gave him no choice.'

The villagers sniggered as she passed, there were whispers everywhere she went, but now, as the verdict was about to be delivered, there were no smiles or laughter in court.

All knew that the six-month break they'd had from Malvolio's clutches might end today.

'Luka Romano Cavaliere—*non colpevole*.'

Despite her anger, Sophie let out a breath of relief and she did lift her eyes to look at him. She didn't expect his eyes to be waiting for hers, yet they were. For a small slice of time they stared at the other and the courtroom faded.

He gave her a nod that apologised, that said he would explain things, that soon he would be with her.

'Here comes the verdict for Malvolio,' Bella whispered.

'Malvolio Cavaliere—*non colpevole*.'

'No!' Bella gasped, and Sophie clutched her friend's hand as the fat brute smiled over in their direction.

Malvolio had wanted Bella for a long time.

Pandemonium broke out as, terrified now and determined to appear loyal to Malvolio, the spectators in the courtroom applauded. Sophie simply lowered her head and tried not to weep.

She knew what was coming.

Her father was so frail he could hardly stand.

Paulo Durante—*colpevole*.

Her father would be taken to the mainland for sentencing, the court was informed, and would serve out his time there.

He would die in prison, Sophie knew that.

She watched him being led away and though she was still angry at him she knew she was the only person that he had so she called out to him, 'I'll be there for you...'

She would be.

There were cheers in the streets as Malvolio left the court a free man, though Sophie didn't hear them and neither did she wait to speak with Luka; instead, she went to Bella's to start packing.

'I'm going to Rome to be near him and you need to leave too,' Sophie urged Bella. 'Malvolio is back, all his yes-men are still here.'

'I cannot leave my mother,' Bella said .

'She will understand...'

'I can't, Sophie, she is so sick.'

There was a knock on the door and Bella went to answer it as Sophie continued to pack.

'No,' Sophie said as Bella returned. 'I don't want to see him.'

'It wasn't Luka,' Bella said, and Sophie looked up when she heard the strain in her friend's voice. 'It was Pino with a message for me. There is to be a big celebration tonight at the hotel, everyone is to be there. I am to work in the bar.'

'No!' Sophie was adamant. 'You are to come with me to Roma.'

'I can't leave her now,' Bella said. 'I know that you have to leave and not just to take care of Paulo—you are the scapegoat now. Everyone knows it is Malvolio but that is not what that will say to his face.' Bella started to cry. 'I don't want my first to be Malvolio. I know you think I should just say no to him.'

'I know that it is not that simple.' Sophie put her arm around her friend, who took a cleansing breath.

'When my mother has gone, and it won't be long, I will come to Rome and be with you. But not now. I need to be here for her in the same way you need to be there for your father.'

There was a knock at the door and Bella went to answer it and after a moment came back and this time, Bella told Sophie, it was Luka here to see her.

'I have nothing to say to him.'

'He says he's not leaving till he has spoken with you.'

He wouldn't leave, Sophie knew it.

Her shame and hurt from the words he had said in court the other day was still there inside her. Her fear, her panic about her father seemed to be swirling into a concentrated storm as finally, for the first time in six months, they would speak.

She stepped out of the small bedroom and there Luka stood in the hall. 'Congratulations,' she hurled at him. 'You and your father walk free, while mine is to be imprisoned on the mainland. Where is the justice?'

'There is no justice,' Luka said. 'Can we go for a walk?'

'Just say what you have to.'

'Not here,' Luka said, and looked over to the bedroom that Bella was in.

'I trust Bella,' Sophie said, 'And, given all that was said, I trust her far more than I trust you.'

'You know why I had to say what I did.'

Somewhere deep down Sophie did. Right there, in the midst of her turmoil, she did know that so she nodded and called to Bella that she was heading out for a short while.

They walked from Bella's home down the street and past the hotel Brezza Oceana, not talking at first. Cars were starting to arrive, there were flowers being brought in through the foyer. Clearly the hotel was preparing for a large celebration.

And, Sophie knew, Bella would be working there tonight and every other night that Malvolio dictated.

Yes, her heart hurt right now.

'Will you be going to the celebration tonight?' Sophie broke the strained silence.

'No,' Luka answered. 'I am having nothing more to do with my father.' They walked further on and they came to the small path that only the locals knew about and they walked down to the cove.

It felt strange being here with Luka when usually she came with Bella, and she told him that. 'We always called it our secret cove. I guess everyone does that, though.' She tried to make small talk but found it impossible, the hurt was too great.

Luka didn't even try.

'Sophie, tomorrow I am leaving for London. I want you to come with me and Bella too. Matteo is also leaving, though no one knows that yet. He will go along with things tonight and make out that he is pleased to see my father released but tomorrow he's getting out.'

'Bella can't leave her mother,'

'Bella has to,' Luka said.

'She won't. I just spoke to her and she says that she can't leave and I understand why. Her mother needs Bella to be working to pay the rent. She used to own her own home till *your* father took it from them to *help* cover the medical bills.'

Luka knew that, he knew it all now, but hearing the slight acid in Sophie's words that inferred his father's dealing were somehow anything to do with him had anger building within him, yet he fought to stay calm.

'I have to support her choice,' Sophie said.

They kept on walking and it was strange that a place could be so picture perfect and yet so sordid.

'Sophie, will you come with me to London?'

'No,' Sophie said. 'I need to be close to my father. I'm going to go Rome and live there.'

'If you come to London with me then I can pay for you to visit him frequently.'

'I don't want you paying for me,' Sophie said. 'God, you're as arrogant as your father. Well, let me tell you—I would rather work as a *poutana* in the bar with Bella than go to London with you. Have you any idea of the shame, to stand the court and hear that?'

'Sophie.' He grabbed her arm and swung her around to face him. 'You know why I said what I did. I did all I could so that what you said to me would have no bearing on your father's verdict.'

But she didn't want to hear it.

'Go and live in London, Luka, and party with your models, who only want you for looks and money. You'll suit each other. Take the head start your father's filthy dealings gave you.'

'He gave me nothing.'

'Please,' Sophie scoffed. 'I'll do better on my own that I ever could with you.'

'Are you sure about that?' Luka checked.

'More than sure.'

'Some welcome,' Luka sneered, and then shook his head. 'I've been in prison for six months, two of them spent in solitary, where the thought of seeing you was the only thing that kept me sane.'

Luka had had a lot of time to think and in that time the only thing that had kept him going had been her and the memory of that afternoon—sheets that had smelt like the sun and the future they had dared to glimpse. He had walked out of court and straight to the jeweller's. It had been closed, of course, but he had gone around to Giovanni's home and asked him to open up, and his first purchase had been the thing he craved most.

A future with the person he loved by his side.

'What exactly did you say to your father?' Sophie demanded. 'I want to hear it.'

Now, instead of looking to the future, Sophie wanted to examine the past.

'I've just been found not guilty, Sophie. I've just had my past and my all my dealings examined. I never thought I'd have to come out to be to be retried by you. I lied under oath for you.'

'I don't care about your lies under oath,' Sophie said, her eyes blazing with anger. 'I care about the parts that were true. You go to London, Luka, you go with your glamorous women, you don't need to take the *peasant* along…'

It was that part that had killed her, that part that made her want to curl up right now and hide for ever, but instead Sophie came out fighting. She had never felt good enough for Luka, and hearing what he had said about her to his father had been more shameful than being paraded half-naked in front of the village. 'You weren't lying under oath then, Luka.'

'It was a row that I had with my father. What I said was wrong, I know that. Sophie, I thought it the moment I opened the door to you and saw you standing there, so beautiful...'

Unwittingly he had hurt her again. The Sophie he had seen that day had been dressed in her finest, but he couldn't know that. All his words did were reinforce her silent fear that if he knew the real Sophie, she wouldn't be good enough.

From the ruins she had to dig deep to find her pride.

'I'll never forgive you for that,' Sophie spat. 'I'll never forget the shame of my first lover calling me a peasant.'

'Well, it was it clearly true.' He hit completely below the belt but, hell, he was hurting. 'Do you really think I want to be standing arguing, with you acting like a fishwife, on the night I get set free? I want champagne, Sophie. I want laughter and a beautiful woman.'

'And?' she demanded.

'That about does it for me,' Luka said, and shrugged her off.

CHAPTER EIGHT

HE DIDN'T FEEL ANYTHING.

Or rather, Luka thought as the car took him from the airport to Bordo Del Cielo , the feelings that he had were perhaps not at they should be on the day of his father's funeral.

Yes, he was grieving.

Just not for Malvolio.

It had been five years since Luka had been back.

At least physically.

More than Luka cared to admit, his dreams regularly brought him back to this place.

The car turned and he looked out at the glittering Mediterranean and then another turn and there spread out before him were his childhood and teenage years.

The church, the houses, the rivers and roads that were all etched in his heart were on view now. Memories of summers and Christmases long gone when he had lived a life with the promise of Sophie in his future.

It had been a promise that he had backed out on, Luka reminded himself.

Today, on the day that his father was buried, when surely there should be a layer of grief for his father, instead it was all for Sophie and for that small slice of time they had been together.

She still resided in his heart.

With the benefit of hindsight he had often rearranged that day in his mind so that they had left for London as soon as she had come out of the shower, before the raid, before everything had fallen apart.

He arrived at the church and as he stepped inside Luka could only give a wry smile for it was practically empty.

Defiant only on Malvolio's death, no one attended.

There was just Angela the maid, sitting midway down the aisle, and Luka gave her a nod and then headed to the front.

There was the sound of the door opening and he turned around because, yes, hope remained.

False hope, Luka thought as Pino, once a young boy on his bike, now a young man, came in and took a seat.

Luka nodded to him also but as he sat through the short service still his mind turned to Sophie.

She should have been here.

Had she cared for him, she would have been beside him today.

The burial was a sad joke.

Malvolio had paid for his own funeral and the huge oak casket with its glitzy trimmings went almost unnoticed, for everyone had chosen to stay at home.

Pino headed off and after Luka had thanked the priest he walked out of the cemetery with Angela.

'I have put on some refreshments,' Angela said, 'back at the house. I wasn't sure how many would be attending. I don't think I'll be hungry for a long time.'

Luka gave a wry smile. 'You know, for all his power and wealth he had nothing,' he said. 'Nothing that matters anyway.'

'I thought Matteo might come with you today. I hear that the two of you are doing very well.'

'He is in the Middle East on business. He offered to come but I really just wanted to do this on my own.'

Or not on his own. Still his eyes scanned the street, hoping against hope that she might yet arrive.

He should leave now.

Luka knew that.

His lawyers were taking care of the estate. Luka could barely stand to hear the details—his father owned Paulo's home and Bella's mother's too.

That was the mere start.

Most of the town had been handed over to his father in times of weakness or ill health, with the promise that Malvolio would take care of everything.

No wonder the church had been practically empty. No doubt the moment Luka left they would celebrate the end of his father's dictatorship.

They would, Luka knew, have reason to celebrate properly soon for he had instructed his lawyers carefully.

He needed nothing from his father's estate. It would take some work and a lot of unravelling but, in time, all the homes that his father had procured through less than honourable means would be returned to their rightful owners or their descendants. The locals would only find that out long after he had left Bordo Del Cielo, though.

They arrived at his car and Luka looked at Angela's tired, strained face.

'How long until I have to leave the house?' Angela asked.

'You don't ever have to leave,' Luka said. Yes, he was handing it over to his lawyers, but he did not want

Angela spending another night in fear. 'I will be transferring the house into your name.'

'Luka!' Angela shook her head. 'Bordo Del Cielo is a popular holiday resort now, the properties are expensive.'

'It is your home,' Luka said. 'Hopefully, now it can be a happier one.' He gave her a small smile. 'Can I ask you to keep it to yourself for a little while?'

Angela nodded tearfully.

'Come back to the house,' she said, but Luka shook his head.

'There are few good memories there...'

'Come back for a little while at least.'

There was one good memory, though, and after a moment of quiet thought Luka nodded.

He hadn't been home since the night of the police raid.

On his release, after pleading with Sophie to join him in London, instead of going to the bar to celebrate his and his father's freedom he had sat on the sand, going over and over Sophie's words.

He went over them again now as he stepped into the kitchen and remembered her sitting on the bench and tending to his eye.

'I might take a look around,' Luka said, and took the stairs, trying and failing not to remember their frantic kisses there, and then went into his old bedroom.

It was like entering a time warp.

Angela must have dusted it but it was just as he had left it.

Luka closed his eyes as he remembered that afternoon before it had all gone so wrong.

He thought of the plans they had made and their hopes for the future. Now, with the wisdom the years had afforded and after so many fleeting relationships that never came close to what he had found with Sophie, he knew that what had been born that day had been a fledgling love. It had to have been for there had been nothing close to the same since. Not just the sex, but the conversation, the sharing, peering into the future with one another and picturing themselves there—not clearly, they'd had but a few hours together, of course, but there had been the chance of a future and it had been stolen from them that same day.

He opened up his bedside drawer, expecting nothing, an old notebook perhaps or a school report. He used to hide them from his father—they had never been good enough. What he found, though, made him sit on the bed with his head in his hands.

Her earring—just a thin gold loop with a small diamond where the clasp met, but it was the only tangible thing he had from that day and he examined it carefully as memories rushed in. He remembered her standing at the door and how that tiny stone and the sparkle it had made had brought attention not to the earring but to her eyes.

She should have been here today, standing beside him. If she cared at all she'd have made the effort, wouldn't she?

'Did you ever look her up?' Angela asked a little later as they drank coffee.

'Who?' Luka attempted.

'The woman you were promised to for half of your life,' Angela said. 'The woman who walked out of this house dressed only in your shirt as the whole town looked on. The woman you shamed in court. I'm sure you don't need me to tell you her name.'

'I had no choice to say what I did in court.'

'I know that.'

'Sophie didn't, though.'

'She was young,' Angela said, and Luka nodded.

'She was more upset about what I said to my father about her being a peasant...' Luka smiled as he rolled his eyes. 'And so, to make things worse, I went and said it again on the beach, the night of my release...'

'To Sophie!' Angela exclaimed, but then smiled. 'She is so like her mother. Rosa could skin you alive with her eyes... I remember the day she turned up here, shouting at Malvolio to leave her family alone...' Her voice trailed off. Even if he was dead, some things still weren't discussed, but Luka nodded.

He could remember that day just a little. Rosa had knocked on the door and had stood shouting down the hallway.

He'd forgotten that, Luka thought. He would have been eight or nine...

'You were younger then too when you said those things and you were also just out of prison.' Angela broke into his thoughts. 'Perhaps it wasn't the time for common sense.'

Again, he nodded.

'So, *did* you ever look her up?'

'I sat in a car outside Paulo's jail day in day out for a month a couple of years ago,' Luka admitted. 'Then I found out that he was in hospital and not even there.'

'You never visited him?'

'I couldn't face him,' Luka admitted. 'He took the fall for my father. When I found out that he had been sentenced to forty-three years...' Luka gave a tight shrug. 'The wrong man was put behind bars.'

'Paulo wasn't entirely innocent either.'

'I know that. I don't know what my father's hold

over him was but surely he could have said no at some point or just left.' Luka gave a tight shrug, weary from thinking about it. 'He didn't deserve forty-three years, though, and for my father to walk free.'

'You never saw Sophie after she left for Rome?'

'Never,' Luka said. 'It is like she disappeared…'

'I am sure she still visits her father.'

Luka nodded. 'Maybe I *should* go and visit him.'

He was older now—he could face Paulo…

Perhaps he could visit him and ask after his daughter.

Maybe he and Sophie deserved a second chance because, as sure as hell, the years hadn't dimmed the memory. Absence really did make the heart grow fonder because Luka was in the agony of recall again.

And still angry again at her words towards him.

He had never compared her to *her* father.

Paulo was no innocent—he knew full well what two visits from him meant.

Never would he have thrown that at Sophie.

She wasn't like her father, though, Luka thought. She was as volatile and explosive as Rosa.

'I'm going to look her up again,' he said to Angela. 'I will go and see Paulo and make my peace with him.'

'And ask where his daughter is?' Angela smiled.

'I have an earring that needs to be returned!' He smiled; he hadn't expected to smile today but he did. It hurt to be back here but it had cemented some things in his mind.

He and Sophie deserved another chance.

'She might be married,' Angela said. 'She might—'

'Then it's better to know,' he said.

It was the not knowing that killed him.

It hurt too much to be here, Luka thought. He wanted

the future, he wanted to explore if there was still a chance for him and Sophie, so he drained his coffee and stood.

'I'm going to head back.'

'Do you want to go through his things first?'

'Just take what you need,' Luka said. 'Get rid of the rest.'

'His jewellery?' Angela said. 'Don't you want that at least?'

'No.' Luka shook his head. He was about to tell Angela to sell it and keep what she made but then he hesitated—no doubt his father's jewellery hadn't all come by honest means and he did not want Angela in trouble for handling stolen goods.

'I will drop it in to Giovanni on the way to the airport,' Luka said, referring to the local jeweller 'He can melt it down or whatever.'

Angela led him up the stairs and into Malvolio's bedroom.

There was nothing he wanted from here.

He opened up a box and stared at his father's belongings with distaste and then Luka's heart stopped still in his chest and then started beating again, only faster than it had been before.

'Can I have a moment?' he said, and somehow managed a vaguely normal voice. He didn't even see Angela leave but she must have because a moment later he looked up from the jewellery box and she was gone, the door had been closed and he was alone.

Luka watched his hand shake a fraction as it went into the heavy wooden box and pulled out a simple gold cross and chain.

Yes, he remembered Rosa.

Luka had heard in court how things worked and

knew that her necklace must have been taken as a souvenir after her death.

Did Paulo know? Luka wondered.

He looked at the door.

Angela too?

He felt sick as he started counting dates in his head. Yes, he remembered Rosa shouting down the hallway, telling Malvolio that it would be over her dead body before she gave up her home.

The next memory?

Her funeral. Paulo, holding a smiling Sophie, who, at two years old, had had no real idea how sombre the day had been.

He remembered his father delivering the eulogy, telling the packed church how he would support his friend and little Sophie.

Even though he had surely been responsible for Rosa's death?

Was that why Paulo had always said yes to his father? Was that the hold that he'd had over him? Had Paulo done whatever had been asked of him just to keep Sophie safe from the same fate?

Poor man.

Luka had always considered Paulo weak.

Now he glimpsed Paulo's fear. He had done whatever it had taken to protect his child, and Luka knew that he had to help free him.

He would get his lawyers onto it this very day, Luka swore there and then. He would get an apartment in Rome and work for however long it took to secure his release.

There would be no contacting Sophie, though, Luka knew.

There could be no second chance for them now.

He knew Sophie well enough, and she would never forgive him if she knew that it had been his father who had killed her mother.

Never.

The glimmer of hope he had just started to kindle, the fleeting hope for some reconciliation with Sophie, died then as Luka pocketed the necklace.

All he could do for her now was fight to set her father free.

CHAPTER NINE

'I SAW LUKA.'

Sophie had always known that she might hear those words one day but when Bella actually voiced them, for a long moment Sophie did not know how to react.

So much so that she said nothing and just lifted her side of the mattress and carried on making the huge king-size bed.

Sophie had known that Bella wanted to speak with her. As well as sharing a very small flat in Rome, they worked as maids in Hotel Fiscella—a luxurious hotel in the very heart of Rome.

The manager, Marco, had, at first, refused to put them together, knowing that they came from the same Sicilian town. However, when a gap in the roster had given him no choice, Sophie and Bella had set out to prove him wrong. They worked very well together, although they chatted a lot!

Now, though, Sophie was silent.

'I just saw him in the elevator when I went to collect the guest list for our floor.'

'He's not on our list? Sophie checked in horror, but thankfully Bella shook her head.

'Looking at the way he was dressed and held himself, he would be on one of the top floors,' Bella said, and that told Sophie he was doing well.

The hotel was indeed luxurious but the top floors were reserved for the rich and famous.

It had been five years since Sophie had last seen him. Five years since that walk on the beach.

She knew that Malvolio had died a few months ago. Her father had been diagnosed as terminally ill on the very same day that she had heard the news. After that she had read that Luka had bought an apartment in Rome and now lived between here and London.

Sometimes Sophie was nervous that she might see him in the street, that she would face him in her maid's uniform when she had sworn she could do better without him. That she might face him in the street was bad enough, but knowing that he was at the hotel was far too close for comfort.

'Why would he stay here when he has an apartment?'

'I don't know,' Bella said. 'But it was definitely him.'

When they had read that Luka Cavaliere had purchased a residence Sophie and Bella had even gone to the library to use the computers and had done a virtual tour of the apartment. It had been a foolish thing to do because Sophie found she could picture herself there and all too often did.

'Did he recognise you?' Sophie asked, but Bella just laughed.

'As if he would even glance at a maid! Though I stood behind the bellboy's trolley just in case he looked over.' she admitted. 'But he didn't.'

'I don't want him to see me like this,' Sophie said in sudden panic. 'I don't want him to see that I am still a chambermaid. What if I have to deliver a meal to his room?'

'Don't feel ashamed.'

'I'm not,' Sophie said. 'I just don't want to give him the satisfaction of seeing how little I have moved on.'

'You won't see him. I heard him say he was going back to London this afternoon.'

'Good.'

'What else do you want to know?' Bella asked.

'Nothing.' Sophie shook her head. 'I don't even want to think of that man.'

It was all that she did, though.

Every night when she fell, exhausted, into bed he was there, waiting for her in her dreams. Every morning she awoke cross with her subconscious and how readily it forgave Luka, for her dreams varied from sweet memories of a sun-drenched childhood to a torrid recall of their one passionate afternoon.

They finished making up the bed in silence and Bella went in to do the bathroom while Sophie dusted the flat surfaces of the hotel suite.

Sophie didn't want to ask questions; she wanted to shrug her shoulders and carry on with her day as if a bomb hadn't just dropped in her world, but, of course, that wasn't possible.

She walked into the bathroom and Bella smiled in the mirror that she was polishing when she saw her friend hovering in the doorway.

'Who was he saying it to?' Sophie asked. 'Who was he speaking with?'

'A woman.' Bella's voice was gentle yet the words hurt so much.

'Was she beautiful?' Sophie asked, and Bella screwed up her nose. 'I didn't really notice.'

'I want the truth, Bella,' she said.

Her friend nodded. 'Yes, she was beautiful.'

'Did she have a name?'

'He called her Claudia.'

'And how did he look?' Sophie asked.

'He looked well.'

'Very well?'

'Well, the last time I saw him he was just out of prison so, of course, he looked better than that.'

Sophie knew her friend was trying to downplay things for her.

'His hair is longer now but still very neat. He still has that scar over his eye.'

'Did he look happy?' Tears were in Sophie's eyes as she asked the question, though she never let them fall. It was ridiculous that the man she hated, the man that had caused her family so much pain could still move her so much. That jealousy could rise in her just knowing Luka was carrying on as he always had—dating and living his life—while she Bella worked as maids in a hotel and could barely make ends meet.

'Luka never really looked happy,' Bella said. 'That, at least, is the same.'

Sophie was quiet.

Bella was right—to others he never looked happy. He was sullen and dark but with her he had laughed and smiled.

She had been privy to such a different side of him.

Knowing that Luka had been here in the hotel had Sophie on edge all day, and it was a relief to get away from work.

All she wanted to do was go home and sleep but instead she changed out of her maid's uniform and into a skirt and a T-shirt and then took the bus. She had to stand nearly all the way to the prison infirmary her father had been moved to.

Once there she put on a ring that had belonged to Bella's mother and signed the visitors' book.

Her bag was searched and she was patted down and then she was allowed in.

'Sophie!' Paulo's face lit up when he saw her walk onto the ward. 'You don't have to come and see me every day.'

'I want to.'

Now that he was in the infirmary, visits could be daily, and Sophie knew full well that he had little time left.

'How is Luka?' Paulo asked.

Her father's mental health had deteriorated throughout the trial and by the time he'd got to Rome he'd been a shadow of himself. He had never been a strong man, and was an exhausted man now.

Sophie just wanted him to know a little peace so she had lied to her father over the years and pretended that she was with Luka.

'He's busy with work.' Sophie smiled, grateful that her father was easily confused and very forgetful. 'He says hello and that he will try to come in and visit you soon.'

'Bella?'

'She's still working at the hotel.'

It was the same questions most days and Sophie knew the routine well. She took out some fruit she had bought for him. A lot of her money went on bringing in Paulo treats, even though she couldn't afford to.

'This is too expensive,' her father said, when she gave him a large bowl of raspberries, which had always been his favourite fruit. When she'd been growing up, they had been a very rare treat.

'Luka can afford it,' she said, and the bitter edge

to her voice had her father frown, and Sophie did her best to rectify her small outburst. 'He's a good man,' she said.

'If he is such a good man, why hasn't he married you?' Paulo asked.

'I've told you that,' Sophie said. 'He knows how much I want you to walk me down the aisle. We are waiting for that day when you are released...'

It was never going to happen. Paulo did not have long left, maybe a few weeks of life, yet his jail sentence was forty-three years.

'I want to see you married in the same church your mother and I were,' Paulo said.

'I know that you do.' Sophie smiled. 'It will happen one day.'

'Maybe,' he said, and Sophie swallowed back tears at the sudden brightness in his voice. 'The director said this morning that things are looking hopeful.'

'Of course there is hope,' she said, and squeezed his frail hand.

'We will know next Wednesday if I am going to get out.'

Sophie looked up and smiled as a nurse came over.

'The director wants to speak with you, Sophie.'

'Thank you,' Sophie said, and stood. 'I'll be back soon,' she said to Paulo, and walked with the nurse, assuming that she was going to get a health update.

She was led through the prison infirmary and to a corridor of offices and there she met a tired-looking woman, who gave Sophie a warm smile and offered her a seat.

'He's more confused than ever,' Sophie said. 'Now he thinks he is getting out of here on Wednesday.'

'He might be getting released,' the director said, and

for a moment Sophie wondered if the chair had been moved for it felt as it the ground had just given way.

'Your father's hearing has been brought forward. We have signed all the forms and have done all we can for him at this end.'

'I don't understand—I didn't even know there was to be a hearing.'

'We are hoping that your father can be released on compassionate grounds. He is no threat to anyone, really he is too weak to go to anywhere other than a hospital or be nursed in your home.' She gave a small shrug. 'Now it is up to the judge to decide but the lawyer who is working on his case is a very good one.'

'I didn't even know there was a lawyer looking out for him.'

'When patients come into the infirmary and their condition is terminal, we try to have their cases reassessed.'

'Why wasn't I told this was happening?'

'It all came about very speedily. When Legal looked at his file they thought there might a possibility for a mistrial but your father does not have time for that. It was thought best to try to get him released on compassionate grounds.' She smiled at Sophie. 'I don't want to get your hopes up but I think in just a few days you might well be able to take your father home.'

Sophie smiled.

It was wonderful news, unexpected and amazing.

And yet it was terrifying too.

She had built a world in her father's mind. One where she lived with Luka in a beautiful flat in Rome, not a scruffy apartment that she and Bella shared.

She had told her father that Matteo and Luka were

still friends, which they were, according to the business press, but she hadn't seen him in years.

The only truth she had told was that Bella worked at Hotel Fiscella, only because once Bella had had to visit on her behalf and had worn a coat over her uniform, which her father had seen.

Paulo was confused enough not to question too many things and there was a lot that he didn't remember.

He simply believed that Luka had kept his word and had got engaged to his daughter.

How could she tell her dying father it had all been a lie?

How could she tell him that she had nothing and that, apart from her friend, she had no one?

'I called you in,' the director continued, but it was as if Sophie was hearing from a distance, 'so that you can start to make plans for his release.'

Sophie managed to thank the director and she even went in to kiss her father goodbye. Once outside again, though, she ran from the hospital and took the crowded bus. When she got off, she raced along the cobbled streets and up the small stairwell, where she wrenched open the iron security door and called out to her friend.

'What?' Bella asked, when she saw her stricken face.

'Pa may be being released...'

Bella let out a shocked gasp. 'That's fantastic news.'

'I know that but how can I bring him here when I have told him that I am engaged to Luka, that we live in a beautiful home?'

'You can't tell him the truth,' Bella said. 'Your father deserves to die knowing that his daughter will be looked after.' Bella's eyes filled with tears. 'My mother didn't know that peace. I think that night Malvolio got released and sent me to work had her go to her grave with a broken heart. It's not going to happen to your father.'

'Oh, so I just produce a luxury apartment? I could just get a photo of Luka, perhaps, and blow it up and sit him in a chair. I know my father is confused but he's not mad...'

'No,' Bella said. 'You are to go and see Luka and tell him that he owes you this much...after the way he shamed you, after all that he said in court, he can damn well go along with things for a while.'

'Do you think I could pull it off?' Sophie said, but then shook her head. 'I can't face him like this.'

'You won't have to,' Bella said. 'I can still sew, I can make you the most sophisticated, elegant woman he has ever seen. You can blow those London women out of the water. He will eat his own words.'

Sophie thought for a moment. 'Luka *could* do it,' Sophie agreed. 'He's a Cavaliere after all. They better than anyone know how to lie under oath.'

CHAPTER TEN

'COULD YOU DIRECT me to Luka Cavaliere's office?'

Sophie stood at a large reception desk and did everything she could to keep the slight tremble from her voice. She was determined to get this right, even if it meant practising her cool façade on the receptionist

'Is he expecting you, Ms…?'

'No, he's not expecting me.' Sophie shook her head. 'If you could just tell me what floor he is on…'

'I'm sorry, but Mr Cavaliere won't see anyone without an appointment.' There was just a slight *something* about the receptionist's voice when she said his name. Her words were tinged with affection and Sophie was quite sure she knew the reason for that.

'For me he would make an exception.' Sophie stared the woman down but it didn't work.

'There *are* no exceptions.' The receptionist smiled her pussycat smile and Sophie glanced at her name badge.

Amber.

'Excuse me,' Amber said as her telephone rang, 'but I need to take this call.'

Sophie stood there as she was summarily dismissed. The beautiful receptionist picked up the phone and started talking but when she had completed the call she blinked, as if surprised to see that Sophie was still there.

'Can I help you?' She frowned.

'You can, Amber,' Sophie responded. 'Please let Mr Cavaliere know that his fiancée is here and that she wishes to see him.'

'His fiancée?'

Sophie watched two spots of colour spread over the woman's cheeks and her cold blue eyes glance down at Sophie's ring finger. 'That's right!' Sophie was the one smiling a pussycat smile now. 'If you could let him know...'

'And your name is...?'

Sophie didn't respond to the question. Luka would know exactly who she was. She pictured his expression when he took the call that would tell him she was back in his life.

A little flustered, the receptionist picked up the phone and relayed the news that Mr Cavaliere's fiancée was there and then gave Sophie a guarded smile. 'I've told his PA and she's going to speak with Mr Cavaliere. If you'd like to take a seat...'

Sophie walked across the elegant foyer to the large leather sofas. She caught sight of herself in the mirror and was relieved for all the effort that she and Bella had made to get to this day.

Bella had, as it turned out, been raiding the bins that they emptied at the hotel for years. Anything that one of the rich guests had thrown out she had squirrelled away.

Beneath Bella's bed were two boxes packed with luxurious clothes.

'This one,' Bella had told her as she held up an ivory silk dress, 'had a little lipstick on the front. She couldn't even be bothered to send it to be dry-cleaned. And these…' She held up some stunning stilettoes. 'They needed to be reheeled, that is all.'

There were coats, jackets, skirts, even nightdresses.

Together they had selected her wardrobe for today and with Bella's skilled hands the rather large ivory dress now clung to Sophie's ripe figure.

The shoes had been reheeled and Sophie's toes had been painted to match her fingernails.

She had flown into London that morning on the red-eye and would be flying back tonight.

The little money they had been saving to fly her father's body, on his death, back to Bordo Del Cielo they had decided to spend on making his last days a dream come true.

Who would guess that Sophie's regular clothes and shoes were in a hired locker at the airport?

Luka must never know.

She had been to a hairdresser's to have her hair put up and then she had changed into the dress Bella had made for her and gone to the make-up counter at an exclusive department store.

She stood as the receptionist came over. 'Mr Cavaliere says you are to go straight up. I'll walk you to the elevator.'

Sophie wanted to turn and run, to ask for a couple of minutes to check her make-up, or for a glass of water for her very dry mouth, but instead she nodded and crossed the foyer.

His office was on the twenty-third floor and her stomach seemed to have been left on the ground as she sailed closer to him.

The elevator doors opened and Sophie was met by a tearful woman who told her that she was the final straw and then let her know that her fiancé was a cheating bastard...

'You can tell him when you go through that his assistant just resigned!'

Sophie merely smiled.

Ah, Luka, she thought, just a little glad for the chaos she had made for him.

Like a witch, she walked through the corridors of his life, delivering little hexes.

She looked around for a moment, taking his world in. There was a large walnut desk, which presumably had been his assistant's because a computer was on and there was half a cup of coffee by its side, as well as a mirror.

There was the quiet hum of the air-conditioning and fresh floral displays stood on the side tables. The carpet was thick beneath her feet—luxury at every turn.

And there, behind that closed door, Sophie knew, was Luka.

The last time she had knocked on his door he had opened it holding a shirt over his cut and naked from the hips up.

She doubted she'd be so lucky again.

She refused to let him glimpse her nervousness by hesitating and she knocked confidently on the door.

'Come in.'

Confidence faded as, after years of self-imposed abstinence her senses momentarily flared in false hope at the return of his voice.

Still, Sophie barely recognised her hand as it reached for the handle on the door, the nails glossy and painted, and it wasn't shaking, as she had thought it would be.

She was ready to face him.

For her father she would get through this.

Into his office she stepped and Sophie stood for a brief slice of time, accepting that again they shared the same part of the planet.

It must be difficult for him also, Sophie knew, and that was confirmed when he didn't turn around. She gave them both a moment to acclimatise to the other's presence—the air was a little thicker there and made no room for the rest of the world.

Still he did not turn and so she spoke to his straight back and broad shoulders.

'Your assistant asked me to pass on the message that she's just resigned. Apparently I'm the final straw.'

Don't turn around, she wanted to warn him.

Not just yet.

Don't let my heart see you until it's beating slowly again, but of course it was too late. Slowly he turned and she met navy eyes that, Sophie knew, were better served warm. Today, though, she was grateful they were cold, for it allowed her to maintain a necessary distance when instinct told her to run, though not from him.

It would actually, Sophie thought, be easier to run across the room and hurdle the desk in her tight dress. It would be far more natural to be in his arms than to simply stand in a room apart from him.

He offered her a seat and she took it.

She told him the reason that she was there—that her father might be being released and of the lies she had told about them.

He pushed every button and so, despite her very best efforts to stay cool, within a few moments she was standing, backed against the desk by him and jabbing her fingers in his chest, telling him that he would do whatever it took to make things right for her father. That he would be her fake fiancé, that he owed her that much.'

Surprisingly, he agreed, but then he told her he would *never* marry her. In fact, he spelt it out. 'I will agree to be your fake fiancé but never your fake husband. Know that now, or get the hell out.'

There was a brief stand-off but finally Sophie sat.

'Do you want a drink?' Luka offered, and reached for the phone. 'I can have some lunch sent up…' He frowned in slight annoyance when his call wasn't immediately answered.

'She resigned,' Sophie reminded him as he replaced the receiver.

'So she did.'

'You could perhaps ring down to Amber,' Sophie said. 'I'm sure she'd be only too happy to assist Mr Cavaliere…'

Perhaps because he heard the disdain in her voice Luka gave a soft, mirthless laugh.

'Have you slept with every woman in this building?' Sophie asked.

'All the good-looking ones,' Luka said, and then shrugged. 'I don't have to explain myself to you.' He stood. 'We'll go and get lunch.'

'I don't want to go out for lunch and sit and reminisce. I want to talk…'

'Sophie, I can assure you that I don't want a cosy lunch and a trip down memory lane. I have a meeting at two that I need to be back for and I'd like to have eaten by then.'

They took the elevator down and Sophie smiled a pussycat smile again at Amber as they walked through the foyer.

'You've got a nerve coming here and calling your-self my fiancée,' Luka said. He was furious that she could, within the space of half an hour, completely disrupt his life. Amber was sulking, Tara was gone and now, given he had just agreed to be her fiancé, the next few weeks would be a sexless hell, lying in bed beside her.

'I have nerves of steel,' Sophie said.

Almost.

Until she'd gone to Rome, she had hardly been out of Bordo Del Cielo and now she was in a foreign city with a man who was so familiar he felt encoded. It seemed wrong not to touch, not to hold hands, but instead to walk painfully apart down the busy street.

They entered a restaurant and were led through to the back—clearly he came here often because they greeted him by name. The waft of the aroma of herbs and garlic made her feel a little sick.

There was a flurry of menus but Luka shook his head. 'No wine.'

'Am I business?' Sophie checked, as the wine waiter walked off.

'If you were business,' Luka said, 'there would be the finest red breathing now.'

'If I were pleasure?'

'Champagne in bed,' Luka said. 'Just one glass for me, though. I'd have to get back to work.'

'So too would Amber?' Sophie flashed.

'I always give her the afternoon off afterwards,' Luka retorted. 'I'm nice like that.'

She was angry and more so when she saw that Luka was ordering for her—no doubt he didn't think her ca-pable.

'I can order for myself,' she flared.

'I'm sure you can,' Luka said, 'but I have about thirty-two minutes before I need to get back, I'm hungry, angry and I'm guessing you still eat pasta… This isn't a nice lunch, Sophie, this is sustenance because I didn't have time for breakfast.'

'Why was that?' She couldn't resist raising her eyebrows and then she knew she had gone too far because he leant across the table and put her straight back in her place.

'Don't ask me about these last years Sophie. You could have been in them, you chose not to be.' The waiter came back with two bowls of pasta and Sophie sat bristling as he refilled her water.

She never cried.

Never.

She almost did now, she could feel this sting at the back of her nose. Oh, it wasn't quite bread and water. But almost. She got pasta and thirty-two minutes of his precious time—she got his attention, but the irritated version of it.

How might it have been?

'So you work as an events planner?' Luka checked. 'Full time?'

'No.' Sophie shook her head. 'I mean yes, but I have cleared my diary, given that he might be getting out of prison…'

'That must have cheered your clients.'

'I handed them over to a friend in the business.'

'Good,' Luka said.

They talked business, or rather they discussed cold facts.

He told her about his Rome apartment and while she was there he called the management and told them his fiancée would be moving in.

'Over the weekend,' Luka said, but as Sophie went to protest he hung up.

'The judgment isn't till Wednesday.'

'You'll need time to get your bearings and move some of your things over. Give your name at Reception and they will give you a key and help with your luggage. I'll be there Tuesday night…'

'Maybe we should wait to see what happens in court.'

'We'll just have dinner, sort out some final details…' Luka glanced at the time. 'I need to get back.'

Sophie went to stand but he gave her a look that had her halt. 'What are you doing?'

'I was going to walk back with you.'

'Why?' Luka asked. 'We have said all that we need to for now. I will see you on Tuesday night. I have a lot to sort out between now and then. Just give me your number in case I need to contact you.'

'I'll contact you.'

'Fine.'

He walked out of the restaurant and Sophie sat there, watching him disappear into the street, and not once did he look back.

'Could I have the bill?' Sophie asked, but the waiter shook his head.

'It's been taken care of'

She looked at the businessmen ordering coffee, at the groups of laughing friends sharing desserts and the loving couples taking their time over a leisurely lunch with wine.

It was a long ride back to Heathrow.

Yet it felt like a very quick flight back to Rome.

She arrived at Fiumicino airport, where Bella was waiting for her.

'*Credeva voi*?' Bella asked.

'Yes, he believed me,' Sophie answered.

Luka believed she was rich.

Luka believed she was successful.

Even at her very best, he still did not want her.

CHAPTER ELEVEN

'THIS COULD HAVE all been yours,' Bella said, as they walked through Luka's apartment in Prati on the eve of judgment day for her father.

They had picked up the keys in Reception and had declined help with her luggage, but as they'd let themselves in both had been blown away.

Yes, they had seen it online, but walking through it was breath-taking. The tall arched windows were beautifully dressed in heavy fabric. The décor was a mixture of antiques yet there was every modern luxury.

'There's an internal elevator,' Bella said. 'Shall we go up to the rooftop?'

Sophie shook her head. 'I'll explore there later.'

It was agony to be here and to know it was his.

Bella had been busy and now in the wardrobe in the main bedroom hung elegant dresses, skirts and jackets and some shoes. Bella had lent Sophie her mother's heavy silver hairbrush and that was in the large bathroom, along with expensive toiletries they had bought. But even with everything they had managed to cobble together over the last few days, even with all their resources pooled and their savings almost spent, it was just a tiny drop in the ocean compared to Luka's obvious wealth.

'Doesn't it make you feel jealous?' Bella pushed.

'I chose not to go to London with him, remember. Anyway, who knows what would have happened if I had gone? We might not have got on,' Sophie pointed out 'One romantic afternoon doesn't mean that we would have lasted a lifetime. And, anyway, I want nothing that has Malvolio's name attached to it.'

'Luka works hard.'

'We work hard,' Sophie said. 'The only difference is we didn't get a step up on the ladder. Our parents didn't give us a share in a hotel to kick our careers off.'

It was easier to resent him, to sound jealous. It was far easier then admitting the truth—that she missed him so much, every single minute of every single day.

And as for the nights…

'What time is he getting here?' Bella asked.

'Any time now,' Sophie said. 'We're going out to dinner to make sure our stories match.'

'Well, just be as expensive as the women where we work. Don't say sorry to staff and don't…' Bella gave her a smile. 'You'll be fine. Oh, I got you a present. Actually, two…'

'Bella!' Sophie scolded when she saw the latest phone. 'We can't afford this.'

'Yes, we can. You can hardly pretend to be an event planner and not even have a phone. When you're done with Luka, I want it if you don't.'

'What's this?' She opened the second present, which was a heavy bottle filled with very expensive perfume. 'Bella…'

'What woman wouldn't have perfume in the bathroom.'

'We didn't have the money for that.'

'Oh, well…'

'You stole this?'

'Yes, I did,' Bella said. 'And I don't feel guilty and I don't feel ashamed. If that's the worst thing I do then I am glad to do it for you.'

Sophie opened the perfume and sprayed it on her wrist and then squirted Bella, who laughed but then it faded.

She had a question of her own.

'Did he say anything about Matteo?'

'Nothing.'

'I thought they were in business together...'

'We really didn't talk that much.'

'I'm scared I'm going to find out that Matteo is married. I know he must think I'm still a whore.'

'Matteo paid for you,' Sophie pointed out.

There was so much shame for them both.

'I still think about him all the time,' Bella admitted. 'Do you think he remembers me?'

'Of course he must,' Sophie said. 'But it was years ago, Bella. If seeing Luka again has taught me anything it is that people move on. Luka is busy with his life, his women. He has long since moved on from those days. So too must we. When all this over, you and I are going to chase our dreams. I don't care what it takes but you are going to go design school and I'm going to have a career.'

'On the ships.'

'Who knows?' Sophie said. 'But I'm not going to spend the rest of my life mourning Luka. I want this over and done with.'

'I'm going to go,' Bella said.

'Thank you.'

Bella forced a smile. 'I want all the details. Imagine you and Luka sharing a bed after all this time...'

Sophie smiled as her friend left but alone she walked nervously around the apartment. The bedroom mocked her, the bed mocked her. It was hard to believe that soon she would be lying in there at night with Luka. That wasn't all that upset her. It wasn't just the thought that he had lain in this bed with others that had bile rising like a volcano.

It was that Luka had had a life, a good one.

But without her.

Alone she walked around and then pulled back the antique gate and stepped into the elevator, it was small but luxurious, and she stepped out to a view that under any other circumstances would have taken her breath away.

Now, again, she was close to tears.

Rome glittered before her, the view better than any from the hotel because you were actually in it. She could hear the noise from the street below and see the Colosseum and the Vatican. The light was fading and soon the streets would pulse with nightlife yet it was not this view she craved.

She had never ached to be back in Bordo Del Cielo till now—there were too many dark memories there. Since seeing Luka, though, she craved to be there. She wanted to get back to her secret cove and to be near water that was so clear and cool that it took the sting out of summer.

Unable to bear it, Sophie headed back down but there was no relief to be had there, for having worked out a room for her father she walked down the main corridor and peered into the bedroom she would share with Luka.

The room was magnificent, better than the presidential suite at the hotel where she worked.

The furnishings were heavy and masculine and it would take more than a silver hairbrush and a few dresses in the wardrobe to detract from the male energy that stopped her from going in.

The bed was wide, dressed in muted jewelled tones, and she could not imagine herself lying there with him.

Worse, she tormented herself by imagining him lying there with another woman.

'Sophie?' His deep voice made her jump and then spin around on her new high heels.

'I didn't hear you come in.'

'Did you expect me to knock?'

'Of course not.' She could hardly bear to meet his gaze. She had seen him angry, she had seen him arrogant and aloof, but she had never seen him like this— there were lines fanning from his eyes and his mouth was grim, his complexion tinged grey, and his tension palpable.

He looked as if he was dreading this just as much as she was.

'Where do you want to go for dinner?' he asked.

'We could have something to eat here.'

'I would guess that we'll be eating here rather a lot,' Luka said. 'If your father gets off, I doubt we'll be going out very much.'

'I don't expect you to be here all the time,' Sophie said. 'We can say that you're busy with work.'

'He's dying, Sophie,' Luka said. 'And if I were engaged to you, if I did love you, your father knows that I would do more than put in a few cameo appearances.'

'Of course.'

'I'll give you a tour,' he offered, but Sophie shook her head.

'I already know my way around.'

'Have you organised a nurse for him?'

'I thought it better to wait and see what happens to-morrow,' Sophie said, although the truth was there was no way she could afford a private nurse for her father.

'I'm going to go to court in the morning,' Luka said. 'I'll text you with what's happening.'

'Why would you go to court?'

'To save you from having to go,' Luka said, and with that simple sentence her heart just about folded in on it-self because that was the type of man she had lost. This was what being loved by Luka would mean. 'Have you any idea how big it is going to be tomorrow with the press and everything?' he checked.

'I'm starting to,' Sophie said. 'I saw on the news that the press are already camping out by the court.'

'They think he's going to be there when the ruling is made,' Luka said. 'Hopefully he can slip out of the in-firmary before the press work it out. Is there anything else that I need to know?'

'I don't think so. We can talk over dinner.'

'I've changed my mind about dinner,' he said.

'Where are you going?' Sophie asked, as he went to walk out.

'What the hell does it have to with you?' he asked.

'If we're supposed to be engaged...'

'The games begin tomorrow, Sophie.' He came right up to her face. 'Tomorrow we lie in that bed, tomorrow we pretend that we care. I've just realised that tonight I don't have to even pretend that I like you, so I won't. I intend to enjoy my last night of freedom before *my* sentence begins.'

He walked off and Sophie knew she should hold her tongue but it had never been her forte. 'Oh, I'm sorry to have thrown such a spanner into your charmed life.'

'Charmed?' Luka turned. 'Tell me, Sophie, what part of my life exactly is charmed? I've worked eighteen-hour days for this. You talk as if it has been handed to me on a plate.'

'The share in a hotel from Daddy was a rather nice start.'

'He had nothing to do with it. I worked for that myself,' Luka said. 'What I didn't say in court was that I knew for years that my father was rotten to the core and that your father was his yes-man. So, tell me more about this charmed life, Sophie. When I came back to London I practically had to go on my knees to my partners at the hotel. Six months in prison takes some explaining. Do you really think my colleagues embraced me on my return? Do you not think that I had to prove over and over that I could be trusted?'

She stood with pale lips as he told her how things had been for him.

'Do you not think that when somebody looks me up and finds out that I was in prison, awaiting trial, for six months that it doesn't slur my name? I took nothing from my father. I have done everything I can to make right what he did. I handed back everything that man gave me. The only thing I couldn't return was the education. You can't unlearn things unfortunately but God knows there are things I've tried to forget...'

He was talking about them, Sophie knew it. He was back in his bed and taking her for the first time with his eyes. 'I washed my hands of Bordo Del Cielo. I only came back that time to rid myself of you once and for all. I should never have opened that door to you!' Even before she could move he grabbed her wrist. 'Slap me again...' Luka warned.

'And you'll slap me back?' Sophie challenged, and she didn't understand because he almost smiled.

Yes, he almost smiled because on so many levels she matched him and in so many ways he adored her. How he would love to end this row in a different way, to kiss her right now into submission, yet he refused that pleasure for himself.

'Slap me again,' he amended, 'and before the finger-marks have faded the engagement will be off and you can tell your father why if you must. I mean it, Sophie, and you should know that I don't give second warnings.'

She stood there and he had won but even as he passed the finish line he kept on sprinting.

'I'm going out now and I'm going to be with a woman who does not question, a woman who is sweet and warm...'

'Give Claudia my love,' Sophie spat, and hoped that the fact she knew his lover's name meant that she sailed past him on shock value alone, but Luka just grinned at the jealous snarl to her voice.

'Claudia?' Luka checked.

'You were with her at Hotel Fiscella.'

'Because Matteo and I are thinking of buying it,' Luka said, and Sophie was grateful that she had handed in her notice as she realised how close she had come to having Luka as her boss. 'Claudia is one of my lawyers.'

'She was there for the purchase of the hotel?'

'No,' Luka said. 'I hired her to get your father released.'

She stood there frozen to the spot, hating how he was always one step ahead, how this man continued to sideswipe her.

'Why?' Sophie asked. 'Why would you hire a lawyer to get my father out?'

No, he didn't tell her about the necklace burning a hole in his pocket and the hellish guilt that had made it his mission to see Paulo freed.

'For this moment, Sophie.' Luka lied. 'So that you would come to my office and ask me to be with you. For the pleasure of lying in bed with you and doing *nothing*...' Black was his smile.

'Why do you hate me so much?'

'You'll work it out,' Luka said. 'I'm going out now. I'll see you tomorrow when the real games begin.'

CHAPTER TWELVE

SHE DIDN'T WANT her father to be released.

Sophie decided she must surely be the most terrible daughter in history because at midday, when still nothing had been said on the news, when still the judge had not ruled, she had this brief fantasy that his application would be denied and she could walk out of the apartment and away from Luka without a single word.

Instead, late in the afternoon, she got a text.

Your father has left the infirmary and will be with you shortly. The judge made his ruling in private for security reasons. It will shortly be announced.

Aside from the hell of what lay ahead, Sophie still wondered what sort of a nightmare her father's release might have been without the well-oiled machine of Luka's life swinging into action.

She saw on the news the crush of reporters both at the court and another group that was now outside the prison infirmary and she shuddered at the thought of her and Bella dealing with this.

Even as the journalists jockeyed for position at the prison gates Paulo was sitting in Luka's home.

'I thought Luka would be here,' Paulo said.

'He was at court,' Sophie said. 'He has been keeping me up to date with all that is going on.'

'It is a beautiful home,' her father said, and then he looked at the view from a huge leather chair. 'Is there a balcony? I would like to breathe fresh air...'

'There's a balcony in your room and there is also a rooftop garden,' Sophie said.

'I would never make the stairs.'

'There's an elevator.' Luka deep voice caught her unawares and again, to the sound of him, she jumped, not that her father noticed.

'Luka!' She heard the sheer joy in her father's voice as he pushed himself to stand and then she watched Luka's eyes briefly shutter as he embraced the old man.

'Thank you,' Paulo said in a heartfelt voice as he took Luka into his arms. 'Thank you for all you did. I know it was you who got me out...'

'Nonsense.' Luka's voice was gruff. 'The judge was right, there were many mistakes made at the trial. You deserve to have your freedom.'

'You knew it was Luka who was behind this?' Sophie checked.

'Of course,' Paulo said. 'There are not many files that just happen to be picked up. I knew that it had to be you.'

'Father?' Sophie frowned because her father sounded far more together than he had in recent weeks. 'Were you pretending to be confused?'

'Sometimes.' He smiled.

'He's not really sick,' Luka said, and then he saw Sophie's horrified expression at the thought that they might be stuck in this lie for ever so he relented. 'That was a joke.'

'Ha-ha,' Sophie said, and then she looked at her father and she knew in her heart that he didn't have long and yet somehow he was here and they were together.

It was agony.

For Paulo the best wine sat breathing up on the rooftop. Sophie had spent the long day waiting for news, cooking her father's favourite pasta sauce, which he ate with relish.

'It tastes of home,' Paulo said. 'Almost.'

She glanced at Luka's plate.

It was untouched.

She watched as Luka poured three glasses and her father reached for his.

'Should you be drinking?' Sophie checked. 'You are on a lot of medication.'

'You are your mother's daughter.' Paulo laughed. 'I just got out of prison.'

'Even so…'

'You worry too much,' Paulo chided.

'Someone has to.'

Luka glanced over at Sophie's slightly bitter retort. She had dealt with so much, that Luka knew—moving so that she could be close to her father, giving up her dreams of working on the cruise liners.

Letting go of them?

Had that been what she had been doing on the beach that night? Luka briefly pondered.

What did it matter now?

The past was closed.

They just had the present to get through and despite Paulo's slight second wind from his release, Luka knew the charade would not play out for long.

'So.' Paulo looked over at Luka. 'What are your plans for my daughter?'

'I learnt a long time ago that it is foolish to make

plans on Sophie's behalf,' Luka responded. 'She is her own person.'

He looked at Sophie's tense expression. There was a curl of thought forming but he soon lost that thread because Paulo was making grand plans.

'I'd like to have a party,' Paulo said. 'We never toasted your engagement.'

'There's no need for a party,' Sophie said. 'We don't need a fuss to be made.'

'I would like to celebrate.' Paulo was insistent. 'Just a small gathering.'

He started to cough and Sophie took him inside, leaving Luka sitting out there.

'Please, Sophie,' her father said as she helped him to bed. 'I want some photos for you to keep. I want a night we can all remember...'

She didn't need photos to remember this, Sophie thought as she came out of her father's bedroom.

'He's asleep,' she said.

'Lucky him.' Luka's response was curt. 'I might take one of the spare rooms—' Luka started, but any hope of pulling that particular piece of wool over Paulo's eyes faded as his bedroom door opened.

'Could you bring me my wine from the table?'

'Father!'

'Stop fussing,' Paulo said. 'And can you show me how the radio works? I would like to fall to sleep to music.'

As Sophie headed up to the rooftop garden he smiled at Luka. 'Where do you two sleep?' Paulo checked. 'Just in case I need Sophie in the night. I won't come in, of course. I'll just knock.'

'Sophie sleeps in that room,' Luka attempted. 'I have the main one.'

'Please!' Paulo was laughing as Sophie reappeared

with his wine. 'Your fiancé is trying to tell me you have separate rooms! I am not that old-fashioned that you have to pretend.'

'Great!' Luka hissed, as they finally closed the door to his room.

'I told you that he'd never buy us sleeping apart.'

'I just never envisaged the hell it would be.'

Sophie went into the bathroom and undressed. She put on a small nightdress and took a few calming breaths before heading out.

Luka wasn't about to scuttle off to the bathroom to change and was still stripping off as she slipped into bed.

'He wants this party.'

'Then he can have one. I will call Matteo,' Luka said. 'I'll ask him to fly in.'

'He might let it slip that we haven't been together very long.'

'Why would he let it slip?' Luka frowned. 'Matteo knows what is going on, he's a good friend. He knows that this is all just a ruse.'

'You've told him?'

'Why wouldn't I tell him, Sophie? We work together, we are in business together, we grew up together. I don't keep secrets from people who matter to me any more.'

'I could ask Bella.'

'Whatever you want. I'll ring him now.'

'But it's nearly midnight.'

'Yes,' Luka snapped. 'I'm early to bed tonight.'

'Can you go one hour without reminding me about your active sex life?'

'Why does it bother you so much, Sophie?'

She didn't answer.

Luka laughed at her non-reaction and got into bed.

He called Matteo and lay chatting to his friend. Yes, it was hell being engaged, he told him, and then he was serious.

'We're going to have a small party for Paulo,' Luka said. 'Will you be able to fly in? Sophie might ask Bella...' There was a pause before Luka spoke again. 'Of course it's not a problem. Bring anyone you choose.'

He hung up.

'He can only make it tomorrow,' Luka said.

'Tomorrow?'

'He has an important meeting to prepare for in Dubai. Is tomorrow a problem?'

'Of course not.'

'Oh, and he's bringing his girlfriend.'

Sophie decided against asking Bella. She knew how crushed she be to see Matteo with another woman.

'I'll keep it simple,' Sophie said, thinking, as she always had to, about money. 'I might just make his favourite meals...'

'Get it catered,' Luka said. 'Today was an exception. I understand you wanted to give him a taste of home tonight but I'm telling you this much—if you were my fiancée you wouldn't have spent the day slaving and making sauce when there are the best restaurants across the street. Get someone to come and dress the garden and organise the music...' He stopped then. 'Sorry, I forget that you're an events organiser.'

Sophie was sure he knew she'd been lying.

'Is he driving you mad yet?' Luka asked, and Sophie gave a reluctant smile, because her father was driving her a little crazy. 'Are you starting to remember why you were only too willing to leave?'

'A bit,' Sophie admitted. 'I am sick of him saying I am just like my mother.'

'She had him under her thumb,' Luka said.

They lay in bed and it felt impossibly awkward, or at least it did for Sophie. Luka seemed completely fine with it. His hand was beneath the sheet and she blinked when she realised he was arranging himself in his underwear, then he saw her shocked look but merely shrugged.

'I've got an erection. I'm just moving it.' He grinned at her shocked expression. 'Don't worry, I'm not going to come near you.'

'You're in a very good mood.'

'I know,' Luka said. 'I thought it would be hell but I'm really enjoying myself. I like seeing your father free and I love watching you edgy and able to do nothing about it.'

Then he did the cruellest thing.

He kissed her on the tip of her nose and two minutes later he was asleep.

CHAPTER THIRTEEN

LUKA WOKE UP AND for the first morning in his life it was the right face on the pillow next to him.

He examined her beautiful face and he looked at where one breast had fallen out of her nightdress. Their legs were loosely entwined, hers over one of his and beneath the other.

She was loyal, she was fierce and she matched him.

He knew their dance, even if it had only been a short one.

He knew the steps, for their souls were familiar.

And she would never forgive him for what his father had done.

If she did, it wouldn't be for long. In the heat of the moment his father's sins would be raised and then hurled at him in her, oh, so Sicilian way.

And he would not live like that.

He wished it were different.

If he could change one thing about her, would he, though?

It would be like trimming the corner off a work of art, or like removing one letter from the alphabet and watching one's words fall apart.

'Why are you staring at me?' Sophie asked as her brown eyes opened to his.

'Because you're in my bed and there is not much else to look at.' Then his eyes drifted down to her exposed breast and he gave a lazy smile as she tucked herself in.

'See,' Luka said, 'it's rude when I rearrange myself, but not when you do.'

'Hard again, Luka?' Sophie smiled.

'That's for me to know,' Luka answered, and didn't even roll over as she climbed out of bed and went to her wardrobe.

She had no idea what to wear. Bella had made her plenty of stunning clothes but none were very practical for making coffee so instead she took out one of his shirts.

'How's the phobia?' Luka asked. 'Last time you put on one of my shirts there were ten policemen in the bedroom. You seem remarkably calm—no flashbacks?'

She didn't bother answering him. Instead, she went to make coffee and didn't look up when Luka came through. He was wearing a suit and looked ready for the office.

'I thought you'd take today off.'

'No.'

'I thought—'

'I have an office here in Rome and I have a lot of work that needs to be done. Anyway, I thought it might be nice for you to have a day with your father, without being on edge with me here.'

'I'm going to take him in some breakfast,' Sophie said.

'The doctor is coming at nine to check up on him,' Luka said, and he put a credit card on the bench.

'What's this for?'

'The caterers and things.'

'I can cover that,' Sophie lied. She really had been

intending to spend the day cooking and doing what she could to prepare for tonight.

'Please, don't say you will get this. You asked me to go along with things as if we were together. Well, that is how it would be. Book the caterers, get the garden looking beautiful. I have never heard of your business so I don't know how easy it will be for you to arrange things with no notice. Use my name, you won't have a problem'

She didn't have a single one.

It was strange to have the world at your fingers, courtesy of the Cavaliere name.

Except people didn't jump in fear when she rang and said that she was organising a last-minute gathering; instead, they seemed genuinely happy to help.

And so she enjoyed herself amidst the saddest of times.

The columns of foliage and scented trees were decorated with tiny lights that would come on at sunset. A string quartet had been arranged and the food had Sophie's mouth watering even as she made her selections.

Hearing her father cough and struggle to catch his breath, Sophie knew this would all be over, long before the credit-card bills came in.

'What's this?' Paulo asked.

'A new shirt and suit.' Sophie smiled. 'They just need you to try it on so they can take it in.'

Yes, to Sophie, Luka's life *was* charmed.

And so she had a beautician come to Luka's home and sat on a velvet chair in the bedroom as her thick black hair was spun into heavy ringlets and her eyelids were painted a smoky grey.

'Red lips…' the beautician said, but Sophie shook her head.

In her bag, still there, was her once-used lip glaze.

She wondered if it would all have dried up but, no, it went on easily.

'Just touch it up through the evening,' the beautician said. 'And try not to play with your hair or the curls will drop.'

Sophie chose her dress from the selection Bella had made. A simple black dress that went with the shoes she had worn on the day she had walked into his office was her choice. She tried it on and let out a small hiss of frustration. The front was far too low and as for the back there wasn't one.

Luka walked in as Sophie stood staring in the mirror, trying to fathom if she'd be safe without a bra.

He saw first her back, glossy and brown, with black ringlets snaking down it. He looked down and saw the muscles of her calves drawn lean in high heels and he walked over, anticipating her slight jump as he came into view in the mirror.

'I'm sorry about all this,' Sophie said.

'Don't be sorry.' Luka shrugged. 'I agreed to go along with this. Of course your father would want a special night.'

'Thank you.'

He looked at her lips and told himself he was imagining things because they were the very lips he had kissed that long-ago day. He looked down at the gape of unrestrained cleavage and thick nipples that jutted from the fabric.

'I forgot to pack my backless bra…'

'Those bras are the ugliest things I've ever seen.'

She could feel a shiver on her back, so light she thought it might be his finger, but she realised he was holding a drink with one hand and removing his tie with the other.

It was the nerves on her spine that were leaping in hope.

'I'll change,' Sophie said, turning to go to the wardrobe, except Luka didn't step aside and she walked slap bang into him.

His drink he held steady.

It was her heart that seemed to spill on the floor.

'You'll wear that,' Luka said. 'You'll wear what turns me on.'

'Why?' Sophie demanded. Why the hell would he do this to them?

'Mortification of the flesh,' Luka answered. 'It's my new game.'

He undid his shirt and she could feel the tense pinch of her nostrils as he took it off and she would hold her breath till he headed for the shower.

He didn't, though.

Instead, he went to the wardrobe and took out a clean shirt.

'Aren't you going to shower?'

'There's no time for that.'

'Luka, please...'

'Do I smell?' He came over and lifted his arm and she simply refused to breathe him in. 'No, I showered this morning. You get me in the raw...'

She wanted him clean and sterile—she didn't want his heady scent.

'See?' Luka smiled at her pale face. 'It's a good game. Well, it is. for me. I keep forgetting you don't like all that business...' He did up his shirt and Sophie chose to get out.

'I'm going to help my father get ready.'

'No need.' His eyes did not leave her alone for a minute. 'I brought a nurse back with me. Another one will take her place at midnight. They come with the best references and I have done the necessary checks.'

'I take care of my father.'

'Of course you do,' Luka said. 'But as a daughter, not a nurse. I was thinking today that if I had a child, not that I ever will, but if I did I would not want them looking after me in that way. Enjoy him as your father now.'

'I can't afford a nurse.' Her words were shrill, her admission reluctantly dragged through strained lips, but Luka didn't even blink.

'You know,' he drawled, 'they're the first honest words to come out of your mouth. We need to head out there. Matteo and Shandy will be here soon, I believe they're getting engaged in a few weeks…'

'Shandy?' Sophie said, resentment prickling for Bella, for her heart would break when she found out that Matteo was about to get engaged. 'What sort of a name is that? Is he bringing a horse?'

'Oh…' Luka gave a low laugh. 'She's back.'

'Who?'

'The *real* Sophie,' Luka answered. 'I keep glimpsing her but then you tuck her away. Bring her out, Sophie. Don't worry, I can handle her.'

The *real* Sophie took the elevator with him up to the rooftop garden.

Her father was there, thanks to the nurse.

And so too were Matteo and Shandy.

'You've done well,' Luka said.

Sophie had. The garden twinkled with lights, the string quartet was softly playing and the waiters were waiting to pounce.

'It's been so long,' Sophie said, and kissed Matteo's cheek.

'Just not quite long enough,' Matteo said, and Sophie jerked her head back.

He hated her too, only she didn't understand why.

'This is Shandy.' Matteo introduced the glossy blonde and Sophie looked at her. With her long legs and slightly protruding teeth, she actually did slightly resemble a horse.

'Shandy.' Sophie kissed her on both cheeks too and met Luka's eyes.

She would behave, Sophie swore.

The food was delicious.

Porcini mushrooms with black truffle pappardelle, the sauce thick and creamy and mopped up with bread rich with herbs and olives, but, Paulo mused, 'It cannot beat Sicilian *panne*...'

'Nothing beats Sicilian,' Sophie said.

She meant it for Bella, for her friend, she meant it to remind Matteo of the woman who was not here tonight, yet it was Luka's eyes she met as she said it.

'No.' She put her hand over the wine glass as the waiter went to pour.

'Enjoy yourself.' Luka smiled. 'I am.'

He liked the real Sophie; he liked watching her attempt to rein herself in as he invited her to come out.

Both were, both knew, playing the most dangerous of games.

Dessert was pure heaven—thick cassata that was as rich and as liqueur-laced as it had been more than a decade ago when he had denied her that kiss.

And then tiny *cannellonis*, the ricotta tart with lemon, refreshing to the tongue.

'Limoncello.' Paulo smiled as he sipped the drink of home, and then he stood on frail legs as Sophie sat.

'Tonight makes up for many things,' Paulo said. 'Tonight I sit with old friends and new...' He raised a glass to Shandy, and Luka and Matteo did the same.

The glass felt like lead to Sophie but she raised hers too.

Then she had to listen to her father say how right she and Luka were. That they were simply meant for each other.

'Luka was twelve when his mother died. I remember Sophie crying that night for his pain.' She had forgotten that. Deliberately. To escape the pain, she had avoided their past and now her father walked them both through it.

For appearances' sake Luka's hand was over hers but it was hot and dry and there was no caress from him as her father exposed the love that was lost.

'When we had a party for Luka moving to London, I remember Sophie coming down the stairs. She had put tissues in her bra. She wanted Luka to notice her...

'"In time,' I told her. But she was fourteen and impatient and did not want to listen to me,' He looked at Sophie. 'Listen to me now. You and Luka's time is now. Don't ever waste it.'

Then it was Luka's turn to speak.

He cleared his throat and thanked their few guests. Out of the corner of her eye Sophie could see that her father was fading. Smiling but fading, and she was so grateful to Luka to have given him this night.

'Paulo, we are so happy to celebrate this night with you. I am very blessed. Some might say that I have a *charmed* life...' He looked at Sophie and with a smile that did not reach his eyes he painted her heart black.

'That is because of you, Sophie…' He offered her his hand and Sophie stood. 'I know you have your ring, but I wanted something to mark this night.'

She opened a box and there was a fine bracelet and she read the inscription:

'*Per sempre insieme.*'

Together for ever.

She wanted to hurl it over the balcony and to the street or throw it across the floor, but instead she handed it to her father, who was putting on his glasses to read what had been written.

'We should go soon,' Matteo said to Shandy.

'Why?' Sophie challenged. 'When we're having so much fun?'

'You could stay here,' Luka offered, but Matteo shook his head. 'It is good to check the hotel out…'

'Where are you staying?' Paulo asked.

'Fiscella,' Matteo answered, and Sophie shivered and hoped that Bella wasn't working there tomorrow. 'Luka and I are thinking of buying it,' he explained to Paulo. 'It is a nice old hotel but it needs a lot of refurbishment. I want to see for myself a few things.'

'Doesn't Bella work there?' Paulo asked, and Sophie tensed, especially when she felt the scrutiny of Luka's gaze.

'She does.'

'Doing what?' Matteo asked.

'She's a chambermaid,' Paulo answered. 'Isn't she, Sophie?'

'Well, I guess it gives her access to a richer clientele.' Matteo's response was surly and, taking Shandy by the hand, he led her to the floor to dance.

'I thought you would wear your mother's earrings

tonight,' Paulo said. 'You wanted them for your engagement.'

'They didn't go with the dress.' Sophie's answer was brittle and Luka noted it.

'Come on,' Luka said. 'Dance.'

I don't want to dance with you, she wanted to say. *I don't want to be in your arms because there I might convince myself that this is real.*

He held her at her waist and she could feel his cheek by hers and it was their first dance and had to be their last because it nearly killed her to be back in his arms.

Yet she didn't want their one dance to end—ever.

'Why did you get me that bracelet? Why would you have engraved "Together for Ever"?'

'What did you want me to have inscribed? "*Né tu letu né iu cunsulatu*"?'

She looked right at him with narrowed eyes as he delivered a very apt Sicilian saying—'Neither you happy nor I consoled.'

'Do you need consoling, Luka?' Her smile was mean with seduction.

'Are you happy?' Luka asked, and saw that her smile struggled to stay on. 'Do you miss it?'

'Miss what?' Sophie hissed, yet she knew what was coming and she was right, for he practically echoed Bella's words.

'Everything we could have had.'

'You ended things with me,' Sophie said. 'You came back to Bordo Del Cielo just to say you didn't want to marry me.'

'Oh, you are so good at rewriting history, Sophie,' Luka refuted. 'I ended the old us, we were just starting anew. It was you that ultimately broke things off.

You who refused to come to London with me. So,' he asked, 'do you regret it?'

If she said that she did, then she admitted her love. And if she admitted her love, then it made the last years wasted, and that shamed her more than being led to a police car dressed in his shirt.

Instead, she clung to her pride as she fought not to rest her head on his shoulder. 'No.'

'Then you're more of a fool than I thought.'

'Oh, I'm a fool now, am I?' Sophie retorted. 'A peasant and a fool.'

'You'll never let it go, will you? Always you let your temper get the better of you,' Luka said into her ear, and she fumed silently in his arms as one by one he took out her faults and examined them as their bodies swayed to the music and turned the other on. 'Your quick tongue...'

'My slow tongue...' Sophie said, and he laughed a dark laugh at her attempt to change the subject.

Yes, the old Sophie was back.

'It won't work, Sophie.'

'Ah, but it already has,' she said, because she could feel him hard against her and certainly, for Luka's sake, one dance must now become two.

'You should be careful who you tease,' he said into her ear. 'I have no problem sleeping with you and then walking away.'

'You would do that, wouldn't you?'

'Oh, yes,' Luka said. 'So don't play with fire.'

It felt strange to be both angry and turned on, to want and to resist.

'Why do you loathe me?' Sophie asked. 'You have a wonderful life. And why does Matteo hate me?'

'Because I'm boring when I'm drunk,' Luka said. 'I guess I tend to complain about you.'

'And why do you hate me so?'

'Many reasons.'

'Such as?'

'You held what my father did against me. You compare me to him when I never did that to you.'

'My father is a good man.'

'Perhaps, but he is not completely innocent.' He dropped a kiss on her burning shoulder and there was nowhere to hide, no row that could be had in the public arena she had made for them, and resistance was agony.

'Don't make him out a saint,' Luka said.

'I don't.' Sophie closed her eyes as his face came back to her cheek.

'What else?' she asked.

'Your inability to back down, to admit you were wrong,' Luka said, and then he warned her what he was about to do. 'I'm going to kiss you now. I'm going to kiss you and there is nowhere you can go and nowhere you can hide, and I am going to remind you what you let go. You are going to taste what you must now miss every day.'

'A small kiss is hardly going to have me on my knees.'

'Who said small?'

'There are people present. My father...'

'Would he not expect us to kiss at our engagement party? Just pull away when it gets too much...'

'Luka, you seem to think I still want you. I told you, I don't want anyone.'

'Oh, that's right—your phobia...'

He pulled his head back so she could see his black smile.

'When you need me to stop, I shall.'

Sophie blinked. She already needed him to stop and he had barely started, but just the graze of his lips was too much, just the press of his mouth was too dangerous.

He was necessarily cruel.

Necessarily because their mouths needed each other, and it was a relief just to give in to mutual want.

The shiver along her spine this time came from his fingers, and it was Sophie's tongue that caressed his.

Just the tip.

That cool, muscular tip that stroked hers enough to remind their scalding bodies of the fire they'd once made.

'Enough for show,' Sophie said, and pulled back.

Just not enough for them.

'I'm going to see Matteo off.' Luka ran a slow tongue over his lips and tasted her again. 'Your father looks as if he needs to go to bed.'

He left her burning.

As Luka saw their guests off, Sophie took the elevator with her father and the nurse.

'It is good to see you so happy.'

'We are happy, Dad,' Sophie told him, as she saw him to his room. 'You can see how Luka takes care of me. You don't have to worry any more.'

'But I do,' Paulo said, then turned to the nurse. 'Can you excuse us, please?'

The nurse nodded and they walked into his room. 'You have no idea how good that feels,' Paulo said.

'What?'

'To ask for privacy and to be given it. You have made my final days happy, Sophie, but there is more that I want. I need to walk you down the aisle. I want to return to Bordo Del Cielo...'

'The journey will be too much for you.'

'Then I will die returning home to my Rosa.'

'Father…'

'Sophie, don't say no to me. Let me see you and Luka marry in the same church that your mother and I did, now, this weekend. I won't see another one, this much I know…'

How could she say no to him?

'I'll speak to Luka.'

CHAPTER FOURTEEN

SHE WALKED INTO the bedroom. Luka was lying on his side, his back to her and the sheet low on his hips.

She didn't know if he was awake or asleep but she knew that she had to tell him between now and the morning that she had told her father they would marry. She headed into the en suite and started to undress then realised she had left her nightdress in the bedroom. Rather than going back in there, she undressed and wrapped herself in a towel then took off her make-up and brushed her teeth.

Luka was going to be furious, Sophie knew.

But, hell, he must surely understand the impossible situation her father had put her in. He was days away from dying—of course he wanted to go home one last time, of course he would want to see his daughter married to the man she supposedly loved.

Loved?

She didn't love Luka, she abhorred him, Sophie told herself, but then she caught sight of her lying eyes in the mirror as she rinsed her mouth.

Her body loved him, she knew, because it hadn't just been hard work and few hours to spare that had kept her from other men, it had been the utter lack of wanting them when she looked at them. She'd had a few kisses that had tasted of plastic compared to being devoured by the man on the other side of the bathroom door.

She stepped into the bedroom.

'Luka…' Her voice was perhaps a little too quiet for someone who was truly trying to wake another, but when he didn't respond Sophie decided that she'd tell him in the morning, and she slipped out of her dress and panties.

'What?'

He didn't turn and Sophie reached for her nightdress as she spoke. 'It will keep till morning.'

'Tell me now.' He turned then and he wished he hadn't for despite the darkness he could see her naked body with arms raised as she pulled on her nightdress.

He should turn away quickly, yet he didn't. Instead, in that brief moment everything he'd imagined was verified. He had been trying to ignore her, willing sleep to come before she slipped into bed beside him and now he had to endure another night fighting instinct.

Sophie met his eyes and denied the sexual tension between them. 'My father…' She kept her voice calm. 'I couldn't get out of it.'

'Get out of what?'

'He wants to go back to Bordo Del Cielo as soon as possible. He wants to visit my mother's grave.'

'I'll arrange the flight, you can go with him. I'll make up some excuse about work as the reason I cannot be there. I never want to go back.'

'He wants us both to go with him, though,' Sophie said. His eyes were fixed on hers and her skin prickled with heat as she continued. 'I've said that we will marry this Sunday.'

He said nothing and she stood there awaiting his response.

'Luka?'

'Are you going to stand there all night or get into bed?'

Sophie took a tentative step forward, pulled back the sheet and slipped in.

Her heart was thumping. The tension in the room was almost unbearable—a mixture of fear at his response and a deep, thick arousal. She knew he was turned on, and so too was she; she could not catch her breath, though she tried to keep it even.

'Did you hear what I said about us?'

'I heard.'

'You didn't respond.'

'I have already told you where I stand on that—I will never marry you.'

'But I've told him that we shall.'

'Then you'd better hope that he dies before the service is due to commence.'

'Luka…' Fury bolted her upright but he pulled her down and pinned her.

'What?' he demanded. 'Say what you were going to.'

'You can't mean that.'

'Oh, I mean it,' he said. 'I'll go along with it, I'll go back home with you and get involved with the preparations. I'll say and do all the right things right up until the church but know this—I won't be standing at the altar when you get there, Sophie. You'll be jilted in front of the town.'

'You hate me so much that you'd do that to me.'

'I hate you as much as I want you.'

'That doesn't make sense,' Sophie said, yet even as the words left her lips she had worked out what he meant. He hated her fiercely, judging by the erection now pressing into her thigh.

'I'll make it clearer, then,' Luka said. 'I hate you as much as you want me.'

'But I don't want you. I don't want anyone,' Sophie said. With every cell in her body she lied and she knew he knew it. 'Will you marry me, Luka? I'm not asking for forever...'

'You miss the very point.'

'Luka, can we start again?' Sophie drew in a breath. 'Can we put the past behind us and start anew?'

'Without examining it?' Luka checked. 'Without accusing?'

'Yes.'

'How very convenient, Sophie, because then you don't have admit you were wrong. You get to wipe the slate clean for as long as it suits you.'

'What does that mean?'

He got up and headed to the safe where her mother's necklace was kept and opened it.

Just hand it to her, he told himself.

Simply give her the benefit of the doubt.

Hand it over to her and see what she says.

'You want a clean slate?' Luka checked.

'Yes,' Sophie said. 'I won't raise what was said in court.'

He stared at the cross and chain; he almost believed she could do it until Sophie spoke on.

'I won't bring up the other women.'

'But. You. Just. Did!' Luka shouted in exasperation, and took out the earring instead of the cross. She was nowhere ready for the truth. 'You're still the fourteen-year-old kid padding her bra.'

'Meaning?'

'You haven't grown up, or rather you haven't moved on.'

'Still the peasant.'

'One row,' Luka shouted, 'one cross word and you hurl the past back at me. So where's the clean slate, Sophie?'

'Keep it down,' she said. 'I don't want my father to hear us row.'

'He can't,' Luka said. 'These walls are soundproof So row away, Sophie, say what you have to. Here…' He tossed her a piece of gold.

Just not the right one.

'My mother's earring.'

'I found it in my bedroom,' Luka said. 'Come on, Sophie, say what you have to.'

'I don't want to row.'

'You want to make love?' Luka checked.

She ran an eye over his naked body and when most might avert their eyes from an angry erection, Sophie frowned.

'I don't think it has love on its mind.'

Uh-oh!

Luka walked over and she refused to flinch as he shredded her flimsy nightdress.

'You'll have sex with me yet you won't go through with the marriage?' Sophie checked.

'Yes,' Luka said. 'And if you knew my reputation you would know many of my girlfriends have complained about the same thing.'

'Ah, but you don't make love to them the way you do with me.'

'You don't know that.'

'I do know that,' Sophie said, and looked right into his eyes. 'Absolutely I do.'

'That's a very confident assumption for someone who's only had sex twice.'

'Once,' Sophie corrected. 'We only did it—'

She never got to finish. His mouth was hard on her hers and he kissed her then as he had wanted to on the dance floor.

He kissed her hard until she was kissing him back, her fingers knotting in his hair.

'Remember, I don't want charity,' Luka said, as his thighs parted her legs.

He made her back down.

With his refusal to go further, he tested their patience to the edge.

'It isn't charity,' Sophie said, as she guided him to her heat.

'Some phobia.'

He exposed her lie and she didn't care, as long as he took her now.

Yet he didn't.

And neither did he leave her hanging on; instead, he knelt up.

'What are you doing?'

'Picking up where we left off.'

He lowered his face to her and confirmed her desire for she was wet and swollen and a moment away from coming to him.

She tried to scramble away from him, but he held her hips down; she wanted them face to face, not this intimate, raw exploration where there was no place to lie.

And, Sophie thought as he pressed his long tongue in over and over again, she was wrong to berate him for past lovers.

She should handwrite them all thank-you notes because his mouth was sucking on her clitoris now and his fingers were probing her along with his tongue, and she was sobbing as she came to him.

'Luka...'

He was kneeling between her parted legs, pulling them apart when they ached to close in on the orgasm he had just delivered her.

'What?' Luka checked, as he nudged a little way in. 'Do you want to me stop?'

He would.

The bastard would.

'Or,' Luka said, 'I go deeper.'

She could hear the sound of them, feel the tease of him that had her beating below again.

'Just come,' Sophie said.

'I told you, I loathe martyrs.'

He rested on his heels and pulled her hips down and carried on his cruel tease, there but not, in but not enough.

'Or,' Luka offered, 'we could try something different...'

'Like?' Sophie asked, and he suppressed a smile.

He could feel her mounting tension, he was holding down her hips as they rose in his hands.

'Something dangerous,' Luka said, and she nodded her head, set now on a rigid neck.

And so he kissed her like the first time.

When they'd tasted sweet and new.

He toppled onto her as he fully entered her again, and he brushed her wet lips with his as she clawed at his back and then gave in.

They made love.

They might well regret it tomorrow, but that was for then.

Now he kissed her like he only ever would kiss her, and Sophie just drank it in.

She smiled and she pushed back his damp hair just

to see him, just to feel it. She stopped fighting and started caressing and they rolled, made love to each other, nipped, sucked and tasted, and came.

And came again.

Guns were down.

Walls were gone.

She accepted his temporary truce as they made up for lost time.

CHAPTER FIFTEEN

'I DON'T UNDERSTAND YOU.'

They were the words he awoke to the next morning. He stared at the face that belonged on his pillow.

'Where did the other earring come from?' Luka asked, because she was wearing both.

'I always carry it in my purse,' Sophie said.

She would carry her mother with her for ever, Luka knew. If the truth was ever revealed she would never forgive and he was right not to trust her with his heart.

Some things were too big to come back from.

'You don't understand me, Sophie, because I won't let you.'

He rose from the bed.

'Will you let me try?'

It was the calmest they had ever been, like sweeping up the debris after a wild party that neither regretted.

'No,' Luka said. 'Sophie...' He sat on the bed and took her hand. 'We had a love that most people never know. You know that saying...better to have loved and lost—'

'I *hate* that saying,' Sophie broke in. 'I hate that saying more than any other. Who wrote that?' Sophie demanded.

'Tennyson.'

'Well, he was wrong.'

'I agree,' Luka said. 'I wish I'd never loved you.'

'But you did.'

'I did.'

'And you don't now?'

Luka wasn't that good a liar so he gave her a kiss instead. A nice one, not a loaded one. A sweet one, if, between them there could be such a thing.

'In a few days this will be over,' Luka said. 'We're going to get back to our lives knowing that we did the right thing by your father. It will be easier on us both once we get to Bordo Del Cielo.'

'How?'

'I'll check into the hotel and, like a good groom, I'll stay well away from the blushing bride-to-be.'

'Not as blushing as I'll be when you jilt me.'

'I can't marry you, Sophie. I can't be your fake husband. I can't stand in a church and exchange vows that I know we can't keep.'

He got up and headed to the bathroom.

'Hey, Luka,' Sophie said. 'I wished I'd never loved you too.'

The calm did not just belong in the bedroom.

A new presence had arrived with the dawn, though no one fully acknowledged it.

The colour seemed to have drained from Paulo's irises, Luka noticed as he wished him good morning.

And as Sophie passed her father his coffee and his shaking hand reached for it, it was a natural transition for her to lift the cup to his lips and help him to drink it.

The nurse stood, about to help, but Sophie shook her head.

'I've got this.'

So too had Luka.

He was so kind to Paulo and so engaged in organising the quick wedding that there were times Sophie
had to catch herself because it felt real.

'What about the evening?' Paulo wheezed.

'The hotel is already holding a function,' Sophie explained, and she looked at Luka, but he shook his head.
There was nothing he could do. It had been the first
thing he had sold. 'The hotel is under new ownership.'

'We don't need that hotel,' Paulo said. 'Before it was
built we would party in the street. I remember my wedding to your mother—we came out of the church and
straight into a feast. Perhaps you could ring Teresa at
the deli and see if she can sort out the food and the
drinks…'

'Pa…' Sophie looked over to where her father sat.
'Why would Teresa want to help us when you—?'

'Sophie.' Luka stopped her from continuing and then
watched as Sophie walked out onto the balcony. He
could see her hands gripping the railing as she fought
not to confront her father. Despite Paulo insisting he
wasn't confused, he seemed to live between the long-
ago past—when Rosa had been alive—and then the
present, as if he had simply erased the damage that had
been caused in between.

'*Scusi*,' Luka said to Paulo, and walked out to join her.

'He gets confused,' Luka said patiently.

'He gets confused when it suits him.'

'No,' Luka said. 'I don't think he can reconcile what
he has done. He needs to go home. I can see that now.'

'No one will be talking to him, though,' Sophie said.
'Have you asked Matteo to be your groomsman?'

'I have.'

'And what did he say?'

'That he'll move things around so that he can be there.'

'I want Bella there too.'

'I'm not sure if that's wise,' Luka said. 'Matteo will be with Shandy. You know a bit of what went down between him and Bella.'

'I believe that it was Bella who went down,' Sophie said. 'And your friend paid for the pleasure.'

'You don't let a single thing go.'

'You refused my offer of a clean slate,' Sophie pointed out. 'So tell your friend that, however uncomfortable Bella's presence might make him, she'll be there.' She rubbed her temples and dragged in air. 'I need to sort out some accommodation for us.'

'That's all sorted,' Luka said.

'How?'

'Come on.' Luka led her back inside then he addressed her father. 'Paulo,' he said in a very practical voice, 'you will be tired after the ceremony. Perhaps we could have a few people back to your home...'

He gave a pale smile as Sophie let herself back in but then Paulo spoke. 'I don't have a home there any more.'

'Yes, Paulo,' Luka said, 'you do. Since his death my lawyers have been sorting out the properties that my father acquired. You have your home to return to. It is all there, nothing has been changed. Angela has been taking care of it.'

For this gift to her father Sophie could almost forgive Luka for not loving her enough to remain in her life.

'I have a home,' Paulo sobbed. 'Your mother's dress will be there, Sophie. You can wear it for the wedding.'

'No!' It was Sophie who interrupted Paulo. 'I'm not wearing my mother's dress. I'm not my mother...'

'Sophie, please,' her father begged, but on this she stood firm.

'I don't want a replica of your marriage, Pa.' She was caught between the truth and a lie. 'I want our marriage to be different.'

She was torn, completely, as she walked out of the lounge and into the bedroom.

'What was all that about?' Luka asked, having followed her in. 'I thought you were trying to give him the wedding of his dreams before he dies.'

'Remember that you said if this was real, if we were in love…?' Sophie turned the tables on him. 'Then my father would know I would not be simply agreeing to everything. My father sees those times through rose-coloured glasses. If we really were marrying…'

'Go on.'

'What's the point in going on?' Sophie demanded. 'Why should I tell you the wife and woman I want to be when you're not even prepared to be there to find out? Why should I trust you with my dreams again when you won't let me into your heart? You can have sex with me. Luka, you can be kind to me, you can argue with me if you must, but don't ask for my private thoughts when we both know that you're planning to walk away from me.' She couldn't continue speaking. 'I'm going to Bella's.'

'We need to get organised for tomorrow.'

'I am organised,' Sophie said. 'We have the church booked, we have your plane to take us. I'll call Teresa and then I'm going out.'

It was amongst the hardest of calls she had ever made. Teresa was as cold and as hesitant as before, but, Sophie guessed, work was work for her and perhaps it was because of the mention of the Cavaliere name that Teresa agreed to cater back at the house for the wedding.

'*Grazie,*' Sophie said, and hung up.

She collected her bag from the bedroom and gave her father a kiss on the cheek.

'How long will you be?' Paulo asked.

'You'll be in bed by the time I'm back.' Sophie smiled. 'I'll see you in the morning. Just think, Pa, this time tomorrow you'll be back in Bordo Del Cielo. You can sleep well tonight, dreaming of that. I love you so much.'

It was getting harder and harder to say goodnight, never knowing if this would be the last time.

She went over and gave Luka the necessary kiss. 'Soon,' Sophie said, as she lowered her head and kissed his mouth then whispered into his ear, 'we'll be living apart…'

'What time will you be back?' Luka asked.

'You're not my husband yet.' Sophie smiled with her lips but not with her eyes and then she moved her mouth to his ear. 'Dawn,' she whispered, 'so, as said, you can sleep well.'

She could not stand another night spent next to a man she could never have so she headed to the door, but Luka followed her out.

'The plane leaves at seven.'

'I'll be back well before then.'

'Tonight might be our last chance to talk…'

'What's the point?' Sophie said. 'There's nothing left to say. We both know what you're going to do to me. You're wrong, Luka, I'm not fourteen, you don't have to prise me from you knee. I'll be at the church, and if you're not…' Sophie shrugged. 'I'll survive. I've had an awful lot of practice.'

She held it together until she made it to the apartment and only there, with Bella, did she finally let her guard down.

'He says he wishes he'd never loved me.'

'At least you have known love… Better to have—'

'Don't,' Sophie warned. 'If you start quoting Tennyson, I'll scream!

'Who's Tennyson?'

'I don't really know,' Sophie said, 'but I don't think he understood the heart…'

But maybe he did, because the thought of never having known Luka's love filled her with dread.

'He's going to jilt me.'

'More fool him,' Bella said.

'And I had a bit of an argument with my father. He wants me to wear my mother's wedding dress and I said no. I don't want a marriage like theirs.'

'I'm already making your dress,' Bella said. 'I guessed that this might happen when Luka agreed to get engaged so I've already started it. I kept some money back from our savings and I bought some chiffon from the market. I will work on it through the night.

'I'm going to be there with you, Sophie.'

'No.' Sophie shook her head because despite her brave words to Luka she could not put her friend through that. 'You have to work, and anyway…'

'Anyway?'

'Matteo will be there and…' Sophie could hardly bear to tell her, but Bella already knew.

'I know that he has a woman,' Bella said. 'And I know that she's stunning. I'd love to come and be your bridesmaid, Sophie. And don't worry about work—as of this morning I am suspended.'

'Bella?'

'I got in a lot of trouble,' Bella said. 'I spilt an ice bucket on a guest's lap when I was delivering the breakfasts to the room.'

'An ice bucket.'

'It was mainly cold water. I tripped but his girlfriend kicked up a fuss and called for the manager. It was a simple accident. The room was dark. I didn't see him— or rather they didn't hear me come in with breakfast... They were otherwise engaged.'

Sophie looked up to the sound of venom and mischief in Bella's voice and her mouth actually gaped for a moment before speaking.

'You threw a bucket of iced water over Matteo?'

'I did.' Bella grinned. 'So, you see, now I am free to be at your wedding and I'm going to make your the wedding dress. Sophie, you're going to be the most beautiful bride.'

'Even if he doesn't get to see me?'

'Oh, he'll see you,' Bella said. 'I'll make sure Matteo takes a few pictures as you arrive.' She hugged her friend and recited a Siclian saying. *'"Di guerra, caccia e amuri, pri un gustu milli duluri."'*

In war, hunting and love you suffer a thousand pains for one pleasure.

'The pleasure will be yours,' Bella said.

'It won't be, though,' Sophie said.

She was tired of the old ways, tired of false pride and sayings that spoke of revenge.

She was tired, so tired of hollow victories.

Maybe she had grown up.

Sophie wanted the man she loved.

CHAPTER SIXTEEN

SOPHIE'S FLIGHT BACK to Bordo Del Cielo was very different from the one she had taken when she had left.

Then she had been nineteen—confused, hurting, angry and just so glad to be getting away.

Now she was confused but the hurt was different.

Paulo was asleep in the bedroom area; Bella was sitting in one of the luxurious chairs with a curtain around her because she didn't want anyone to see the dress she was making for her friend.

Sophie sat beside Luka, staring out of the window and watching the land she wanted to love but which had cost her so much come into view.

'I was wrong,' Luka said, and she turned.

'Oh, you are so wrong,' Sophie said. No doubt he was talking about something else but all she knew was that he was wrong not to give them this chance.

Luka gave a soft, wry laugh as if he knew what she was thinking. 'I thought you were lying when you said that you were an events planner but I know few women who could organise a wedding in a couple of days.'

'It's easy to when you know...' Sophie shrugged. 'Well, let's just say I'm not too worried about how the cake is going to look and whether Teresa has had enough notice.' She looked right into his eyes. 'How could you even consider doing this to him, Luka?'

'How could you have done this to us?'

His words didn't confuse her, they ate at her instead.

She remembered standing on the beach, confused and ashamed and shouting, when their mouths should have been kissing.

She remembered hurling the sins of his father at him when she should have loved him first.

The plane came in to land and they sat in silence, but as they hit the tarmac, as they hurtled down the runway, Sophie didn't care if the plane lifted now and took them away.

But it came to a halt and they were home.

'I'm not perfect...' Sophie turned to him '...but I'd fight for us.'

'Nice speech,' Luka said. 'Tell me, though, Sophie—when did you ever fight for us? Did you come to my father's funeral? You would have known I had no one, the hell it would be to come home...'

'I was going to,' Sophie said, 'but I had just found out that my father was terminally ill.'

'He still is,' Luka replied, unmoved. 'You've held up the death card and I'm here. That's not an excuse not to show up on the day you would have known I needed you the most.'

He accepted no excuses for her carelessness with their love.

Did she sit there now and tell him the truth?

That he was right?

It hadn't been her father's illness that had stopped her contacting him.

Did she tell him she couldn't have afforded it?

Would a man like Luka accept as an excuse that she'd had no money? That he'd have had to wire her the fare?

'Did you fight for us on the beach, when I pleaded with you to come with me?' Luka asked.

'No.'

Her single word moved him. She did not kick up with her usual defence as to how he had shamed her in court.

'So when did you fight for us, Sophie?'

'I'll fight now.'

Luka said nothing.

He just stood as the passengers disembarked.

'I'll see you to your home,' Luka said.

It was a strange ride.

Her father never stopped coughing. There was the angel of death in the car with them and turned backs on the streets as Sophie looked out.

Yet it was home.

And it was somehow beautiful.

'Do you remember...?' She stopped.

Eight years old to his fourteen, she had found Luka crying for the first and last time, washing blood from his face in the river.

'Did you fall?' she had asked.

'Yes, I fell.'

They had sat eating nectarines and she had looked at his bruised, bloodied nose and closed eye.

'One day,' Sophie had said, 'you will be taller than him.'

'Who?' Luka had asked, because then he had still been loyal to his father.

'Taller than any man in this town,' she had said.

'I remember,' Luka said, and she did not turn or jump to the sound of his voice.

Here it felt normal.

Here they were as entwined as the vines and the roots beneath them.

They passed the school where she had left at fifteen to work in the hotel.

'I cried the day I left,' Sophie admitted. 'I wanted to learn all the poems. I wanted to sort out the maths…'

'You have the cleverest head on the planet,' Luka said.

'Yet I can't work us out.'

'We're here,' Bella said, and Sophie looked as they turned from the hotel and into her street.

It was the same, except different.

The neighbour's house had changed and was *tastefully* renovated. 'It smells of London.' Sophie winked as she waved to her weekender neighbours.

'I'll leave you here,' Luka said, having helped Paulo up the path.

'You're not going to come in for coffee?'

'I'm going to go and check into the hotel,' Luka said, once he had ensured everything was okay. 'And then I am meeting with Matteo.'

He didn't want to go in.

He didn't want to see just how poor his father had kept them.

'I might go for a walk,' Bella said. 'I would like to look at my old home, even if there are other people living there…'

Sophie looked at Luka but he gave her a slight shake of his head and pulled her aside. 'I haven't told everyone what I am doing. I don't want anyone feeling beholden. My lawyer will contact people once I've gone. Bella will find out soon enough that she has a home.'

Thank God for the nurse, because she took an exhausted, overwrought Paulo to his room for some oxygen and medication.

'It is your last day as a single woman,' Paulo wheezed. 'You should go out with Bella.'

'I'm just happy to be home.'

Sophie was. Though it felt so strange to be back.

Happy her father was settled, she set to work. There was a lot to be done and also there was Teresa to pay.

She walked into town, trying not to look up. She didn't want to see Malvolio's home spreading out over the top of the hill.

She didn't want to glimpse the bedroom where she and Luka had first made love and she averted her eyes as she passed the church where tomorrow he would leave her standing.

Sophie walked into Teresa's deli and, just as they had the last time she'd done so, the people in the deli fell silent. Angela was there, chatting with Teresa and a couple of other locals, and Sophie felt her cheeks turn to fire as she stepped up to the counter.

'I've come to pay for the catering for the wedding tomorrow.'

'*Gratuitamente*,' Teresa said, and Sophie was about to slam the money down, as she had all those years ago, but she chose not to.

She was older and wiser now, even if she'd prefer not to be at times.

'Teresa, I know it must be difficult for you to know that my father is back. He just wants to see Luka and I marry...' Just as Sophie always did, she held back her tears. 'That is all we are here for, to give my father some peace in his final days. Soon we'll be gone and out of your lives for good.'

'Sophie?' Angela asked. 'How is Paulo?'

'He's weak. He just wants to be home and to see me married.' She put down the money. 'We don't want any trouble.'

She walked out of the deli. A part of Sophie wanted to go to the beach, to sit there a while and remember days when life had seemed so much simpler, but instead she made her way home.

Bella was back from her walk and busy finishing off the dress, and Sophie dealt with the flowers and cleaning the house, as she had done so many times before. But then Paulo awoke and declared that he wanted to visit his wife's grave.

It was a long slow walk to the hill.

And agony to walk back down.

Spare me from your grief, she wanted to plead to her father as the nurse took him, weeping, to bed.

'Another walk?' Sophie smiled as Bella again headed out with a full face of make-up.

'Who knows who I might bump into?' Bella smiled.

Almost the moment she left there was a knock at the door and, no, it wasn't Bella to recheck her make-up, it was the priest.

'Do you want to let your father know I am here?'

Sophie nodded.

He looked so tired when she went into his room and Sophie knew then that tomorrow might not be the embarrassment she was dreading. Luka had been right. The journey, no matter how luxurious, had depleted him and visiting Rosa seemed to have taken the last of his strength.

'The priest is here,' Sophie said. 'Do you want me to send him through?'

'Please.'

She went out to the garden and lay on a sun lounger

and tried not to think of what was happening. Her heart seemed to still as she felt a shadow fall over her and she looked up into the strained features of Luka.

'You're crying.'

'No,' Sophie corrected, 'because I never cry. I don't think I know how to. I'm just tired.' She looked up into navy eyes. 'The priest is in with my father. He is making his confession. I would expect him to be some considerable time.'

He sat down by her knees on the sun lounger but she shrank away.

'Please, don't be a hypocrite,' Sophie said. 'Don't offer me your arms and then remove them tomorrow. I'm drained, Luka. I'm tired of being a parent to my father. I'm exhausted from absorbing his tears so I'm going to sit and watch the sunset and then I'll get up and put on my green dress, as per tradition, for a Sicilian bride on the eve of her wedding.'

'About tomorrow—'

'I'm not even thinking about tomorrow, Luka,' she interrupted. 'The day will bring what it shall bring and I'll survive it.' She looked up as the priest came out and stood to see him out.

'He's made his confession.'

Luka heard the priest's reedy voice as Sophie saw him out.

It was, Luka knew, time for him to make his confession.

Just not to Sophie.

Paulo was sitting in bed, holding his rosary beads and a picture of Rosa, but he turned and smiled as Luka made his way over and joined him.

'Is it good to be home?' Luka asked.

'It is,' Paulo said. 'I have made my confessions. Most of them anyway.' He looked at Luka. 'How long will you two pretend to be together for? Till after my funeral?'

'What are you talking about, Paulo?'

'I'm not a fool. I've always known that Sophie was lying to me. I knew, with what you said about her in court, that you were over before you even started.'

'She doesn't forgive easily.'

'She is like Rosa.' Paulo smiled. 'Even if I believed at first you were together, we do see the news in prison. I've read about your affairs and your scandals. I've seen the many beautiful women that you've dated.'

'You went along with it?' Luka frowned as he sat on the edge of the bed.

'She thought it made me happy knowing she was being taken care of.'

'Yet here you are you are. pushing for us to get married, even though you know it is a ruse. Why?'

'Because for all the mistakes I have made in my life, that wasn't one of them. You two are right for each other. I hoped that maybe being forced to spend time together you both might see that. It didn't work though.'

'No,' Luka admitted.

'It's time to be honest,' Paulo said. 'Now, while we still have time to be.'

Luka gave a small nod.

'You paid people a lot of money to work on my case these past months. What happened to make you suddenly want my release?'

'I always thought you were weak,' Luka admitted. 'I saw you as my father's yes-man but then I found something and I realised then that you had been protecting the person you love most.' He went into his pocket and handed Paulo the cross and chain. 'I found this amongst my father's things.'

Paulo let out a small cry as he took his beloved wife's cross and chain and pressed it to his lips.

'You knew her death was my father's doing, didn't you?'

'Not at first but eventually I did,' Paulo said. 'Malvolio wanted to build the hotel on the foreshore but there were families, including Rosa and I, who did not want to sell our homes.' He took a moment to take some long breaths from his oxygen mask and then continued speaking. 'I said to Rosa that we should move away and just leave Boro Del Cielo but she would not be run out of town—she said that someone had to stand up to him.' It was the most difficult conversation. With every sentence Paulo paused to breathe. 'Rosa went to see him to give him a piece of her mind. A few days later there was a car accident. I didn't connect the two at first. I was grieving and Malvolio was the white knight, the friend...' He started to cough.

'Enough,' Luka said.

'No.' Paulo was insistent that he finish. 'He said to put differences aside—he organised the funeral when I could not. He spoke at the service when I had no words. When I told him that I could not stand to be in the home we had loved he moved me here...' Paulo looked around at what had been his and Sophie's home. 'It took a few months for me to come out of the fog and start to see what had happened. He had got us out of our home by any means. By then I knew what he was capable of. He never threatened that harm would come to Sophie— instead, he said how lucky she was that he would look out for her, that our children would one day marry.'

'But the implication was there?' Luka asked, and Paulo nodded.

'When did you know?' Paulo asked.

'About Rosa?' Luka checked. 'When I found her necklace amongst my father's things, although I knew that he was corrupt long before that. It's the reason I rarely came home.'

'You came home that day to end things with Sophie?'

'I did,' Luka said. 'I just wanted to break all ties with this place. It wasn't that easy, though.'

'Love never is,' Paulo said, and held out the chain to Luka.

'Why are you giving this to me?' Luka asked.

'I would have liked to be buried holding it,' Paulo admitted, but then he shook his head. 'If I was then Sophie would have to know what had happened.' Paulo spoke his absolute truth. 'She would never forgive you, Luka. I know my daughter and the fact that your family was involved in her mother's death is something that she would not be able to forgive. Take the necklace and throw it the ocean when I am gone,' Paulo said. 'I will take your secret to the grave.'

'It's not my secret,' Luka said.

'It can be,' Paulo said. 'Sophie loves you and you love her. You do not need this hanging over you. Please.' He gave the cross and chain one final kiss and handed it back to Luka. 'Never tell her the truth. There is no need.'

Luka pocketed the chain and walked out from the bedroom to the lounge. There was Sophie and she gave him a tired smile.

'How is he?'

'He's okay.'

'You?'

Luka didn't answer. There was lie in his pocket and he didn't know how to handle it. Her own father had told him that their love could not survive it, but as he went to walk off Sophie halted him.

'I was wrong, Luka. I should have come to London with you that night.'

'Why?'

'I just should have. I was angry and I blamed you.'

'When did you decide this?'

'Just now.'

'Five years after the event,' Luka sneered. His emotions were everywhere. 'You let it fester for five years.'

'Luka…'

'So what happens when the shoe drops, Sophie? What happens when the next bombshell hits? Am I to wait another five years for you to come around? Am I to wait again for you to swallow that Sicilian pride?'

'You refuse to give me that chance.'

'I do.'

CHAPTER SEVENTEEN

'REMEMBER HOW WE used to sit here?' Bella said, as they sat bathed in sunrise with their calves dangling in cool water.

'I do.' Sophie smiled. 'I also remember the terrible row I had here with Luka.'

'It is a glorious day for a wedding.'

'A wedding that isn't going to happen,' Sophie said.

'He loves you,' Bella said. 'I can see it in him. Luka would not leave you standing in the church. He would not have come to Sicily just to shame you.'

'He told me he would never go through with it. Is it wrong that I wish my father would die before three p.m., just to spare him the shame?'

'I think so.' Bella smiled.

'Luka is as stubborn as I am.' Sophie sighed. 'He accuses me of being Sicilian as he trips on his own pride. I'm going to be jilted.'

'You could always have a fall this morning.' Bella smiled again. 'Slip on one of those rocks up there…'

'I could,' Sophie said. 'Or I could get a cramp, swimming, and you have to save me but I swallowed so much sea water that I was too weak to make it to the church…'

They laughed, they sat at the water's edge and laughed, and it felt so good to do so.

'Let him jilt me,' Sophie said. 'Let's really give the people of Bordo Del Cielo some scandal again. The girls are back in town!'

'Sisters in shame,' Bella said.

Sophie looked at her dear friend, who was terrified about today too.

'Are you scared to face Matteo?'

'I'm ashamed to face him.'

'He paid for a night with you, remember. You wouldn't be a whore if it wasn't for his money.'

'I know,' Bella said. 'If he tries anything I will tell him he can't afford me now!'

They laughed again and then Bella stood. 'Come on, we have a lot to do today.'

'You go back,' Sophie said. 'I might just sit here a while.'

'I will give your pa breakfast.'

'Thank you.'

Alone she sat and stared out at the water and at the cargo ships and cruise liners so far out on the horizon.

Out of reach for ever.

She was going to cry.

It hit her as surely as the sensation that she might vomit.

It felt like thunder rising in her chest and, like a cat hiding, she moved to the shelter of the cliffs and curled into her knees and wept.

For the father she would soon lose.

For the future devoid of Luka.

But most of all for the love she *had* known.

A love that could never be replicated or surpassed. She was exhausted, not just from the past but already from a future without him. How she loathed the poets she did not understand, but even with a lifetime to study them she wanted one that matched her, that told her how to deal with a future without Luka in it.

'You're going to startle,' Luka said. 'As you do every time I approach.'

'Well, I've never had the chance to get used to the sound of your voice,' she said, and wiped her eyes and looked up. 'So, yes, every time we meet in the future, expect me to jump. How did you know I was here?'

'Bella told me. She is sitting in the morning sun with your father. Matteo and I met her walking back…'

'Walking back from what? Your stag night?'

'There are no bucks' nights in Sicily,' Luka said. 'We did our best, though. We drank at the hotel till it closed and then walked along the shore.'

'You should go,' Sophie said. 'It's bad luck to see me on the morning of the wedding.'

'We've had our share of bad luck,' he said. 'How is your father this morning?' he asked, and this time she didn't accuse him of not caring.

She knew that he did.

'He will live to see his daughter jilted.'

Luka sat down beside her.

Paulo would know why he could not go through with the wedding. It should not be her father who would have to explain things to Sophie. It was for that reason he sat down to tell her, and braced himself for the most difficult conversation of his life.

'Why do you hate me, Luka?'

'As I said before, there are many reasons.' It should be odd that he took her hand to break her heart, but to Sophie it wasn't. 'Remember the night we parted? How angry you were, how you refused to give me a chance to explain? How you compared me to my father?'

'I was nineteen years old then.'

'No, Sophie, that's my excuse when I go over that time,' Luka said. 'I was younger, I was just out of prison, I had no idea what was going on. I had said things in court that I regretted, things I know I would handle better if they happened today. I'd run rings around that barrister now.'

'I know that you would.'

'I've changed,' Luka said. 'You haven't.'

'You mean I'm not sophisticated enough for you?'

'I mean your fire remains.' He snapped his fingers in front of her eyes. '*That* is how long it takes for you to make up your mind, Sophie—you decide things in an instant and nothing will change your mind.'

It was true, Sophie knew, for almost the second he had opened the door to her she had fallen in love and nothing had dimmed that.

'Almost nothing changes my mind,' Sophie refuted. 'I regret the words I said. I was confused, I was hurting…'

'I know that,' Luka said. 'How long did it take for you to see things from my side? To calm down?'

'I don't know.'

'Nearly five years,' Luka said. 'It has taken you until we are on our knees, till we are all but over, for you to see things from my side.'

'No, I knew almost straight away.'

'What did you do about it?' Luka challenged. 'Did you try to look me up in London? Did you do anything to let me know that you were wrong?'

'No.'

'Only now will you admit that you can see things from my side, that you were wrong.'

'Are you saying that I have to be perfect?'

'No,' Luka said, 'I love your stubbornness. You would

argue the sky was purple. I love your fire and that you are pure Sicilian yet it is what will ultimately tear us apart.'

'I don't understand,' she said. 'Is it because I lied?'

'Tell me your lies,' Luka said. 'Let's do this once and for all. Tell me your lies and secrets and I'll tell you mine.'

'Why?'

'Because the truth can't hurt us any more than this does.'

'I'm poor,' Sophie said. 'Bella and I are as poor as church mice and we fooled you with my wardrobe and phone.'

Luka just smiled.

'You knew that?'

'Not really. Though I did wonder about you being an events manager,' Luka admitted.

'I'm a chambermaid.'

'You were when I met you.'

She loathed that she hadn't moved on but he melted that fear with four words. 'I loved you then.'

'You don't care?'

'I don't care about money and things. I admit that I like not having to worry about it and, yes, I like nice things but, at the end of day, if it all falls into the ocean I would survive without it. My father had more money that a team of accountants can trace and yet he was the poorest man I have ever known.'

'I'm sorry.'

'For what?'

'For not being there for his funeral.'

'It doesn't matter.'

'It does. My father has done a lot of things wrong but I still love him.'

'My father did worse.'

'The hurt is more, then,' Sophie said. 'I don't think you can ever remove love. Even when by others' standards it deserves to be removed, even by your own... Love is not a whiteboard, Luka, it doesn't come with an eraser.'

'I can't make a good man out of him,' Luka said, 'but there were times when my mother was still alive that I remember with some affection. After that...' He shook his head. 'So what are your other lies?

'I feel like I trapped you that day we first made love. That you didn't see the real me. I am the peasant you despise. When you opened the door I was dressed in my finest with my mother's earrings, some make-up that I was trying out for our engagement, the dress...'

'Sophie, I hate that I said that to my father about you. I can't take it back, just explain that it was a row between him and I. It should never have been replayed in court. As to trapping me, well, I spent six months in prison, and within that time I spent two very long months alone when I thought about that day a lot... Do you think, when I replayed that time, I recalled that you were wearing your mother's earrings?'

He moved his head and he kissed the lobe of her ear, kissed it with such tenderness that it was as if it was the most important layer of skin that had ever existed. 'Do you think,' he asked, 'when I touch you that I remember the make-up?' His mouth moved to her eyelids and again he was so gentle and Sophie started crying because she knew, she just knew that right here, right now, he was kissing her goodbye; she just didn't understand why. 'I promise you, Sophie,' he said, his mouth moving down her neck, 'when I recalled that time, not once did I think of the dress you were wearing. I thought of these...'

He slipped the knot from her top and her breasts were naked to the morning sun and to his mouth.

'When I go over that time,' Luka said, and his fingers moved up her dress and to the silk of her panties, which were damp as he slid them down. She moaned as his fingers slipped into her. 'I remember you naked... I remember taking you for the first time, and the noises you made.'

He pushed her slowly down and onto her back. It was Sophie who slipped off her panties as Luka unzipped. Half-dressed but naked to the very soul, she stared into his eyes.

'When I come, every time I remember this...'

He seared inside her, and his face was over hers, and Sophie didn't try to hold back the tears as together they revisited that day.

'I remember you coming. I remember how I tried so hard not to.'

He moved up on his elbows and looked down at her. 'I don't want to come because when I do...'

'You're going to leave me, aren't you?'

How could he be making love to her while nodding that, yes, they were over?

She had lived in the moment just once in her life. That afternoon when the dog had ceased barking, when the surroundings had faded, Sophie had glimpsed the present, and she found it again now.

The past slipped away and the future was unseen, and she kissed the man she loved. She kissed his mouth and his rough cheek, she kissed the scar she had closed and, try as she might not to just yet, she started to come to him.

'Don't,' Sophie begged, because once Luka came it was over, but his tide was coming in.

She knew from the only body she truly knew—his.

His moan was one of pain as he released because it signalled the end, but even in the last throes Sophie might have lost her heart but her head remained and she looked into his navy eyes as he offered her one last chance.

"Will you fight for us?' Luka asked.

He pulled out, he dressed and then he dressed her and he asked her again. 'Now, with what I have to tell you, will you fight for us as you promised?' He went on, 'Will your words still be kind and wise when we face a test?' He placed a gram of gold in her hand and it felt like a weighted ball, with no burden lifted, as he handed it over to her.

'I found it when my father died. I came back to Bordo for the funeral and I was going through my father's things.'

'Your father did this... You...' She halted, tripped over her words. She tried to remember she was fighting for them but she was breathless on the ropes in her mother's corner.

'You see, Sophie, with this you can win every row. You can take the shame of what my father did and give it to me over and over. But I can't live like that. The reason I will never marry you is this—I have lied under oath to protect your family. It didn't work. I have lied on the Bible, I have attempted over and over to edit the truth. No more. I will not stand in a church and lie and take you as a temporary wife when the truth is I will love you for ever.'

Anger, rage, fury, hissed at an unknown target.

'I don't care if you're poor. I don't care if you have

lied, cheated…whatever…' Luka continued. 'You do what you have to to survive but I know my limits, Sophie. I know I love you. I accept you but I cannot compromise with this. I cannot take more of his shame. I cannot say sorry any more for a person I am not. Know that.

'I love you,' Luka said. 'I love the life we could have, but I care about myself too. I have dreams and ambitions and I will never be brought to my knees again for that man.'

'Luka, how long have you known?'

'When he died.'

'And you never guessed before then?'

This was her mother who had died—*her mother*!

'I need to know. How long have you had your suspicions?'

'I can remember your mother coming to our house. She was angry at my father for trying to get them out of their home. Your father had warned her they should leave yet she refused…' Luka tried to look with adult eyes at a child's past and then he lost his cool.

'I won't let you do this to us, Sophie,' he shouted. 'You want facts? I found out for sure a year ago. I have known for a lifetime he was rotten to the core. If you want a dissection then get a dead frog—they don't bleed and anyway their blood is already cold. Mine's warm. My heart beats. I won't let you do it to me.'

She came out fighting then.

Sophie pushed herself off the ropes that bound her and entered the ring.

For them.

'You criticise me for comparing you to your father, yet over and over you compare me to my mother. Not just you,' Sophie said, 'but my father, the whole town does. "She is like Rosa..."' The only sound was silence. 'I am like her, just as you are like your father. But you are not him. You are arrogant, you are clever and you are strong, but you are good. I am fierce, I have a temper, but I would listen when the man I love told me that we had to leave. Did I march to your father and demand Bella's freedom of choice?' Sophie shouted. 'No. I offered to and when she said no, when she said she must stay, I respected her choice...as I have to respect that you can't marry me.'

'I can never be your fake husband, Sophie.'

She looked at him.

'Can we get past this?'

'I don't know,' she admitted. Questions were swirling, dates and times and anger and blame, and Luka smiled at her honest answer.

'You get to decide, Sophie. I'll be there today. Jilt *me* if you think I deserve it for what he did. Score your point for your fleeting victory but I win because I know you will regret it for ever if you don't show up today. No one ever shall, or ever could, love you as much as I do.'

'You love me so much that you invite me to end us—?'

'I love you so much,' Luka interrupted, 'that I won't relegate us to a poor future. I would rather have sex with a stranger for the rest of my life than lie next to you cold and blaming. I would rather have half a marriage, half a life, half of me, if I cannot have all of you. For you to deny me that part of you...for you to hold me hostage...' He shook his proud head. 'Fight with me about things if you want to, be every inch Sicilian. Call me on what my father did once. I might get that, but if you call me on it twice...'

And Luka dared accuse *her* of being Sicilian!

'I don't give second warnings,' Luka said. 'My father was responsible for the death of your mother. I will not let his sins, or your anger, bring me to my knees. If you walk into that church,' Luka warned, 'then you'd better know that it's for ever. You only walk towards me if you can love me more than the shadows of our past. If you can't, then it is better for both of us that you walk away.'

Luka did the nicest thing then.

Her breast was precariously close to falling out again so he redid the tie to her halter-neck and rearranged her dress. He looked after her in a way that no one ever could and he demanded that she match that care.

Always.

'Show up or don't,' Luka said. 'Hate me at your own peril.'

'What will you do if I don't turn up?'

'Nothing,' Luka said. And it was, for Sophie, the darkest response he could deliver. 'If you don't show for our wedding then nothing will happen, not ever. I will wish you luck for the future, I will accept that our love could not survive. I'll be proud of you for having the guts to admit it and,' he added, 'I will get on with my life.'

He left her on the rocks.

He left her spinning like a Catherine wheel.

There was a retort she could deliver.

A proud last word, perhaps.

There was comeuppance still to be had.

Or there was a shiny new future?

CHAPTER EIGHTEEN

'YOU LOOK WONDERFUL,' Bella said.

It was possibly the most beautiful dress in the world and might, Sophie knew, remain unseen.

He had left her with seven hours to grow up.

She was down to twelve minutes.

'Are you scared he won't show up?'

It was no longer a town of secrets but what had happened on the beach Sophie had kept to herself.

This was between her and Luka.

She was scared that *she* might not. Scared that her rapid tongue could not hold its fire.

Sophie pulled out the necklace.

I love you, she said in her head to her mother. *I come from you but I am not you.*

'It looks like the one in the photos that your mother wore,' Bella said, as she helped her to put it on.

'It is the one my mother wore,' Sophie said, and she felt Bella's hands pause on her naked shoulders.

Bella knew, Sophie realised.

Here there were secrets even amongst the very closest of friends.

Her mother would probably have known and would have told Bella the truth long ago. The whole town would have been able to see what a small child could not.

Rosa had gone and confronted Malvolio.

A few days later she had died.

'Why didn't my father insist that they run?' Sophie asked. She knew the answer—Rosa, with her stubbornness and pride, had been right to want to stay.

Dead right.

'Can you ever forgive him?'

'Malvolio?' Sophie scoffed. 'Never.'

'I mean can you ever fully forgive Luka for what Malvolio did?' Bella asked, but hushed as Paulo walked in.

'Their names don't belong in the same breath,' Paulo said, his eyes filling with tears when he saw that Sophie was wearing Rosa's chain.

'But they do belong in the same breath,' Sophie corrected. 'Just as I belong in the same breath as my mother. Just as I look like her and act like her at times. I'm not her, though.'

'I know that.'

'Even if she's not here, I've learnt from her...'

'The cars are here,' Bella said.

'Go,' Sophie said to Bella. 'I will see you at the church.' She gave her friend a hug. 'Good luck with Matteo.'

She stood alone with her father.

'You are your mother's daughter. That is not always a compliment. I wanted to leave here, to get away. She told me to stand up to him, to fight for what was right.' Sophie stood as her father shook his head. 'So I did. I had our tickets booked to leave. I wanted to get out of here...'

'You were right.'

'I would rather have been wrong.'

'Malvolio *is* Luka's father,' Sophie said. 'At times

they will belong in the same breath. I don't want a marriage where there are things that cannot be discussed or names that can never be mentioned. I nearly lost Luka, not once but twice. I am not going to do that again. I shan't make the same mistakes as...'

'Me?'

'As so many people did,' Sophie said, more aware than ever how words could hurt so very much. 'You did the best that you could for me. I know that.'

'Not really.'

'Yes, really.' Sophie smiled at her father. 'You got one thing very right—you chose the perfect husband for me.'

'You and Luka belong to each other.'

'We do.'

It wasn't just the bride who was nervous on a wedding day, Luka was finding out.

The groom stood at the altar when, for the longest time, he had thought that he never would.

Luka had long ago accepted that he and Sophie were over and, given that he had known he would never love like that again, he had decided he would remain single.

Until this morning.

This morning he had chosen for their sakes to take the biggest gamble of his life and to reveal the truth.

Her own father thought that Sophie could never forgive him and Matteo too was tense.

And so he stood on his wedding day not even knowing if Sophie would show up.

He didn't care about the public reaction if the bride didn't show.

He cared only about them.

'Whatever happens—' Matteo started, but Luka halted him.

'She'll be here.'

He had confidence in them, in the love they had found that long-ago afternoon.

And he was right to.

He turned around and there was Sophie, dressed in a simple white dress that reminded him of yesteryear. Today her black hair was worn down, as he preferred, and dotted with summer jasmine. In one hand she loosely held a bunch of wild Sicilian poppies and they were as sexy and as decadent and as heady as her.

The delighted, stunned look on her face when she saw the packed church was something he would remember for ever.

They loved her and understood too just how hard it had been for Paulo.

He was home, where he belonged, and ready now for his daughter to leave properly.

She walked towards him and Luka could see the glimmer of her mother's cross.

Guilt, fear, shame left him as her eyes met his.

Sophie walked and then, as her father let go of her arm, she ran—those last few steps she ran—to the shield of his arms and the freedom they afforded her.

To him.

Luka kissed the bride before the service had even started.

They needed that moment even if it made the priest cough.

'You're here,' he said.

'So are you.'

'Always.'

Paulo stood, even though he was offered a seat.

Luka turned just once and his eyes met Angela's and thanked her.

She, he was sure, was the one who had told the rest of the townsfolk to give these people the chance they deserved and to forgive Paulo now, while they still could.

Their vows were heartfelt.

'I love you,' Luka said. 'I always have and I always will.'

'I love you,' came Sophie's response. 'I always have and I always will.' Then she deviated from the priest's words for she made a small addition. 'And I shall *try* to remember that in all that I say and do.'

No one understood why the groom laughed.

Matteo was the perfect groomsman, even if cynicism was written all over his face, for just yesterday Luka had told him this wedding would never take place, that it was a sham.

But for now he went along with it and handed over the rings.

And tried not to glance at the bridesmaid!

Luka slid on the ring and then he too deviated from tradition, for he went into this pocket and took out another ring and placed it next on her finger.

It was rose gold and the diamond was emerald cut and stood high, and Bella stared at it for a moment, her eyes filling with tears.

She remembered staring in Giovanni's window and a diamond catching her eye.

The hope that when Luka got out, that one day...

There wasn't time to dwell on it for now.

They were man and wife.

The church bells were ringing loudly in Bordo Del Cielo today and as they stepped out, it was to a *true* Sicilian celebration.

The street was lined with tables and dressed in ribbons and flowers, the trees were lit with lights that would glow brighter as evening fell.

Angela and an old friend were helping Paulo out of the church.

'Dance with your father,' Luka said.

She did.

And to hear him laughing and proud was the best medicine for both of them…but then she was back to Luka's arms.

She glanced over his shoulder and smiled. Bella and Matteo were dancing a duty dance, not that it looked like duty for Bella—her eyes were closed and her head was resting on his chest. Only Matteo looked as if he was struggling.

'He's angry,' Luka said. 'He thinks that she is still…' He looked down at Sophie. 'I want to catch up on all the years we have missed, I want to know everything.'

'You shall.'

'Your father is so happy.'

'He wants us to have a baby now.' Sophie smiled.

'You could lie and say you are…'

'Knowing him, he would live for another nine months just to make sure that we were telling the truth.'

'We are,' Luka said. 'This is for ever.'

'That ring?' Sophie asked. 'Is it from Giovanni's?'

Luka nodded. 'As soon as I got out of court I went and bought it. I wanted to take you to London, not as a friend or a date. Those months in prison had taught me many things…'

Sophie could hardly stand to think of all she had dismissed that day, all the foolish pride she had held onto just to be right.

'I can afford something nicer now.' Luka offered.

'Nothing could be nicer,' Sophie said. 'It belongs with me.'

'So do you.'

EPILOGUE

SOPHIE LAY IN that delicious place between sleep and waking and for a moment she thought she was dreaming.

The lap of the sea, the slow motion of rising and falling with the waves, and Sophie knew she was awake.

She was on honeymoon with Luka.

They were taking their time to sail from Corsica to the Greek islands, stopping where they chose to and just enjoying the journey.

Life was better than she had ever dreamed it might be.

It had been an emotional time. Her father had held on long enough to know that Sophie was expecting a baby. He had seen a summer and a winter in his beloved town and finally he now lay with Rosa.

Sophie lay there thinking about the past months.

It had been Sophie who had thrown her mother's necklace in the grave. It was her mother's, not hers.

She didn't want to wear it day in, day out.

Instead, she wore her mother's earrings, for they spoke of the happiest days with Luka.

And there had been so many of them.

Yes, she was stubborn, but never about that.

'Morning,' Luka said.

'Where were you?'

'Thinking,' he said. 'About us. Are you happy?'

'So happy.' she said, and then looked into his navy eyes. 'And cross with myself for all the time we wasted.'

'We needed that time,' Luka interrupted. 'We were young, there was a lot of pain and little of it was of our making.'

'Even so.'

'We know that what we have is precious,' he said, and she nodded. 'Had I married you when you were nineteen you might have always resented that you never got to work on the cruise liners.'

'No.'

'Yes.'

He smiled and always it made her stomach fold over and in on itself. He was so stern and serious with others, but so open with her.

'And had we got together after the court case and then later found that chain...' Luka thought about it. 'I needed to find out about my father away from you.' It was Luka who brought the name up at times and he was so grateful that her eyes didn't flash in anger; instead, they could hold his gaze as they explored the pains of the past. 'This is our time.'

'So you don't think I was wrong?'

'Sophie...'

'I didn't make us waste all those years?'

'Sophie,' he warned, but he was smiling. 'Come on, let's go and see the sunrise.'

'No, come back to bed,' she grumbled, but Luka shook his head and she got out of bed, put on her sarong and tied it then headed up to the deck.

The sky was gorgeous and just dipping out of navy and the stars were fading.

'Where are we?' Sophie asked, and then she paused as for the first time she saw her home from the sea.

The sun was rising over Sicily and their yacht was close enough that she could make out the familiar landscape—the church where they had not only married but where both their parents rested. She could make out Luka's home, the beach where they had made love.

'I used to sit there every day with Bella,' Sophie said. 'Dreaming of the future, wondering what our lives would be like. I used to picture myself on a cruise liner out on the seas...'

'And now here you are.'

'I'm here with you,' Sophie said, and then she told him a deeper truth, one she hadn't told Bella. Not because she was scared to, she simply hadn't dared admit it to herself, for it had seemed pointless that long-ago day.

'Even though I didn't want to be married, I wanted you then. I wanted it all, I just didn't know how it could happen. How I could be out on the ocean and sailing the seas and somehow be with the man I loved. Yet here I am.'

'We can dock,' Luka said. 'Spend a couple of days there if you wish.'

Sophie thought about it. The people would make them more than welcome. They had their homes back and Bordo Del Cielo was thriving now.

Yet there was no need to go back, no need to visit.

Not now

One day maybe.

They were having a daughter, and they would take her back and, far more gently than they both had, she would learn about her past, about the pain and the beauty of the land that ran through her veins.

But not now.

Now, as Bordo Del Cielo awoke, it was Sophie and Luka that were the glint of a boat on the horizon.

They were out there, together, and living their dreams.

* * * * *

'I honoured you with a gift. The most important gift a man can give to a woman. I made you my wife and you threw it in my face.'

Prudence gaped at him, shock washing over her in waves. She opened her mouth to deny his claim but the words clogged her throat. *His wife?* Surely he didn't really think that they were actually married? Her heart was pounding and the palms of her hands felt suddenly damp. *Married?* That was ridiculous! Insane!

Dazedly she thought back to that day when she'd been led, giggling and blindfolded, to his great-uncle's trailer. Laszlo had been waiting for her. She felt a shiver run down her spine at the memory, for he'd looked heartbreakingly handsome and so serious she had wanted to cry. They'd sworn their love and commitment to one another and his great-uncle had spoken some words in Romany, and then they had eaten some bread and some salt.

Her pulse was fluttering, and despite her best efforts her voice sounded high and jerky. 'We're not married,' she said tightly. 'Marriages are more than just words and kisses. This is just another of your lies…'

Her voice trailed off at the expression of derision on his face.

'You're going off topic, *pireni*. We're still married. I'm still your husband. And you're my wife.'

Louise Fuller was a tomboy who hated pink and always wanted to be the prince—not the princess! Now she enjoys creating heroines who aren't pretty pushovers but are strong, believable women. Before writing for Mills & Boon® she studied literature and philosophy at university and then worked as a reporter on her local newspaper. She lives in Tunbridge Wells with her impossibly handsome husband, Patrick, and their six children.

This is Louise's stunning debut
for Mills & Boon® Modern™ Romance
We hope you love it!

**Visit the author profile page at
millsandboon.co.uk.**

VOWS
MADE IN SECRET

BY
LOUISE FULLER

Published in Great Britain 2015
by Mills & Boon, an imprint of Harlequin (UK) Limited,
Eton House, 18-24 Paradise Road, Richmond, Surrey, TW9 1SR

© 2015 Louise Fuller

ISBN: 978-0-263-25070-1

Printed and bound in Spain
by CPI, Barcelona

VOWS
MADE IN SECRET

To my husband, Patrick, who provided inspiration
not just for the love scenes but the emotional conflict!

CHAPTER ONE

SCOWLING, A LOCK of dark hair falling onto his forehead, Laszlo Cziffra de Zsadany stared at the young woman with smooth fair hair. His jaw tightened involuntarily as he studied her face in silence, noting the contrast between the innocence of the soft grey eyes and the passionate promise of her full mouth.

She was beautiful. So beautiful that it was impossible not to stand and stare. Such beauty could seduce and enslave. For such a woman a man would relinquish his throne, betray his country and lose his sanity.

Laszlo smiled grimly. He might even get married!

His smile faded and, feeling restless and on edge, he leant forward and squinted at the cramped, curled inscription at the bottom of the painting. Katalina Csesnek de Veszprem. But even though his eyes were fixed intently on the writing his mind kept drifting back to the face of the sitter. He gritted his teeth. What was it about this painting that he found so unsettling? But even as he asked himself the question he shrank from acknowledging the answer.

Anger jostled with misery as he stared at the face, seeing not Katalina but another, whose name was never spoken for to do so would burn his lips. Of course it wasn't so very like *her*; there were similarities, in colouring and the shape of her jaw, but that was all.

Disconcerted by the intense and unwelcome emotions stirred up by a pair of grey eyes, he glanced longingly out of the window at the Hungarian countryside. And then he froze as he heard an unmistakable hooting. It was bad luck to hear an owl's cry in daylight and his golden eyes narrowed as he uneasily searched the pale blue sky for the bird.

From behind him there was a thump as Besnik, his lurcher, sat down heavily on the stone floor. Sighing, Laszlo reached down and rubbed the dog's silky ears between his thumb and forefinger.

'I know,' he murmured softly. 'You're right. I need some air. Come.' Standing up straight, he clicked his fingers so that the dog leapt lightly to its feet. 'Let's go! Before I start counting magpies.'

He wandered slowly through the castle's corridors. The wood panelling on the walls gleamed under the low lights, and the familiar smell of beeswax and lavender calmed him as he walked down the stairs. Passing his grandfather's study, he noticed that the door was ajar and, glancing inside, he saw with some surprise that the room wasn't empty; his grandfather, Janos, was sitting at his desk.

Laszlo felt his chest tighten as he took in how small and frail Janos appeared to be. Even now, more than six years after his wife Annuska's death, his grandfather still seemed to bear the burden of her loss. For a moment he hesitated. And then, softly, he closed the door. There had been an almost meditative quality to his grandfather's stillness and he sensed that Janos needed to be alone.

He wondered why his grandfather was up so early. And then he remembered. Of course. Seymour was arriving today!

No wonder Janos had been unable to sleep. Collecting art had been his hobby for over thirty years: a personal, private obsession. But today, for the first time ever, he would reveal that collection to a stranger—this expert, Edmund Seymour, who was arriving from London.

Laszlo grimaced. He instinctively distrusted strangers and he felt a ripple of dislike for Seymour—a man he'd never met, and to whom he had never so much as uttered a word, but whose company he would now have to suffer for weeks.

Pushing a door open with his shoulder, he glanced warily into the kitchen and then breathed out slowly. Good! Rosa wasn't up. He wasn't ready to face her gimlet eye yet. Apart from his grandfather their housekeeper was the only other person from whom he couldn't hide his feelings. Only, unlike Janos, Rosa had no qualms about cross-examining him.

Pulling open the cavernous fridge, he groaned as he saw the cold meats and salads arranged on the shelves.

And then, despite the rush of cold air on his face, and the even colder lump of resentment in his chest, he felt his mood shift and he closed the fridge door gently. Food had been a comforting distraction during his grandmother's long illness. But by the time of her death it had become a passion—a passion that had led to him financing a restaurant in the centre of Budapest. The restaurant had been his project: it had been a risk, and a lot of hard work, but he thrived on both and he was now the owner of a staggeringly successful chain of high street restaurants.

Laszlo lifted his chin. He was no longer just Janos's grandson but a wealthy, independent businessman in his own right.

He sighed. Not that he wasn't proud of being a de Zsadany. It was just that the name brought certain responsibilities along with it. Such as Seymour's impending visit. He gritted his teeth. If only the blasted man would ring and cancel.

As if on cue, his mobile phone vibrated in his pocket. Clumsy with shock, and a ridiculous sense of guilt, he pulled it out with shaking fingers: it was Jakob! Relief, and the tiniest feeling of regret, washed over him.

'Laszlo! I thought you'd be up. I know you'll have forgotten, so I've just rung to remind you that we have a visitor arriving today.'

Laszlo shook his head. Typical Jakob—ringing to check up on him. Jakob Frankel was the de Zsadany family lawyer, and a good man, but Laszlo couldn't imagine letting his guard down with him or any other outsider. Not any more: not after what had happened the last time.

'I know you won't believe me, Jakob, but I did actually remember it was happening today.'

He heard the lawyer laugh nervously.

'Excellent! I've arranged a car, but if you could be on hand to greet—?'

'Of course I will,' Laszlo interrupted testily, irritated by the tentative note in the lawyer's voice. He paused, aware that he sounded churlish. 'I want to be there,' he muttered roughly. 'And let me know if I can do anything else.' It was the nearest he got to an apology.

'Of course. Of course! But I'm sure that won't be necessary.' Jakob spoke hurriedly, his desire to end the conversation clearly overriding his normal deference.

Laszlo murmured non-committally. For most of his life Janos's hobby had seemed a strangely soulless and senseless exercise. But Annuska's death had changed that opinion as it had changed everything else.

After her funeral life at the castle had grown increasingly bleak. Janos had been in a state of shock, inconsolable with grief. But once the shock had worn off his misery had turned into a kind of depression—a lethargy which no amount of time seemed able to heal. Laszlo had been in despair; weeks and months had turned into years. Until slowly, and then with increasing momentum, his grandfather had become almost his old self.

The reason for his recovery, like all catalysts for change, had been wholly unexpected. A stack of letters between Annuska and Janos had reminded him of their mutual passion for art.

Tentatively, not daring to hope, Laszlo had encouraged his grandfather to revive his former hobby. To his surprise, Janos had begun to lose his listless manner and then, out of the blue, his grandfather had decided to have his sprawling collection catalogued. Seymour's auction house in London had been contacted and its flamboyant owner, Edmund Seymour, had duly been invited to visit Kastely Almasy.

Laszlo grimaced. His grandfather's happiness had over-ridden his own feeling but how on earth was he going to put up with this stranger in his home?

Jakob's voice broke into his thoughts.

'I mean, I know how you hate having people around—' There was a sudden awkward silence and then the lawyer cleared his throat. 'What I meant to say was—'

Laszlo interrupted him curtly. 'There are more than thirty rooms at the castle, Jakob, so I think I'll be able to cope with one solitary guest, don't you?'

He felt a sudden, fierce stab of self-loathing. Seymour could stay for a year if it made his grandfather happy. And, really, what was a few weeks? Since Annuska's death time had ceased to matter. Nothing much mattered except healing his grandfather.

'I can manage,' he repeated gruffly.

'Of course…of course.' The lawyer laughed nervously. 'You might even enjoy it. In fact, Janos was only saying to me yesterday that this visit might be a good opportunity to invite some of the neighbours for drinks or dinner. The Szecsenyis are always good fun and they have a daughter around your age.'

In the early-morning light the room seemed suddenly grey and cold, like a tomb. Laszlo felt his fingers tighten around the handset as his heart started to pound out a drumroll of warning.

He took a shallow breath, groping for calm. 'I'll think about it,' he said finally. His tone was pleasant, but there was no mistaking the note of high-tensile steel in his voice. 'I mean, our guest may simply prefer paintings to people.'

He knew what his grandfather really wanted, and why he had inveigled Jakob into suggesting it. Janos secretly longed to see his only grandchild married—to see Laszlo sharing his life with a soulmate. And why wouldn't he? After all, Janos himself had been blissfully happy during his forty-year marriage.

Laszlo's fingers curled into his palms. If only he could do it. If only he could marry a perfectly sweet, pretty girl like Agnes Szecsenyi. That would be worth more than fifty art collections to Janos.

But that was never going to happen. For he had a secret, and no matter how many dinner dates his grandfather engineered, a wife was most certainly not going to result from any of them.

'Now, you *have* read my notes properly, haven't you, Prue? Only you do have a tendency to skim…'

Pushing a strand of pale blonde hair out of her cloud-grey eyes, Prudence Elliot took a deep breath and counted slowly up to ten. Her plane had landed in Hungary only an hour ago, but this was the third time Uncle Edmund had rung her to see how she was doing: in other words, he was checking up on her.

Edmund paused. 'I don't want to sound like a nag, but it's just… Well, I just wish I could be there with you…you *do* understand?'

His voice cut through her juddering, panicky thoughts and her anxiety was instantly replaced by guilt. Of course she understood. Her uncle had built up the auction house that bore his name from scratch. And today would have undoubtedly been the most important day of his career—the pinnacle of his life's work: cataloguing reclusive Hungarian billionaire Janos Almasy de Zsadany's legendary art collection.

With a lurch of fear, Prudence remembered the look of excitement and terror on Edmund's face when he'd been invited to the de Zsadany castle in Hungary. His words kept replaying in her head.

'The man's a modern Medici, Prue. Of course no one actually knows the exact contents of his collection. But a conservative valuation would be over a billion dollars.'

It should be Edmund with his thirty years of experience sitting in the back of the sleek, shark-nosed de Zsadany limousine. Not Prudence, who felt she could offer little more than her uncle's reputation by proxy. Only Edmund was in England, confined to bed, recovering from a major asthma attack.

Biting her lip, she glanced out of the window at the dark fields. She hadn't wanted to come. But she'd had no choice. Edmund owed money, and with debts mounting and interest accruing on those debts the business was in jeopardy. The fee from the de Zsadany job would balance the books, but the de Zsadany family lawyer had been adamant that work must start immediately. And so, reluctantly, she'd agreed to go to Hungary.

She heard Edmund sigh down the phone.

'I'm sorry, Prue,' he said slowly. 'You shouldn't have to put up with my nagging when you've been so good about all this.'

Instantly she felt ashamed. Edmund was like a father to her. He had given her everything: a home, a family, security and even a job. She wasn't about to let him down now, in his hour of need.

Taking a deep breath, she tried to inject some confidence into her voice. 'Please try not to worry, Edmund. If I need anything at all I'll ring you. But I'll be fine. I promise.'

He rang off and gratefully Prudence leant back against the leather upholstery and closed her eyes until, in what felt like no time at all, the car began to slow. She opened her eyes. Two tall wrought-iron gates swung smoothly open to let the limousine pass, and within minutes she was looking up at a huge, grey stone castle straight out of a picture book.

Later she would realise that she had no memory of how she got from the car to the castle. She remembered only that somehow she had found herself in a surprisingly homely sitting room, lit softly by a collection of table lamps and the glow of a log fire. She was about to sit down on a faded Knole Sofa when she noticed the painting.

Her heart started to pound. Stepping closer, she reached out with one trembling hand and touched the frame lightly, and then her eyes made a slow tour of the walls. She felt light-headed—as though she had woken up in dream. There were two Picassos—pink period—a delightfully exuberant Kandinsky, a Rembrandt portrait that would have sent Edmund into a state of near ecstasy, and a pair of exquisite Lucian Freud etchings of a sleeping whippet.

She was still in a state of moderate shock when an amused-sounding voice behind her said softly, 'Please—take a closer look. I'm afraid the poor things get completely ignored by the rest of us.'

Prudence turned scarlet. To be caught snooping around someone's sitting room like some sort of burglar was bad enough, but when that someone was your host, and one of the richest men in Europe, it was mortifying.

'I'm so—so sorry,' she stammered, turning round. 'What must you...?' The remainder of her apology died in her throat, the words colliding into one another with a series of shuddering jolts as her world imploded. For it was not Janos Almasy de Zsadany standing there but Laszlo Cziffra.

Laszlo Cziffra. Once his name had tasted hot and sweet in her mouth; now it was bitter on her tongue. She felt her insides twist in pain as around her the room seemed to collapse and fold in on itself like a house of cards. It couldn't be Laszlo—it just couldn't. But it was, and she stared at him mutely, reeling from the shock of his perfection.

With his high cheekbones, sleek black hair and burning amber eyes, he was almost the same boy she had fallen in love with seven years ago: her beautiful Romany boy. Only he most certainly wasn't hers any more; nor was he a boy. Now he was unmistakably a man: tall, broad-shouldered, intensely male, and with a suggestion of conformity that his younger self had lacked. Prudence shivered. But it was his eyes that had changed the most. Once, on seeing her, they would have burnt with the fierce lambent fire of passion. Now they were as cold and lifeless as ash.

She felt breathless, almost faint, and her hand moved involuntarily to her throat. Laszlo had been her first love—her first lover. He had been like sunlight and storms. She had never wanted anything or anyone more than him. And he had noticed *her*. Chosen *her* with a certainty that had left her breathless, replete, exultant. She had felt immortal. The knowledge of his love had swelled inside her—an immutable truth as permanent as the sun rising and setting.

Or so she'd believed seven years ago.

Only she'd been wrong. His focus on her—for that was what it had been—had burnt white-hot, fire-bright, and then faded fast like a supernova.

Prudence swallowed. It had been the ugliest thing that had happened to her. After the fierce bliss of what she'd believed was his love, that disorientating darkness had felt like death itself. And now, like a ghost from paradise lost, here he was, defying all logic and reason.

Surely he couldn't be real? And if he was real then what was he doing *here*? It didn't make any sense. She stared at him, groping for some kind of answer. Her stomach lurched as she remembered the last time she'd seen him: being pushed into the back of a police car, his face dark and defiant.

Laszlo didn't belong in a place like this. And yet here he was. Standing there, as though he owned the place.

She felt her stomach lurch. In the back of her mind, pushed down in the darkness, she'd always imagined that he'd drifted into bad ways. So to watch him saunter into the room was almost more than her brain could fathom. Helplessly, she racked her brain for some shred of explanation.

'Wh—what are you doing here?' she stammered, her voice sounding small and shrunken, like a soul facing purgatory.

Laszlo stared at Prudence, his handsome face cold and blank. But inside it was as though he was falling from a great height. His mind was racing, explanations tumbling over one another, each one more desperate and untenable than the last. And all the time, like a silent movie, the short, doomed pretence of their love played out before his eyes.

Aware that he was playing for time, he felt a rush of anger. But words had literally failed him—for he had blotted out all traces of her so completely that just looking at her made him feel dizzy.

'I could ask you the same question,' he murmured.

And then, with shock, he remembered that it had been only that morning that his hunger-fuelled brain had conjured up her memory. He shivered as the hairs stood up on the back of his neck and he remembered the cry of the owl he had heard earlier. Had he somehow summoned her here?

The part of his mind not numb with shock pushed the suggestion away irritably: of course he hadn't. Clearly she hadn't come looking for him, for her own shock was unmistakable. So what exactly was she doing here?

Eyes narrowing, he stared assessingly at her and waited for answers.

White-faced, Prudence stared back at him dazedly. She must have fallen down a rabbit hole, for what other explanation could there be? Why else was Laszlo Cziffra here in this isolated castle in the Hungarian countryside? Unless—her blood turned cold—could he be working for Mr de Zsadany?

Her mind cringed from the possibility and, remembering his blank-eyed indifference when she'd told him she was leaving him, she felt suddenly sick. But that had been seven years ago. Surely after all this time they could treat each other with at the very least a polite neutrality? But instead of cool curiosity, he was watching her with a sort of icy contempt.

'I don't understand—' She broke off, the colour draining from her cheeks as he walked slowly across the faded Persian carpet towards her. 'What are you doing here?' she said again. 'You *can't* be here.'

Watching the shock on her face turn to horror as he approached, Laszlo felt the floor yaw beneath him like a wave-tossed ship. But he had no intention of revealing to Prudence how strongly he was affected by her presence. Or her evident dismay at seeing him again.

Breathing deeply, he steadied himself. 'But I am,' he said slowly. 'Why are you trembling, *pireni*?'

She tried to ignore it. Just as she was trying to ignore how handsome he was and his nerve-jangling nearness. But the familiar word of endearment seemed to grow to a roar inside her head, drowning out her answer to his question.

For what felt like a lifetime they stood, staring at one another in silence, as they had done a hundred...a thousand times before.

The man's voice, when it came, startled both of them.

'Ah, there you are! I'm sorry I'm late. The traffic was terrible.'

A plumpish, middle-aged man, with thick, dull blonde hair and a panicked expression on his face, hurried into the room. Turning to Prudence, he shuffled some files under his arm and held out his hand.

'I'm so sorry to have missed you at the airport, Miss Elliot. You got my message, though?'

Still speechless with shock, Prudence nodded. She had felt a momentary spasm of relief at the man's arrival. But now it would appear that her relief was premature. For his words had made it painfully clear to her that Laszlo's presence was a shock only to *her*.

The man glanced cautiously at Laszlo and cleared his throat. 'I see you two have already met. So let me introduce myself. Jakob Frankel. I work for the law firm that represents Mr de Zsadany. May I say on behalf of the family how grateful we all are for you stepping in at the last moment. It was really very kind of you.'

Laszlo felt his guts twist. His brain was struggling to give meaning to what was happening. Jakob *had* told him that Edmund Seymour was ill and that someone else was coming in his place. Typically, he'd forgotten—for one stranger was no better or worse than another. But suddenly Jakob's words seemed to take on a new and wholly unpalatable significance: Seymour's replacement was *Prudence Elliot*. And that meant she would be living under his roof for the foreseeable future!

'It's my pleasure,' Prudence said hoarsely.

The lawyer nodded and, looking nervously from Prudence to Laszlo, said, 'Everyone is most grateful.'

Prudence smiled weakly and opened her mouth to speak but Laszlo interrupted her.

'Miss Elliot could buy her own castle with the fee we're paying her. I don't think she needs our gratitude as well.'

Flinching at the undertone of hostility in his voice, Prudence felt rather than saw Laszlo's dark, probing gaze turn towards her. Her breath, suddenly sharp and serrated, tore at her throat and she touched her neck nervously. She still had no idea what he was doing here but he must be important, for the lawyer was clearly deferring to him. The thought somehow exhausted her, and she felt suddenly on the verge of tears.

This wasn't supposed to be happening. It was bad enough feeling out of her depth professionally. But now there was Laszlo, staring at her with those cold, dismissive eyes, and all she could think was that he could still make her feel like nothing. How he had made her feel like nothing seven years ago. Swallowing, she gritted her teeth. At least she'd fought for their relationship; he, on the other hand, had been too busy doing whatever he'd done to get himself arrested.

And she *wasn't* nothing. In his words, she was being paid enough to buy a castle to do this job and that was what she was there to do. Her job. It didn't matter that once upon a time, her love hadn't been good enough for him.

Lifting her chin, she turned towards the lawyer. 'You're very kind, Mr Frankel,' she said clearly. 'Thank you for allowing me to come. This is a marvellous opportunity for me. I just hope I can live up to your expectations.'

'Oh, I wouldn't worry about that,' Laszlo murmured softly. 'We have very low expectations.'

There was another long, tense moment of silence and then Frankel gave a nervous laugh. 'What Mr Cziffra is trying to say—'

'Is that Miss Elliot and I can take it from here,' Laszlo finished smoothly.

The lawyer looked at him doubtfully. 'You can?'

'I think I can manage.' Laszlo's voice was as cold and

flat as an Arctic ice floe and Prudence shivered as Frankel nodded, his plump face flushed.

'Of course,' he said hastily. 'Of course.' He turned towards Prudence.

'You'll be in safe hands, Miss Elliot! After Mr de Zsadany, no one knows more about the collection than his grandson.'

The shock was like a jolt of electricity.

Prudence felt her whole body still and then start to shake. The room was spinning at the edge of her vision. Janos Almasy de Zsadany was Laszlo's grandfather! But how could he be? Janos Almasy de Zsadany was a billionaire several times over. Laszlo was a Romany—a traveller who lived in a trailer. How could they possibly be related?

With an almost painful stab of hope she wondered if she had misheard Frankel and she turned to Laszlo, expecting, praying he would still be staring at her with the same cold, uninterested expression. But she saw instead that he was staring at her with a look of pitying scorn and horror.

Her stomach convulsed with fear. Frankel was telling the truth.

Heart thumping, feeling dizzy and sick, she glanced numbly at the lawyer. But he seemed unaware of the turmoil he had created with his simple statement of fact. Fighting her misery, she glanced back at Laszlo. There was no denial on his face—no embarrassment or confusion, and she stared at him, unable to ignore, even in her misery, his luminous, impossible beauty.

He looked up and she flinched as he met her gaze, the softness of his mouth only seeming to emphasise the hard challenge in his eyes.

Frankel coughed. 'Right. In that case I'll be on my way. Goodnight, Miss Elliot! I'll see myself out, Mr Cziffra.'

'Thank you, Frankel.' Laszlo stared steadily at Prudence, his eyes glittering like shards of yellow glass. 'Enjoy the rest of your evening. And don't worry. I'll take good care of Miss Elliot.'

Prudence felt her stomach turn to liquid as Laszlo turned towards her and nodded.

'I promise I'll give her my full and undivided attention.'

The table lamps felt suddenly like spotlights, and although the room was warm she felt cold and shivery. She watched Frankel leave with a mounting sense of dread, every nerve in her body straining to breaking point. She wanted to run after the lawyer and beg him to stay but her body was rooted to the spot. Numbly, she stared at the paintings on the wall. Just moments ago they had given her such innocent pleasure. But not any more. Now they seemed like cruel-eyed onlookers, mocking her stupidity.

The anaesthetic of shock and bewilderment was starting to wear off and she felt a sudden stabbing surge of irritation. Okay, it was awkward and stressful for both of them to be thrown together like this, but surely she had a far greater reason to be upset than him? Surely she deserved some answers here? Her lip curled. In fact, how could he just stand there and not offer one word of explanation?

Glancing at his expressionless face, she gritted her teeth. Quite easily, it would appear. Her chest tightened. He hadn't changed a bit. He was still putting the onus on her to resolve everything. As though he were a witness rather than a central protagonist in what was happening.

'Pretending I'm not here isn't going to make this go away!' she said slowly. Willing herself to stay as cool as she sounded, she lifted her chin and met his gaze. 'We need to sort this out.'

Laszlo stared at her. '"Sort this out"?' he echoed softly. His mouth tightened as he suppressed a humourless laugh. There was nothing *to* sort out! Except out of which door he would throw her! 'Is that what we need to do?' His eyes met hers. 'So. You're Seymour's replacement?' he said coolly.

Heart thumping against her ribcage, Prudence nodded. Keeping her eyes straight ahead, she cleared her throat. 'And you're Mr de Zsadany's grandson!'

She fell silent and waited for his answer. But he did nothing more than nod. Turning her head, she clenched her fists: the words *incorrigible* and *impossible* were ricocheting inside her brain. Was that it, then? No explanations. Not one word to acknowledge the impact and implication of those words.

As though reading her mind, Laszlo sighed. His eyes looked through her and past her as he spoke. 'My mother was Zsofia Almasy de Zsadany. She was Janos's daughter and only child.'

It was like hearing a marble statue speak and her heart flinched at the chill in his voice.

'She met my father, Istvan, when she was sixteen. He was seventeen, a Kalderash Roma. Both their families opposed the match but they loved each other so much that nothing could keep them apart.'

His eyes gleamed and she felt a jolt of pain at the accusatory barb of his words.

'They were married and I was born nine months later.'

Prudence stared at him numbly. Who *was* this Laszlo? And what had he been doing living in a shabby trailer in England? Had he been rebelling? Or estranged from the de Zsadanys? Her head was swimming with questions. From knowing next to nothing about him she suddenly had so much information she could hardly take it all in. But her heart contracted as she realised that even the small things he had shared with her had been half-truths.

'Why were you there? In England, I mean?'

He frowned. 'After my parents died I spent time with both my families. My grandfather wanted me to go to school. To be educated. So I stayed in Hungary during term-time, and in the holidays I went and visited my father's family, wherever they happened to be living.' His eyes gleamed remorselessly. 'I wanted to be loyal to both my mother *and* my father.'

She forced herself to meet his gaze. 'I see,' she said slowly. 'But you didn't want to be open and honest with me?' She felt a sudden rise in tension as his eyes slid slowly and assessingly over her rigid frame.

'No. I did not,' he said finally.

Prudence gaped at him, her pledge to stay calm and detached now completely forgotten. 'Didn't you think it might have been better, not to say *fairer*, to share the whole truth with me?' she said furiously. 'You know—the fact that your grandfather was one of the richest men in Europe? And that you lived in a castle surrounded by priceless works of art?'

He looked away from her and shrugged. Prudence felt almost giddy with rage. How dare he just stand there and shrug at her? As if it didn't matter that he'd lied to her. As if *she* didn't matter.

'What difference would it have made?' he said flatly. 'There were lots of facts you didn't know about me—why focus on that one?' His face twisted. 'Unless, of course, it wasn't the truth you wanted to share. Maybe there were other things you'd have liked to share. Like my grandfather's money.'

The breath seemed to snarl up in her throat. 'How can you say that?' She stepped towards him, her body shaking with anger. 'How can you even suggest—?' Her head was spinning, nerves humming with rage and frustration. 'Don't you dare try and twist this, Laszlo. You lied to me!'

Laszlo's face was suddenly as pale and rigid as bone and she had to curl her fingers into her hands to stop herself from flinching at the hostility in his eyes.

'I didn't lie,' he said coldly. 'I *am* half-Romany and I *did* live in a trailer.'

'Oh, that's okay, then,' Prudence said sarcastically. 'Maybe it was your other half. The half that lived in a castle. Perhaps *he* lied to me?'

Anger was bubbling up inside her, her breath burning her throat. *She* wasn't the one who'd lied about who she was. She winced as her nails dug into her skin. Had he actually told her the truth about anything?

Laszlo met her gaze. 'You believed what you wanted to believe.'

Prudence shook her head in disbelief. 'I believed what you encouraged me to believe,' she said furiously. 'There's a difference.'

There was a dangerous silence and then his eyes narrowed.

'You're missing the point, Prudence. It doesn't matter what someone believes if they don't have faith.' His voice was ragged, frayed with a bitterness she had never heard before. 'Without that it's all just words.'

She sucked in a breath. 'Yes, it is. *Your* words. The lies you told me.' Her heart was pounding; her hands were tight fists against her sides. 'Don't try and turn this into some philosophical debate, Laszlo. I'm upset because you lied to me and you took away my choices.'

'So now we're even,' he said coldly.

CHAPTER TWO

SHE STARED AT him blankly. Even? *Even!*

'What that's supposed to mean?' She flung the words at him, wishing they were sticks or stones or better still bricks. But he didn't reply. Instead he made an impatient sound and she watched helplessly as his face closed tight like a trap. Her muscles were aching with the effort of not picking up a lamp and beating him to death with it. How could he *do* that? Just switch off in the middle of a conversation and take himself outside of it?

Feeling a familiar cold, paralysing panic, she wrapped her arms around herself. But of course she didn't need him to answer anyway. She knew exactly what he was talking about.

An undertow of defiance tugged at her frustration and slowly she shook her head. 'No, Laszlo. If you're talking about the fact that I ended our relationship, then we are *not* even. Not even close to being even.'

Her whole body was suddenly shaking and she wrapped her arms more tightly around herself. Walking away from Laszlo and from her romantic hopes and dreams had been hard—one of the hardest things she'd ever done—and it had taken every ounce of willpower she'd had. But if he'd wanted to, if he'd wanted her, he could have stopped her; she'd given him every chance to change her mind. Only he'd barely uttered a word when she'd told her that she was leaving him. Certainly not the sort she'd craved. He'd let her go and that had been his choice.

A sudden, suffocating misery reared up inside her as, with a shudder, she remembered just how cold and unapproachable he'd been.

She stood rooted to the spot, numbed and struck dumb at her own stupidity. No wonder he'd been so secretive—smuggling her into his trailer and carefully sidestepping her requests to meet his family. Fool that she was, she'd been too dizzy with love, too in thrall to the way her body had softened and transformed beneath his touch, to wonder why. Besides, she'd been flattered at the start, at least, for she'd believed that he wanted her all to himself. He'd stolen her heart and her virginity in quick succession and all the while he'd been living a lie.

She looked at him wearily. But why did this lie matter, really? After all, she couldn't change the past. Or change the fact that he hadn't loved her enough to fight for her. Her mouth twisted. This discussion was a dead end. There was no point in trying to talk about their relationship now: it was seven years too late. And besides, she had a new life now. Maybe not the one she'd been hoping for, but a good life, and she wasn't about to let him pick up her world and smash it to smithereens.

Her pulse fluttered into life and she glanced at the door, wishing she could go back in time to the moment before she'd walked through it. And then, with a start, she remembered that even if that had been possible it simply wasn't an option. Edmund needed this job. That was why she had come to Hungary. And she needed to focus on that fact and not get sidetracked into a post-mortem of her romantic past.

She took a calming breath. The cataloguing was more important than her feelings. Not that she had any feelings for Laszlo any more. At least not any that should get in the way of what was essentially a job like any other. Their relationship was history and, while clearly she would never have chosen to meet him again, let alone work with him, there was no reason not to treat him like any other client—albeit one who was difficult, bordering on the socially inept.

Fighting down the urge to bolt through the door, she lifted her chin and met his gaze. She wasn't going to let his inability to let go of the past upset her. She would be calm and efficient—a detached professional.

'This is getting us nowhere, Laszlo,' she said firmly. 'I'm here to do a job for you and your grandfather.'

Biting her lip, she paused, her muscles tightening again. Did Janos know about her relationship with his grandson? That could be awkward. But then her body relaxed. Somehow she didn't think so. It was a long time ago, and they'd never met, and Laszlo had probably had hundreds of girlfriends since her. Her cheeks grew suddenly hot and quickly she pushed that thought away.

'I know he wants to start on the cataloguing as soon as possible, so why don't we put aside our differences and try and concentrate on making that happen for him? Can we do that? Can we call a truce?' She gave a small, tight smile and clenched her hands into fists to stop herself from crossing her fingers.

Laszlo stared at her speculatively. She wanted this job. It was obvious from the conciliatory note in her voice and the slight increase in tension around her shoulders. His gaze drifted hungrily over her neck to the pulse beating in the hollow at the base of her throat. To anyone who didn't know her she looked like the perfect English Rose, pale and demure. But he knew the other Prudence. The one beneath that calm, poised exterior, who had wrapped herself around him with passion and fervour. That contrast, and the knowledge that he alone possessed that other, hidden Prudence, had excited him unbearably. With a spasm of disbelief, he realised it still did.

Feeling his body stiffen, he lifted his gaze and smiled at her almost mockingly. 'Since you put it so nicely—'

She stared at him warily. She hadn't expected him to come round so easily. But then, with Laszlo you never knew what to expect. 'Thank you,' she said stiffly. 'I must say I'm a bit surprised—'

He smiled coolly. 'I know how much women love surprises.'

Nodding, she forced herself to breathe slowly. Perhaps she could make this work. She just needed to stay focused on what was important: the fact that Laszlo was nothing more than a client. She looked up and found him watching her. A tingle of heat ran down her spine. She could almost see his desire—feel him wrapping it round her like a dark velvet cloak.

Her cheeks were burning. Quickly, before the sudden softness in his eyes could rattle her even more, she looked away. She was here to work and it didn't matter that she and Laszlo had once shared a passion so pagan, so consuming, that the outside world had ceased to exist. Now their relationship needed to work only on a business level.

She met his eyes. 'And I know men hate delays.' She paused and cleared her throat. 'So I suggest we discuss what happens now.'

Laszlo stared at her. A peony-pink flush had crept over the skin on her throat and his gaze drifted down over the pale grey blouse that clung to the soft swell of her breasts, then lower still to where the smooth downward curve of her hips and waist pressed tight against the fabric of her skirt. She was so close they were practically touching and, breathing in the familiar scent of jasmine, he found himself almost paralysed with longing again.

Breathing in sharply, he gritted his teeth. He had spent so long hating her, hating what she had done to him, that he had never supposed that he might still want her.

And yet apparently he did.

He stared at her, confused. He wanted her. But he also wanted to punish her. And yet even that wasn't wholly true, for he couldn't help but admire her. After all, how many other women—particularly one as shy and unworldly as Prudence—would stand their ground in this situation? Not that it surprised him. She had always possessed that quality of being in a state of quiescence, of teetering on the edge. His jaw tensed as her misty grey gaze rested on his face. Only now was not the time to be thinking about Prudence's finer qualities. Better to concentrate on her flaws.

'You tell me. Talking was always your thing, wasn't it? For me, actions speak louder than words.'

He watched colour creep across her cheeks. Saw the moment that she relaxed, the tension leaving her body, making it softer and more vulnerable.

Prudence felt her cheeks grow warm. She needed no reminder of how eloquent his actions had been. Particularly not now, when she needed to keep her thoughts in some semblance of order. But his smile was like a beam of sunlight breaking through cloud. She just wanted to follow it…place herself in its path.

Focus, she told herself firmly. She cleared her throat and began to talk quickly. 'As I said before, I know how keen your grandfather is to begin the cataloguing. So I think we should push on with the original timeframe.'

He stepped towards her and she tensed, her body suddenly a helix of tendon and muscle.

'You're the expert,' he murmured.

Blushing, Prudence swallowed. His voice was such a captivating mix of soft and seductive. She felt heat begin to build inside her and for one brief moment allowed herself to remember the touch of his fingers, travelling over her skin with the virtuosity of a concert pianist. How the rippling rhythms of their bodies had quickened and inter-twined to a breathless cadence.

Prudence took a deep breath. Surely she couldn't still ac-tually find him attractive? She must have more sense than that. But what had sense got to do with lust? No woman alive could stand next to Laszlo Cziffra and feel nothing.

Somewhere in the castle a door slammed and Prudence started forward with surprise. For a moment her hands grazed his chest as she swayed against him and then, breathing unsteadily, she teetered backwards. They were standing inches apart now. He was so close she could feel the heat of his skin. Her heart was pounding as though she'd been running and her body was trembling helplessly. He smelt of newly mown hay and rain-soaked earth and she felt almost dazed with longing as every inch of her reacted to him.

'Castles were built to keep out arrows and cannon fire. Not draughts,' he said drily.

Still horrified by the revelation that her body apparently had no loyalty to her heart, Prudence dragged her gaze away, hoping that he hadn't noticed or, worse, correctly interpreted her physical response to him.

'Weren't they?' she mumbled, her cheeks flushing. 'Wh—what was I saying? Oh, yes. The timeframe. Three weeks is a typical estimate for a preliminary assessment. It's important to be thorough at that stage.' She frowned. 'And don't worry. If I have any problems I can speak to Mr Seymour. In fact, I'll be in close contact with him the entire time.' She gave a small, tight smile. 'I find it help-ful to have another point of view. For clarity.'

Her smile faded and she stared at him nervously, aware of a sudden stillness in him, a slight narrowing of his eyes, although she couldn't quite understand what had changed. But then, why should she care? She was here to work, and Laszlo's moods were no longer her concern.

Clearing her throat, she straightened her shoulders and forced herself to ignore the undertow of apprehension tugging at the back of her mind. 'A-and obviously I'm happy to discuss any concerns Mr de Zsadany has,' she stammered. His eyes clashed with hers and despite herself she felt another twinge of foreboding.

'Obviously...' he said coolly. 'I know how you love to discuss problems.'

Her heart was thumping hard. There it was again: a tiny but deliberate dig. He was taking what was nothing more than a casual, unpremeditated remark and making it something personal, to do with the past. *Their* past. She felt sudden swift anger. Hadn't they agreed to call a truce? This was going to be hard enough as it was, without him making a difficult situation worse with his snippy double-edged comments.

Her mind was so churned up with emotion it took her another couple of moments before she understood just *how* difficult the situation was going to be. For it wasn't as if she was just going to *work* with Laszlo—her blood seemed to still in her veins—she was going to have to live with him too.

A tremor grew at the back of her neck. Of course she would have to live with him. But not like this. Not dreading his every remark—not deliberately having to misunderstand his every insinuation. She needed to make it clear now that she would not tolerate being treated like that.

'I don't *like* discussing problems.' Returning his gaze coldly, she lifted her chin. 'It's just that I think communication is key to a successful relationship.'

She had meant to sound assured, without being overtly confrontational. But she knew the moment she spoke that it was the wrong thing to say. For he went entirely still and his eyes locked onto hers like an infrared missile seeking its target.

Swaying, she took a faltering step backwards. 'I didn't mean us—'

'Don't bother! I already know pretty much all there is to know about your views on relationships.'

Watching the shock and confusion bloom on her face, Laszlo felt a surge of satisfaction.

His voice was little more than a rasp. 'You explained them to me in great detail when you walked out on me— *Prudence.*'

She flinched as he turned towards her and spat her name into the air as though it were a poison he had inadvertently swallowed.

'In fact...' He paused, his lip curling with contempt. 'You made it abundantly clear how pitiable I was to have ever imagined that our relationship might work, given the range and depth of my flaws.'

'N-no. I didn't—' Prudence began shakily, shocked and unnerved by the level of venom in his voice. But her voice died as he stepped towards her and she saw real anger in his eyes.

'Oh, but you did.' His face was tight with emotion. 'Only you were wrong. They weren't *my* flaws. They were yours!' he ground out between gritted teeth. 'You were just too weak and snobbish—'

'I was *not* weak and snobbish.' The injustice of his words melted her shock and suddenly she was coldly furious. 'I just didn't want to pretend any more.'

'Pretend what? That you loved me?' His face was blunt, angular with hostility.

Liquid misery trickled through her. 'That we had anything in common.'

He shook his head. 'Like loyalty, you mean? Maybe you're right. We certainly felt differently about *that*!'

'You don't need to tell me about the differences between us,' she snapped, stung into speech by the censure

in his voice. 'I know all about them. They're why our relationship didn't work. Why it could never have worked.'

Her throat tightened as he looked at her coldly.

'Our relationship didn't fail because we were different.
It failed because you cared more about those differences
than you did about me,' he snarled. 'Tell me, *pireni*, how
are you finding my communication skills now? Am I making myself clear enough?'

Her heart gave a sudden jerk as abruptly he turned and
walked towards the fireplace.

For a moment she stood frozen, gazing speechlessly at
his back. Anger was building inside her, displacing all other
feeling, and suddenly she crossed the room and yanked
him round to face her.

'That's not true! I *did* care—' She broke off. Rage, hot
and unstoppable, choked her words. 'Don't you dare try and
tell me what I felt.' She set her jaw, her eyes narrowing. 'If
I cared about the differences between us it was because,
yes, I thought they mattered. Unlike you, I like to talk about
the things that matter to me. And, crazy though this may
sound, I try and tell the truth. But what would *you* know
about that? The truth is like a foreign language to you.'

She watched his eyes darken with fury, the pupils seeming almost to engulf the golden irises.

'The truth?' he said savagely. 'You left me because you
thought I wasn't good enough for you. *That's* the truth.
You're just too much of a coward to admit it.'

Silently, Prudence shook her head. Not only because she
was disagreeing with him but because she was too angry
to speak. She hadn't even known she could feel that angry.

Finally, she found her voice. 'How dare you talk to me
about the truth when we're standing here in this castle?
Your castle. A castle I didn't even know existed until today.'
Her eyes flashed with anger. 'And just because I wanted to
talk about the leaks in the trailer and the fact that we didn't

have enough money to buy food for more than a couple of days didn't mean I thought you weren't good enough!'

'Those things shouldn't have mattered. They didn't matter to *me*,' Laszlo snarled.

'I know!' she snarled back at him. 'But they did to me. And you can't punish me for that fact. Or for the fact that it worried me: how we felt differently about things. We disagreed about stuff and that was going to be a problem for us sooner or later, only you wouldn't admit it,' she raged at him. 'So it wasn't me who was a coward. It was you.'

She took a sudden step backwards as he moved towards her; his face was in shadow but the fury beneath his skin was luminous.

'I am not the coward here, Prudence,' he said quietly, and his dispassionate tone was frighteningly at odds with the menacing gleam in his eyes.

Prudence felt her insides lurch. Beneath the chill of his gaze her courage and powers of speech wilted momentarily and she felt suddenly defeated. Suddenly she didn't want to talk any more. What was the point? Judging by the last twenty minutes it would only hurt more than it healed.

When at last she spoke, her voice was defeated. 'This is going nowhere,' she said wearily. 'I know you're angry. We both are. But can't we just put our past behind us? At least until after the cataloguing is complete?'

Laszlo stared at her, his eyes glittering with fury. 'The *cataloguing*? Do you know what my grandfather's collection means to him? Or why he decided to have it catalogued?' He shook his head. 'After everything that's happened between us, do you really think I'd trust *you*, of all people—?' He broke off and breathed out unsteadily.

Prudence felt a stab of fear. What was he trying to say? 'But you can,' she said shakily. 'I'll do a good job. You have my word.'

He winced as though she had ripped a plaster from a

scab. 'Your *word*?' he repeated. He tilted his head. 'Your word…' he said again.

And this time the contempt on his face felt like a hammer blow. Her mouth had gone dry.

'I—I only meant—' she stammered, but he cut across her words with a voice like a flick knife.

'It doesn't matter what you meant. We both know that your word is worthless.'

'What are you talking about?'

Balling his fists, feeling sick to his stomach, Laszlo shook his head. He felt an odd rushing sensation in his head, like a sort of vertigo, and words and memories hurtled past him like debris from an explosion. What kind of woman *was* she? He had long known her to be snobbish and weak-minded, but this—this refusal to acknowledge what she'd done—

His jaw tightened.

'I honoured you with a gift. The most important gift a man can give to a woman. I made you my wife and you threw it in my face.'

Prudence gaped at him, shock washing over in waves. She opened her mouth to deny his claim but the words clogged her throat. His *wife*? Surely he didn't really think that they were actually *married*? Her heart was pounding; the palms of her hands felt suddenly damp. Married? That was ridiculous! Insane!

Dazedly she thought back to that day when she'd been led, giggling and blindfolded, to his great-uncle's trailer. Laszlo had been waiting for her. She felt a shiver run down her spine at the memory, for he'd looked heartbreakingly handsome and so serious she had wanted to cry. They'd sworn their love and commitment to one another, and his great-uncle had spoken some words in Romany, and then they had eaten some bread and some salt.

Coming out of her reverie, she stared hard at him wordlessly. There had been no actual marriage. It had been no more real than his love for her. But it had been part of the fantasy of their love. And now he was destroying that fantasy. Taking the memory of something beautiful, innocent and spontaneous and turning it into a means of hurting her.

Her vision blurred and she felt suddenly giddy, as though she were teetering on the edge of a cliff-face. 'You're despicable! Why are you doing this? Why are you trying to ruin that day?'

'Ruin it?' His features contorted with fury. 'You're the one who did that. By walking out on our marriage.'

Her pulse was fluttering and despite her best efforts her voice sounded high and jerky. 'We're not married,' she said tightly. 'Marriages are more than just words and kisses. This is just another of your lies—'

Her voice trailed off at the expression of derision on his face.

'No. This is just the ultimate proof of how little you understood or respected my way of life. For you, my being Romany was just some whimsical lifestyle choice.' He watched the blood suffuse her face and felt a spasm of pain. 'You liked it that I was different—an outsider. But you didn't expect or want me to stay like that. You thought I'd just throw it off, like a fancy dress costume, and become "normal" when it came to the rest of our lives.' His eyes hardened. 'That's when you started whining about the mess and the moving around. But that's what we do. It's what *I* do.'

'Except when you're living in a castle,' she said shakily.

His gaze held hers. 'You're going off topic, *pireni*. It doesn't matter where I lived then or where I live now. We're still married. I'm still your husband. And you're my wife.'

She felt a stab of shock—both at the vehemence in his

voice and at the sudden spread of treacherous heat at his possessive words.

Turning her head, she swallowed. 'What happened in that trailer wasn't a wedding, Laszlo. There were no guests. No vicar. No witnesses. We didn't give each other rings. We didn't even sign anything. It wasn't a wedding at all and I'm not your wife.'

Laszlo forced himself to stay calm. He had too much pride to let her see that her horrified denial had reopened a wound that had never fully healed—a wound that had left him hollowed out with misery and humiliation.

Shaking his head, he gave a humourless laugh. 'Oh, believe me, *pireni*, I wish you weren't—but you are.' His fingers curled into the palms of his hands. 'In my culture a wedding is a private affair between a man and wife. We don't register the marriage, and the only authority that's needed for it to be recognised is the consent of the bride and groom.'

Prudence felt a vertigo-like flash of fear. She shook her head. 'We're not married,' she croaked. 'Not in the eyes of the law.'

The change in him was almost imperceptible. She might even have missed the slight rigidity about his jawline had the contempt in his eyes not seared her skin.

'Not your law, maybe.' He felt a hot, overpowering rage. 'But in mine. Yes, we were married—and we still are.'

Closing her eyes, she felt a sudden, inexplicable sense of panic. Laszlo clearly believed what he was saying. Whilst she might have viewed the ceremony as a curious but charming dress rehearsal for the vintage-style white wedding she'd been planning, the marriage had been real to him. Nausea gripped her stomach. What did it really matter if there was no certificate? It didn't mean that the vows they'd made were any less valid or binding.

Heat scorched her skin. *What had she done?* She looked

up and his gaze held hers, and she saw that he was furious, fighting for control.

'Laszlo, I didn't—'

His voice was barely audible but it scythed through her words and on through her skin and bone, slicing into her heart.

'This conversation is over. I'm sorry you had a wasted trip but your services are no longer required.'

Prudence looked at him in confusion, her face bleached of colour. 'I—I don't understand...' she stammered. 'What do you mean?'

Laszlo rounded on her coldly. 'What do I *mean*?' he echoed. 'I mean that you're fired—dismissed, sacked. Your contract is terminated and this meeting is over. As of this moment I never want to see your face again.' He turned back towards the fire. 'So why don't you take your bags, turn around and get out of my house? *Now.*'

CHAPTER THREE

PRUDENCE FELT THE floor tilt towards her. She reached out and steadied herself against the back of an armchair. 'You can't do that,' she said slowly. 'You can't just fire me.'

'Oh, but I can.'

Laszlo turned and looked at her, full in the face, and a shudder raced through her as she saw to her horror that he meant it.

'But that's so unfair!' Her voice seemed to echo around the room and she gazed at him helplessly.

'I don't care.'

He spoke flatly, his jaw tightening, and with a spasm of pain she knew that he didn't. Knew too that it wouldn't matter what she said or did and that it had probably never mattered. She had lost the job the moment Laszlo walked into the room. She just hadn't realised that fact until now.

She stared at him, shock and disbelief choking her words of objection. But inside her head there was a deafening cacophony of protest. He couldn't fire her. What would she tell Edmund? And what about their debts to the bank and the insurance company?

'No.'

The word burst from her lips like a flying spear. Laszlo stared at her calmly. Firing her seemed to have lanced his fury and he seemed more puzzled than angry at her outburst.

'No?' he murmured softly. 'No, what?'

She glared at him, her cheeks flooding with angry colour. 'No, I won't leave. I know I made a mistake, but it all happened years ago—and anyway you can't fire me for that. Apart from anything else it's got nothing to do with my ability to do this job.'

'It's got *everything* to do with your ability to do this job,' Laszlo said coldly. 'You lack conviction and loyalty and I don't employ people without those qualities.'

Prudence sucked in a breath, hating him more than she had ever hated him before. 'Stop it!' she hissed. He was so self-righteous and hypocritical. How dare he act as if he had the moral high ground? He'd lied to her. And he was the one who'd broken the law and been arrested for who knew what! Perhaps he should examine his own failings first instead of focusing on hers.

She opened her mouth to tell him so and then closed it again. There was so much history in this room already. Why add more? She breathed out slowly.

'Stop sitting in judgement on me! You're not some innocent victim here, Laszlo. You lied. Maybe that doesn't matter to you, but it does to me.' She stopped, her breathing ragged. 'Only I'm not using it to get at you. I wouldn't stoop that low.'

Laszlo looked at her for one long, agonising moment.

'Really?' he said coolly. 'I wonder...' He ran his hand over the dark stubble grazing his chin. 'Just how badly do you want this job, Prudence? Are you prepared to beg for it?'

She felt nausea clutch at her stomach. 'You're a monster!' His eyes were cold and implacable.

'This is payback! Firing you makes us quits, *pireni*! And, believe me, you've got off lightly. If there were still wolves in Hungary I'd throw you to them. So if I were you I'd walk out of here while you still can.'

Prudence stared at him, her chest blazing with anger.

'What does *that* mean? Are you threatening me?' she asked tightly.

Laszlo stared at her in silence, his eyes glittering with mockery. 'Threatening you? Of course not. But this discussion is over, so I think you should accept that and walk away.' His jaw tightened. 'That shouldn't be a problem for you. After all, you've had lots of practice.'

Anger swept through her. 'Oh, you think you're so clever, don't you? Well, let's get one thing clear. This discussion is *not* over.'

He gazed at her impassively in silence. Finally he said, almost mildly, 'Then I suppose you'd better start talking. Although I'm not quite sure what difference you think it will make.'

She stared at him in confusion. How did he *do* that? Only moments earlier his anger had been incandescent beneath his skin. Now he was prepared to grant her an audience. It was impossible to keep up with him. She gritted her teeth. But hadn't it always been this way between them, though? With her trying to chase the moods which ran like quicksilver through his veins?

She lifted her chin. But the blood was humming in her ears and she felt suddenly hot and stupid in the face of his cool composure. Was she just expected to somehow plead her case while he stood there like some hanging judge? Fixing her gaze on the wall behind him, she swallowed.

'I admit I made mistakes back then. But you're punishing me for them *now*. How is that reasonable or fair?' She paused and heat burnt her cheeks as he stared at her. For a moment his eyes fixed on her, as though her words had meant something to him, and then he shook his head slowly.

'Fair?' he echoed. '*Fair!* Since when did you care about fairness? You dumped me because you didn't want to live in some tatty trailer.' His eyes hardened. He, on the other hand, would have been content to sleep under the stars if she was with him. Shaking his head, he gave a humourless laugh. 'How was that fair to me?'

Blood colouring her cheeks and collarbone, Prudence flinched, his bitterness driving the breath from her lungs. It was true—she *had* said words to that effect—but she hadn't meant them, and whatever Laszlo might think, she'd been so madly in love then that she would have lived in a ditch with him if he'd asked.

All she'd wanted was for him to repudiate her fears that he'd lost interest in her or, worse, found someone else. Only he'd been so dismissive. And bored. As if she was a nagging child. So it had been impossible to tell him the truth, for that would have meant revealing the depth of her love. She'd been too upset to do that, but just angry enough to want to provoke him and hurt him for not loving her. And so instead she'd lashed out at him about the mess and the cold and the rain.

Prudence felt a trickle of misery run down her spine, but then, almost in the same moment, she shook her head, anger filling her. He was taking what she'd said out of context and—surprise, surprise—ignoring the part he'd played.

Damn it! Unlike her, he'd actually thought they were married! So why hadn't he done more to make it work between them? Did he think that relationships just sustained themselves? A lump formed in her throat. It certainly seemed that way. She'd gone to him for reassurance but he'd left her no choice but to walk away, and it had been the hardest choice she had ever made. Even talking about it now made her heart swell with grief.

She lifted her chin. 'We're not going to go there, Laszlo. I am not going to talk about the past with you any more.' Heart thumping, she took a breath. 'If you wanted to discuss our relationship you should have done so at the time. Frankly, now it's irrelevant.'

Her grip tightened on the chair as he stepped towards her. She felt her stomach swoop. Close up, his beauty was radiant and piercing—like a flaming arrow. His eyes were more golden, his skin smoother, the angles and shading of his cheekbones almost too perfect to be real.

'I don't agree. I think it's entirely relevant, given that you have brought our past back into my life.'

Her mouth trembled. 'That's not true, Laszlo. It was you who contacted Seymour's.'

She stared at him indignantly. If he hadn't wanted anything to do with her then why had he chosen to use her uncle's firm? Only of course he didn't *know* it was Edmund's business. He didn't even know her uncle's name, let alone what he did for a living. She shivered. Somehow now didn't seem like the best time to tell him.

Trying to ignore the pounding of her heart, she swallowed. 'I know how you hate being responsible for anything, but this is *your* mess.'

'And we both know how you hate mess, Prudence,' he said smoothly.

'I didn't care about the stupid trailer!' she snapped, her temper rising. 'You just focused on that and wouldn't listen to me. It wasn't a criticism of you, or your precious Willerby Westmorland! It's just who I am.' Her heart was thumping so hard it hurt. 'I don't like mess. I like things tidy and in order and that's why I'm good at my job. Maybe if you'd thought about that instead of sneering at me—'

'I'm not sneering, *pireni*.' His face shifted, and meeting her angry gaze, he shrugged. 'And you're right. Maybe I did focus on that remark—'

He stopped and Prudence gaped at him speechlessly. Was that some kind of apology?

His eyes locked with hers and he sighed. 'But I'm not going to change my mind, Prudence. You do understand that, don't you?'

'Yes,' she said stiffly. 'But, given that it's probably not just your decision to make, I've decided it doesn't matter.'

Laszlo frowned. 'You think there's a higher authority than me?'

His eyes gleamed with sudden amusement and she felt her stomach flip over.

'I hope so—for Mr de Zsadany's sake.' Wondering again if Janos knew of her relationship with Laszlo, she felt a stab of pain. He was such a fraud. Why, if he'd believed himself to be married, had he kept her existence secret?

Forcing herself to stay focused, she lifted her chin. 'Seymour's is the best there is. Giving this job to another firm would only demonstrate how unqualified you are to have anything to do with the cataloguing.' Hers eyes flashed challengingly at him. 'I mean, you don't even *like* art!'

'I appreciate beauty as much as the next man,' Laszlo said softly.

'Really?' Prudence retorted. 'How do you work that out? The only time we went to see an exhibition together you spent your entire time in the café.'

Laszlo shrugged, his gaze sweeping slowly over her face until heat suffused her skin.

'I can think of better things to do in a darkened room. You, of all people, should know that.'

Prudence stared at him, trembling, dry-mouthed; her body suddenly a mass of hot, aching need. He let the silence lengthen, let the tension rise between them.

'Or have you forgotten?' he murmured finally. 'Perhaps I should jog your memory.'

He watched her eyes widen and felt his groin tighten in response. But almost immediately he closed his mind to the tormenting tug of hunger.

'But I digress. I don't need to like art, Prudence. I just want to support my grandfather and be there for him—'

'Good luck with that!' Prudence interrupted him crossly.

'*Being there* for someone generally requires an element of reliability or commitment, you know.'

She glared at him as his gaze rested on her accusing face.

'Meaning...?' he asked slowly.

'Meaning that *you* can't commit to the next five minutes.' She stared at him incredulously. 'Don't you know yourself at all? Trying to pin you down to a time and place is like asking you to give up your soul or something.'

A slight upturn of amusement tugged at the corner of his mouth. 'Ah, but at least you admit I have a soul.'

And then suddenly he smiled, and it felt like the sun on her face. Despite her brain warning her not to, it was impossible not to smile back—for it was a glimpse of the Laszlo she had loved so very much. The Laszlo who, when he chose, had been able to make her laugh until she cried. But then her smile faded and she reminded herself that *this* Laszlo had cold-heartedly used his power to avenge himself, regardless of the consequences to her or her family.

She frowned. 'Life can't always be improvised. Sometimes you have to do boring things too—like learn lines and turn up on set on time.'

Laszlo stared at her, a muscle working in his jaw. 'You're comparing our relationship to a film?'

'Yes. I am.' Prudence lifted her chin. 'A very unmemorable silent film, with poor casting and no plot.'

She felt the hairs stand up on the back of her neck as he smiled again and shook his head slowly.

'I think your memory is playing tricks on you, *pireni*. There were some very memorable scenes in our film. Steamy too. Award-winning, even.'

'For the best short film?' she snapped.

'I was thinking more hair and make-up,' he said, his eyes glittering.

She couldn't resist. 'Yours or mine?'

'Oh, definitely mine,' he whipped back.

There was a silence, and then both of them started to laugh.

Prudence stopped and bit her lip. 'Can't we stop this—please, Laszlo?' She saw the indecision on his face and for a moment she faltered, and then she said quickly, 'It's brutal. And senseless. We're just going round and round in circles, and all this name-calling isn't going to change the fact that your grandfather wants his collection catalogued and I'm here to do it. So let me do it, Laszlo: for him. For your grandfather.'

Their eyes locked: hers bright and desperate, his, dark and unreadable. She swallowed hard, trying to find the words to change his mind.

'If I lose this contract you won't just be punishing me,' she said steadily. 'Other people will suffer—people you've never met…people who've done you no harm.'

She held her breath and watched his face, trying not to let her desperation show.

'Please, Laszlo. Please don't make this personal. Just let me do my job and then I'll be out of your life for ever.'

There was a tense, expectant silence as he studied her face. She wanted this job, badly, and he wondered idly just how far she would go to get it back. Immediately prickling heat surged through him and his groin grew painfully hard. He gritted his teeth, shocked by the intensity of his body's response.

It would be easy to give her a chance. His chest tightened painfully. But why should he? After all, she had never given their marriage a chance, had she? His face hardened. Did she really think that she could somehow emotionally blackmail him into forgetting the past and the harm she had done to him? And what about his family? What about *their* pain?

He remembered the long days and nights spent watching his grandmother's health fade, the years spent living with the guilt of not having given her the great-grandchildren she'd so longed for.

Prudence held her breath, watching a sort of angry bewilderment fill his eyes. The tightness around her heart eased a little: maybe all was not lost yet.

'Can't we just forgive and forget?' she said softly. He looked up and she hesitated. 'Please, Laszlo. I don't believe you really want to do this.'

His face was stiff with tension. Slowly he shook his head. 'Then you clearly don't know me at all, Prudence.' His mouth was set in a grim line. 'I *want* to let you stay. For my grandfather's sake, you understand. But I can't,' he said simply. 'You see, I'm half Kalderash Roma. We don't forget or forgive.'

He paused and his voice, when he spoke again, was like the sound of a tomb sealing.

'And you're still fired.'

Prudence gazed at him in shock, her ragged breathing punctuating the silence in the room. A sense of impotent despair filled her and then something else: a hot and acrid frustration that burnt her stomach to ash.

'I see. So it's not your choice.' Her hands curled into fists. 'How convenient for you to be able to blame your stubbornness and your spite on genetics.'

His narrowed gaze held hers. 'I'm not blaming genetics. I'm blaming *you*.'

'But not yourself?' She stared deep into his eyes. 'Nothing is ever your fault, is it, Laszlo?' she asked flatly. 'You just saunter through life, expecting everyone around you to take responsibility for the nasty, boring bits.' Smiling bitterly, she shook her head. 'I thought husbands and wives were supposed to give and take. Not in *our* marriage, though!'

She tensed as he stepped towards her, his eyes suddenly gleaming like wet metal.

'So now you're my wife? Interesting! As my charms

clearly weren't sufficient to persuade you of that fact seven years ago, I can only imagine that my grandfather's wealth is a more compelling reason for you to belatedly acknowledge our marriage.'

Prudence glared at him. 'How dare you? I couldn't care less about your grandfather's wealth.'

'Just about my poverty?' he said bleakly.

'No!' Biting back the hundred and one caustic responses she might have made, she shook her head. 'This isn't about wealth or poverty. This is about what's happening here and now. About how you're prepared to make everyone suffer—me, Edmund and all the people who have worked so hard to make this happen.' She ticked them off on her fingers. 'All because you're so blinkered by your stupid male pride that won't see sense!'

'And you're so blinkered you couldn't see beyond my trailer to the people living inside,' snarled Laszlo.

'That's not true,' Prudence said hotly. 'If I didn't see those people it's because you would never introduce me to anyone.'

His eyes narrowed. 'You're such a hypocrite. You didn't want to be part of their lives any more than you really wanted to be part of mine.'

For a moment she didn't reply. It was true. She hadn't wanted to be part of his life: she'd wanted to be all of it. As he'd been all of hers.

She shook her head. 'You don't know what I wanted.' She shivered on the inside. He never had.

Feeling suddenly close to tears, she clenched her fists, struggling to find a way past her misery.

'Fine! Have it your way! I was everything you say and worse,' she said flatly. 'That doesn't mean I'm not good at my job. But if you fire me you'll never know. Until you're stuck with a second-rate replacement.' She paused and shot him a challenging glance. '*If* you can find one, that is.'

'Oh, that shouldn't be a problem. I had no trouble replacing you last time,' he said softly. He watched the colour leave her face.

'I'm not surprised,' she said hotly. 'Being the grandson of a billionaire and owning a castle must have a lot of pulling power with a certain kind of woman.'

Watching his eyes narrow at her insult, she felt a flicker of triumph that blotted out the misery of his words.

'It's nice to know that you took your wedding vows so seriously,' she snapped. 'Having vilified *me* for not believing our marriage was real. Who's the hypocrite now?' Breathing deeply, she let her eyes meet his—steel clashing with bronze. 'We could stand here trading insults all night, Laszlo, but this isn't about our personal qualities. It's not even about us. There are other people involved. Not just people, but family. Just remember how anxious your grandfather was to get started. Don't his feelings count?'

She paused as, with a jolt, she suddenly realised that Mr de Zsadany was sort of her family too. Shock swept over her in waves. She stared at him, legs shaking, stomach plummeting. Suddenly she had to know for certain.

'Is that why he chose Seymour's?' she blurted out. 'Because he thinks I'm your wife?'

Laszlo stared at her calmly. 'No. He doesn't know we're married. No one does except my cousin and my great-uncle. I didn't see the point in upsetting everyone.' His eyes hardened to stone. 'Especially not my grandfather. He wasn't strong enough to deal with it.'

She felt dizzy, sick with wretchedness. 'I'm sorry. I really am.' It sounded so inadequate, even to her. 'But surely that makes this easier? My staying, I mean?'

She took a step back from the white heat of his anger.

'*Nothing* about you being here is easy.'

'I just meant—'

'I know what you meant,' he said bleakly. 'I know you better than you know yourself.'

Her misery gave way to fury. 'Stop being so sanctimonious. You've just spent the last half-hour telling me how contemptible I am for not believing in our marriage but you didn't even tell anyone about us.'

She glowered at him.

'You don't actually feel any more married than I do, do you, Laszlo? What's upsetting you is the fact that *I* didn't think our marriage was real.' Biting her lip, she pushed a strand of tousled blonde hair behind her ear. 'That's what this is really about. That's why you're punishing me. Not because you really care about our marriage. If you did then how could you treat me like this? I mean, do you honestly think that any *normal* man would fire his own wife?'

She flinched as he raised his eyebrows, his lips curling in disbelief and contempt.

'That would depend on the wife...' he said slowly.

He studied her face, noting the small frown between her eyes, the delicate flush colouring her cheeks. She was so disingenuous! His feelings about their marriage might not be consistent or rational, but at least he hadn't deleted its very existence. He frowned. He should hate her—and he did. And yet his body was responding to her just as it had done in the past.

She shook her head. 'You can't use our marriage against me, Laszlo. Married or not, you never really let me in.'

She swallowed. Except when they'd made love. But there was more to a relationship than just lovemaking. Like trust and honesty and a willingness to share.

Sighing, she shook her head. 'I get that your life was complicated. I even sort of see why you didn't tell me everything at the start. But nothing changed after we "married". You still kept me on the outside.'

She met his gaze, her hurt and anger clearly visible in her eyes.

He felt his chest tighten painfully. 'You didn't give me a chance. You barely managed to stay around long enough to digest the bread and salt we shared at our wedding. Besides, you're just talking about details.'

'Details?' Prudence stared at him incredulously. '*Details!* Your grandfather is a billionaire and you call that a *detail*.'

She shook her head. She felt light-headed—almost dizzy. How could he stand there with that contemptuous look on his face as if he was the one who'd been tricked?

'You're unbelievable! You deceived me. And you kept on deceiving me.' Her voice sounded jagged. 'Not just about some tiny, stupid detail but about who you *were*. Don't you see how that makes me feel?' She stopped abruptly, like a train hitting the buffers.

Laszlo's face was cold and stone-like. 'I imagine it feels no worse than realising my background had some bearing on your feelings for me.'

The contempt in his eyes seemed to blister her skin.

'Besides, my grandfather's wealth is not pillow talk: I don't discuss the state of his finances with every woman I sleep with.' He gave a short laugh.

Prudence felt the room lurch as the implication of his words sank in. She clenched her hands together to stop them shaking.

'I wasn't "every woman". I was your wife. Or have you forgotten?'

He shook his head slowly. 'I try to forget every day, *pireni*. One day I may finally do so. But, either way, I will never forgive you. And you're still fired.'

There was a frozen silence. Prudence could taste rust in her mouth—the corrosive tang of failure. Her body felt limp, spent, her mind reduced. She had no words left inside—or none that had the power to reach him anyway. It was over.

And now that it was, all she wanted to do was get away from him as quickly as possible, with all that remained of her dignity.

'Fine. Then perhaps you could call me a taxi for the airport? I should like to leave as soon as possible.' Her head suddenly felt impossibly heavy, and she pressed her hand against her temple.

Laszlo watched her. Even though anger still festered inside him, he found himself reluctantly admiring her courage in defeat.

'If that's what you'd prefer,' he said.

His voice was that of a stranger: polite, solicitous, but remote. It pricked her like a needle and she felt a cold, creeping numbness begin to seep through her body at this poignant reminder of the irrevocable shift in their relationship.

'Our car is at your disposal, of course.'

Prudence shook her head. 'Thank you, but no thank you,' she said stiffly. 'I'd be happier making my own way.' She hesitated and then, lifting her chin, said flatly, 'I don't know what you're going to say to your grandfather, but please would you pass on my apologies for what's happened? I really am sorry for any inconvenience this may have caused him. And I'm also sorry not to be meeting him. He sounds like a remarkable man.'

Pausing, she stared fixedly at a point above his head.

'And there's something else—' Noticing the irritation on his face, she shook her head. 'It won't take long.'

He nodded but suddenly she found she couldn't speak. She knew what she needed to say—she just wasn't certain of how to say it. She just knew that as long as she remained 'married' to him her life would never be her own.

Gritting her teeth, she drew a quick breath—for what more had she to lose?

'If I'd known you were here I never would have come.

But…' She paused and took another breath. 'But I'm glad now that I did. Seeing you again has made me realise that I need to draw a line under what happened between us.'

Her face felt suddenly hot and dry and her unshed tears felt like a burden of lead. But she would not cry. Not until she was on that plane home.

Watching his eyes narrow, she smiled stiffly. 'Don't worry. I'm not going to go over it all again. Let's just agree that we were both too young and we made mistakes.' She hesitated. 'But we're older now, and wiser, and so we can put them right.'

'Put them right?' echoed Laszlo. His words were expressionless but there was a glimmer of emotion in the hammered gold of his eyes.

'Yes,' Prudence said flatly. She swallowed. 'I mean obviously neither of us wants to meet again. So I think we should take this opportunity to sort our relationship out once and for all.'

The air felt suddenly tight around her. Gasping, she lifted her chin and found herself on the receiving end of a bone-chilling stare.

'I see. So what exactly are you suggesting?' Laszlo said softly.

Prudence tensed. Whatever inner strength she had, it wasn't enough. Not nearly enough to dig a hole big enough to bury the past and the pain. And she was done with digging. She needed closure. Something formal. Something that would let her get on with her life. And now maybe she'd found it.

'Our marriage is over. We both accept that. All I'm suggesting is that we make it official. I think we should get a divorce, however we do that.'

Her voice trailed off and there was a small, tight pause. Her cheeks felt hot.

Suddenly her heart was beating like a drum and she

found herself babbling. 'It's been seven years, Laszlo. Our lives have moved on. We just need to tie up all the loose ends.'

It was the wrong thing to say. She watched his shoulders stiffen with a tension that thinned the air between them.

'Is that what I am?' he said, his gaze probing her face with such fierce intensity that suddenly she was holding her breath. 'A *loose end*?'

She ignored his question. 'I don't want this hanging over me. Without a divorce we'll both be trapped by something neither of us wants any more. I want my freedom.'

'Freedom?' Laszlo demanded.

She flushed. 'I want closure. I want to move on,' she said urgently.

'You want to move on...' Laszlo lifted his eyebrows. He looked at her impassively but there was a dangerous glint in his eyes.

'Stop repeating everything I say! Yes, I want to move on.' Prudence jerked her chin up. 'I have a career now. And if I meet someone...'

Suddenly he was no longer coolly aloof but intent and alert.

'Did you have a particular someone in mind?'

He spoke softly—courteously, even—but there was no mistaking the hostility and challenge in his voice.

Prudence stared at him, transfixed. 'No. I don't. Not that it's any concern of yours.'

His eyes clashed with hers and she tensed in their glare.

'No concern of mine? And how do you come to that conclusion, *pireni*?'

'Easily,' she said irritably. 'We haven't seen or spoken to one another for seven years. We have no claim on each other whatsoever.'

Laszlo's eyes lifted to hers and with shock she saw passion and possession in their burnished depths. 'And yet here you are: my wife.'

Heat rose up round her neck, coiling tendrils over her face and throat.

Shaking her head, she took a small, hurried step back from the intensity of his eyes.

'You know what? Forget it! Let's just leave it to the lawyers.'

Her heart was thumping and her palms felt suddenly damp as he shook his head slowly.

'I don't believe in divorce.'

She stared at him in silence, her skin prickling beneath his gaze. 'So what are you saying?' Her voice rose. 'That we carry on as though none of this happened?' It was her turn to shake her head. 'Laszlo, that's *insane*! Why on earth would you want to do that? You don't even *like* me.' She paused, her colour rising betrayingly. 'And I certainly don't like *you*!'

'Is that right?'

He gave her an infuriating smile and she gritted her teeth together.

'Yes, it is. It's been a long time since I've been susceptible to your charms.'

Her pulse twitched at the lie and she had to clench her hands to stop them covering the tips of her breasts, which were pushing treacherously against the thin fabric of her blouse.

'Are you sure about that?' he whispered.

Transfixed, Prudence caught her breath. Her skin was taut and tingling, as though a storm was about to break, and as his eyes travelled questioningly over her trembling body she felt a slow, rippling swell of tension rise up inside her. He stepped towards her and her stomach plummeted. She knew she should protest, or push him away, and she opened her mouth. But no words came, for something in his gaze had drained the last atom of resistance from her.

'Let's just see, shall we?' he murmured softly.

Imprisoned by a hope, a longing she knew she should resist, she felt her body melt as he brought his lips down on hers with a fierce urgency. And then there was no one but him, his insistent mouth on hers, and a swimming giddiness tugging her down into darkness.

He tasted sweet and salty. And hot. Her eyelids fluttered and her mouth opened and then she was kissing him back greedily, her lips bruising against his. And all the time heat was climbing inside her, spiralling upwards. Frantically she squirmed against him, pressing her body to his, her hands tugging at his shirt, plucking clumsily at the buttons.

He kissed her hungrily, with lips that formed no words but spoke of danger and of something like belonging, and his kisses made her feel fearless and strong.

She heard him groan, and then abruptly he released his grip and stepped away. She opened her eyes and stared at him, confused, feeling a coldness against her skin where moments earlier she had felt the pressing warmth of his lips and fingers. Her body was trembling like a leaf in the rain and hastily she clutched at one of the armchairs for support.

There was a long, pulsing silence and then Laszlo shook his head and said quietly, 'Not susceptible?'

Prudence gazed at him, dazed; her brain felt fogged and her lips were tingling and tender from the heat of his kiss. She could hardly believe what had just happened—what she had let happen.

'We shouldn't have done that,' she said shakily. 'It was a mistake.' She took a step backwards, her eyes darting frantically around the room.

Laszlo studied her coolly. 'No. Our marriage was a mistake. That…' He stared mockingly at her swollen mouth.

'That was just a demonstration of how little you know yourself.'

Somewhere in the castle a clock began to chime and, frowning, Laszlo glanced at his watch. His face darkened and he shook his head, his mouth set in a grim line.

'It's too late now for you to catch a flight home.'

There was a tense silence and then finally, in a voice that made her stomach turn in on itself, he spoke.

'You'll have to stay here tonight.'

He stared at her coolly, his eyes dark and implacable.

'But don't get any ideas. I'm only letting you stay out of the goodness of my heart.' His eyes glittered. 'Nothing's changed, Prudence. You have one night and one night only.'

She found herself holding her breath as he studied her face.

'After that I don't ever want to hear from you or see you again,' he warned softly. He studied her coldly. 'A word of advice, though. I wouldn't bother trying to pursue this matter outside of this room. The stakes are too high. It won't just be your pride that gets hurt.' He paused, his eyes fixed to her face. 'I'll ruin Seymour's too.'

In other words, she just had to accept her dismissal in silence. *Unfair dismissal,* her brain screamed. He couldn't just fire her like this.

Only he could. And he had.

Worse, there was nothing she could do about it. The De Zsadany Corporation was a huge, global company that had almost limitless funds and an entire publicity department at its disposal. She felt a shiver of apprehension. There was no doubt in her mind that if she tried to challenge Laszlo he'd use every weapon in his armoury to wipe not just her but Seymour's off the face of the earth.

It was bad enough that she was going to have to tell him that she'd lost the de Zsadany contract; she certainly wasn't going to do anything else to jeopardise Edmund's livelihood.

She shivered at the intensity in his expression as he spoke again.

'I don't suppose you'll want to hang about, so I'll arrange for a taxi to be waiting at…shall we say six-fifteen?'

Prudence nodded mutely.

'Good.' His mouth twisted into a grim smile. 'And make sure you're in it. Otherwise you, your family and all those nice people at Seymour's will live to regret it.'

And with that he turned and walked out of the room.

Her heart pounding erratically, Prudence stared after him. A rising hysteria was scrabbling inside her like a trapped animal. She'd ruined everything—and not just for Edmund.

She shivered. Seven years ago she'd vowed to forget him. Some mornings she'd barely been able to drag herself out of bed. Only one thought had kept her from pulling the duvet over her head: that in time she would be able to think of Laszlo Cziffra with nothing more than a bruised sadness. And one day she might just have managed it.

Her face quivered. One fervid, feverish kiss later and how foolish that hope seemed. For now she saw that it didn't really matter how much time she had. Seven years or seven hundred—it would make no difference. It would never be long enough for her to forget Laszlo and how he had made her feel.

Prudence lifted a hand to her mouth, remembering the burning heat of his kiss. How he could apparently still make her feel.

CHAPTER FOUR

LASZLO WOKE WITH a start. His room was dark and cold but it was not the cool night air which had shaken him from sleep. He shivered and rolled onto his side, feeling his heart drumming against his chest. It had been a long time since 'the dream' had woken him—so long he had almost forgotten the mixture of apprehension and panic that followed in its wake. Of course the feeling of dread would subside, but Prudence Elliot wasn't just haunting his dreams now. She was here, in his home, sleeping under his roof, her presence tugging at him like a fish hook.

Scowling, he rolled onto his back. In the darkness, he felt his cheeks grow warm.

Last night Prudence had accused him of being a coward and a liar. Her accusations—so unexpected, so bitter—had left him breathless; and now they lay lodged under his heart, cold and solid like stone. He rolled back onto his side, trying to shift the memory of her words, but the empty space beside him seemed only to strengthen their tenacity.

He felt misery swell in his chest.

Once upon a time he had imagined Prudence lying next to him in this very bed—had imagined bringing her to the castle as his new bride, even pictured her face, her surprise and excitement. He frowned. And now she was here. Only she was sleeping in a guest room and she had come not as his wife but as an unbidden, unwelcome intruder.

He grunted crossly. No matter. She would be gone soon enough. His breathing sounded suddenly harsh in the darkness, and anger, frustration and resentment fused in a rip tide of emotion.

Gritting his teeth, he shifted irritably beneath the sheets, knowing that sleep was inconceivable now. He fumbled in the darkness for the bedside lamp and a soft light illuminated the room. Squinting, he rolled onto his side. What the hell was wrong with him? Prudence's imminent departure should have comforted him, so why was the thought of it making him feel more tense?

He swallowed. Guilt. That was why. Picturing his grandfather's disappointment, he frowned through the ache in his chest. But what choice had he had? Working with her, living with her, would have been intolerable. Laszlo shivered, his jaw tightening. Firing her had been the right, the only thing to do. And it should have been the end of it. Only then she'd told him she wanted a divorce.

He winced inwardly: *divorce*. She'd thrown the word at him carelessly, almost as an afterthought. But to him it had felt like a punch to the head. Grimacing, he punched the pillow in return and lay back again. She had been so insistent—she who had never known her own mind, who had questioned every tiny detail. Demanding her freedom! Freedom from something she'd never even believed in.

The only thing that had mattered had been hurting her and proving her wrong, and so he'd kissed her. And, feeling her melt against him, he'd felt a surge of triumph. Only now the triumph had faded and he was lost—swept far away, a stranger to himself, his entire body a quivering mass of frustrated desire.

Damn her! He shouldn't be feeling like this; after all, he hated Prudence Elliot. A muscle flickered in his jaw and suddenly, remembering her mouth beneath his, his body instantly and painfully tightened. He rubbed his hands tiredly over his face. Okay: he wanted her. That was un-deniable. Maybe *hatred* was the wrong word. It certainly didn't do justice to this whole set of feelings that were plaguing him now. Not that he even really knew what they were. Just that his life had grown infinitely more compli-cated and less certain overnight.

Abruptly he tired of his thoughts and hoping to shift the uneasy, shifting mass of arguments inside his head, he switched off the lamp and stared at the window, watching the light creep under the curtains. And then, feeling sud-denly drained, he slid down under the bedclothes and sleep came at last as the sun began to warm his room.

It was time to leave.

Pressing herself into the corner of the taxi, Prudence sat back and, closing her eyes, said a silent farewell to Kastely Almasy. It should have been a relief to leave, to know that this was the end. But as the car accelerated down the drive she was fighting hard not to give in to the sense of failure and desolation that filled her chest. How could it have come to this?

Sadly, she remembered the first time she'd seen Laszlo. It had been at a funfair, and even though she'd been almost intoxicated by the lights and the noise, the screaming and too much sugar, she had still lost her footing when she'd noticed him standing slightly aloof from the crowd. His dark-eyed beauty had been like a shot of neat alcohol. A rushing, teasing dizziness she could still remember. In that moment, she had fallen swiftly and irrevocably in love and later lying in his arms, she had felt invincible in the sanc-tum of their intimacy.

Prudence sat up straighter, her jaw tightening. But that had been seven years ago. Now all that remained of that exhilaration and ecstasy was a crushing hangover. She sighed irritably. Tiredness was making her self-indulgent.

Last night sleep had eluded her. Images from the evening, dark like wine, had spilled and spread through her dreams: Laszlo's brooding gaze, the sensual curve of his mouth, his strong hands reaching out to pull her closer...

Her body stilled as she remembered the fierce, vivid pleasure of his kiss and how badly she had wanted him to keep kissing her and touching her and—

Abruptly, her eyes opened. And what? She caught her breath. Wasn't letting him kiss her a big enough mistake? Perhaps she should sleep with him too, just to make her humiliation complete? Maybe then the message would get through to her. That his kiss had been nothing to do with passion and everything to do with power.

She should have slapped him or pushed him away—or better still run away. But of course she'd done nothing of the sort. Her body had been utterly beyond her control— her hunger, her need for him, hot and unstoppable like lava. Even though he'd been so cruelly vindictive and unreasonable, everything and everyone—her family, her career, her pride—had been surrendered to the honeyed sweetness of his lips and the warm, treacherous pleasure gathering inside her.

Wincing, Prudence bit her lip. What had happened last night shouldn't have happened. But it wasn't surprising that it had. Last night their past had dropped into the present like an atom bomb. She and Laszlo had been like the survivors of a blast, staggering around, unable to speak or hear. Physical intimacy had been inevitable, for they had both been wounded and needing comfort. And besides, sex had always been the way they'd communicated best.

She stared bleakly out of the window, feeling the comet's tail of his caresses trailing over her skin, and then she shivered, feeling suddenly empty and drained. Now was not the time to be indulging in fantasies. Laszlo Cziffra might still be her 'husband' but he was not her lover. He was the enemy, and that kiss had been a ruthless demonstration of his power—not some resurrection of the passion they had once shared.

She lifted her chin, feeling anger effervesce inside her. How dare he twist what had been beautiful and blissful between them for his own ends! He was a monster! A bullying, manipulative monster. For all that talk of being married was just that: talk. After all, what kind of a husband would sack his own wife?

Seething with frustration, she glanced out of the window at the wall that edged the estate, her thoughts scampering in every direction. How could he just fire her anyway? She frowned. She, or rather Seymour's, had been hired by Mr Janos de Zsadany—not Laszlo Cziffra!

She felt another spasm of anger and then suddenly, unthinkingly, leant forward and hammered on the glass behind the taxi driver's head.

'Stop! Stop the car, please!'

She was out of the taxi before it had even ground to a halt and she caught a glimpse of the driver's startled face as she half stepped, half fell onto the road.

'S-sorry,' she stammered breathlessly. 'I didn't mean to scare you. It's just that I've realised there's something I need to do back at the castle.' She felt her cheeks burn as the man stared at her incredulously. 'I just remembered it. Just then,' she said hurriedly. 'So I'll just go back and...'

Her voice tailed off as he frowned and, suddenly remembering that she needed to pay, Prudence reached hastily into her handbag. But the driver shook his head.

'No. No need. It is settled. No need for money. But no need to walk. I take you back, yes?'

Prudence felt a sudden twinge of alarm. What exactly was she doing? And then, with shock and something like excitement, she realised that she didn't know—and what was more, she didn't care. All her life she'd made plans and followed the rules and what good had it done her?

She shook her head. 'No,' she said firmly. 'No, thank you. It's not far and I'll enjoy the walk. If you could just get my suitcase from the boot?'

She waited impatiently as the driver got out of the car and went round to the rear of the vehicle, releasing the boot to take out her case. He placed it beside her and she pulled up the handle and tilted the case back onto its wheels. She smiled her thanks at the driver and then turned and, heart thumping in her chest, began to walk back towards the castle.

Part of her expected to hear the driver call out, or turn the car round, but nothing happened and after a few moments she realised that for the first time since she'd agreed to go to Hungary she felt oddly calm—happy, even.

Finally she reached the tall iron gates. She stopped and drew a deep breath and, reaching out, pulled firmly on the handle. And pulled and pulled—and pulled again, and again, with increasing desperation. But it was no good: the metal creaked but the gates stayed obstinately shut.

For a moment Prudence stood pink-cheeked and panting, and then she let out a low moan. Of course—they were electric. She glanced wildly around for a bell but there wasn't one. There wasn't even a nameplate. How was she supposed to get back in?

She stared up and down the road but there was no sign of anyone, and finally she turned back to the gates, feeling her earlier bravado slip away. So that was that. Her one and only act of rebellion—over before it had even started. Looking up, she stared sadly at the stone wall.

Or was it?

Frowning, she glanced down at her high-heeled court shoes, and then in one swift movement she had kicked them off and tucked them firmly into her suitcase. Perfect! She took a couple of steps backwards and stared assessingly at the wall, and then, with as much strength as she could manage, she hurled her midsized case upwards. Holding her breath, she watched as it flew high into the air and over the top of the wall. It landed with a heavy thump on the other side.

Sighing in relief, she grabbed hold of one of the damp stones and began to pull herself up. It was easier than she'd thought it would be, and climbing down was easier still. She had just stepped back from the wall with a self-congratulatory smile when abruptly she felt a sudden rise in tension. The air stilled and her skin began to prickle. And then the breath seemed to ooze out of her lungs like a balloon deflating as she heard a familiar voice.

'Good morning, Miss Elliot! I'd like to say it's a pleasure to see you again but we both know that wouldn't be true, don't we?'

Prudence reluctantly turned round to find Laszlo watching her, his hands in his pockets, his face, as usual, unreadable. Dressed casually in jeans and a black polo shirt, his hair tousled, he looked younger, more carefree than he had done last night, but there was an intensity to his stillness that felt almost predatory to her.

'This dropping in on me is becoming a bit of a habit, isn't it? If I didn't know better I'd say you had designs on me,' he observed slowly. 'I must say that I'm a bit surprised— although perhaps *surprised* isn't the right word. *Shocked* might be better; or *outraged*—or perhaps *offended*. Given that you appear to be in the process of breaking into my home.'

Laszlo thrust his hands deeper into his pockets. Actually, as he'd watched her clamber down the wall he'd felt something closer to fear than anger—for what would have happened if she'd fallen and he hadn't been out walking the grounds?

Even though she was back on solid ground, Prudence felt her nerves scrabbling frantically for a footing. A sidelong glance at Laszlo did nothing to improve her composure: he seemed almost preternaturally calm. But there was no point in her having come back if she was going to let him intimidate her from the outset and, gritting her teeth, she held her head high and met his gaze defiantly.

Finally he shook his head and said lightly, 'So. Did you come back to rob me? Or just to check that you'd finished me off with your suitcase?'

Prudence stared at him, her face white with shock. 'Of course I didn't come back to rob you!' She stopped speaking suddenly, momentarily confused. 'Wh—what do you mean, finish you off?'

Laszlo raised his eyebrows. 'What do I mean?' he repeated quietly, his expression cryptic. 'I mean I was taking an early-morning stroll, quite happily minding my own business, when suddenly I was nearly poleaxed by *that*.'

He glanced behind him and Prudence saw her suitcase lying on its side in the grass.

'That *is* yours, isn't it?'

She bit her lip and he watched her eyes darken, the black swallowing the grey, and then slowly she was smiling, and then she burst out laughing.

'I'm sorry,' she mumbled. 'It's not funny. I'm sorry—I really am.' She bit her lip again and tried to stifle a giggle as he shook his head, his eyes gleaming and golden beneath their dark lashes. And then, just as suddenly, his jaw tightened and it felt as if a bucket of cold water had been thrown into her face.

'It's a miracle you didn't injure someone. My grandfather often rises early and walks around the grounds.' He looked at her evenly. 'But I suppose no one was actually hurt, so I'll accept your apology. However, that doesn't explain why you're sneaking over my wall just minutes after I saw you leave in a taxi.'

Prudence felt her face turn hot with embarrassment and

fury. 'I wasn't *sneaking*!' she snapped. 'I had to climb over the wall because the gates were locked.'

Again Laszlo raised an eyebrow.

'Indeed they are,' he said softly. 'They keep out unwanted visitors. Usually.'

Feeling clumsy under his cool scrutiny, but refusing to be intimidated, she turned to face him. 'I am *not* an unwanted visitor. I am here to do a job—a job I was hired to complete by your grandfather. You might want to send me packing but it's not your choice to make.'

Laszlo studied her impassively. He'd thought nothing could ever surprise him again after finding Prudence in his sitting room last night, but that was before he'd watched her scramble back into his life over a huge stone wall. And now she was refusing to leave unless his grandfather agreed to it.

Fingering his phone in his pocket, he looked away and gritted his teeth. It would be the work of moments to call the taxi driver back and double…triple his fare to take her away. So why was he hesitating?

He glanced back at her and his groin tightened. *That* was why! He felt heat slide over his skin and wondered if she had any idea how incredibly sexy she looked. Was this really the same shy girl he'd married seven years ago? Standing there barefoot on his lawn, her hair tumbling over her shoulders, her breasts thrust forward like a modern-day Semiramis.

He shook his head, to clear it of this arousing, unsettling chain of thought, and as if on cue she stepped forward, eyes flashing, ready for battle. 'I won't leave on your say-so, Laszlo. You'll have to drag me kicking and—'

'Okay. Okay.' He raised his hands in surrender. 'Give me your bag!'

Prudence looked up at him suspiciously. 'Wh—why would I want to do that?'

Their eyes met and the silence between them rose and fell in time to the sound of her heartbeat.

'So I can carry it for you. I don't usually conduct business on the lawn. Let's go somewhere more private. And safer!'

She heard the smile in his voice and, glancing up at him, she felt her stomach flip over as his eyes locked on hers. 'Trust me. This lawn's actually much more dangerous than it looks.'

She felt the hairs rise on the back of her neck and suddenly breathing was a struggle. 'No, thanks,' she said hoarsely, averting her gaze. 'You probably just want to throw me in the moat or something.'

Laszlo shook his head and looked up at her speculatively through thick dark lashes.

'That definitely won't happen.' He paused, the corners of his mouth tugging upwards. 'We haven't had a moat since the sixteenth century.' Glancing up at the sky, he frowned. 'Besides, it's about to start raining. I'm too much of a gentleman to leave you to your one-woman protest, and rain means my hair is going to get wet. And you know what happens when my hair gets wet...'

Shaking her head, she gave a small reluctant smile. 'Gentleman? More like gentleman of the road!'

He winced as a drop of rain hit his shoulder. 'Come on, *pireni*! You know how much I hate it when my hair goes curly.'

Breathing unsteadily, her heart banging against her ribs, Prudence frowned.

'I promise I won't do anything you don't want me to,' he said lightly.

He watched the colour spread over her cheeks as she hesitated, and then she nodded. And then the clouds split apart and they ran as rain thundered down.

'This way!' he shouted over his shoulder as water

splashed at them from every direction, and then, as one, they burst through a heavy close-boarded door into an enormous empty barn. 'We'll have to wait here until it stops!' He glanced down at her feet. 'Are you okay? You didn't cut yourself or anything?'

He had to yell to make himself heard and she shook her head dumbly. Was she okay? She was in a barn, alone, standing with a soaking wet, panting Laszlo. How was that ever going to be okay?

Her eyes fixed on his rain-spattered shirt, the definition of hard muscle clearly visible against the damp fabric. Instantly she felt a familiar tingling ache low within her pelvis: she knew exactly what lay beneath that shirt. She could feel a yearning deep inside for the ceaseless touch of his hands, his lips—

And then the air slammed out of her lungs as he suddenly shook his head like a dog.

Abruptly she heard the rain stop.

He looked up at her and Prudence felt her pulse jump.

'I don't want to have to drag your grandfather into this, Laszlo. I just want you to give me my job back,' she blurted out.

Laszlo studied her calmly. 'I know what you want,' he said slowly, and his shimmering golden gaze slipped over her skin in a way that made her stir restlessly inside.

Flustered, almost squirming with tension, she lifted her chin. 'Do you?' she said challengingly.

His eyes gleamed and the trace of a smile curved his lips for the briefest of moments—and then his smile faded. Staring at her broodingly, he let his gaze drift over her soft pink mouth and felt his body respond instantaneously. It had always been like this with Prudence—this fierce, relentless tug of physical need like a terrible, aching hunger that must be satisfied.

He frowned. He felt as if he was teetering on the brink of something.

'Okay,' he said softly. 'You can stay. The job is yours.'

Heart thumping, Prudence bit her lip. Had he really changed his mind? Or was this some sort of cruel game? But one look at his face told her that incredibly, unbelievably, he was telling the truth. She turned away to hide her confusion as instead of relief a spasm of doubt ran through her body.

'And you're sure about this?' she said slowly, looking up at him and frowning. 'Only it all seems a bit sudden. You changing your mind like this.'

Laszlo forced himself to meet her eyes. He was just going to have to hope that she accepted his volte-face as evidence of his impulsive nature. But the truth was that he was struggling to make sense of his decision too. 'You know me, Prudence. I can't resist a fork in the road. It's in my blood.'

Prudence stared at him suspiciously. She could hardly refute his claim; his mercurial moods and erratic behaviour had overshadowed their entire relationship. However, if this was going to be a business relationship, they needed to deal in fact. It didn't mean that he could try to fob her off with some flowery, meaningless nonsense.

'You're going to have to do better than that, Laszlo.' She shook her head. 'Why have you changed your mind?'

There was a loaded silence and then he shrugged. 'Seymour's are the best, and I want the best for my grandfather.' He surveyed her calmly. 'So, do we have a deal, then?'

She nodded slowly.

His smile tightened. 'But don't think that just because I've changed my mind anything has changed between *us*. I may be willing to forget the past for my grandfather's sake, but I haven't forgiven you.'

Nor was he entirely sure that he'd done the right thing,

letting Prudence stay. But it would be for only a matter of weeks, and *he* would be calling the shots. Breathing out slowly, he felt a twinge of satisfaction—for now that he'd rationalised his behaviour, he saw that it would be immensely gratifying to have his beautiful English wife at his beck and call.

Staring defiantly at his face, Prudence clenched her fists, resentment curdling in her throat. She should be feeling relieved—ecstatic, even—for she'd fought to keep her job. But now the full consequences of having achieved that goal were starting to dawn on her and she felt more cornered than anything. He was in control here and she knew that. Worse—he did. And even worse than that was the knowledge that she still responded to the maleness of him with an eagerness that shocked her.

Her pulse leapt. Could she really do this? Work and live with Laszlo? Remembering the heat of his lips on hers, she felt her body still and her breath snag in her throat. How could she still want him? After everything he'd done and said? It was incomprehensible. But while her heart might have hardened against him, her body still melted at his touch. Not liking that fact didn't make it any less true.

She turned to face him and found him watching her impassively. Looking away again, she swallowed. If ever she was weak and stupid enough even to *imagine* kissing him again, she'd need to remember that look—right there—to remind herself that Laszlo had coldly and without any compunction discarded her. No kiss and no caress, however sublime, could change that.

'I understand,' she said crisply.

It was on the tip of her tongue to say that receiving his forgiveness was not exactly top of her agenda, but she had no desire for yet another confrontation—and then she sucked in a breath as she realised that her inadequate instinct for self-preservation was the least of her worries.

'What about your grandfather?' she said abruptly. 'What are you going to tell him? About us?'

For a moment he said nothing, and she held her breath, and then he turned to look at her, his eyes so golden and fierce it was like looking into the sun.

'What would you have me tell him? That I've deceived him for the last seven years?'

His voice seared her skin and she shook her head. He looked away, his mouth thinning to a grim line. She swallowed and took a stinging breath, hating herself but knowing that there was no avoiding it.

'And my contract?'

Laszlo studied her for a moment. 'Will be signed this morning. But until then shall we shake on it?'

Prudence stared at him in silence, her skin prickling. Taking a deep breath, she nodded and offered him her hand. His fingers brushed against hers, and then she gave a sharp cry of surprise as his hand slid over her wrist and he jerked her towards him, hard and fast, pulling her body close to his lean, muscular torso.

'Let me go,' she said, trying desperately to yank herself free.

She struggled against him but he simply drew her closer, clamping her body against his until he felt her resistance subside.

'No. Not until you and I have got a couple of things straight.'

Prudence gritted her teeth. 'Isn't that something to do when we sign the contract? You know—with a lawyer present.'

Her stomach flipped as she felt him weave his fingers through her hair, his hand holding her captive.

'You'll get your contract, Prudence. But we need to lay down a few ground rules just between the two of us.'

He tilted her face up towards him and her skin grew warm beneath his glimmering hypnotic gaze.

'Firstly, you're here to work. And whatever you might like to think, *I'm* your boss and I'll be working closely with you on this project. This is something my grandfather has asked me to oversee. So if you don't think you can stomach taking orders from me then I suggest you climb back over that wall right now.'

Clenching her hands into fists, she counted to fifty under her breath. Finally, after a long pause, she said stiffly, 'I understand.'

Their eyes met and he nodded.

'Good. Secondly, you will restrict your remarks to matters relating to the cataloguing. You will most certainly not discuss anything to do with our previous relationship or the existence of our marriage with anyone. And I don't just mean my grandfather.'

Prudence stared at him, her mouth trembling. 'Oh, don't worry—I don't intend to tell *anyone* about our marriage; it's not something I actually go around boasting about.'

His hand twisted in her hair and she squirmed in his grip as he jerked her closer. 'Finally,' he said softly. 'Something we can agree on.'

Her eyes slammed into his like thunderclouds colliding with the sun and then she shook her head wearily. She was beginning to wish that she'd just stayed in the taxi.

'You know what? I actually don't want to have anything to do with you when I'm not working. That's *my* ground rule. I came back for my job and that's what I'm going to do: my job. Not gossip about a marriage I didn't even know was real and that quite frankly was so long ago and so short I can't really remember it anyway!'

His eyes met hers and she held her breath, her blood humming in her veins.

'Oh, but I can,' he murmured.

His hand slid down her neck, cupping her chin, the thumb strumming her cheek, stroking slowly, steadily, until she arched helplessly against him, feeling his hard strength, his raw desire, and wanting more of both.

'I can remember every single moment.'

Prudence swallowed. She opened her mouth to speak, tried to lift her hands and push him away, but her brain and body refused to co-operate. Her head was spinning and she could feel her insides tightening, desire mingling with frustration and anger. And then he shifted against her so that the hard muscle of his thigh pushed against her pelvis.

She moaned softly, tipping her head back as his lips caressed her neck, moving slowly, deliberately over her throat and back to her mouth, and then her lips parted and he lowered his mouth to hers. Tingling currents of sensation snaked across her skin and, reaching up, she curled her fingers through his hair and drew him closer, gripping him tightly, for it felt almost as though she might disappear into the kiss itself.

And then, slowly at first, and then with a jolt, her brain seemed to awaken from a deep sleep and she broke free of his arms.

The air on her skin felt sudden and sharp, like a knife, and she rubbed her hand against her mouth as though to remove all traces of his dark, compelling kiss.

'We shouldn't have done that.'

Her voice was raw, her breathing coming in panicky little gasps. It had been wrong. And stupid and dangerous. A shudder ran through her. But how could it be wrong when it had felt so good and so right?

Laszlo watched her shake her head, a fierce, urgent heat flaring in his belly. He wanted her so much he could hardly stand. And she had wanted him—she still did. He could see that in the dark turbulence in her eyes and in the convulsive trembling of her skin.

'What are you talking about?' His voice was taut, his breathing fraying apart as he spoke.

'I don't want that—I don't want you—' she began.

Laszlo cut her off incredulously. '*That* was you not wanting me?'

Biting her lip, she shook her head, too horrified by the violence of her response to him even to try to dissemble her desire for him. 'No. I *do* want you.' Shivering, she took a step backwards, staring at him with wide-eyed agitation. 'But we can't. It would be wrong—' She looked frantically past him, trying to locate the door in the gloom of the barn.

Laszlo frowned. 'Wrong? How could it be wrong? We're married—'

It was her turn to look incredulous. 'It's not about whether we're *married*, Laszlo!' She shook her head again. 'It's not appropriate, our doing that, when—' She was struggling for words. 'I mean, you hate me.'

'I don't hate you,' he said slowly, and he was surprised to find that it was true. He didn't.

There was a shocked silence and she met his gaze.

'But you don't like me, and I don't like you, and we certainly don't love one another.' Her voice sounded wooden but her breathing was calmer now and she lifted her chin. 'This is just sex.'

'This is *not* just sex,' he said, speaking with slow, clear emphasis. 'You clearly haven't had much in the way of sexual experience if you think *that* was just sex.'

Her face coloured. 'You're right. I haven't. But when I make love to someone it will be because I love them and *only* because I love them. Not because of anything else.'

Knowing just how good that 'anything else' could feel, she clenched her fists against the treacherous warmth seeping over her skin.

'So, no, Laszlo. I'm not going to have sex with you in a barn even though we may be married.'

Crossing her arms in front of her body, she stared at him defiantly.

Laszlo studied her in silence. Had he really thought she would sleep with him? And would he have respected her if she had? He smiled grimly. Would he have respected *himself*? After all, he'd kissed her twice in twenty-four hours, each time telling himself it was the last time—each time, telling himself it was a mistake, that whatever desire he felt was just some reflex kicking in…a habit from the past. But why, if that were true, did he want to keep on repeating those mistakes? And go on repeating them.

He felt his body stir again and frowned. His mistake had been to believe he was over her—for he saw now that, like a virus in his blood, his longing for her had simply lain dormant until she'd walked back into his life yesterday and turned him inside out.

His jaw tightened. He needed some way to cure himself of this sexual power she had over him. Only he was so wound up he was finding it hard to think. All he knew was that his body was pulsing with frustration.

'Okay,' he said finally. He watched her breathe out. 'Look. We've both had a lot to take in. And we're still coming to terms with—' he waved his hand towards the roof of the barn '—everything. So I think we should cut ourselves a bit of slack. How about we go up to the castle and have some breakfast?'

Prudence nodded wordlessly. Her brain was in overdrive. Why had she said she 'might' be married to Laszlo? And why did the thought of being his wife make her stomach turn over and over in helpless response to him? Her mouth tightened. It was foolish and distracting. Even if she accepted his version of events, it was still not something of which she needed to be reminded. Particularly as she seemed determined to give in to the intense sexual chemistry between them at every opportunity.

Pushing back her shoulders, she reached behind her neck and smoothed her hair into a ponytail. Her body clearly had very poor judgement when it came to men and she would need to be on her guard at all times—otherwise this arrangement simply wouldn't work. And that was what she was here to do: work. Not concoct some parallel life in which she and Laszlo were happily married.

She realised that he had spoken again. 'Sorry—what did you say?'

He stared at her speculatively. 'I said that I'll introduce you to my grandfather after breakfast. And then we can sort out where you're going to sleep. It shouldn't be a problem. We have twenty bedrooms at the castle. Eighteen spare, that is.'

His groin tightened painfully as an image of her lying naked beside him in his bed slid into his head and he took a deep breath. Maybe their sleeping under the same roof was not such a good idea after all. Not unless he was prepared to sleep standing upright under a cold shower.

Prudence was clearly having the same thought.

'Why don't I just stay in a hotel?' she said quickly.

'That won't be necessary.'

A muscle flickered in his cheek. There was another option—only up until that moment the mere thought of suggesting it would have appalled him. But nothing was the same any more. Looking up at Prudence, he cleared his throat. 'There's an empty cottage on the estate. It's small. But it's clean and private and a lot cosier than the castle.'

His eyes blazed.

'Just don't get *too* cosy! As soon as the cataloguing is complete I want you out of my life and I never want to see you again.'

CHAPTER FIVE

'AND THIS IS one of my favourite pieces in the entire collection!' Janos de Zsadany took a step back and stared intently at the portrait of a girl clutching an open green fan. 'Annuska and I gave this to Zsofia for her sixteenth birthday.' He turned towards Prudence and gave the faintest of smiles. 'I think secretly she'd been hoping for a horse. But thankfully she was enchanted.'

Prudence gazed at the portrait. 'It's beautiful!' she said slowly. 'Were you specifically looking for a Henri?'

Janos shook his head. 'No. Not at all. But when Annuska and I saw this painting we both knew it was the one. She reminded us so much of Zsofia. Not just in colouring. It's her expression.' He smiled ruefully. 'My daughter often used to look at me like that. You know—that mixture of love and exasperation.'

Prudence bit her lip. She had suddenly realised that they weren't talking about some random young woman but Laszlo's mother. 'I'm sure it was just her age,' she said hesitantly.

She felt suddenly sick with guilt. Janos was talking so openly about such a private matter with the woman who was secretly married to his grandson. But what choice did she have? She sighed. It had been easy enough to agree with Laszlo not to discuss their marriage with anyone. It was not even that hard to convince herself that it was all for the best. Only now, faced with Janos's gentle courtesy, their subterfuge made her feel shabby and sly.

She sucked in a breath and managed a polite smile. 'Whatever your reasons, it was a good choice, Mr de Zsadany.'

Janos laughed. 'I think so too.' He beamed at her. 'I think we're going to get along very well, Miss Elliot.' He frowned. 'But could I suggest we do away with all these formalities, or we'll spend most of our time together repeating each other's names. Please call me Janos!'

Smiling, she shook his hand. 'Prudence,' she said firmly. 'And thank you, Janos, for making me feel so welcome.'

He bowed. 'No. Thank *you* for making this happen. You've made an old man very happy. And, as sorry as I am that Seymour was unable to be here, I'm in no way disappointed by his replacement. Don't worry, though! I won't tell anyone. It can be our little secret.'

'A remote castle in Hungary and a beautiful woman with a secret. How intriguing! It sounds like the plot for some kind of historical romance.'

They both turned to find Laszlo watching them from the doorway. His eyes fixed on Prudence and then his gaze shifted to his grandfather, his face softening into a smile.

'So!' He walked into the room and stopped in front of the painting, frowning. 'What's the big secret, then?'

He was still smiling, but his voice was blunt—like a knife against a whetstone. Since her arrival he'd been tormented by dreams of Prudence naked in the barn, and yet every time he'd met her she'd been polite but glacially remote. His smile tightened. It was an icy aloofness that appeared to be reserved only for him, for she'd established a sweetly flirtatious rapport with his grandfather.

Shaking his head, Janos patted his grandson on the arm. 'Oh, I was just trying to reassure Prudence that her presence here was in no way a disappointment. In fact, I'm rather hoping she might agree to be a charming, if sadly temporary, addition to our bachelor evenings of chess and backgammon.'

Forcing herself to look straight ahead, Prudence managed a faint smile. 'That would be lovely, Mr de— I mean Janos. But I wouldn't want to intrude.'

Janos shook his head. 'Not at all. You're a long way from home,' he said firmly. 'And while you're our guest it's our job to make you feel welcome—isn't it, Laszlo?'

Prudence caught her breath as Laszlo gave the ghost of a smile and nodded slowly. 'Of course, Papi,' he said stiffly. 'But right now you need to go downstairs and find Rosa. Apparently you're supposed to be discussing curtains?'

Janos frowned. 'Ah, yes. The curtains. I hadn't forgotten. I just rather hoped Rosa had.' He ran a hand over his face and cast an apologetic glance towards Prudence. 'If you'll excuse me, my dear? Perhaps, however, I can persuade you to join Laszlo and myself for lunch?'

Watching Janos leave, Prudence felt a pit open up in her stomach and the air seemed suddenly to swell in the pulsing, steepening silence. Since arriving at the castle three days ago she'd made a point of staying in the cottage outside of work hours, and had hardly seen Laszlo except at mealtimes, when she'd found his marked courtesy towards her both grating and depressing. Only now here they were: alone. There was nowhere to hide from his dark, probing gaze. Or from the fluttering, shivery anticipation squirming inside her.

Biting her lip, she reached up to tuck her hair behind her ear before remembering that, as usual for work, she'd tied it back into a low ponytail.

'I don't have to come to lunch. I could say I have work to do. Or that I've got a headache.' She spoke quickly, desperate to say something before her body began to slip apart and she couldn't even think straight, far less talk.

Laszlo stared at her, his face expressionless, and then he

said coldly, 'I'd rather you didn't keep lying to my grand-father, Prudence.'

She glared at him. 'I'm not lying. I *do* have work I could be doing.' And, turning, she began to rifle pointedly through a pile of papers on the desk.

'And the headache?' Laszlo said relentlessly.

Gritting her teeth, Prudence turned back to face him. 'Also true—and standing right in front of me!' she snapped.

Laszlo stared at her for a long, long moment, until finally he began to drift around the room. From the corner of her eye, she watched furtively as he walked up to his mother's painting and idly ran a finger down the frame.

'Don't you have somewhere to be?' she snapped finally.

Turning, he shrugged, and then in a voice that made the hairs on the back of her neck stand upright, he said mildly, 'I have a cure for headaches.'

His eyes locked onto hers and she felt heat break out on her skin. Clenching her fists, she gave him an icy glare. 'So do I. Painkillers. In my handbag.'

Laszlo frowned. 'You shouldn't take pills for a headache. They're not a cure. You need to treat the cause, not the symptom.'

Prudence glanced at him irritably. 'I'm sorry, I didn't know you were a doctor. Is that another of your parallel lives?'

A muscle flickered in his cheek. 'I don't like you taking drugs.'

'It's a painkiller!' she said through gritted teeth. 'And I'd be grateful if you kept your remarks to matters relating to the cataloguing. That is unless you think my drug-taking is affecting my job—'

She gazed at him in astonishment as he began peering under tables and rifling through canvases. 'Be careful! Don't touch them without gloves.'

She hurried across the room, and then her feet stuttered to a halt as he turned to face her.

'Wh—what are you doing?' she stammered. His eyes rested on her face and, legs shaking, she pressed her knees together as her body tightened automatically in response.

'I'm looking for your high horse,' he said softly. 'Or is he in stables with all the others?'

Prudence swallowed. 'Very funny! I don't know why you're making fun of me. It was you who said we couldn't discuss anything apart from the cataloguing. I'm just following the rules.'

'But I make the rules. And I can change them too.'

She held her breath as his eyes locked onto hers. Then, abruptly, he walked towards the window and glanced outside.

'What you need is some fresh air,' he said smoothly. 'And some sunlight. A walk, maybe. You used to like going for walks.'

Prudence licked her lips. A sudden, all too vivid memory of where a walk with Laszlo might lead flashed into her head and she felt heat rise up inside her. Cheeks burning, she fumbled for the remnants of her anger—for something that would banish the slow, treacherous thickening of her blood.

'Okay. I'll go for a walk before lunch. Satisfied? And now, if you don't mind, I have work to do.'

Desperate for him to be gone, she put her hands on her hips and stared pointedly at the door. But instead of leaving he simply stood and watched her in silence until she thought she would scream.

'Why are you still here?' she snapped finally. 'Don't you have some suits of armour you could polish or something? I thought you had a job running a restaurant.'

He shrugged, shook his head. 'A chain of restaurants actually. But no. I'm entirely unoccupied.'

Her eyes narrowed. In other words, he was bored. And she was—what? The entertainment? 'Well, I'm not,' she said flatly. 'So why don't you go climb your towers and survey your estate?'

'Turrets…' Laszlo murmured. 'From the Italian *torretta*. They help protect a castle from hostile intruders. At least, they're supposed to.' He raised an eyebrow. 'I'm ready when you are,' he added softly.

Prudence felt a niggle of dread. 'Ready for what?'

He frowned. 'Our walk, of course.'

His eyes were fixed on her shocked face and she shook her head. Her heart was suddenly pounding so hard she could hardly hear herself.

'I said no, Laszlo!'

She took a step back and Laszlo stared at her mockingly.

'Come on! You need some fresh air. And besides, Rosa gave me some linen to bring over to the cottage. I'll never hear the end of it if I let you carry it. So either I can come with you now or I can drop by later.'

Prudence stared at him in silence; she felt like a mouse cornered by a cat. But surely she was being over-anxious? She glanced down at her demure navy blouse and olive-coloured work trousers. It wasn't as though she was dressed for seduction. Besides—she bit her lip—she didn't want him turning up at the cottage at night!

'Fine. Let's get it over and done with, then. But I'll need to take one of these boxes back with me, so you'll have to wait until I've sorted out the paperwork.'

Five minutes later she was walking resentfully towards the cottage, trying to ignore the fact that Laszlo was strolling alongside her, clutching what appeared to be nothing more burdensome than a pile of tea towels. To add insult to injury, the document box she'd chosen to bring with her seemed to have doubled in weight since they'd left the castle and her arms now felt as if they were on fire.

'Here. Let me.' A lean brown hand reached out towards her.

'I can manage,' she muttered, but Laszlo ignored her feeble resistance. Tugging the box out of her hands, he tucked it under his arm before continuing to saunter calmly by her side.

Determinedly she carried on walking, staring fixedly at the horizon until finally, and to her infinite relief, she saw the roof of the cottage come into view.

She stopped and turned towards him.

'Thanks very much. I think I can take it from here.' Looking up at him, she blinked, feeling suddenly hot and stupid as he smiled at her coolly.

'You know, it's hotter than I thought,' he murmured, glancing up at the midday sun. 'Perhaps I could just grab a glass of water?'

She caught the glint in his eye and gritted her teeth; he'd be asking for a pot of tea and biscuits next. Quickening her pace, she marched across the grass, fuming in silence.

Suddenly he was beside her again. 'Why aren't you talking?'

Eyes flashing with fury, she spun round to face him. 'Mainly because I have absolutely nothing to say to you.'

She watched the corner of his mouth tug upwards.

'Oh, I think you've got plenty to say to me,' he said softly.

Feeling hopelessly out of her depth, she let out a breath and pointedly looked in the other direction.

Laszlo watched her intently. 'Perhaps you're right,' he murmured. 'I've always thought talking was overrated and I can think of much better things to do with your mouth.'

Her chest grew tight. Things were getting too complicated. Breathing was suddenly difficult, and hastily she began to walk down the sloping path that led towards the cottage. The path was still damp from some overnight rain, and as her shoes slithered beneath her she almost fell. Her heart jerked as Laszlo reached over and caught her hand to steady her.

'Careful,' he warned softly. 'Or is walking with me so traumatic you'd rather break your own neck?'

Knocked off balance by the unexpected gentleness in his eyes, she stood half swaying against him. Her blood was singing and heat and confusion crackled under her skin. Looking up, she saw that the sky had grown dark. The air felt suddenly viscous and heavy. A storm was coming.

'It's these shoes. The soles are slippery,' she mumbled, her cheeks suddenly hot.

'Don't worry. I've got you,' he said calmly.

Holding her breath, she felt his grip on her hand tighten as the first drops of rain splashed onto her face.

They ran towards the cottage, stopping at the door to face one another.

'I guess I don't need that water any more,' he said hoarsely.

Heart pounding, Prudence stared at him. She knew he was giving her a choice. But what choice was there really? Wordlessly she stepped towards him and then, by way of reply, she reached up, slid her arm around his neck and pressed a desperate kiss against his mouth.

Groaning, he pulled her against him, pushing the door open with his body and kicking it shut behind them both. Her mouth parted beneath his and he pulled her towards him, capturing her face between his hands. Grunting, he pulled lightly at the knot at the nape of her neck, tugging her hair free, weaving his fingers between the silken strands.

She moaned, curling her fingers into his shirt, and he deepened the kiss, slowly, languidly sliding his tongue between her lips, teasing her, tasting heat and sweetness. He felt her stir restlessly against him and he groaned softly, his groin tightening in response as she kissed him back, pressing her mouth to his, then catching his lower lip between her teeth.

Senses swimming, he lifted his mouth, his breath snagging in his throat as her hands slid under his shirt, and then he turned his head, breaking the kiss. His pulse seemed to trip and stumble as the scent of her, warm and clean and sweet, filled his nostrils.

'Prudence...' he murmured softly. She looked up at him and his stomach clenched, his body growing painfully hard. He saw the struggle within her eyes that so sharply echoed his own. 'Don't be afraid. I won't hurt you.'

The tension inside him was fast, dark and swirling, like a spring tide rising. He could barely breathe for wanting her. Suddenly he was fighting to stay calm.

Reaching out, he touched her cheek gently. 'Do you want this?' he asked roughly. The air felt suddenly thick in his throat and he could barely speak. 'Do you want me?'

She looked up at him and their eyes met, and then she nodded, and her face seemed suddenly to open and uncurl like a flower feeling the sun.

Slowly he let out his breath, and as he traced his thumb over the soft fullness of her mouth, he heard her gasp. A fierce heat engulfed him, for it was the sound of surrender. Desire leapt in his throat and, leaning forward, he lowered his head, brushing his lips over hers.

'I want to see you. All of you,' he whispered hoarsely.

In the darkness of the room her eyes looked feverish, almost glazed, and her soft pink mouth was trembling. Reaching out, he undid the fastening of her trousers and gently pushed them down over her hips. Straightening up, he watched dry-mouthed as she unbuttoned her blouse with trembling hands and shrugged it off, so that she was undressed except for the palest pink bra and panties.

Time slowed and Laszlo gazed at her, heart thudding, wordless, waiting. Heat seemed to burn every inch of him and his head was spinning wildly.

'Take them off,' he said finally, and slowly she unhooked the bra and peeled it from her shoulders.

His breath rasped in his throat as he stared at her small upturned breasts. She was so beautiful. Helplessly, he reached out and pulled her towards him, sliding his hands slowly up her thighs, over her hips and waist to her breasts, his thumbs brushing against them until he heard her cry out in pleasure.

Then suddenly, he was guiding her back towards the sofa, tugging his shirt off at the same time, wanting to feel the touch of her skin against his. Breathing deeply, he wrenched off his shirt. His eyes never leaving her face, he moved swiftly towards her, straddling her legs and pressing his mouth against the petal-smooth softness of her throat, then lower to the curve of her breast. His lips grazed the rose-coloured nipple, feeling it quiver and harden, and then his mouth closed over the tip, his tongue sliding over it, taking his time.

Blood was roaring in his head, swelling and rolling, humming like a cloud of bees about to swarm. Blindly he reached out and cupped her bottom, lifting her against him. He heard her gasp, felt her arch closer as his hands moved slowly over her hips and between her thighs. He felt her still beneath him as his hand caressed the apex of her thighs, brushing over the already damp silk. Gently he slid her panties over the curve of her bottom. Her fingers gripped the muscles of his arm and she whispered his name, and then her hand moved down over his chest and stomach and she was tugging at the buckle of his belt.

He groaned as she unzipped him, her fingers curling around him, freeing him. Trembling, his breath quickening in his throat, he shifted his weight, moving between her knees, spreading her legs. Her hips lifted to meet him and he pushed up, entering her with a gasp. He heard her answering moan of pleasure and began to move, thrusting inside her.

She clutched him tighter, her body shuddering, her hands tangling through his hair, pressing against him, pressing and pressing—and then she tensed and he heard her cry out. As he felt her flower beneath him he thrust hard, his muscles rippling, his breath choking in his throat and his body spilling inside her.

He lay still and spent. Her body was still gripping him tightly, and gently he caressed her warm, damp skin, feeling the spasms of her body fade. The sound of the rain was deafening now and he was grateful, for it blotted out the frantic beating of his heart.

Breathing unsteadily, he buried his face in her neck, trying to sort out his thoughts. It had been inevitable, he told himself bleakly. Since that moment in the barn the sexual tension between them had been ratcheted up to breaking point. Every single time they'd met it had felt like a minor earthquake. And today, finally, they'd snapped. His heart began to beat faster. It was only natural.

He frowned. But that didn't make it right. He glanced down at the woman lying in his arms. In the barn, he had ached with wanting her. Her refusal to give in to the powerful sexual attraction they had for one another had been infuriating, not to say painful. He sighed. But now he wondered whether by giving in to that hunger he'd merely set himself up for another sort of discomfort.

His breathing slowed. Hypothetically, it was easy to fall into bed with a woman to whom you had no commitment. There was no need for post-coital conversation or affection. No need even to see her again. But Prudence wasn't just any woman. She was his wife and pretty much nothing about their relationship was easy.

Feeling her shift against him, he frowned. Now he'd added another layer of complexity to their already tangled relationship. In fact, he was struggling to work out how to even describe what was going on between them— for while he was ostensibly her husband, he was also her boss...and now her lover.

Lightly, he traced a finger down her arm. He must have been crazy to let her stay and work for him, and crazier still to end up sleeping with her. But how was he supposed to resist her when everywhere he looked she was there? Laughing with his grandfather or bending over a notebook, her bottom jutting so alluringly towards him... His face darkened as he felt her stir beside him. It was too late to worry about resisting her. The only question that remained was what he should do next.

Shifting his weight slightly, he turned his head and stared down into her face.

Prudence looked up at him in silence. Her head was still spinning but she didn't want to speak anyway. For to speak would be to break the spell. Drifting her fingers over the flat muscles of his stomach, she bit her lip. It had felt so good—too good, she thought, heat colouring her cheeks as she remembered the sharp intensity of her climax. But then, making love with Laszlo had always been shockingly exciting. It was hardly surprising that her body still responded to him so fiercely.

She felt a twinge of alarm. Hardly surprising, but not particularly sensible. Her eyes closed. There was nowhere to hide from what she'd done.

She'd made love with Laszlo. A man who had broken her heart seven years ago and made her feel worthless and stupid. A man who, she'd since found out, had lied to her for the entire length of their relationship but who held her responsible for ending their affair. Her eyes opened. Oh, if that wasn't messy enough, he was both her boss and apparently her husband too.

She shivered and, frowning, he pulled her against the warmth of his chest.

'You're not cold, are you?'

She managed a weak smile. 'No. I was just listening to the storm. I think it's moving off.'

Laszlo reached out and cupped her chin with his other hand. 'It's not, you know. It's right here. In this room. Can't you feel it?'

His fingers began to drift languidly over her stomach and lower, to the triangle of soft curls at the top of her thighs. She knew she should push him away, tell him to stop, but already she could feel her pulse quicken in response.

'We need to get dressed,' she whispered quickly, for soon she wouldn't be able to speak or think or even be aware of anything except the ruthless seeking rhythm of his caresses. 'For lunch.'

His fingers stilled and then she felt a sharp tug, like a fish hook in her stomach, as his warm palm slid over her breast, pulling gently at the nipple until she felt soft and hot and aching inside.

'I can't wait that long,' he murmured, catching her hand and pushing it down towards his groin. 'I'm too hungry.'

Without giving her a chance to reply he lifted her hips and drew her against him, his mouth stifling her soft gasp of excitement. And even though something deep inside her knew she was heading for disaster she arched herself willingly against him as the fierce heat swept over her again.

CHAPTER SIX

GLANCING UP AT the window, Prudence frowned as a few small drops of rain hit the glass. Mr de Zsadany—she still thought of him as that privately—had given her the afternoon off and she'd been hoping to walk into the nearby village. Now that plan would have to wait. She sighed. Not that it mattered really; she had a stack of books by her bed or she could even just watch some old black and white movie on TV.

She bit her lip. Only that would mean going back to the cottage. Her face flared, as it did every time she remembered that scene inside the living room: she and Laszlo, their bodies fused together, moving effortlessly against and inside each other, outside of time and reality. Her happiness had been absolute—and for the first time in such a long while she had felt savagely alive.

Only now, back in reality, she had to face facts. She'd simply picked up from where she'd left off seven years ago. Only at least then they'd actually been in love—or she had. And to Laszlo, at least, she had been—her mind shrank from the words—his wife.

Crossly, she snatched up a pile of papers and stuffed them without her usual care into a file. Now she was nothing more than a fool and a clichéd fool at that. She shook her head. The castle might be a romantic setting but the truth was more prosaic: she'd just slept with her boss. Like some naive heroine in a lurid story, she'd allowed herself to be swept away by a tide of fate and coincidence. And lust!

She blinked. What was *wrong* with her? She had practically *invited* him to have sex with her. Her stomach clenched and she felt a pang of queasiness. How *could* she? Knowing what she knew about him and how he felt about her. For someone who'd vowed never to fall for his charms again, she'd certainly fallen into his arms with almost embarrassing alacrity.

Biting her lip, she picked up a paperweight and thumped it down on top of a pile of certificates. Who was she trying to kid? What had happened between her and Laszlo had been inevitable. But also horribly confusing. Lying in his arms had felt so natural, so familiar—as if she still belonged to him. And afterwards, when he'd pulled her against him, kissing her passionately right up until the moment before he'd calmly ushered her into lunch, that too had felt as if it meant something.

She frowned. But it hadn't. What they'd shared had just been sex. And after seven years of occasional dates and virtual celibacy, what she'd been feeling had simply been loneliness and lust. Only it had been impossible for her to see that, because intimacy with Laszlo shouldered out all rational thought.

She sighed. It was too late for regrets. All she could do now was keep her distance. Which shouldn't be hard, given that shortly after she'd let him take what he wanted he'd simply disappeared, slipping away like a swallow at the end of summer.

Picking up a box of files, she glanced round the empty room dispiritedly and sighed. Wouldn't it be wonderful if she could make her longing for him disappear just as easily?

An hour later, hair newly washed and dressed in a faded sundress, she wandered slowly around the garden behind the cottage. She felt slightly calmer now, restored by the fresh air and the sunlight. The rain had stopped, the sky was a clear blue and a light wind brushed her bare legs as she crossed the lawn.

With a cry of pleasure she spotted a cherry tree and, after pulling down a handful of the gleaming dark fruit, she bit into one. It was perfectly ripe and a sharp sweetness filled her mouth.

And that was when she saw him, walking slowly towards her across the grass.

It was all she could do to keep breathing. She stood, tracking him with her eyes, until he stopped in front of her. There was a roaring sound in her ears and her pulse scampered like a mouse across the floor as his gaze met hers—golden, steady and unwavering.

'I've been looking for you,' he said quietly.

Skin prickling, she stared at him in silence, hardly able to believe it was him.

'It's my afternoon off,' she said finally, glancing at him and then quickly looking away. 'Can't it wait until tomorrow? I'll be back at work then.' The gentlest of breezes caught her hair and, suddenly conscious of his focus, she felt her face grow warm.

'It's not work-related,' he said softly.

Their eyes locked and Prudence flushed. 'Then we have nothing to discuss.'

He laughed softly. 'In other words, we have a lot to discuss. Let me guess: you're mad at me for going off like that?' He lifted his hands in a gesture of surrender. 'I'm sorry I disappeared. I had to be somewhere. But if it's any consolation I've been thinking about what happened a lot.'

Prudence stared at him in silence. 'Did something happen?' she said slowly, trying to affect an air of nonchalance. 'I didn't notice. Just like I didn't notice that you'd disappeared.'

A slow smile spread across his face and then, shaking his head, he reached out towards her. Her heart contracted. It would have been so easy to give in, to let him take her into his arms, to lean in to his warmth and strength. But instead she raised her hands, curling them into fists.

'Don't!' she said fiercely. 'Don't even think about it! Honestly, Laszlo. You're unbelievable. Did you really just think you could roll up after two days and expect to carry on like before?'

His eyes narrowed. 'I said I was sorry. What more can I say?'

She stared at him helplessly. 'What *less* could you say? You didn't even say goodbye. But don't worry, I'll say it for you now. Goodbye.'

She turned to walk away but he reached out and grabbed her arm.

'Let go of me!' Jerking her wrist, she tried to pull herself free, but he merely tightened his grip.

'I'm sorry, okay?'

Shaking her head, she tugged herself free of his hand. 'It's *not* okay. How could it ever be okay?' She grimaced. 'Laszlo. We broke the rules.'

'I'm aware of that. But I don't see why you're getting so upset about it. We're both consenting adults.'

Gritting her teeth, she took a step towards him. 'It's not that simple.'

His face stilled and her skin seemed to catch fire beneath his gaze.

'Oh, but it was. Simple and sublime.'

She caught her breath, achingly aware of just how sublime it had been. How sublime it had always been. For a moment she hovered between desire and anger, and then anger won.

'It's not simple and you know it. It's a mess,' she snapped.

He studied her dispassionately. He hadn't intended to

argue with her. On the contrary, he'd been looking forward to seeing her again despite the fact that she was right: it *was* a mess. He smiled grimly. After they'd made love he'd held her in his arms, trying to rationalise his behaviour, and on some levels it had been easy to explain. It was perfectly natural for any man to be attracted to any woman— and what man wouldn't be attracted to Prudence? She was beautiful and clever and poised.

His face tightened. Only then he'd started to think about their marriage, and about lying to his grandfather, and suddenly he'd wanted to be free of the tangled mess of his thoughts. A flush coloured his cheeks. And so he'd simply walked out, fully intending to stay away until the cataloguing was complete. Only after just two nights he'd changed his mind, driven back to the castle by a sudden inexplicable need to see her smile.

She wasn't smiling now. Her face was taut and strained, and he knew that his sudden disappearance had angered and hurt her. *Hell!* Why couldn't she just accept his apology and move on?

He stared at her coldly, his dark hair falling across his forehead. 'What do you want me to say, Prudence? I thought you enjoyed it. I certainly did.'

She was staring at him as though he were speaking in Mandarin.

'This isn't about whether I *enjoyed* it or not.'

'Then you really don't know yourself at all, Prudence. You slept with me for the same reason I slept with you. Because what we have is incredible. Physically, we couldn't be better matched.'

Prudence blushed, heat seeping over her throat and collarbone. There was a loaded silence.

'Fine. I agree,' she admitted finally. 'But that doesn't change the fact that our doing what we did makes everything so much more difficult. Even you must see that.' She stared at him agitatedly. 'I can't believe you just *left*. That you didn't think we should at least have one tiny conversation about it.'

He shrugged and glanced across the lawn, his gaze drifting away towards the horizon. 'What's there to talk about?'

'Everything!' she cried. 'You. Me. Us. My job. Our marriage. Where do you want to start?'

He stared at her, his golden eyes reflecting the early-afternoon sun. 'At the beginning.' He gave her an infuriating smile. 'When we got married. Which makes you my wife.'

She gazed at him helplessly. 'Only I don't feel like your wife, Laszlo! It still doesn't feel like a real marriage to me. But even if it did we haven't been together for seven years. We broke up—remember? And now we've crossed a line.' She bit her tongue. 'I know couples who split up do end up sleeping together and it's understandable. I mean, everything's so familiar and safe and easy.'

Feeling his steady gaze on her, she paused, blushing, for none of those adjectives bore any relation to her intimacy with Laszlo.

She glowered at him. 'But they have a one-night stand! They don't have to live and work with each other afterwards. We do—and I don't even know how to describe our relationship any more, let alone how to make it work.' She felt a spurt of anger. 'Everything's so messy and confusing, and you just stand there and do nothing like it's all going to just fall into place—'

'And what are *you* doing, *pireni*?' he interrupted her harshly. 'I fail to see what you think you're actually achieving here. You're just asking me unanswerable questions.' His mouth twisted. 'What happened between us in the cottage isn't the problem, Prudence. *You* are. You turn everything into an inquisition. Hell, seven years ago you turned our relationship into an inquisition.'

Prudence choked in disbelief. 'An *inquisition*? Did you ever stop and think *why* I asked all those questions?' She shook her head, bunching her hands into fists. 'No. Of course not. Our relationship was never about me, was it? It was only ever about you and your needs.'

Misery washed over her in waves and she curled her fingers into the palms of her hands to distract herself from the pain.

'I asked questions because I wanted answers. I wanted to know you; to understand you. But you made me feel like I was an intruder in your life. When you were there you never wanted to talk and then you'd disappear for days and I wouldn't know where you were. And you just expected me to put up with it.'

Laszlo shook his head in frustration. 'Not this again. You knew I didn't have a nine-to-five job. You knew I sometimes worked away for days at a time. And you knew I'd be back.'

'No, I didn't.' Her voice sounded suddenly loud and harsh. 'I *didn't* know that.'

Her whole body was shaking and she stopped, breaking off as she saw from his face just how baffling and irritating he found her insecurities. She bit her lip. She'd had reason to feel like that. Only aged twenty-one she had felt too unsure of his love, too aware of how boring he found any sort of soul-searching, to blurt out her life story.

'I didn't know,' she said again, more quietly this time, for the old pain was welling up, making her hurt inside.

'Meaning what, exactly?'

His face was like stone and she looked away from it. 'I know it sounds crazy but I *didn't* know that you'd come back. Every time you disappeared I thought that was it. And I couldn't bear it.'

Laszlo said nothing and she felt the pain inside her spread. But had she really thought he would want to understand now, after seven years of hating her, just because they'd had sex again?

'Why did you feel like that?'

His voice was so gentle it startled her, and she looked up, half thinking that someone else must have asked the question.

'Did you feel like it right from the start?'

She nodded slowly, suddenly deprived of speech. Looking up, she saw him frown.

'But if you felt like that,' he said softly, 'then why did you stay with me?'

Prudence sighed. There in that one sentence was why their relationship had ended. For surely he knew the answer to that—just one look at her face had been enough for her Uncle Edmund to guess the truth.

She'd stayed because she'd fallen deeply and desperately in love with him.

Those few short weeks with him had been the most incredible, the most exciting time in her life. Exciting but terrifying, for Laszlo had unlocked a part of herself that she'd denied and feared in equal measure: a part of herself that she'd spent most of her life trying to repudiate or forget.

And here, now, after everything they'd done and said, she was afraid of giving too much away. Or, worse, destroying the memory of their time together, the time when she'd loved him and believed he loved her. Her lip quivered. She might no longer love Laszlo, but part of her still wanted to protect and preserve her memories.

'Like I said, I was acting a little crazy.' She smiled weakly.

Laszlo studied her. 'You were never crazy. Anxious and insistent, yes. And sweet, gentle and sexy.' His gaze rested on her mouth. 'Not crazy, though.' He paused, his eyes cool and unreadable. 'But why does that mean you didn't think I'd come back. I mean, I admit I was unreliable. But I was *reliably* unreliable: I always came back.'

He was attempting a joke and she tried to smile. But instead, to her horror, she felt hot tears sting her eyes and she shook her head.

Laszlo stared at her with a sort of bewildered anger and then his jaw tightened. 'So you're saying it's my fault? I made you feel like that?'

But Prudence didn't answer; she couldn't. Not with Laszlo standing so close. He wouldn't understand her fear, the creeping uncertainty. He was just so certain of himself—so sure and utterly without doubt.

'Please. Tell me. I want to know,' he said slowly.

Some roughness in his voice made her lift her head. And then, after a moment, he reached out and touched her hand, uncurling it with his fingers.

'I might even be able to help.'

Heart pounding, she took a deep breath. 'It wasn't you.' She gave him another weak smile. 'Although you didn't help much.' Her heart twisted. 'It was me. I was just waiting for it to happen. Waiting for you to leave and not come back. Like everyone else.'

She felt close to tears again, remembering the waiting, fearing, hoping that it would be different—

'Who's everyone else?' Laszlo frowned, his face darkening. 'You mean other men?'

Prudence laughed. 'What other men? There haven't been any. Not really since us—and certainly not before.' She shook her head, frowning. 'No. I mean my mum—and it's a long story. You won't want to hear it.'

Laszlo stared at her intently. 'I do want to hear it. Tell me about your mum.'

His face was focused on hers, the golden eyes calm

and dispassionate and yet warm like the sun. She let out a long breath.

'My mum met my dad when she was nineteen. They got married and had me. And then he left her.' Her mouth trembled. 'He came back, though. He always came back after a bit. While he was away she'd be frantic, and sometimes she'd go out looking for him.' The skin on her face felt suddenly scorched. 'Or for someone who'd make her forget him. She'd leave me. On my own. For hours. Sometimes all night. I hated it, being alone in the house in the dark.'

She swallowed, lowering her gaze.

'I always knew when she was going to go out. And I'd try and stop her. Stall her by asking questions.' She bit her lip; her questions to Laszlo seven years ago had stemmed from the same fear. Letting out a long breath, she shrugged. 'She nearly always went out, though. Then one day my dad never came back. Just cleared out their bank account and disappeared. It turned out that he was married already— to two other women. So really they weren't even married,' she said flatly.

'And you thought I'd do that to you?' Laszlo's voice was neutral but his mouth was set in a grim line.

Prudence couldn't meet his eyes. 'I suppose, deep down, I did. I assumed the worst.'

And that was why she'd walked away. Because she'd been scared. Scared that the worst was already happening, and that if she stayed her life would settle, like her mother's, into a pattern of rows and pleading and disappearances and lies.

Looking up, she met his gaze and they stood staring at one another, the silence between them broken only by the humming of the bees and the faint sound of a tractor on the breeze.

'I didn't give you much reason to hope for the best, did I?' Laszlo said softly.

He scanned her face, seeing what he'd failed to see before: a young woman seeking reassurance. Not once had he stopped and thought to ask himself *why* she had been so anxious. Instead he'd convinced himself that her constant need for reassurance had demonstrated a feebleness of character unbecoming in his wife.

Reaching out, he pushed an unsteady hand through her hair and pulled her gently towards him. For a moment he imagined burying his face against the doe-soft smoothness of her neck, but then he frowned.

'You were my wife. I should have known these things about you. And the fact that I didn't is my fault,' he said slowly. 'But you're right. You *did* assume the worst. Only I'm not your dad.' She stiffened at his words and he grimaced. 'And you're not your mum, Prudence! From what you've just told me, she doesn't sound like the sort of maddeningly stubborn woman who'd climb over a massive wall to demand her job back.'

Blushing at that image of herself, she looked up at him. He smiled at her slowly, his eyes glittering with an emotion she didn't recognise.

'I wasn't that stubborn until I met you,' she said carefully, her grey eyes issuing him with a challenge.

Watching the colour return to her cheeks, Laszlo felt a flicker of admiration rise inside him. She was brave. Braver than he'd thought. Braver than himself. He knew just how hard it was to reveal the truth about yourself to anyone.

Loosening a strand of her hair, Laszlo curled it round his finger. If only they could go back to bed, so she could curl her body around his as she'd done at the cottage.

As though she could read his mind, she looked up and sighed.

'So what are we going to do? You said you'd been think-ing about us a lot?'

They were back where they'd started. He frowned. 'Not us. It. About *it*. The sex.'

Her shoulders felt leaden and she was suddenly more tired than she had ever been in her life.

'Of course. My mistake!' she said wearily. 'I seem to be making a lot of those. Look, Laszlo. What happened between us isn't going to happen again. I don't want to sleep with you—'

'Yes, you do,' Laszlo interrupted her, his voice sharp and sure like a scalpel. 'You want me as much as I want you. And until you stop torturing yourself about that it won't stop, whether you're in London or in Hungary, mar-ried to me or not. You told me you wanted a divorce so you could move on. But you didn't even know we were mar-ried. Now that's *crazy*, Prudence.'

A muscle tightened in his cheek.

'I agree. We need to move on but what's holding us back is not some vows we made. It's this thing we have. This incredible need for one another. I'll "divorce" you, if that's what you want. But you need to accept that no piece of paper, or whatever it is you're hoping to get, is going to bring you physical closure.'

Prudence felt herself frown. What he was saying made sense. Being unaware of her marital status hadn't stopped the memory of him casting a shadow over her sexual rela-tions with other men. A light blush spread over her skin. Their touches, their kisses, had seemed like insipid, infe-rior copies of the fierce, primal passion she had shared with Laszlo. But how was she ever to move on if she couldn't stop this burning want she had inside her for him?

She shook her head. 'I don't understand. Are you say-ing you *do* want a divorce?'

His eyes darkened. 'The divorce is irrelevant. You have

to face the truth. We want each other. And that want is holding us back from living freely.'

'What are you suggesting?' she asked slowly.

He studied her face. The air was suddenly thick between them.

'I think we should keep on sleeping together,' he said softly. 'The truth is we both want to. And maybe that's what we need to do to get each other out of our systems for good.'

She stared at him, stunned into silence not just by his words but by her body's instantaneous response to them.

Finally, she shook her head again. It wasn't worth the risk. 'So your solution to this mess is to make our lives more complicated? What happened at the cottage was understandable—'

'It was incredible,' he corrected.

Ignoring his comment, and the traitorous heat rising up inside her, she forced herself to concentrate. *'Understandable,'* she repeated firmly. 'But it was spontaneous. A one-off. What you're suggesting would be deliberate and repeated. We can't do that.'

'It's nothing we haven't done before.' He spoke quietly but his eyes were fierce.

She blinked. 'No. Laszlo. *I* haven't done this before. Had an affair with my estranged husband, who doesn't even like me and also happens to be my boss! It's just wrong on so many levels.'

His gaze flickered over her face and he smiled a smile that lit up his eyes like the sun, spreading radiance and warmth over her.

He shook his head, his eyes glittering. 'No. What we share could never be wrong, Prudence,' he said softly. 'I agree, it's not a conventional arrangement, but what we have is so extraordinary, so overwhelming. Look, I don't know if it'll work, but when I'm holding you in my arms it feels like we know everything about each other. It's like our own perfect private communion.'

Gazing up into his face, Prudence felt herself wavering. She knew she should turn him down but the pull of his words was so powerful. She could no more resist him than the tide could resist the tug of the moon.

Laszlo let out a breath. His heart was pounding. Looking down, he saw with surprise that his hands were shaking and he wondered why. He gritted his teeth. It was frustration, he told himself. Two days spent thinking about Prudence's delectable body and his own body was hovering on the edge of meltdown. Particularly with her standing so close, looking so desirable.

And she was so very beautiful. Her eyes were shimmering like beaten silver and he could smell the sweet honeyed fragrance that clung to her skin and hair. But truthfully it wasn't just about her beauty. It wasn't even about the sex. Her bright enthusiasm for art, her doggedness in getting back her job, her sweetness with his grandfather—all charmed him, delighted him.

'It's not just the physical,' he said finally. 'I like spending time with you.'

Prudence swallowed. Her grey eyes flashed with reproach. 'Only when it suits you.'

Seeing the indecision in her eyes, he was on the verge of simplifying everything by pulling her into his arms and melting her resistance with the heat of his kisses. But something held him back—some confused idea that this was not the moment for passion.

Besides, he had something better in mind.

CHAPTER SEVEN

'COME WITH ME. I have something I want to show you.'

He held out his hand and after a moment Prudence took it. They walked slowly together over the rough, springy grass until finally they reached a copse of stunted, low-branched trees and he stopped and gently disengaged his hand.

'What are we doing?' she asked.

'We're meeting him here,' he said, turning to face her.

'Meeting who? Where? We're in the middle of a field.'

Grinning, he shook his head. 'We're meeting my cousin. And this is not a field. It's an apple orchard. My apple orchard,' he said softly, taking her hand in his again. 'A long time ago the estate used to make all its own cider.'

Biting her lip, she looked at him nervously. 'Your cousin? Won't that be a little awkward? I mean, he knows we're married...'

Her voice sounded shrill and shaky and, frowning, Laszlo pulled her towards him.

'Take it easy. I have about thirty cousins. This is a different one.' Gently, he pushed a strand of hair behind her ear. 'This is my cousin Mihaly.' He paused and studied her face speculatively. 'He doesn't know we're married. Only my great-uncle and my cousin Matyas know.'

He grimaced.

'And they're not here. Not that they'd say anything to anybody anyway,' he said slowly. 'I promise. You'd have more luck having a conversation with Besnik than you would at getting a word out of either of them.'

Squeezing her hand, he squinted into the horizon. 'There he is.'

He lifted his arm and waved at the outline of a man riding on horseback.

'That's Mihaly.'

Feeling somewhat calmer, Prudence let out a breath as he raised his hand to greet his cousin.

'Mihaly! How are you?'

Smiling shyly, Prudence turned to where Laszlo was waving and then gasped softly. Not at the dark-haired man sliding off the bare back of a sleepy-eyed white cob, but at the caravan behind the horse.

'Oh. That is so beautiful,' she whispered. 'Is that a *vardo*?' Blushing, she glanced at Laszlo and he nodded slowly.

He dropped her hand and walked swiftly towards his cousin. The men hugged one another and then Laszlo turned. Reaching towards Prudence, he tugged her forward by the hand.

'Mihaly, this is Prudence. She's working for my grandfather. Prudence—my cousin Mihaly. He's like a brother to me and he's a good friend. Just don't let him sing to you.'

Mihaly grinned and inclined his head. 'And don't let *him* play a guitar.' He winced. 'I'm still having trouble in this ear. And now, cousin, where do you want me to put this—because I need to be getting back.' He turned towards Prudence and grinned sheepishly. 'My wife is having our fifth child any time now, so I need to get home as soon as possible.'

After much manoeuvring, Laszlo and Mihaly finally managed to guide the *vardo* between the apple trees and across the fields to the cottage. Having detached the shafts from the pulling harness, Mihaly waved cheerfully and rode away.

Prudence stared at the *vardo* in wonder. 'When I was a little girl I had a storybook with a picture of a *vardo* in it. But I've never been this close to one before,' she murmured.

'Take a look inside.' Laszlo gestured towards the *vardo*. 'There's a bed and a dresser and a stove.'

Prudence climbed up the steps and then trod lightly inside the *vardo*. It was just perfect, with intricately painted roses and castles and bright embroidered cushions. She swallowed and climbed back down.

There was a moment's silence and then Laszlo said quietly, 'So, what do you think?'

His voice sounded hesitant and, glancing across, Prudence saw that his expression was strained—anxious, almost. Guiltily she remembered how he'd accused her of shunning his family. Clearly he wanted to know what she thought of his cousin.

She smiled. 'He seemed nice.'

Laszlo laughed. 'Not Mihaly! The *vardo*. Do you really like it or are you just being polite?' He stared at her, his gaze intent, a line of doubt on his forehead.

'N-no, of course I'm not just being polite,' she stammered. 'It's beautiful. Really. You're very lucky,' she said teasingly. 'A castle *and* a *vardo*! That's just plain greedy.'

He grinned, and then his expression shifted, grew serious. He looked at her levelly. 'Actually, the *vardo* isn't mine. I've just been holding on to it for someone.'

She held her breath, sensing a tightness in him—a sort of eagerness. 'Whose is it?' she whispered. But even before he could reply she already knew the answer to her question. 'Is it mine?' she asked hesitantly.

He nodded, watching as her look of shock and confusion turned to happiness. 'It was supposed to be my wedding gift to you.'

He hadn't planned on telling her that the *vardo* was hers. He'd simply wanted to show it to her, for he'd known that it would soften her. A woman would have to have a heart of stone not to be ensnared by the romanticism of a real gypsy caravan.

She turned to smile at him and he smiled back. But his smile was hollow, for seeing her genuine pleasure made him feel shabby and manipulative and he felt a stab of jealousy. With shock, he realised that he wanted to *share* in her happiness. That he actually *liked* making her happy.

A muscle flickered in his jaw. 'It's more of a curio than anything. We wouldn't have lived in it, obviously—'

'Why not?' She frowned, instantly defensive. 'It's beautiful and romantic and it's got everything you need—'

'Everything but a toilet and a shower and hot running water.' He smiled ruefully. 'Give me a Willerby Westmorland any day!' His eyes gleamed. He watched her with mild amusement. 'And there's nothing romantic about not being able to wash,' he added drily.

'Why did Mihaly have it?' She glanced up at him tentatively.

His eyes met hers. 'He and my uncle restore *vardos*. They've been holding on to it for me.'

He paused and Prudence felt her face grow warm.

'That's where I went the other day,' he said softly. 'After I ran away. I went to my uncle's and I remembered it was there. Only I couldn't bring it back because one of the wheels was damaged. So Mihaly said he'd bring it over to me today.' His golden eyes moved over her face like the sun. 'I wanted you to see it before you leave,' he added calmly.

His matter-of-fact tone went some way towards taking the bite from his words but Prudence still heard the blood rush inside her head and felt her stomach clench as she came crashing down to earth. But of course she was going to leave. Her contract wasn't permanent and Laszlo had just agreed to divorce her. So why did she feel so cold? As though she'd suddenly stepped into the shadows?

Pushing that troublesome question away, she took a step towards the *vardo*.

'Is it really mine?' She turned to face him. 'I mean, could I spend the night here?'

He took so long to answer that she thought he hadn't heard her, but then he stared at her, his eyes impossibly gold and translucent, like clear new honey, and nodded. She hesitated, suddenly tongue-tied and blushing.

'I mean, with you.'

The words caught in her throat and the air felt suddenly charged around them. Their eyes locked and then slowly he walked towards her. Sliding his hands through her hair, he tipped her face to his.

'Me? Stay in your caravan?' Frowning, he pretended to think. 'Are you sure? I don't know. That sounds complicated,' he whispered.

She pulled away from him and held out her hand. 'Then I think we should keep things simple,' she murmured. 'Stick with what we do best.'

And then, taking his fingers in hers, she began to lead him up the steps into the *vardo*.

Prudence woke to the sound of birdsong. The *vardo* was warm with sunlight and for a moment she lay sleepily on her back, revelling in the ache of her body. Then, rolling over, she reached out and touched the space beside her in the bed. The sheets were still warm and, closing her eyes, she breathed in Laszlo's clean, salty, masculine smell.

In the last few days when they'd been together every private moment had been spent in bed. And every night Prudence lost count of the number of times they made love. At first, despite lack of sleep, she hadn't wanted the morning to come, for fear that daylight would break the spell between them. But on waking that first morning, without any apparent effort on their part, everything had fallen quite naturally into place, and now their days and nights had slipped into a pattern.

Most mornings Laszlo would wake long before she did—often before dawn. Sometimes he would get up and dress and return, waking her with breakfast. Other times he would reach out for her in the darkness, pressing her body against his, the beat of his blood in time to her heart...

At the memory of the way his mouth sought out hers, of his hands so gentle, yet demanding, she felt a familiar ache deep inside her pelvis that made her press her legs together. Blushing, she gave a squirm of pleasure. The sex was so good, and his desire for her was so intoxicating, so quick, so urgent—like pollen bursting from a flower. He made her feel so alive, utterly unlike herself. Lost in him she became passionate, brave and wanton.

She bit her lip. But soon it would be over. She would be back in England and back to a life without passion; a life without Laszlo. Slowly she rolled out of bed and sat up straight. A hard knot was forming in her stomach. She had spent the last week living in the moment, trying not to think, and more particularly trying not to think about the future. Easy at first, with the days and nights stretching out ahead of her, to do just that. Easy, too, to accept the rationale for what they were doing and ignore the fact that physical intimacy encouraged the senses to play all kinds of stupid, dangerous tricks on the mind.

Sighing, she lay back down and rolled onto her side. She had no one to blame but herself, for Laszlo had never offered anything other than sex. In fact, he couldn't have made it clearer that their affair was simply a finite means to an end—a way for both of them to find sexual closure. But being with Laszlo seemed to be doing little to reduce her hunger for him. Instead the hours she spent in his company seemed only to remind her why she'd fallen in love with him seven years ago.

'I don't normally like talking about work over lunch...' Janos paused and glanced apologetically around the dining room table. 'But I just wondered, Prudence, how you think the cataloguing is going?'

Prudence frowned and put down her fork. It was a perfectly reasonable question, but there was a tension in the old man's voice that made her hesitate and, looking across at him, she felt a ripple of concern when she saw that he looked drawn and tired.

'It's early days,' she said slowly. 'But we are making progress.'

Looking across at his grandfather, Laszlo frowned. 'You look a bit pale, Papi. Are you feeling all right?'

Janos shook his head. 'I'm fine, Laci. I'm just being a silly old man.'

Laszlo frowned. 'I doubt that,' he said firmly. 'What's up? Is something worrying you about the cataloguing?'

The old man shook his head. 'It's nothing, really. It's just that it all seems to be taking so much longer than I expected.'

Prudence felt her chest squeeze tight with guilt. All she'd been thinking about for the last few days was Laszlo; everything else—Edmund, England and even the cataloguing—had been pushed to the periphery of her mind.

'Please don't worry, Janos,' she said quickly. 'I should have warned you. This part is always incredibly slow-moving. There's always lots of gaps in the paperwork.'

'Particularly when a collection is owned by a forgetful old fool who can't remember what he bought or when and where he bought it?' Janos said slowly.

Prudence shook her head. 'Not at all. You'd be surprised how many people own art that's worth thousands of pounds—hundreds of thousands of pounds—and yet have no paperwork at all.'

'They need Prudence to come to their rescue,' Janos said, his smile returning.

Laszlo leant back in his chair, his face impassive. 'They can't have her. She's ours!'

His eyes gleamed with an intensity that made her lose the thread of what she was saying and she felt her skin turn to liquid.

Resisting the tug of his gaze, she cleared her throat. 'I'm sorry you've been worried. I know it can be a bit overwhelming...' She hesitated. 'I don't know how you feel about this, but I'm sure Edmund would be a good person to talk to about it.'

Janos nodded slowly. 'Certainly, my dear—if you think he'd be happy to give me an opinion?'

Grimacing, she laughed. 'Knowing Edmund, I'm sure he'll be more than happy!' She bit her lip. 'I don't always like what my uncle has to say, but maddeningly he's quite often right.'

Her words were simply meant to reassure Janos but, feeling a prickle of heat on her skin, she looked up and found Laszlo watching her.

'Is that so?' he said flatly. 'Your *uncle* is a man of many talents!'

His eyes locked onto hers and her heart began to pound, for she saw that while his face was still and calm, his eyes were alive with anger.

'How *fortunate* for all of us,' he said slowly.

Laszlo felt a sickening wave of nausea. His stomach twisted. Edmund Seymour was Prudence's *uncle*!

It was as though a tide had receded, revealing jagged rocks beneath a calm blue sea.

It was bad enough that he hadn't known until now exactly who Edmund Seymour was in relation to Prudence. But for her to suggest that Seymour now be allowed to give his 'opinion'— It was intolerable.

He gritted his teeth and then, turning to his grandfather, smiled gently. 'Papi, I'm going to sort this out. I want you to take the rest of the day off.'

He held his hand out towards his grandfather.

'You can go and put your feet up and read one of those interminable Russian novels you like so much.'

Waving away Janos's words of protest, he chivvied his grandfather out of the room.

'No, Papi. I insist. Prudence and I can manage.'

At the door, Laszlo stopped and turned, and she felt her pulse slam against her skin as his eyes fixed coldly on her face.

'Oh, don't ring your uncle just yet. I've got an opinion of my own I'd like to share with you first. Wait here!'

A moment later, her face still scalded with colour, Prudence sat staring nervously around the dining room. Looking down at her plate, she pushed it away. Could she have misunderstood the implication of his words? But she knew she hadn't, and she knew that something had happened to change the mood between them. She frowned. Only *nothing* had happened. Part of her job was to reassure the client, and that was what she'd done. Her mouth tightened into a grim line. It most certainly *wasn't* part of her job to try to second-guess Laszlo's moods.

Ten minutes later she bit her lip in indecision and then, abruptly pushing back her chair, she stood up. Typical Laszlo! Telling her to wait and then forgetting all about her. She shook her head irritably. Unlike him, she actually had work to do. But first she would ring Edmund. After all, what possible objection could he really have to her speaking to her uncle?

Laszlo caught up with her just as she reached the cottage. 'Where the hell do you think you're going? I told you to wait!'

His voice, dark with fury, swung her round mid-stride. She stared at him, struck by the cold, angry beauty of his face.

Forcing herself to stay calm, she shrugged and said flatly, 'I did wait. But you didn't come back and I have notes to write up. So, if you don't mind—'

'Oh, but I *do*. We need to talk.'

She flinched at the biting tone of his voice but drew her head up to meet his gaze. 'I'm sorry you feel like that, but I'm busy now,' she said carefully. 'Maybe we can talk later.'

Turning, her heart pounding in her chest, she walked quickly up the path and opened the front door of the cottage. Before she could shut it, Laszlo had followed her into the living room.

'What are you doing?' She stared at him furiously. 'You can't just barge in here!'

'Don't you *ever* walk away from me.' His face was twisted with anger. 'I told you to *wait*!'

She lifted her chin, eyes blazing. His high-handed manner was setting her teeth on edge. 'I did,' she shot back at him. 'But if you think I've got all day to sit around and wait for you—'

'My grandfather was upset. I was trying to make him feel better. But maybe you don't care about that.' His eyes were hardening like lava cooling.

'That's not true, Laszlo. I *do* care about your grandfather,' she said shakily. 'And I want to help. That's why I'm going to speak to my uncle.'

She stared at him in helpless silence as he shook his head. 'No, you're not.'

His voice scraped over her skin, hostility palpable in every syllable.

'Not if you want to keep this job!'

Prudence took a step backwards, the unfairness as much as the autocratic tone of his command leaving her feeling almost winded. She felt dizzy. He'd gone completely mad. That was the only explanation.

'What *is* your problem? You're not making any sense. If Edmund hadn't been ill he'd have been here instead of me. And you were fine with that. Only now you're telling me I can't even *ring* him?'

Incandescent with anger, Laszlo stared at her. She was right. His behaviour was irrational. Except that it wasn't. Only he couldn't explain that to her. Not while he was still reeling from this revelation that Edmund Seymour was the man who had ruined his life.

His chest felt tight and he took a calming breath. Finally, he said flatly, 'We made a deal. I told you that if you couldn't work for me then you should leave.'

'Any deal we made *didn't* include pussyfooting around you when you're having some sort of temper tantrum!' She glared at him. 'This has nothing to do with our deal and you know it. You're just angry because I wasn't where you wanted me to be. Well, now you know what it feels like!'

There was a moment's savage silence and then she took a breath. What were they doing? Tearing each other apart over a phone call?

Feeling suddenly calmer, she shook her head and said slowly, 'I didn't just leave to make you angry. I really did—really *do*—have a lot of work to do.'

She bit her lip. Had they naively expected that the anger and resentment from their past would magically dissipate just because they'd started sleeping together again? If so, they'd been grievously mistaken. The fragile peace they'd shared for more than a week was over, and sadly she realised that it had been as illusory as every other aspect of their relationship.

'But my advice would still be to contact Edmund.'

His eyes narrowed. 'I see. I suppose you think you know better than I do what's best for my grandfather?'

Biting her lip, she nodded. 'In this instance—yes. He's worried about the cataloguing and Edmund can help him,' she said simply. 'Sometimes you just need a different point of view to solve the problem.'

Catching sight of the ineffably contemptuous sneer in his eyes, she felt a ripple of anger snake over her skin.

She took a deep breath. 'You know, the trouble with you, Laszlo, is you're just so certain you're right you just can't imagine that there might be another point of view.'

'Not true.' His voice was dangerously soft. 'I know everything there is to know about other points of view. Particularly your uncle's.'

There. He'd said it. It was as though he'd taken off a particularly scratchy sweater. She stared at him, her eyes blinking in time with her scattering thoughts. 'What do you mean? You've never even spoken to my uncle. He spoke to your grandfather and Jakob.'

He smiled slowly and she felt the breath squeeze out of her lungs.

'Not about the cataloguing...' he said softly.

'I don't understand,' she said faintly.

'Then let me explain.'

His voice seemed to slice her bones away from her flesh and she felt her legs starting to sway.

'Seven years ago I went to your home.'

Her head jerked up and, despite the pain in his own heart, he felt a sharp sting of satisfaction at the shock in her eyes.

He looked at her steadily. 'I went to talk to you.'

Prudence's heart seemed to stop. 'I don't believe you,' she said weakly.

'That doesn't stop it being true.'

His voice trapped her, pulled her in. 'You're lying,' she whispered.

But she knew that he wasn't, and her face felt hot, and she suddenly couldn't breathe. Looking up, she saw the anger and the pride in his eyes. She took a step backwards.

Watching her back away, Laszlo felt a ripple of rage—even now she was trying to evade what she'd done.

'Only you were out. Shopping…' He spat the word out with derisive emphasis. *'Shopping!'* There was a tense, choking silence and he shook his head. 'How do you think that made me feel? To find out that while I was sitting in some stinking police station my wife was out shopping.' He laughed without humour. 'Sorry. My mistake. You didn't actually think we were married, did you?'

She clenched her fists. She had resolved never to mention his arrest. But now his sneering contempt unleashed the pent-up fear and pain.

'What should I have been doing? We were over. Your criminal activities were no concern of mine.'

'They took me in for questioning. And then they released me without charge,' he said slowly, his face tight with hostility. 'Only you didn't know because you were out *shopping.*'

She shook her head, trying to stay focused. He didn't have the upper hand here—didn't have it full stop! All he'd done was lie and deceive her.

She glowered at him. 'We were over—'

'We were *not* over. We'd had a row. Do you really think I'd just let you throw away our marriage like that?' he said savagely. The air was quivering between them.

Prudence shook her head. 'I asked you how much effort you'd give to make our relationship work.' Her voice broke. 'Do you know what your answer was? You said that *any* effort was too much!'

'I was just angry with you! I'd just walked in the door. I was tired. I wanted a shower.'

Eyes blazing, she stepped towards him. 'And that meant you could give up on our relationship?'

'No. But as you keep on reminding me, I had to go to the police station!' His mouth twisted. 'I couldn't leave. You, on the other hand, were free. I came to find you as soon as I got out. You didn't come to see if I was all right.' He stopped and shot her a look of pure exasperation. 'I know that you didn't think our marriage was real. And, yes, we'd broken up. But didn't you feel bound to me in *any* way?'

The bitterness in his voice felt like a slap to her face.

There was a pulsing silence and then he shook his head. 'I could never work out what had changed. You seemed different that day. Not yourself.'

Prudence stared at him, trying to keep her expression steady. She could feel something like panic building up inside her.

He gave her a long, hard look. 'But then I met your uncle and it all kind of fell into place.' Smiling grimly, he nodded. 'You're right about his opinions, by the way. I didn't like what he had to say. In fact, I was quite upset by his point of view. But funnily enough I wasn't surprised by it.' He looked across at Prudence, his eyes glittering with sudden savage fury. 'But then, how could I be? I'd already heard it before—hadn't I?'

Prudence stared at him, frozen to the spot, struggling to swallow her shock. 'I don't understand...' Her voice shrivelled as she felt the blistering anger of his gaze.

'Oh, I think you do.'

There was a moment's dead silence and then, in a voice that chilled her bones, he went on.

'When I'm struggling with something, I always find it helpful to have another point of view.'

She felt the blood drain from her face as she recognised her own words.

Watching her reaction, he clenched his jaw. 'It was quite eerie, actually. Hearing your words come out of his mouth. It was a faultless performance. You must have rehearsed a lot.'

'N-no…' Prudence stammered. 'No. It wasn't like that.' She shivered as the temperature in the room plummeted.

'It was *exactly* like that, Prudence. Or are you telling me he told you to stand by your man?'

Looking at her paper-white stricken face, he felt suddenly sick inside.

'No. I thought not.'

A muscle flickered in his jaw and he regarded her for a long, excruciating moment.

'You should have waited to hear what I had to say. But you didn't. You chose to listen to someone who'd never met me. Who despised the very idea of me.'

Laszlo leant forward, his face dark with fury.

'Do you know he called me a liar and a charlatan? Told me he knew all about my "sort".'

He gave a humourless laugh and Prudence felt her cheeks burn. She shook her head desperately.

'He didn't mean because you're a Romany,' she mumbled.

Laszlo smiled derisively. 'Please! Do you think I'm stupid?'

Miserably, Prudence shook her head. 'No. But I know he wasn't talking about that. He was just worried about me. About where it would all end. I think he thought I was turning into my mum.'

She looked away, fighting tears; fighting memories.

'You'd been gone for ten days, Laszlo. I didn't know what to think. I'd left so many messages, and then Edmund came home from work and found me crying.' She gave a small strangled laugh. 'I think it really scared him.' She drew a jagged breath. 'Especially because I hadn't really told him and Daisy much about us. Just that I was seeing someone I'd met at the fair.'

Prudence stared blankly around the sitting room. 'I *did* talk to Edmund, and he gave me advice. But he didn't change my mind,' she said slowly. 'When I came looking for you—after I'd spoken to him—I still wanted us to work. I would have done anything to be with you.' She paused and shivered, her lip trembling. 'But, like I told you before, you didn't even try and reassure me.'

Her voice petered out and Laszlo frowned. It was true. He *hadn't* tried to reassure her. And he saw now that the repercussions of her parents' bigamous marriage had affected not just Prudence but her aunt and uncle too. They had looked after her, brought her up. His breathing was suddenly harsh. How must it have felt for Edmund to see the girl he thought of as a daughter weeping hysterically over a man? A man who seemed in many ways to resemble her perfidious father?

Prudence took a breath and looked up at him sadly. 'Edmund told me what he thought I should do. But he also said that the decision must be mine.' She bit her lip and her eyes felt suddenly hot with tears. 'And it was. You didn't seem to care one way or another. That didn't seem to be a good basis for a relationship. So I ended it.'

Her stomach was contorting, as though her misery was actually alive inside her.

'Edmund didn't wrong you. All he and Daisy have ever done is try and protect me. You can think what you like. The truth is our relationship ended not because of other people or their opinions but because the sum of what we held back was greater than what we shared. We only really shared our bodies.'

Laszlo stared at her in silence. She had never looked

more beautiful or vulnerable. But for once he couldn't lose himself in the soft beauty of her face. His skin was prickling with what he knew to be guilt. Guilt and regret. Having grown up in the shadow of her mother's disastrous love affair, she'd met him before she'd had a chance to realise that she wasn't her mother but her own person.

Now he understood just how lonely and frightened she must have felt when confronted by his baffling absences and moodiness. His head jerked up, his cheeks burning. He had told her he would never forgive her for what she'd done. Now he saw that it was he who needed forgiveness. He had been her lover and, in his mind at least, her husband. The one man who should have restored her faith in men and, more importantly, in herself.

And what had he done to reassure her?

Nothing.

No wonder she had sought comfort from the one man who had always been there for her and never let her down.

'You must love them very much,' he said finally.

He saw the flicker of emotion in her grey eyes.

'They're not perfect.' She smiled weakly. 'But they're my family, Laszlo, and I love them. I trust them too.'

'More than you trusted me?'

His question caught her off guard and she swallowed hard. She was so tired—more than tired…she was drained. Meeting his gaze, she saw from the tension around his eyes that her answer mattered to him. It would be easier to placate him; quicker to give him some glib answer that would end this row, so she could crawl off and lick her wounds. But she was done with lying to him. No matter what the consequences, she wanted to confront the past—the whole of the past. Not keep holding back or editing out the most painful parts.

Finally, she nodded.

The gold of his eyes began to flicker with outrage.

'What did you *want* me to say?' she said, annoyed by his reaction. 'Haven't you learned *anything* from the past? Our marriage might be over but I want—' She stopped. Her voice had turned husky with emotion but she didn't care. 'I need to be honest with you. And I'd like to think you want that too. So the answer is *yes*, Laszlo. I trusted them more than I trusted you. Or myself.'

His mouth set in a grim line, Laszlo stared at her for a long moment.

'I want to be honest with you as well,' he said quietly. 'You were right to have doubts about me. Right not to trust me.'

She stared at him dazedly. 'Wh—what do you mean?' she stammered. She felt almost physically sick at the expression of guilt and remorse on his face.

He watched her in silence, a muscle working in his jaw. 'I was holding back. Holding back the truth about my grandfather. And you sensed that and that's why you didn't trust me. Add that to all my comings and goings, and I'd say you had a very strong case for ending our relationship.'

He sucked in a breath.

'In fact, I'm surprised you stayed with me for so long.' His face tightened and then slowly, his hand shaking slightly, he reached out and stroked her cheek. 'I've not always been a kind person, *pireni*. Or a fair one.'

He let out the breath.

'When you broke up with me I blamed your uncle. And then I blamed you.' He gave a small, tight smile. 'And then I blamed both of you.' He sighed. 'But I can't blame anyone but myself for what happened. All I did was fuel your doubts and then get angry that you doubted me,' he said quietly. 'Too angry to look deeper.'

He opened his mouth to say something else and then stopped.

Prudence felt her spine stiffen, her hurt somehow tempered by the inevitability of the familiar way his face closed over. Had she really expected Laszlo to open up to her? Surely she knew him well enough to know that he would always have secrets to keep.

Frowning, Laszlo glanced away from the tears gleaming in her eyes. He didn't want to hurt her. She had been so open, so brave. But there was so much he couldn't explain.

'I'm sorry about everything,' he said slowly, 'but I'm glad we had this conversation.' There was a moment of uneven silence, and then his face creased and he added softly, 'And I'm glad you're here.'

He saw the pull of his words on her face and then his chest tightened as he watched a tear trickle down her face.

'Don't cry!' Impulsively Laszlo reached out and brushed his fingers gently over her cheek. Their eyes locked and then he sighed again. 'We certainly didn't make it easy for ourselves, did we, *pireni*? I just assumed that our marriage would somehow magically work, and you were convinced it would fail!'

He tilted her face to his and cupped her chin in his hand.

'We didn't get everything wrong, though, did we? I mean, most couples would kill to have the sort of chemistry we share.'

She knew he didn't really mean his words to be taken seriously, but something about his remark depressed her. It was the truth, probably, she thought miserably. For Laszlo, any discussion about their relationship would always lead back to that one thing.

Glancing down at her, Laszlo frowned again. He knew he'd hurt her, and he wanted more than anything to pull her into his arms, but much as he desired her he suddenly didn't want to use sex to blot out emotion.

'Look, don't worry about the cataloguing.' He paused and took a breath. 'I'm going to ring your uncle later and

talk it all through with him. You don't think he'll recognise my voice, do you?'

Prudence hesitated a moment, her grey eyes searching
his face. She knew he was trying to make amends and
it was novel at least to have Laszlo be the one to make a
peace offering. Shaking her head, she gave him a weak
smile. He grinned at her and his obvious relief that he had
made her smile made her heart wobble.

'Good. I don't want him charging over here to rescue
you.' He paused. 'You don't *want* to be rescued, do you?'

Prudence shivered. Of course she didn't—but it might
have been better if she had. Her feelings were becoming
more and more confused, and harder and harder to contain.

She shook her head. 'No. I don't want to be rescued.'

His face flushed and she felt her pulse start to quicken,
for he looked heartbreakingly like his younger self.

'I promise I'll be on my best behaviour,' he said slowly.
'I won't say or do anything annoying.'

She laughed softly. 'Let's not tempt fate!'

Looking down at her, Laszlo smiled crookedly. 'How
reassuringly superstitious of you,' he said softly. 'My sweet
Romany wife.'

She gazed at him, hypnotised by the soft darkness of
his eyes and the even softer darkness of his voice. And
then her heart twisted inside, for Laszlo's words were not
a promise for the future but a simple statement of fact.

Trying to ignore the tangle of emotions her thoughts
provoked, she glanced at one of the clocks—surely sense
demanded she should leave before she said something she'd
regret?

'I should go and find your grandfather, but he usually has
a nap about now.' She bit her lip. 'I don't know what to do…'

Laszlo frowned. 'Maybe I can help with that.'

Sliding his fingers through her hair, Laszlo pulled her
towards him, his expression thoughtful.

'Let's see...' Turning her hand over, he stroked the centre of her palm and then, lifting her hand, slowly ran his tongue along the lifeline until she squirmed against him. 'Hmm...' he murmured softly. 'Your skin's so smooth it's difficult to read the future. But...'

His gleaming golden gaze rested on her face, making her feel hot and tingly all over.

'I *can* see that there's a tall, dark, handsome man in your life.'

Prudence wriggled free and shook her head, trying not to laugh. 'Really? I wouldn't say Jakob is tall.'

He grinned at her. 'The man I'm talking about is definitely not a lawyer. He's just as smart, but he's witty and cool and sexy...'

He laughed softly as, heart pounding, she tugged her hand away. 'And bordering on the delusional?' she said quickly.

She wanted him so much. And when he held her close like this, his body so warm and hard against hers, everything inside her seemed to unravel and fly apart.

Hoping fervently that her feelings weren't showing on her face, she took a deep breath and lifted her chin. 'Or maybe you just need your eyes tested?'

He smiled—a long, curling smile that whipped at her senses.

'Quite probably. No doubt my eyes have been damaged by years of living in this gloomy castle.' He pressed his body against hers. 'Maybe I should keep you where I can see you,' he murmured possessively.

And then his hand tightened in her hair and, dropping a fierce kiss onto her lips, he pulled her into his arms.

CHAPTER EIGHT

FROM THE WINDOW of his bedroom Laszlo stared out at the cloudless blue sky and scowled. Rising early, he had gone for a walk before breakfast in the fields that surrounded the estate. Usually he enjoyed the silence and the crisp, early air—but not today. For once he had found it hard to take pleasure in the peace and beauty. Instead his thoughts had been dogged by scenes from last night. And now yesterday's conversation with Prudence was playing on repeat inside his head, so that rather than slip back into bed beside her, he'd returned to the castle.

His chest grew tight. Feeling distinctly uncomfortable, he closed the window. But there was no way he could shut out the unpalatable truth. He had treated her badly. And a weaker person—the person he'd so arrogantly assumed Prudence to be—would have been crushed.

Only she hadn't been crushed. And she hadn't given up either. In spite of her youth and inexperience, and in the face of his evident and repeated reluctance to talk about anything, she had still tried to make it work. His mouth tightened. And it was still the same story now. When fate had thrown them together he had used his power and position to punish her, but even then she hadn't walked away. She'd just climbed over the wall and refused to leave.

He suddenly grinned. He loved it that she was so bloody-minded. And beautiful. And brave. She was everything he'd wanted in a wife. And then his smile faded. Why was he using words like *wife* and *love*? He didn't *love* Prudence, and soon she wouldn't even be his wife. In fact, soon she wouldn't even be in the country. With a growl of frustration he clenched his hands. Everything seemed to have backfired. Letting Prudence back into his life and into his bed seemed to be having quite the opposite effect to the one he'd imagined.

For a start, sleeping with Prudence didn't actually seem to be killing his desire for her. If anything he wanted her more. In fact, he couldn't imagine a time when he *wouldn't* roll over in bed to find her lying next to him.

Worse, the anger he had felt when he'd found her in his study seemed to have faded to be replaced by a sort of nervous anticipation. He gritted his teeth. If he hadn't known better, he might have said that he had some sort of *feelings* for her.

A muscle flickered along his jaw. Only of course that would be ridiculous. His 'feelings' were just a trick of the senses. As Prudence had so rightly pointed out yesterday, the only time they ever felt comfortable being open and honest with one another was during sex, and no doubt his emotions were just the after-effects of intimacy. Add to that his guilt at having treated her so shabbily and it was no wonder he was feeling confused.

He let out a breath, pleased to have found a rational explanation for his discomfort. Glancing out of the window, he could just see the roof of the *vardo* and, whistling softly, he turned towards the door.

Sifting through the papers in his lap, Janos gave a small cry of triumph and beamed at Prudence.

'I've found it. *Finally.* That *is* a relief!' Glancing up, he looked at the grandfather clock in the corner of the sitting room and frowned. 'I can't imagine where Laszlo is.' He shook his head. 'Sometimes I think he's less house-trained than Besnik. At least Besnik remembers mealtimes.'

Closing her laptop, a blush creeping over her cheeks, Prudence said shyly, 'Actually, he told me he's going to be a little delayed.'

Her blush deepened. She was still reeling from the unfamiliar experience of Laszlo earnestly *telling* her that he was going to be late.

Studiously avoiding Janos's eyes, she added, 'I think there was some problem over at the top field.'

Janos gave her a searching look. 'I see.' There was a pause, while Prudence gazed in concentration at the lid of her laptop, and then he said slowly, 'I think I might need to speak to your uncle later.'

Prudence looked up at him. 'Wh—why?' she stammered. 'Is there a problem?'

Janos shook his head, a small smile tugging at the corners of his mouth. 'Don't look so worried, my dear. I'm just wondering whether I can persuade him to let you stay for ever! First you manage to single-handedly organise forty years of paperwork concerning my collection, and now—far more impressively—you've trained my grandson to apprise you of his movements.'

Prudence drank a mouthful of coffee, finding it suddenly difficult to swallow. 'I don't think that's all down to me,' she said, blushing again.

Janos laughed. 'It's certainly not down to *me*! But don't worry. You won't have to stay in this draughty old castle for ever. I know you must be missing your family.'

She smiled. 'I did miss them at first. But you've made me feel so welcome. And I love the castle,' she said simply. 'It's such a perfect setting for all your beautiful things.' Biting her lip, she paused. 'Actually, it really reminds me of one of my favourite places—the Soane's Museum in London. Sir John Soane used to live there, with all these incredible works of art and sculptures and clocks—just like you do there. It's an amazing place.'

She shook her head slowly.

'Edmund says I treat it like church: I always go there if I have something to celebrate or if I feel sad—' She broke off in astonishment as the clocks throughout the castle began to strike the hour. 'Is that the time? Perhaps I'd better just run down and tell Rosa that Laszlo is—'

'Laszlo is what?'

Dressed casually in jeans and a faded grey sweatshirt, Laszlo strolled into the room, Besnik following at his heels. Reaching his grandfather's armchair, he bent down and kissed Janos gently on the head, then turned to Prudence, his gleaming gaze making her stomach flip over.

They shared a brief burning silence and then he said, almost conversationally, 'That I'm starving? Or that I'm on time? Hard to say which would give her greater pleasure!'

Dropping onto a sofa, he sat back and his eyes drifted over her lips. Her breath stuck in her throat.

'How are you today, Prudence? Are *you* hungry too?'

His voice was teasing and warm, and she felt a corresponding heat across her skin. She glanced nervously over to Janos, for she was always worried that he would sense the tension between her and Laszlo. But she saw with relief that he had returned to sifting through his paperwork. She still disliked having to lie to him, but it was not for much longer. And then she would be back in England and she would have to lie only to herself.

She felt a jolt of misery. *Don't go there,* she told herself, sitting up straighter. *This was only ever going to be temporary. Nothing has changed.*

She took a deep breath. Only it had. She hadn't meant it to change, but it had. Like a tsunami warning, a cool voice inside her head kept urging her to get away from the strike zone. But she couldn't. Her only option was to stay detached. It was only sex, after all.

She shivered. But what was going on inside her heart had nothing to do with sex. Her lower lip quivered as miserably she realised that Laszlo had been right all along. A piece of paper meant nothing. For in her heart she would always be married to Laszlo.

Shifting in her seat, she tried to steady her nerves. *It's all in your imagination,* she told herself angrily. But it wasn't. She loved him, and all she really wanted to do was forget everything that had happened between them and start again.

Looking up, her eyes collided with the stinging intensity of his gaze and she felt a spasm of pain—a pain that she knew no amount of distance in time or place would ever lessen. She might be in love with him, but he had simply and expediently reduced their relationship to the physical.

Heart pounding, fighting her misery, she looked away and said hastily, 'I'll just go and tell Rosa you're here.'

'Not necessary,' Laszlo said softly. 'I told her on my way up. Oh, and Jakob rang to say he'd be over this evening.'

He sat back, letting his long legs sprawl negligently in front of him, but despite his relaxed pose Prudence could almost see the restless energy coming off him in waves.

For a moment the room was silent, and then Janos looked across at his grandson thoughtfully. 'Incredible. You're on time *and* you remembered to give me a message!'

Laszlo shrugged. His face was neutral, but his feet were tapping out a rhythm on the carpet. 'Just keeping you on your toes, Papi.'

Janos studied his grandson benignly. 'There's nothing wrong with my toes. You, on the other hand, are about to wear a hole in one of my favourite rugs. Did Jakob say what time he'd be over?'

Frowning, Laszlo pretended to think. 'He did. Now,

what did he say...? Oh, yes. About eight.' He grinned at his grandfather. 'Oh, ye of little faith!'

Shaking his head, Janos laughed. 'I'm impressed, but still a little shocked.'

'I don't see what the fuss is all about,' Laszlo grumbled. He turned to Prudence, a curve of amusement tugging at the corner of his mouth. 'What do *you* think, Prudence? Can't a leopard change his spots?'

Conscious of Janos's presence, she bit her tongue—but the desire to tease overwhelmed her. 'I'm not sure. Is that how you see yourself? As a leopard?'

She paused, mesmerised by the hunger burning in his golden eyes and the rough shadow of dark stubble grazing his jaw.

'You're more like a wolf really,' she murmured, her blood slowing in her veins at the intensity of his gaze. 'A tamed wolf that'll come inside the house but only if the door is left open.'

Their eyes locked and she felt a shiver of quicksilver run down her spine. Suddenly her heart was pounding, and the only sound was the rain falling on the window and the strained intake of their breath.

And then Janos cleared his throat. 'I believe the word you're looking for is *liminal*,' he said mildly. 'It means to occupy a space on both sides of a boundary—or in this case threshold.'

For a moment Prudence stared at him blankly, all thoughts, all words gone. And then, colour burning her cheeks, she straightened up abruptly and the spell was broken.

'Liminal... I must remember that,' she said weakly, finding speech at last.

Janos nodded. 'I believe architects often refer to hallways as "liminal" spaces.'

Prudence shifted in her chair, uncomfortably aware that she'd been too consumed with longing to hide her emotions. But if Janos was aware of her feelings he was hiding it well, for he merely smiled and returned to reading his papers.

Her heart was thumping painfully hard. Breathing out, she looked up and found Laszlo watching her almost hungrily through the thick dark lashes that fringed his eyes.

'If I'm a wolf, does that mean you're a lamb?' he said softly. Her heart lurched against her ribs.

He was exactly like a wolf: a predatory, single-minded wild animal. And she felt exactly like a lamb that had stumbled into his lair. Only perhaps because finally—privately—she had admitted her love for him it suddenly felt like the most important thing in the world to disagree.

Taking a deep breath, she summoned up a casual smile. 'Oh, I'd probably be something very prickly and shy—like a hedgehog.'

Laszlo grinned slowly. 'Hedgehogs aren't always prickly. When they relax and feel safe their quills lie flat.'

Their eyes met and she had to curl her fingers into the palms of her hands to stop herself from reaching out and pulling his mouth against hers. 'Then what happens? You eat them, I suppose?'

She blushed as he lifted an eyebrow.

'That would depend on the hedgehog.'

Janos shook his head. 'He's teasing you, my dear. He's never eaten a hedgehog in his life.'

Smiling weakly, Prudence sat up straighter, flattening herself against the back of the chair. Her skin felt hot and prickling, quite as if she were growing spines, and she had to ball her hands into fists to stop herself from rubbing her arms.

'What about you, Janos?' she said quickly, turning away as Laszlo mouthed the word *coward* at her. 'What animal are *you* like?'

Janos put down his papers and frowned. 'Judging by

the state of my memory, I ought by rights to be a gold-fish,' he said ruefully.

They all burst out laughing.

Grinning, Laszlo reached across and squeezed his grandfather's hand. 'You're such a fraud, Papi! Your memory's better than mine. And as for Prudence——' He shook his head. 'Hers is *too* good! I'd like her to forget the odd thing.'

He paused and, unable to resist the pull of his gaze, Prudence looked up helplessly.

He gave her a crooked smile and then his expression shifted, grew suddenly serious. 'Actually, there's quite a lot of things I'd like her to forget.' He hesitated, as though groping in his mind for a word or phrase, and then said quietly, 'Quite a lot I'd want to change too.'

She stared at him uncertainly, her stomach suddenly churning with nerves and confusion. His voice was strained—she might even have described it as anxious. But of course that must be her nerves playing with her imagination, for his face was neither.

Something passed through his eyes, and then abruptly he stood up and walked over to his grandfather.

'Papi! I've got some news! Something I want to share with you!'

Looking up, Janos chuckled and shook his head slowly. 'I *knew* there was something. I don't know about a wolf, but you've been like a cat on a hot tin roof all morning! Come on, then—out with it. What's your news?'

'Kajan is here!' Laszlo spoke softly but his eyes were bright.

Prudence smiled politely. She had no idea who Kajan was, but his arrival was obviously welcome, for both men were beaming at each other.

'He arrived last night, after you'd gone up to bed. I helped him set everything up in the top field. Everyone else should be arriving today.'

He hesitated and Prudence felt her scalp begin to prickle, for she could hear the pent-up excitement in his voice.

'Mihaly wants to christen Pavel this weekend. And they've asked *me* to be his godfather.' Then he grinned as Janos stood up shakily and pulled his grandson into his arms.

Watching them together, Prudence felt suddenly utterly out of place—as though she had gatecrashed a private party. Inside, her heart felt leaden. Lying in his arms that morning, her body aching and sated, their closeness had felt like the natural, unfeigned intimacy of any normal couple—it had been easy to pretend to herself that theirs was just an ordinary relationship.

But now, like a spectator watching from the sidelines, she felt a stab of despair. Who was she kidding? She had no right to stand up and congratulate her lover with a hug. Nor would she ever see his godfathering skills put into practice with their own children.

Forcing herself to push away that troubling thought, she smiled brightly and said, 'Congratulations. That's wonderful!'

Releasing his grandfather, Laszlo turned towards her. She was about to repeat her congratulations when something on his face stopped her.

'Thanks.'

He stared at her with such bleakness that she felt cold on the inside.

And then his face twisted into a smile as his grandfather patted his arm and said shakily, 'I'm very, *very* proud of you. I'm sorry, my dear!' Janos glanced at Prudence. 'It's just that this is quite a moment for both of us.'

She smiled at Janos. 'Of course it is! And I'm very pleased for both of you.' Her gaze flickered towards Laszlo and she said carefully, 'What are your duties? Is it quite a hands-on role?'

His eyes fixed on her face and she saw a ripple of some nameless emotion stir the surface.

Then, glancing away, he shrugged and said stiffly, 'It can be.'

His voice was flat, with no trace of his earlier joy, and she could almost see him withdrawing from the conversation—withdrawing from *her*. She stared at him in misery and confusion.

'I'm sure Mihaly will want you to be involved,' she said slowly. 'He obviously thinks a lot of you.'

He shrugged. There was a short, tense silence and then, not looking at her, he said coolly, 'I'm his cousin. Relatives are always chosen to be godparents.'

'I didn't know,' she said stiffly.

'Why should you?'

The coldness in his voice held a warning. It felt like a slap to the face and, biting her lip, she looked away. She felt suddenly foolish and tired—for how could she ever have imagined that they were close?

Oblivious to the tension in the room, Janos beamed. 'He's following a great tradition, Prudence. Both his father and his father's father had many godchildren between them, and I know Laszlo will be the same. He is much loved.' His face softened and he glanced at Prudence conspiratorially. 'And this will be good for him. Being shut up in this castle with only an old man for company has made him far too serious about life.'

Avoiding Laszlo's gaze, Prudence licked her lips. 'He *can* be a little intense,' she said carefully.

Janos snorted and Laszlo looked up and shook his head. 'I *am* still in the room, you know,' he said drily.

Prudence eyed him sideways. His mood seemed to have shifted again, and not for the first time she wondered what actually went on inside that handsome head of his. She watched in silence as he sighed in mock outrage.

'Some of us don't spend all day just looking at pretty pictures, Papi. So, now that my character is slain—laid bare and lifeless for all to see—can we move on? I've got a lot to organise.'

He was smiling again and Janos laughed.

'Is that right? I'll remind Rosa of that later!' Reaching into his jacket pocket, he pulled out a small leather-bound notebook and a fountain pen. 'We're all going to be very busy for the next few days. You too, my dear,' he said, smiling warmly at Prudence. 'Outsiders don't generally get to go to Romany gatherings, but you're our guest, so you'll be welcomed as one of the family.'

Prudence felt the blood drain from her face. She glanced anxiously across at Laszlo, to gauge his reaction to Janos's words, but he was leaning forward unconcernedly, scratching Besnik's ears. Perhaps he hadn't heard—for surely if he had he would be making some sort of objection? After all, he wouldn't actually *want* her mixing with his family. It had been nerve-racking enough meeting Mihaly.

Janos looked up and frowned. 'I imagine Kajan will be wanting a *bolimos* after the christening?' He turned towards Prudence. 'Kajan is the most senior member of the Cziffra family. Between the two of us, we brought Laszlo up.'

Feeling slightly sick, Prudence nodded weakly. If only Laszlo would pay attention!

She felt a swell of relief as he looked up distractedly and frowned. Thank goodness! Now he would intervene and tell Janos that she couldn't possibly come to some intimate family gathering.

But after a moment, he simply nodded and said, 'Yes. I was thinking we might hold it in the barn. We'll need that much room for the tables and the dancing.'

Janos glanced across to where Prudence sat, quietly frozen, looking at her hands. 'A *bolimos* is great fun. It's like a huge feast and party combined. And the whole *kumpania* turn out for one. Men, women, children... So you'll have a chance to meet everyone.'

Prudence forced herself to smile. 'That's really very kind of you, but I don't think I should intrude—'

Frowning, Janos glanced up at the clock. 'Nonsense. Laszlo—make Prudence see sense. I am going to find Rosa, and then we'll all have a glass of champagne to celebrate.'

Wordlessly, Prudence watched him leave, and then, turning to Laszlo, she said breathlessly, 'Why didn't you say something? You know I can't come!'

He narrowed his eyes. 'Seriously? You're worried about *intruding*? Shall I remind you of how you got your job back?'

'Of course I'm not worried about intruding,' she said crossly. Why was he being so obtuse? 'If you won't say something then I'll have to speak to your grandfather...'

He frowned. 'It's just a christening and a party.'

She looked at him incredulously. 'But you don't know who's going to be there. What if someone recognises me?'

He shrugged. 'They won't. But even if they did, like I said, they wouldn't say anything.' He studied her for a moment with that mixture of bafflement and irritation she knew so well, and then, at last, he said softly, 'Besides, they won't remember you. There were always loads of *gadje* girls hanging round the site. I doubt they could tell any of you apart.'

Prudence shivered. She felt numb inside. How could a few randomly combined words cause so much pain? And how could he be so insensitive, so brutal when he'd been so loving just hours ago? But then, love had nothing to do with his earlier tenderness during sex. His kisses and caresses were simply designed to excite and arouse. Any impression of feeling was a mistake on her part.

'I see.'

Her response was automatic. She'd just needed to say something—anything to slow the suffocating, relentless misery rolling over her. And it worked, for anger was slowly supplanting the exhaustion.

'Let's hope that's true for both our sakes. And now I think I'll go and look at some pretty pictures!'

She stood up quickly, but he was quicker.

'I'm sorry!'

His voice was so taut, so savage that it took her a moment to understand that he was apologising.

'What?' she said dazedly. 'What did you say?'

She watched him shake his head, saw muscle tighten beneath his shirt and thought that she must have misheard him.

And then he said quietly, 'I'm sorry. I shouldn't have spoken to you like that. I didn't mean what I said.'

His words seemed to be scrabbling out of his mouth, and with shock she saw that there was fear and misery in his eyes.

'I'm sorry,' he muttered again. 'Don't go. Please.'

Prudence regarded him in silence. Even though he'd hurt her so badly, she felt an urge to reach out and comfort him. Stifling it, she lifted her chin. 'Why did you say it, then?'

He shook his head again. 'I don't know. To hurt you, I suppose.'

She stared at him. 'Why do you want to hurt me?' she said slowly. 'I thought we were past all that. You said you wanted me to forget and that you wanted to change—'

Laszlo grimaced.

'And I meant it,' he said shakily. 'But then, when I told my grandfather this morning about being a godfather, I just kept thinking about all the lies I've told him and how badly I treated you—' His face twisted. 'I just don't think I can stand up in front of all those people and make promises.'

Prudence swallowed. She felt helpless in the face of

his uncertainty, for Laszlo had always been so sure, so secure in his beliefs.

'Why not?' She looked up at his face and then, taking a breath, reached out and took his hand. 'Why not?' she repeated.

He stared down at her hand almost in bewilderment, and for a moment Prudence thought he would push it away. But instead his fingers tightened on hers and she had to bite back tears.

'Surely you, of all people, don't need to ask me that?' he said quietly.

His eyes fixed on her face and she realised with astonishment that she did. She had actually forgotten what had happened between them. Her breath stilled. Forgotten and forgiven—for of course she loved him, and what purer form of love was there but forgiveness?

'Mihaly wouldn't have asked you to be a godparent if he didn't think you could do it.'

He looked away, his face creasing with frustration. 'I told you. Mihaly chose me because I'm family. And family comes first,' he muttered hoarsely.

Prudence's eyes blazed. 'And who knows that more than you? Janos told me how you stayed with him the whole time your grandmother was ill. And you're still here now, taking care of him.'

She paused, her words and the emotion behind them choking her.

'Look at *me*!' she commanded. 'You even let me stay to make him happy. Despite everything that had happened between us you let it go. For *him*.' She shook her head. 'You're strong and loyal and kind. And I think you'll be a wonderful godfather.'

There was a moment's charged silence and then Laszlo lifted her hands to his lips and kissed them tenderly. 'So.

When did you become my number one fan, *pireni*?' he murmured unsteadily.

Lost in the golden softness of his gaze, she let out a long, shaking breath. 'I'm not saying there's not room for improvement...' she said slowly.

He smiled and she saw that his misery and confusion was fading and his confidence had returned too, and also a peace that hadn't been there before—as though something...some burden...had been lifted from his shoulders.

'Is that so?' he asked lightly. 'Perhaps you could give me a little bit of guidance. Point me in the right direction!'

He ran his hand lightly down her arm, his fingers brushing against her breast. She nodded, grateful that his words required no answer, for her mind was struggling to think of something other than the touch of his hands on her skin.

But even as she let him pull her closer her relief was tinged with confusion. Not so many days ago she had hated Laszlo. Now she was championing his cause, and with a joy almost like a jolt of pain she realised that for the first time ever he had needed her.

She felt his hand moving rhythmically over her back, lower and lower. But what did any of that matter really? She might love Laszlo, but for him this relationship was only ever going to be about great sex. Nothing would change that. But she could change how she reacted to that fact like when she'd been a child and she'd wanted a star for her birthday. Eventually she'd got over it and settled for a dolls' house. That was what you did when you wanted the impossible. You took what was offered instead. And if all Laszlo could offer was passion, then she wasn't going to dwell on the impossible.

'Why are you shivering? Are you cold?'

'No,' she said and swallowed.

Gently, his breathing not quite steady, he pulled her closer. She felt the warmth of his body against her and some of her confusion seemed to go away. And then his arms tightened and, leaning against him, she reached up and pulled his mouth onto hers, kissing him with fierce desperation.

Blindly, he pulled her closer, pressing her against him, deepening the kiss, tasting, teasing, tracing the shape of her lips. Prudence whimpered. Her skin was squirming with tension, drops of pleasure spreading over her skin in rippling concentric circles. She could feel her body melting; feel his hardening, the swollen length of his arousal pressing against her pelvis.

His grip tightened in her hair and she felt him shudder—and then he groaned softly and pushed her away.

'Wh—what's the matter?' She took a step backwards, gripping his shirt to steady herself. 'Why have you stopped?'

Laszlo gave a strangled smile. 'I want to tear all your clothes off.' He glanced over his shoulder. 'But Rosa will be up here any minute. We need some place private.' He felt a flash of panic: he sounded like some gauche teenage boy.

'So take me somewhere private. Somewhere I can tear your clothes off,' she said slowly.

Groaning, he lowered his mouth and kissed her fiercely. And then from the hallway there was the sound of voices and laughter and he tore his lips away from hers. They stared at each other, panting, and then finally he held out his hand.

'Come with me!'

CHAPTER NINE

HAND IN HAND they ran, giggling like teenagers, past an open-mouthed Rosa, along corridors and up staircases, until finally he stopped and they stood panting in front of a door.

Heart thudding, feeling a knot of tension in her stomach, Prudence stared at him. 'Where are we?'

He was silent, and then abruptly he leant forward and, tipping her head back, kissed her hard—kissed her until she couldn't think or speak or breathe.

He lifted his head and stared into her eyes. 'Somewhere private,' he said softly. 'My bedroom.'

With infinite tenderness he ran his fingers over her trembling cheek, his eyes fixing on hers.

'You don't need to worry about being disturbed. No one comes up here but me.'

She stared at him for a long moment, her chest tightening, for she knew he was trying to let her know that this was important to him. Wordlessly, she nodded, her breath sharpening at the blazing, possessive intensity of his gaze, and then his head dropped and his mouth captured hers, parting her lips and kissing her passionately.

Suddenly he was pushing her backwards, through the door and across the room to the bed. Her hands slid over his back and through his hair, and then she cried out hoarsely as his lips slid down her neck and over her throat and collarbone, grazing her nipples through the thin fabric of her blouse.

One hand was on her hip, the pressure making her squirm against him. Her eyes closed as his warm breath caressed her throat. She felt cool air on her thighs as slowly his fingers pushed up the hem of her skirt. And then his hands moved higher and gently he pulled the silken strip of her panties from her.

He lifted his head and gazed down at her, breathing unsteadily, his eyes dark with passion. 'You are so beautiful,' he murmured. 'And I want you so much.'

Dry-mouthed, she watched him slide down the bed. 'What are you—?'

But her words died on her lips as he dipped his head and lowered his mouth to the small triangle of damp curls at the top of her pelvis. She gasped, squirming beneath his touch, almost frightened at how badly she wanted him to keep touching her. Her pulse was pounding; her skin felt hot, burning with a fierce white heat. Inside she was tightening, her body tugging her towards the darkness.

Curving her back, she balled her hands into fists, curling and uncurling as she felt his warm, flickering tongue probe and caress. Suddenly her head was spinning. She clutched him closer and a fluttering, dancing pleasure shimmered over her skin, growing faster and stronger, quickening in time to her pulse, until finally her body tensed and she arched her pelvis against his mouth, burying her hands in his hair.

She lay spent and shaken, and then he slid back up the bed. She shuddered helplessly as his tongue found the soft swell of her breast. Moaning softly, she pulled frantically at the buttons of his fly, her breath stuttering in her throat as she felt the hard, straining male flesh as she eased his jeans down.

At the touch of her hand he groaned and, reaching out

blindly, she pulled him inside her. His hips lifted to meet hers and he thrust deep inside, then deeper still, his mouth capturing hers. She gripped his arms, her body throbbing in response, moving and shifting frantically against him. His hands tightened convulsively in her hair and his mouth sought hers. Her muscles clenched and, digging her nails into his back, she cried out loud as her entire body jerked against his. And then she heard his own cry as he tensed, arched and drove himself inside her.

Later, their bodies aching and sated, they lay entwined on his bed.

'I meant to ask you something, earlier.'

His deep voice broke into her thoughts and she tipped her head up to gaze at him. 'What is it?'

He smiled, his eyes lighting up as they moved over her face and body. 'I wanted to ask you why you came back. The second time, I mean.'

She frowned. 'I told you. To get my job back.'

He nodded. 'But there are other jobs. Surely no job was worth having to put up with me?' Raising his eyebrow, he studied her face, watching the slow flush of colour spread over her skin.

'I didn't want to let my uncle down.'

She looked up at him, her eyes wide with misery and confusion, and he felt a sudden fiercely protective rush towards her.

'You didn't. But if you'd told him who I was he wouldn't have wanted you to stay—?'

She shook her head. 'I couldn't tell him. He needs the money,' she said flatly. 'Edmund's stupidly generous with everyone and he's got in a muddle. Anyway… Your fee will make everything okay. That's why I had to come back.'

His eyes were warm and clear, like single malt whisky. 'I see. So you put up with me to make your uncle happy? Despite everything that happened between us, you let it go? For *him*.' He shook his head. 'I think that makes *you* pretty strong and loyal and kind too.'

Recognising her words, Prudence blushed.

Laszlo frowned. 'You know, we might be more like one another than we care to admit. I think if we'd concentrated on how similar we are, rather than focusing on our differences, we could've made it work.'

Smiling, she slid her hand low over his belly, watching his eyes close with relief—for her sadness was almost too much to bear beneath his gaze. They had wasted what they might have had and yet she knew that one word from him and she would have given their marriage another chance.

But Laszlo was only talking about the past. Words like *if* and *could've* held no promise of a future they might share. Her throat was suddenly thick and tight with tears, and then she felt his hand curl underneath her and, closing her eyes too, she let the fire building inside her consume her misery...

Later, running her hand lightly over his hair-roughened skin, still intoxicated with happiness at how much he'd wanted her, Prudence buried her face against the hard muscles of his chest.

'You smell gorgeous,' she murmured. Tilting her head back, she met his eyes. 'Like woodsmoke and lemons and salt, all mixed up.'

Laszlo held her gaze and then gently kissed her on the lips. 'How is that "gorgeous"? It sounds like kippers to me.'

Laughing softly, she cuffed him playfully around the head and then, giving a shiver of pleasure, snuggled against him. She felt ridiculously happy and safe. Outside the sun was shining weakly, and she could hear birds singing, but it was what was inside his room that mattered. Just her and Laszlo: perfect and complete. Here they could laugh and kiss and touch, and the uncontrollable, intrusive demands of the outside world would just pass them by.

Drowsily, she pressed herself against him.

She didn't remember falling asleep. With a sigh, she rolled over onto her side and, opening her eyes, found Laszlo, fully clothed, sitting on the edge of the bed watching her.

'You got up…' she murmured sleepily, stretching out under the sheets.

Smiling, he lowered his head and kissed her—a teasing caress of a kiss that made her feel hot and tense, made her want him all over again.

'Why don't you come back to bed?' She sat up, the sheet slipping down over her body, exposing her breasts, and watched his gaze darken and grow blunt and focused. She shivered with anticipation.

'I want to….'

He ran his fingers over the smooth, flat curve of her abdomen and she swallowed as a prickling heat spread over her. 'But…?'

He glanced at her regretfully and then shook his head. 'But I can't. I just went downstairs to grab some food and my uncle collared me—now I've got to paint the barn with my cousins.' Glancing from her breasts to her reproachful face, he groaned. 'Don't look at me like that! If I don't go down they'll come looking for me—'

Glancing towards the door, he frowned and picked up one of his sweaters from a nearby chair.

'In fact, I wouldn't put it past them to come barging up here anyway. Let's get you decent.'

Prudence frowned. 'I can just get dressed and go.'

She watched his face shift, grow hesitant, and then he shook his head slowly.

'No. I don't want you to leave.'

Her heart gave a tiny leap. His desire for her to stay was obviously nothing more than that: desire. But he clearly didn't want her to leave, which was something.

Feeling suddenly wicked, she leant against the pillow and let the sheet slip even lower. 'Won't they knock?' she asked mischievously.

He glared at her. 'No. They won't. Now—arms up,' he said firmly.

Pretending not to notice how aroused he was, Prudence raised her arms with exaggerated slowness. Swearing softly under his breath, he slid the jumper down and over her head.

'That's better,' he said, breathing out. Grimacing, he shook his head. 'You are going to pay for that later, *pireni.*' His body stiffened painfully as he heard her breath quicken. 'Damn it!' Shaking his head, he laughed softly. 'You have got to stop taking advantage of me. Or at least feed me first. If we hadn't missed lunch I'd never have gone downstairs and Kajan wouldn't have collared me.'

Food. Lunch.

Prudence stared at Laszlo, frozen in horror as her stomach suddenly gave a loud grumble of complaint.

'Oh, no! W-we missed lunch!' she stammered, staring at him in dismay.

Laszlo shrugged.

'It's cool. I saw Papi and told him you were lying down.'

She gaped at him. 'Up *here*?' she squeaked. 'You told him I was in your bedroom?' Her cheeks felt suddenly hot, and she felt panic rising like a storm inside her.

Laszlo frowned. 'I'm thirty, Prudence, not fourteen. I don't have to ask permission to take people up to my room. Anyway, don't look so worried.' He leant forward and kissed her. 'He was fine about it. He told me to let you sleep. Said that you'd been working far too hard. And Rosa was just worried that you'd starve. Which reminds me…'

Pausing, he stood up and walked across to the chest of drawers, picked up a plate covered with a napkin.

'I made us a picnic.' He grinned, his eyes gleaming.

'Oh, and there are cherries. Unless you want to wait till I get back for dessert?'

She rolled her eyes at him and laughing softly, he sat down on the bed beside her.

While they ate he told her stories about the castle and explained some of Hungary's complicated history. Then, when they'd finished, they fed each other cherries until there was nothing but stones and stalks left. Finally Prudence looked up and kissed him softly on the lips.

'Thank you. That was delicious. Some quite surprising taste combinations. I like that.'

She was teasing him and he grinned.

'I know you like to mix your flavours up.'

She shivered as his warm hand touched the bare skin of her leg.

'But what if I could only give you bread and cheese? Would you be happy with that?' he asked slowly.

'Yes,' she said softly. 'If you were there I'd eat old shoe leather.'

His eyes were dark and unreadable and then, glancing away, he looked round the room speculatively. 'Maybe you should just stay here in the tower? You could be my very own Lady of Shalott.'

She looked at him levelly, trying to ignore the steady, soft touch of his hands. Trying to stop herself from reading too much into his remark. She smiled. 'Doesn't she die alone and heartbroken?'

Laszlo frowned.

'Yes, she does. I'd forgotten that part. I wasn't really thinking about the poem. I just remember the painting by Waterhouse.' He smiled at her mockingly. 'Okay. What about Rapunzel? She saves her prince and they live happily ever after.'

Not trusting herself to speak, Prudence glanced away. *Could* she save Laszlo? Would he ever let her get close to him? She felt a flicker of hope. Maybe they could live happily ever after—maybe that was why fate had thrown them back together.

Her breathing slowed. Wrapped up in his bed sheets, it was easy to forget that none of this was real, for his words were so seductive. But her relationship with Laszlo would end soon, and there would be no happy-ever-after. And his words were designed to captivate and ensure that he got what he wanted. She sighed. What she had wanted too, at the beginning. Only now she wanted more.

And then, remembering how he'd held back from her just yesterday, she felt her stomach tighten. There was no point in hoping for any kind of reconciliation. What kind of marriage could they really have without trust and openness on both sides? Not that Laszlo had any interest in rekindling their relationship anyway. To him, this was and had only ever been a finite fling. Any seduction on his part was simply a means to an end. She needed to remember that when his poetic words started making her believe in fairy tales.

Composing herself, she smiled. 'I'm not sure. I don't remember Rapunzel throwing suitcases at her prince,' she said teasingly.

He gave her a crooked smile. 'That's because her pointy hat got in the way.'

She giggled as he reached over and pulled her closer.

'Not that you've thrown anything at me for days. Except the odd insult!' His eyes moved across her face slowly. 'I meant what I said. About you staying. I mean, why does all of this have to end?'

His arm tightened around her waist.

'I admit when you arrived it was difficult. We had a lot of things to sort out. But that's done now.'

His face was tense with concentration; she knew he was choosing his words carefully.

'We could just carry on doing what we're doing, couldn't we? We both want it. And I want you more than I've wanted any other woman.'

She felt a twitch of longing between her thighs, but it was tempered with sadness. It was flattering to be so desired, only she wanted so much more. But the thought of leaving him was so dreadful to contemplate that there was really no point pretending that she would refuse a relationship on whatever terms he offered.

'Just you and me? Just the two of us?' she said lightly.

He nodded, but his expression was suddenly serious. 'Just the two of us,' he echoed. 'That could work.'

Silence fell and then abruptly, Laszlo stood up.

'I'd better go. But you'll stay, won't you?'

She nodded slowly and watched him leave and then, sighing, she fell back onto the pillows.

She hadn't meant to fall asleep again. But somehow she had. It was the second time she had woken up in Laszlo's bed. Only this time she was alone in his room, and she felt his absence like an ache inside. Hugging his jumper against her body, she drew some comfort from his scent, and then rolling over, she gazed around the room.

It was a beautiful room, with high ceilings and deep, wide-set windows. Unlike all the other rooms she'd seen at the castle, there were no paintings or mirrors on the pale grey walls and it was sparsely furnished. Just an armchair, the curved wooden bed she was lying on and a chest of drawers.

And then she noticed the photograph.

For a moment, she stared at it blankly, wondering why she hadn't noticed it before, for it was the only ornament in the room. Then, pushing back the sheets, she walked across the carpet and, feeling slightly guilty, reached out and touched the framed black and white photograph.

Her mind was humming. Thoughts and feelings were buzzing through her head. And then she breathed in sharply. The two people in the photograph were Laszlo's parents. She was sure of it. The family resemblance was there in every line and curve of their faces. They were so beautiful, so young. But what drew her eye was not their youth or beauty—it was the intensity of their focus. They literally seemed to have eyes for no one but each other.

Prudence swallowed. She had never seen a photo of her own parents together. In fact, the only picture she had of her father was from a newspaper. Someone—probably Aunt Daisy—had cut out the report of a trial involving her father. She'd found it, yellowing and fading, hidden inside a book.

She was gazing so intently at the photograph that she didn't hear Laszlo come in.

'Pick it up, if you want.'

Jumping slightly at the sound of his voice, she turned round, a faint blush colouring her cheeks. 'You always seem to catch me snooping,' she grumbled.

Watching her worry the soft flesh of her lower lip, he felt a sudden twitch of desire. Even wearing his tatty jumper, with her hair tousled from sleep and her pink mouth bruised from his kisses, she looked sexier than hell.

He gave her a faint smile. 'Snooping…breaking and entering? Prudence, I have a feeling you're not in Surrey any more!'

There was a short, tense silence and then he reached out for her as she stepped towards him and they kissed fiercely.

Lifting his head, he dragged his mouth away from hers. 'I missed you.' He felt her arms tighten around him.

'I missed you too,' she murmured, burying her face against his chest.

Finally she gestured towards the photograph and frowned. 'Sorry…' She hesitated. 'They're your parents, aren't they?'

He nodded slowly, his golden eyes studying her warily. 'Yes.'

'Is that before or after they were married?'

'After,' he said shortly.

She wanted to ask more, but the brusqueness of his tone seemed to discourage any more talk in that direction, so instead she glanced around the room and said lightly, 'It's not how I expected it to look. Your room, I mean.'

'What were you expecting? Shawls and knick-knacks and bargeware?' Seeing from her guilty expression that she had, he grimaced and shook his head. 'I've had my fill of castles and roses—excuse the pun. But why do you care what my room looks like?' And then he frowned. 'Oh, I get it. You think it somehow reflects *my soul*.'

His earlier tension seemed to have shifted and his eyes were laughing down at her.

She blushed. 'I did an Art History degree, remember? I can find tragedy and torment in two squares of maroon and red.'

Grinning, he took her hand and held it against his lips. 'So what do you think my room says about me?'

She lifted her head. 'I think it says you ran out of picture hooks. Either that or you're a philistine.'

She yelped as he made a grab for her.

'Just because I don't want a bunch of Old Masters cluttering up my walls, it doesn't make me a philistine.'

He spoke flippantly, but there was an edge to his voice and she turned to face him.

'I was joking. Truly. I know you're not a philistine,' she said slowly.

She watched his face grow taut.

'Because of my grandfather?' He shrugged. 'That's rather a simplistic point of view. I would have thought you'd be the first person to understand that blood can be no thicker than water.'

He looked away, and her cheeks burning, Prudence stared at his profile helplessly. There was something pushing to get out from behind his anger. Something that he'd wanted and failed to tell her yesterday and she needed to find some way—some words—to reach him.

Holding her breath, she followed his gaze. He was looking at the photograph of his parents.

'What were they like?'

He was silent so long she thought he wasn't going to reply, and then his shoulders rose and fell and he said quietly, 'They were perfect.'

Her heart was suddenly pounding. It was an odd word to use, but it was the way he said it—so wearily, so unhappily—that made her feel as though she were breaking in two.

Her eyes fixed on the photograph.

'You look a lot like your mother,' she said carefully. 'But your eyes are just like your father's.'

Laszlo watched her glance anxiously from the photo back to him. 'At least I inherited *something* from them.'

He hadn't meant his remark to sound so sharp, and his neck tensed as she turned to look at him.

'What does that mean?'

Instead of answering he gave a casual shrug and leant forward, intending to kiss her. Kiss away his pain and confusion.

But, stepping backwards, she stared at him confusedly. 'I want to help—'

'I don't want your help!'

He spoke quickly—too quickly—and she lifted her head, her eyes suddenly darker than steel, her voice glacier-cold. 'But you *do* want to have sex with me?'

As he met her gaze, he felt relief, for her anger was so much easier to respond to than her concern. 'I don't see a connection.'

'I want you to stop pushing me away.'

'I don't push you away. I can barely keep my hands off you.'

'I'm not talking about that. That's just sex.'

She looked away. There was a pulsing silence. A muscle flickered in his jaw and he groped for something to take the pain from her eyes. And from his heart.

'I'm sorry. I don't want to.' His face was suddenly stiff with tension. 'I'm not trying to push you away—' Prudence stared at him anxiously. She could almost feel the weight of misery in his heart.

'But you are pushing *something* away. Or someone…?'

It was conjecture—nothing more than a feeling—but his face tightened.

'Is it your mum and dad?'

He looked almost dazed, and then his eyes seemed to scramble away from hers. There was a silence, and then he said quietly, 'I let them down. And not just them. My grandparents too.'

'I don't understand…' she said slowly. And then suddenly—incredibly—she did. 'Are you talking about our marriage?'

Even as he nodded, she was shaking her head.

'No. Laszlo. That doesn't make sense. None of them knew about our marriage. So how could you have let them down?'

His face quivered. 'You're right. You *don't* understand.' He frowned. 'Even now people in my family talk about my parents. They were so perfect together. And they made everything look so effortless. Marriage. Love. Life.'

He grimaced. Even the difference in their backgrounds had been no obstacle to their happiness; instead their passionate belief in each other had simply blurred the lines between the Romany and non-Romany world.

'And you wanted to be like them.' It was a statement not a question.

After a brief hesitation he let out a breath and nodded. 'I wanted what they had. That passion—that rightness.' He gave a twisted smile. 'I think, actually, it'd be more accurate to say that, as their son, I *expected* it. As my right. And I thought I had it.'

'Why?' she whispered.

And she was suddenly more grateful than she'd ever been that it was his turn to speak, for she couldn't have opened her mouth again without crying.

'I met you.' He smiled again, but this time his smile seemed to illuminate his whole face. 'And I was desperate—no, *determined* not to lose you. We married and everything was perfect. At first.'

She stared at him, feeling a spasm of nausea. 'And then I ruined it?'

Abruptly he grabbed her arms and shook her, his face tightening with anger. 'No. You *didn't* ruin it. You were just young and nervous and inexperienced.'

She struggled against him, words tumbling haphazardly from her lips. 'You were young too.'

'Spoilt and arrogant is what I was! I was used to getting what I wanted,' he said harshly. 'And what I wanted was for you to make our marriage work—because I sure as hell wasn't going to. I just assumed everything would fall into place.' His eyes fixed on her face. 'I was wrong.'

'We were both wrong!' she raged back at him.

His hands dropped to his sides and he let out a ragged breath. 'I thought it'd be easy.'

He frowned, remembering how inadequate he'd felt. How lonely too—for he'd been too proud to admit his problems to anyone.

'Only it *wasn't*. And when it got hard I blamed you. I pushed you away,' he said quietly. 'I'm the one that ruined everything, *pireni*! I hurt you and I lied to you, and because of my arrogance and stubborn pride I let you go when I should have done everything in my power to make you stay. And then I had to lie to both my families. All my grandmother wanted was to see me happily married before she died, and I messed that up too.'

His voice cracked and he lowered his head.

'I never meant to hurt you, Prudence. You have to believe me. I just wanted it to be perfect.'

Feeling tears prick the backs of her eyes, Prudence shook her head. 'I know,' she said softly. 'And I don't blame you for what happened.'

Her throat tightened. It was no wonder he'd reacted so badly when their marriage had seemed to falter.

Reaching out, she took his hand and squeezed it. 'You know this morning, when you said we're more alike than we thought? You were right. Our parents' marriages influenced us way too much.' She laughed weakly. 'I actually think it was some kind of miracle that we even got together in the first place.'

Gripping his hand, she dragged him across the room.

'Listen to me, Laszlo!' She picked up the photo, brandishing it like a weapon. 'I've spent years looking at photos, paintings and sketches. And it's true what they say: every picture *does* tell a story. And this is *their* story. Not yours.'

She put the frame down carefully.

'I don't have a photo of you, but if I did it would tell me your story. The story of a young man who made some mistakes but who is loyal and devoted to his family and who has learned to forgive and trust.' Her eyes flared. 'You haven't let *anyone* down. Your parents' marriage may have looked easy from the outside, but you only knew them as a child. And I'm sorry that your grandmother didn't know about our marriage, but you made her very happy, Laszlo. And you took care of her—just like you're taking care of Janos now.'

He caught hold of her arm and pulled her tightly into his arms, burying his face in her hair. 'I don't deserve you,' he murmured.

For a long, long time, he just held her, his warm breath on her neck. Then at last, he sighed.

'Talking is so tiring. How do women do so much of it?'

She pulled back slightly and smiled up at him. 'We *are* the stronger sex,' she said quietly.

He nodded, his face serious. 'Stronger. Wiser. You're probably the wisest woman I've ever met, Prudence Elliot. The most beautiful. Most compassionate. Most forgiving.' He sighed again.

'If only I could make a proper Hungarian goulash I'd be perfect,' she said shakily.

He smiled weakly. 'I've had enough of perfection. I'm happy with what I've got.'

Standing on tiptoe, she pressed her mouth against his. 'Me too!'

He kissed her back fiercely and then, groaning, broke away from her. 'You know, all that talk about goulash has made me think about food again. How about we go downstairs and show Rosa where she's been going wrong all these years?'

Later, lying with Prudence curled against his body, Laszlo felt strangely calm. He'd told her everything, and she'd listened while he talked. Not once had she judged him. Instead she'd given him the courage to face his fear. A fear that had chafed at him for so long and corroded his relationship with the only woman he'd ever loved.

Closing his eyes, he felt his heart contract almost painfully.

The woman he still loved. His wife.

His hand tightened around her body and he was suddenly close to tears, for he had so nearly lost her again.

And then he almost laughed out loud as he remembered their teasing conversation of earlier. For he was the one who was trapped in the tower, and *she* had rescued *him*.

Abruptly, he felt his chest grow tight. And then, like a balloon popping, his happiness burst. His relationship with Prudence would soon be over and all his thoughts of love and marriage were just speculation and hope. At no time had Prudence even hinted that she wanted to give their relationship another chance.

He frowned. Come to that matter, he hadn't either.

In fact, he'd made it pretty clear that their relationship was nothing more than a cathartic fling that would terminate at the same time as her period of employment at the castle.

Opening his eyes, he stared bitterly at the photograph of his parents. He needed to show Prudence he'd changed. Words wouldn't be enough this time. But, having convinced her that all he wanted was a loveless affair, how was he going to persuade her that he wanted to give their marriage another chance?

CHAPTER TEN

'ARE YOU READY?'

Laszlo's voice drifted up the stairs, causing Prudence to glance in dismay at the discarded clothes strewn across her bed. So far she was wearing only her underwear and her shoes.

'Nearly!' she called out quickly.

'Nearly? How is that possible? You've been up there for hours...' His voice trailed off as he stepped through the doorway. 'Nice dress,' he said slowly. 'Where's the rest of it?'

She glared at him. 'This isn't the dress. It goes underneath.'

His eyes slid over the sheath of satin.

'And what goes underneath that?' he murmured softly.

'Nothing. That's the point.'

He grinned. 'It's a very good point. Very convincing, in fact.' He walked across the room and kissed the corner of her mouth. 'Although if you took it off I think your point might be clearer still.' He pulled her towards him and kissed the soft hollow at the base of her neck.

She looked into his eyes and gave him a teasing smile. 'Really? You don't think it might be a little risqué for the party?'

She squirmed against him and he looked down at her, his gaze darkening.

'Hell, yeah! I'm the only person who gets to see you

naked,' he growled, lowering his mouth onto hers and kissing her fiercely.

Head spinning, Prudence clung to him, feeling heat—scorching, dizzying heat—wash over her. Just as she thought her legs would give way, she heard him swear softly under his breath.

Groaning, he broke the kiss and released her. 'I can't believe we have to go to this damn party. I've already spent all day with my family.'

He stopped and stared incredulously at the pile of clothes on the bed.

'You're not going to say you don't have anything to wear, are you?' he said slowly.

'No. Yes. I don't know… It depends.'

He frowned. 'On what? What about the dress you chose in Budapest?'

She bit her lip. 'I did get a dress. Only now I'm not sure if it's more of an evening one than party.'

Laszlo winced. 'Can't it be both? We *are* going to an evening party, after all.' His eyes lit up hopefully. 'If you're really worried then maybe we should just stay here?'

Smiling, she shook her head. 'Nice try! But we're not bailing. What would your family think?' She frowned. 'I don't know why you don't want to go anyway.'

Throwing himself down onto the bed, he pushed the dresses to one side and pulled a pillow behind his head. 'Because I want to stay *here*,' he said sulkily. 'And, as it's taken you nearly two hours *not* to get ready, I think the party will probably be ending by the time you're dressed.'

Laughing, Prudence picked up a scarf from the back of a chair and threw it at him. 'It's easy for men!' she said, reaching round and sweeping her long blonde hair into a loose topknot. 'They just put on a suit!' Glancing at him, she felt her smile fade and gave a small cry of exasperation. 'Only you're not!'

Winding the scarf around his neck, he looked up at her calmly. 'Not what?'

'Wearing a suit!'

Looking down at his jeans and shirt, Laszlo frowned. 'What's wrong with this?'

She glowered at him crossly. 'You're joking, aren't you? Laszlo! I thought you said everyone was dressing up?'

He shrugged. 'They are. And I *have* dressed up; this is the shirt I bought yesterday. Anyway, it's my party—I can wear what I like.' Reaching out, he grabbed her hand and pulled her next to him on the bed. 'What's wrong?' he said gently.

'I don't want to let you down in front of your family.'

'How could you ever let me down? If it hadn't been for you I might never have gone through with being Pavel's godfather.' He pressed her hand to his lips and kissed it tenderly. 'Besides, you'd look beautiful wearing that rug.' He glanced at the riotously patterned Afghan carpet on the floor and grimaced.

Stroking his hair off his forehead, she smiled weakly. 'They won't be looking at me anyway. You're the godfather, remember?' Her eyes grew soft and misty. 'The very handsome, very serious godfather.' She hesitated. 'I'm so proud of you.'

He pressed his thumb against her cheekbone. 'You're a good person,' he said softly, leaning forward so that his warm breath tickled her throat. 'Good enough to eat.'

His words excited her unbearably, and she could feel heat pooling between her thighs. Cheeks burning, she gritted her teeth, trying to stay calm. 'You don't want to spoil your appetite. And I need to get dressed,' she said lightly.

He sighed. 'I still don't really get why you're so worried, *pireni*. Although I suppose I'd probably feel the same if I was in your shoes.'

Summoning up a smile, Prudence looked down at her

high-heeled black court shoes. 'If you were in my shoes I think you'd bring the party to a standstill!'

He grinned. 'Don't tempt me!'

His eyes met hers and she felt a shiver of desire run over her skin as Laszlo ran his hand slowly up her leg and then abruptly rolled to the other side of the bed.

'You know what? I don't care what you wear.' He groaned. 'But you *have* to put some clothes on or I won't be responsible for what happens.' He stood up. 'In fact, just to be on the safe side, I'm going to go back to the castle. If I put a couple of fields and metre-thick stone walls between us I might just be able to keep my hands off you until after the party!'

He paused and pulled her scarf more tightly around his neck.

'Oh, and I *might* change into something that's a bit more "evening and party wear"!'

She giggled and their eyes met.

'I'll be back to pick you up later...ish.' Blowing her a kiss, he grimaced and shook his head. 'The things we do for love!'

After he'd gone, she spent at least ten minutes mulling over his words. Finally she roused herself. It was just a phrase—a jokey remark that people used all the time. She would be crazy to read anything more into it.

Twenty minutes later she slid a lipstick across her lips and stared critically at her reflection in the dressing table mirror.

She turned her head from side to side. The neckline was perhaps a little lower than she'd normally wear, and her pinned-up hair would probably not survive the dancing, but overall she was satisfied. Still staring at her reflection, she bit her lip. She seemed to be looking at two separate versions of herself. One was serene and cool, the deep smoky grey of the long silk dress highlighting her classic English rose skin and fair hair. The other Prudence was visible only in her eyes, which were dark, apprehensive. Aroused by Laszlo's imagined response to her transformation.

She heard a knock at the door and felt a stab of excitement. *Laszlo!*

Heart pounding, she opened the door—and took a step backwards, her hand over her mouth. He looked impossibly handsome in a classic black dinner jacket, his snowy white shirt unbuttoned at the neck, bow tie hanging loose around the collar.

'It—it's a dinner jacket,' she stammered.

He glanced down at himself nonchalantly. 'This old thing? I found it at the back of my wardrobe,' he murmured.

He smiled, his teeth gleaming in the darkness. She saw the flare of approval and desire in his face and felt her body respond.

'You're beautiful, Prudence,' he said softly. Reaching out, he tugged gently at a tendril of honey-coloured hair, shaping the curl between his fingers. 'I love your hair up like this. You're like a goddess—an Aphrodite.'

Prudence stared at him breathlessly. He was more beautiful than any god she could name. And sexier too, with his shirt open and his eyes dark and teasing.

'That would explain why I can't ever seem to get warm. I should really be on some hot Greek mountain,' she said lightly, her heart banging against her chest.

He studied her in silence. 'Speaking of cold...are you going to invite me in or shall I just wait out here?'

She blushed. 'Sorry. Of course—come in. I just need to get my bag.'

Shutting the door behind him, Laszlo pulled off his jacket and hung it carelessly over the back of the sofa. He sat down in one of the armchairs, picked up a magazine and began to flick through it.

After a moment he sighed and put his feet up onto the

coffee table. 'What do women put in their bags anyway?' he said idly.

Prudence smiled. 'All the things men keep in their jacket pockets. Money, keys, lipstick…'

'I don't have any lipstick,' Laszlo said sadly.

She laughed softly. 'You don't have any money or keys either.'

Grinning up at her, he tugged her leg and she let herself fall into his lap.

'Is that so? How would you know? Or have you been going through my clothes as well as breaking into my house?'

He shook his head and, laughing, she wriggled free of his hands. Standing up, she pulled down his jacket and began patting the pockets one by one.

'See?' she said triumphantly. 'Empty. Oh—' Her fingers touched something small and rectangular and then suddenly she was holding a small velvet-covered rectangular box.

'What's this?'

Frowning, Laszlo stood up. He paused and then swore softly under his breath. 'Damn it!' He shook his head and then smiled ruefully. 'That was—is actually for you.'

She stared at him, too shocked to speak. 'For me?' she said finally. 'What is it?'

His eyes met hers and he laughed quietly. 'Open it and see!'

Heart pounding, she felt her mind dance forward as she lifted the lid—and then she gasped. 'Oh, Laszlo. It's beautiful.'

He nodded. 'It's to match your eyes.'

She stared at the luminous grey pearl necklace in silence, shivers running up and down her spine. 'It's truly lovely. But I didn't get *you* anything,' she said, looking up at him anxiously.

A dark flush coloured his cheeks. There was a pause, and then he shook his head slowly. 'It's not from me.' He cleared his throat. 'It's from my grandfather. He would have given it to you himself, but he got tied up on the phone and he wanted you to have it before the party.'

Prudence blinked 'Your grandfather?' She swallowed. Her skin felt hot and raw; his gaze was blistering her skin. She felt stupid and naive. Keeping her gaze averted, she breathed in deeply. 'That's so sweet of him. But I can't possibly accept it.'

Laszlo frowned. 'You must. Please. He chose them himself as a thank-you for all your hard work.'

She bit her lip. 'He didn't need to thank me. Not with something as beautiful as this. Shall I wear it tonight?' she said shakily.

Nodding, he reached out and took the necklace gently from her hand. 'It's not as beautiful as you. Now, stand up and turn round!'

She turned away, feeling her skin tingle as his warm fingers slid over her.

'There! Let me see…'

She turned back towards him slowly and lifted her head. Their eyes met and her pupils shrank beneath the intensity of his gaze.

'You don't need any jewellery. Your eyes and lips are your jewels,' he said roughly.

Breathing deeply, he stepped away, his eyes narrowing.

'And now I'd like to give you *my* gift. I'm sorry it doesn't quite match up to my grandfather's.' He smiled ruefully. 'If he'd been any other man I would have punched him on the nose. But what could I do? He's my grandfather!'

'*Your* gift?'

He reached down and pulled a small embellished leather bag from beneath his shirt. 'It's a *putsi*. It means "little

pocket". It's traditional for Romany women to carry one.'
He looped the cord over his hand and held it out to her.

'It's beautiful,' she croaked.

Her heart was racing, and she knew that her feelings
were all over her face, but she was too happy to care. Her
whole body felt as though it were filling with light.

With hands that shook slightly, she turned the bag over.
It rattled softly. 'Is there something inside it?'

He nodded. 'Amulets. Magic charms.' He shrugged.
'They're supposed to bring good luck. Ward off evil. If
you believe in that sort of thing.'

She nodded, unable to speak.

'Just don't open the bag,' he said, deepening his voice
dramatically. 'Or the magic will fail.'

Shivering, she looked up with wide, uncertain eyes.

He pulled her towards him, laughing softly. 'I'm kidding. You can open it if you want.'

She began to pull clumsily at the drawstring and then,
looking up, saw him watching her. Her fingers faltered.

'I think I'll wait,' she said slowly. 'Save my luck for
later.'

Gently, he reached up and stroked her cheek. 'You don't
need luck.' He glanced at the soft curve of her waist beneath the clinging silk and frowned. 'But if we don't go
right now there's no amulet on earth that's going to stop
me ripping that dress off you!'

'I'm ready!' she said hastily.

Reaching down, she picked up her small beaded evening bag, opened it and put the *putsi* inside. Then, looking up, she smiled at him shyly.

'Thank you, Laszlo. I'll keep it close to me always. And
I love it just as much as the pearls.'

He watched her coolly, back to his old inscrutable self.

'It's my pleasure. And I'm pleased.' He grinned. 'Utterly unconvinced, but pleased.'

He turned towards the door but she put her hand on his arm. 'Wait!' Their eyes met and then she blushed and pointed to his neck. 'What about your bow tie?'

Glancing down, he frowned. 'Oh... I gave up,' he said simply. 'Papi can do them in his sleep, but he was busy on the phone, and every time I tried to talk to him he shooed me away,' he grumbled.

Their eyes met and she burst out laughing. 'You are *such* a spoilt baby.' She reached out and did up his top button. 'Your grandfather was probably talking to the caterers. Now, lift your chin!' Deftly, Prudence twisted the black silk between her fingers. 'Turn around!' Stepping backwards, she stared at him assessingly. 'Perfect!' she said softly.

He grinned slowly. 'Me? Or the bow tie?'

Rolling her eyes, she picked up the pashmina she'd had the foresight to buy at the airport and slid it over her shoulders. She let out a breath.

Laszlo looked at her enquiringly. 'Ready?'

'No. But do I have a choice?'

He kissed her lightly on the lips. 'Not any more. Come on! Let's go!' He gave Prudence his arm and, opening the front door, stepped into the night air.

She gave a gasp of surprise, for, leading away as far as the eye could see, hundreds of tiny flickering flares edged the path up to the castle. 'That's so pretty!'

Shaking his head, Laszlo laughed. 'They're supposed to stop us breaking our necks. But I suppose they *do* look a bit like fireflies.' His golden eyes gently mocked her excitement. 'It all adds to the magic of the occasion. For the women and children!'

Prudence laughed. 'Don't make me use my *putsi*,' she said teasingly.

'There's nothing wrong with a bit of magic.' Laszlo grinned. 'I'll remind you of that later, when my Uncle Lajos starts doing conjuring tricks.'

The noise of laughter and music greeted them as they walked along the gravel path towards the barn and Prudence squeezed Laszlo's arm nervously.

She had enjoyed the christening more than she'd expected. The tiny church had been bright with sunlight and filled with flowers. And seeing Laszlo hold Pavel in his arms, his unguarded face still with pride, she could have wept with love and envy. Laszlo's family had been polite and friendly. But now the darkness felt intimidating, and she suddenly wished that she was walking in as his wife.

Shivering, she pushed the thought away. 'It sounds like the party's already started,' she said quickly. 'How many people are coming?'

Laszlo shrugged. 'I don't know. Probably a hundred—maybe more.'

Prudence felt her feet stutter to a halt. 'A—a *hundred*?' she stammered. 'A hundred people?' She stopped and stared at him incredulously. 'Why didn't you tell me?'

He gazed at her with a maddening lack of concern. 'I thought you knew? Did you think it was just the guests from the christening?' He laughed softly. 'No. This is *everyone*.' Frowning, he took her hand in his. 'Does it matter? I mean, they're all family...'

Swallowing, she smiled weakly. 'Is that why there were more women than men at the church?'

He grinned. 'They didn't all come to the church. A lot of the men think that priests take away your manhood. Mine seems fine, though!' His eyes gleamed in the darkness.

She knew he was teasing her, trying to make her relax, but she couldn't. Feeling suddenly queasy with panic, Prudence clutched his arm more tightly.

Laszlo gave her hand a comforting squeeze. 'You did the hard part this morning. It'll be fine. They're going to love you. Trust me.'

Trust: how could so much be wrapped up in that one little word? 'Okay.' Heart pounding, she nodded. 'Okay. But you have to trust me too, Laszlo. That's how trust works.'

In the darkness, she couldn't tell if he'd taken in her words or not. She opened her mouth to speak again, and then, behind them, the door to the barn opened and light and noise and colour hit her like a physical blow.

'Laszlo! *Laszlo!*'

Prudence stared in astonishment round the barn. All around her, hands were reaching across and patting Laszlo on the back, pulling him by the arm, calling out his name. Turning towards her, he grinned and shouted back something in Hungarian, or maybe Romany. But the noise in the barn made it impossible for her to do anything but smile and nod.

Children were running around, darting through the crowds of smartly dressed adults, laughing and shouting. Some men dressed in dark suits and waistcoats were singing, stamping in time to guitars, and men and women, old and young, were dancing in a mass of people that seemed to fill one end of the vast barn.

Laszlo guided her into a part of the barn that had been screened off as a cloakroom. He turned to her and grinned. 'Now, *this* is a party. A Romany party!' he whispered in her ear.

She nodded. 'A hundred people?' She glared at him accusingly as he led her back into the main barn. 'There must be well over two hundred!'

He glanced round the room. 'Nearer three, I'd guess.' His eyes were light and teasing.

She shook her head. 'You're *incorrigible*, Laszlo Cziffra! You knew *exactly* how many people were coming—and I bet you were always going to wear a dinner jacket, weren't you?'

'No.'

His smile sent shivers up and down her spine.

'I was always going to wear a suit. But then I thought tonight was special—'

He turned as a dancing couple barged into him and apologised. She blinked in confusion. What did he mean by 'special'? She felt his hand tighten on hers and looking up, found him watching her, his gaze fierce and glittering.

'We need to talk.'

Wordlessly, she nodded—and then, glancing over his shoulder, she noticed a middle-aged couple watching them curiously.

'Not here,' she murmured, flinching as another couple skimmed past Laszlo's back.

Frowning, he put his arm round her protectively. 'Shall we go outside? It's quieter there…less chance of injury.'

'Yes.' She paused. 'But could we find your grandfather first? I want to thank him for the necklace.'

Laszlo studied her face and then nodded slowly. Scanning over the heads of the dancers, he pointed across the barn. 'He's over there! And there's Mihaly too.' He gripped her hand tightly. 'Don't let go. I don't want to lose you.'

He turned and began to push his way through the crush of people, pulling her behind him. Every few metres he was stopped by guests and Prudence found herself being introduced to a baffling array of people. Finally they reached the other side of the barn, where tables and chairs had been set up and trestles of food and drink lined the walls.

'Laszlo!' Mihaly reached out and yanked his cousin into a crushing embrace. He took a step back and, glancing down at Laszlo's suit, grinned wickedly. 'What's this? They've got you being a waiter at your own party?'

Pushing Laszlo under his arm, he sidestepped in front of Prudence and bowed.

'Miss Elliot! You look beautiful! I wonder, may I have this dance with you?'

He gave a yelp that turned into a laugh as Laszlo grabbed him from behind and punched him on the arm.

'No. You may not!'

Still laughing, Mihaly held out his hand to Prudence. 'Don't listen to him, Miss Elliot.' He gestured towards an elderly woman sitting by the dance floor, a walking frame by her side. 'That's my great-aunt. Laszlo danced with her once! Just *once!*'

He and Laszlo both burst into laughter, but there was no mistaking the possessive note in his voice as Laszlo pulled her against him. 'Prudence won't be dancing with anyone but me. And *you're* going to need a walking frame too, cousin, if you don't back off!'

Trying to ignore the warm rush of pleasure at his words, she glanced anxiously over to where Janos was talking to another elderly man. 'I must just speak to your grandfather,' she said quietly.

Janos broke off his conversation as she approached him. He smiled warmly. 'You look quite lovely, my dear.'

Prudence blushed. 'Thank you so much, Janos. It's such a beautiful necklace.' Standing on tiptoe, she reached up and kissed Janos gently on the cheek.

Smiling, he patted her on the hand. 'It's my pleasure.' He glanced over Prudence's shoulder to where Laszlo and Mihaly were still fooling around with each other. Sighing, he shook his head. 'They act like children when they get together, but it's nice for me to see Laszlo having fun.'

His face clouded.

'I know it must appear to you that he's had a charmed life, living here in a castle surrounded by priceless works of art. But he's known a great deal of unhappiness,' he said quietly. 'He's seen so much sickness and death and grief.' He smiled sadly. 'Of course I love having my grandson live with me, but he's spent far too much of his life cooped up in the castle with me.'

He hesitated.

'We're too shut off here. It's made him push away the world. Turn away from life itself. But you coming here has changed that. He seems so much happier.'

Prudence blushed. 'I don't think I can really take the credit for that.' She swallowed. 'But I'm glad he's happy. He deserves to be. Even though he's so incredibly annoying and stubborn...' Her mouth twisted. 'I don't think I know anyone quite like him!'

Janos burst out laughing. 'Nothing you can't handle, I imagine?'

She laughed. 'No. I think we've pretty much worked out our differences.' Biting her lip, she hesitated. 'But I think it's not just Laszlo who's changed. You've changed too.'

Janos nodded. 'Yes. I have.' His eyes flickered with excitement. 'And there may be more changes to come. But none of it would have happened without your hard work and patience.'

Prudence glanced down to the necklace gleaming at her throat. 'Hmm... Pearls for patience? I think I should quit while I'm ahead.'

Janos smiled. 'It's a fair exchange! And happily Laszlo actually remembered to give you the necklace.' He frowned. 'I wasn't entirely sure he would. He can be a little forgetful.'

'Jakob's not forgetful!' Laszlo slid between his grandfather and Prudence. 'What are you talking about, Papi? He's got an excellent memory. Or were you casting aspersions on *me*?' He smiled mischievously at Janos, who shook his head and began to speak in Hungarian.

For a long moment Laszlo said nothing. His expression didn't change, but something in his gaze seemed to reach out to her—she could almost feel his hands on her skin, even though they were standing apart.

Finally both men nodded and then, his face softening, Laszlo held out his hand. 'Dance with me?'

Prudence felt the air squeeze from her lungs and for a moment time seemed to stop—and then slowly she smiled. The rest of the party passed with unconscionable speed. Later, Prudence would try to piece the evening together. She had danced and eaten, and talked until her voice was hoarse from trying to compete with the music. And then finally the music had slowed and the lights had dimmed and Laszlo had held her tightly against him. They'd danced until suddenly Janos had been there, telling them that he was tired and was going to go home to bed.

'I'll walk you home, Papi. I could do with some fresh air,' Laszlo said, pulling his dinner jacket from the back of a chair. He turned to Prudence, his eyes locking onto hers. 'Shall I come back for you?' he asked quietly.

She shook her head. 'No. I'll come now.'

Smiling, he slipped his jacket over her shoulders, and together the three of them walked up to the castle.

Inside the hall, Janos turned and frowned.

'Are you all right, Papi?' Laszlo stared at his grand-father.

'Oh, I'm fine. The fresh air's just woken me up.' Janos hesitated. 'I wonder... Do either of you feel up to a night-cap?'

Glancing at one another, they both nodded simultane-ously.

Janos beamed. 'Wonderful. Let's go and warm up.'

In the study, a fire was flickering in the grate. Laszlo leant over and banged the glowing logs with a poker, and flames leapt up as though defending themselves.

'Sit down by the fire, Papi. Prudence—come here,' he ordered.

Janos sat down and glanced apologetically around the room. 'I'm afraid I may have been a little disingenuous.' He smoothed an imaginary crease from his trouser leg. 'You see, I have something I want to discuss with you both. I was going to wait until tomorrow...' Lifting his head, he frowned. 'But it's been playing on my mind.'

Prudence looked down at her hands in her lap, feeling Laszlo's gaze on the side of her face.

'So? What is it, Papi?'

Janos paused. He looked alert and animated, the vigour in his eyes belying his age. 'I'm thinking about making some changes. And I'd be quite interested in hearing what you think.'

Laszlo raised his eyebrows. 'Not the moat again, Papi?' he said slowly.

Janos shook his head and gave a reluctant smile. 'No. Not the moat. Although it *does* have something to do with the castle.' Pausing, he glanced across at Prudence. 'It was you, my dear girl, who gave me the idea.'

Prudence gaped at him. 'I did?' she said incredulously.

There was a moment's silence, and then Laszlo cleared his throat. 'So. Don't keep us in suspense, then, Papi. What's the big idea?'

Smiling, Janos shook his head. 'You're just like your mother. Always so impatient.' He looked up at his grandson, his expression tender and hopeful. 'All my life I've been surrounded by beauty. Now I'd like to share my good fortune with other people.' He paused again, his eyes bright, almost feverish with excitement. 'And that's why I want to turn the castle into a museum.'

CHAPTER ELEVEN

THERE WAS A stunned silence in the room. Finally Laszlo shook his head. 'I'm sorry. Did you just say you wanted to turn the castle into a *museum*?' He gave his grandfather a long, searching look. 'Why on earth would you want to do that?'

Janos raised his hands placatingly. 'To give something back, Laszlo.'

Laszlo frowned. 'You *do* give something back. Quite a lot of "something", if that last meeting we had with the accountants is anything to go by.'

Janos shook his head. 'Yes. I give to charity. But this would be different.'

His frown darkening, Laszlo began pacing the room. 'Different?' He gave a short laugh. 'It would definitely be *different*. And disruptive—and intrusive. Have you really thought what it would be like to have a bunch of people wandering about in our home?' Stopping in front of his grandfather, he stubbed the carpet with the toe of his shoe. 'I just don't understand why you would want to do this. And why now?'

He shot Prudence a questioning glance.

'*Is* this something to do with you? What did you say to him?'

She stared at him, confused. 'I—I don't know—' she stammered.

Reaching out, Janos patted the chair beside him. 'Laszlo!

Laszlo! Sit down. Prudence and I were talking about her life in England and she mentioned the Soane's Museum. That's all.'

Prudence watched as Laszlo allowed his grandfather to pull him into the chair.

Janos frowned. 'I'm so sorry.' He glanced at Prudence apologetically. 'I should have waited until tomorrow. We're probably too tired and emotional after the party to be having this sort of conversation.' His voice trembled. 'It was thoughtless of me. I suppose I've just had this idea buzzing around my head for so long now that I forgot it would be new and shocking to you.' He sighed. 'And I just wanted to share it with you both.'

Taking his grandfather's hand, Laszlo squeezed it hard. He looked so young and troubled that Prudence turned away.

'I'm sorry, Papi,' she heard him say softly. 'Of course I want to share your idea. I just wasn't expecting it.' He smiled weakly. 'But I want to hear all about it. So—how will it all work?'

Janos smiled back at him. 'It's not going to happen overnight. Someone from the Museums Committee is coming over in a couple of weeks, to take a look at what we've got here, and then I think there will be a lot of long but necessary meetings. Quite possibly the castle will be ready for visitors by the end of next year.'

Laszlo nodded slowly. 'And how will that work? I mean having visitors. You're not expecting me to give guided tours or anything?' He spoke lightly but his face had tightened.

Laughing, Janos shook his head. 'No, Laszlo. You won't be giving tours around the castle. We won't have much to do with the visitors at all.'

Laszlo frowned. 'Given that they'll be wandering around our home, I think we *will*.'

There was a long, strained pause and then Janos coughed.

'The castle won't *be* our home when it's a museum, Laszlo. By the time it opens to the public we'll have moved out.'

'Moved out?' Laszlo said slowly. 'Moved out of the castle?' He shook his head. 'Papi... What are you talking about? This is your home. *Our* home. It's been in our family for hundreds of years!'

'I know—and I love this castle. It's been an enormous privilege to own such an incredible building. But, my darling boy, it's not a home any more.' He put his hands on his grandson's shoulders and said roughly, 'This castle is a museum in everything but name. And we both need to accept that and move on.'

For a moment the room hummed with a silence that was broken only by the spitting of the fire, and then finally Laszlo nodded.

'I know,' he said quietly. 'I suppose it's just that it's taken me a long time to think of it as home and now—' He cleared his throat. 'But you're right. It's ridiculous, the two of us rattling around here like this.' He managed a small smile. 'Have you told Rosa yet?'

Shaking his head, Janos frowned. 'Not yet. I wanted to speak to you first.' He screwed up his face. 'I must admit I'm a little worried about telling her.'

Laszlo pursed his lips. 'She'll be fine once she gets used to the idea.' He smiled. 'And as long as she gets to fuss around *you* she'll be happy wherever she lives.' Looking up at his grandfather, he hesitated. 'Which sort of brings me to my next question... Where exactly are you planning on us living?'

Janos let out a breath. 'That would rather depend on Prudence.'

Prudence felt her fingers curl painfully around her glass as both men turned to stare at her. 'M-me? Why does it depend on *me*?' she stammered.

'Because I was rather hoping that after the cataloguing is complete you might consider staying on,' Janos said gently. 'That's why I want you to be here now. So I can ask you if you would like to be the museum's curator.'

Prudence stared at him speechlessly. Stay on? In Hungary? With Laszlo?

Finally, she found her voice. 'I—I'm not... I don't know what to say...' she faltered.

Janos laughed. 'Of course you don't. How could you? Please don't look so worried, Prudence. I'm not expecting you to give me an answer right now,' he said hastily. 'I'm just hoping you might think about it over the next few days. Or weeks. Take as long as you like.'

Heart pounding, Prudence gave a weak smile. 'Thank you. And thank you for thinking of me,' she said slowly.

Janos laughed. 'My dear, I didn't think of anyone else.' He frowned. 'I must confess before you came I was quite worried about how everything would work. You know—having a stranger in our home. But you coming here has been a blessing.' He glanced across to Laszlo, his lined face creasing into a smile. 'And you're part of our family now—isn't she, Laszlo?'

Almost intoxicated by hope and longing, Prudence glanced across at Laszlo—and her bubbling happiness began to ebb away. For, meeting his gaze, she saw from his face that he shared none of her pleasure or excitement.

She felt panic clutch at her chest as he stared at her in silence, smiling unsteadily, a strange, unfamiliar light glittering in his eyes.

Abruptly he stood up and cleared his throat. 'I'm going to go back to the party. Make sure everything's okay. And you need to get some sleep, Papi. It's been a very long night for you. And this can wait until morning. We don't want to push Miss Elliot into a decision she regrets.'

Her body tensed as he turned, but he didn't even look at her as he walked out of the room. Pain and panic tore through her as she watched him leave. For one terrible, agonising moment she wanted to go after him and pull him back. Demand that he stay and explain. But she stopped herself. Laszlo had never been much good with words, but on this occasion he didn't need to be. He didn't need to explain anything. His actions were loud enough.

He didn't want her to stay.

He didn't want her at all.

It was nearly time to leave. The *vardo* gleamed in the late-morning sun. Gently Prudence ran her hand over the gold-painted scrolls and garlands and bouquets of flowers. It was truly a labour of love. For the craftsman who'd made it, at least. She bit her lip.

Slowly she walked up the steps, touching, feeling the wood smooth and warm beneath her fingers. Picking up a pillow from the bed, she closed her eyes and inhaled: woodsmoke and orange blossom. It was his scent, but even as she inhaled it seemed to fade. Opening her eyes, she crawled onto the bed and stared bleakly out of the window. From where she lay the castle seemed to fill the tiny square of glass entirely, blocking out the light.

Just as Laszlo had dominated her life from the moment she'd met him seven years ago.

Rolling onto her back, she closed her eyes.

They had come so close to making it work.

Yesterday, for the first time ever, he had opened up to her about so many things. His family…his fears. Her breath caught in her throat. He had needed her emotionally—wanted her support. And she had let herself believe that it meant something, for it had felt as if something had changed between them. As if there had been some shift in the fundament of their relationship.

Her heart gave a painful lurch. But of course, as with so much of their relationship, nothing was what it seemed.

She shivered, remembering Laszlo's face when Janos had called her one of the family. She could have ignored his reaction. Let it go. As she'd let so many other things go because she'd feared losing him. But she didn't fear losing him any more.

On the contrary—what she'd feared most was that she wouldn't be strong enough to leave him.

Her eyes grew hot and damp. It had been so, so hard the last time. She drew in a breath. But she had got over it eventually. And she would do so again. In time, and with distance between them. Which was why she'd gone to find Janos that morning and told him that she needed to go home for a few days. She'd used the excuse that she needed to talk through his offer with Edmund and he'd agreed immediately, as she'd known he would. Jakob had even pulled strings so that a seat had been found for her on a plane leaving that evening.

Opening her eyes, she covered her mouth with her hand, trying to hold back her misery. Part of her wanted to stay. The part that felt as if it was disintegrating. But what would be the point? Her love wasn't enough for Laszlo; *she* wasn't enough for him.

She lifted her chin and the knot of misery in her stomach began to loosen. She was not about to crumble. Laszlo might not love her but she still had her self-respect. And if she wanted to avoid the same fate as her mother, diminished and worn down by unrequited love, she needed to get away from him.

That meant leaving Hungary. And never coming back.

It was the first time she'd acknowledged that fact— if not out loud then in her head. But she knew it was the right—the only choice she had. She needed to be where her judgement wasn't skewed by her heart. That was why she was going home to her family.

She glanced up at the sky and frowned. And why she needed to start packing.

Back at the cottage, suitcase packed, she walked dully from room to room, checking for anything she might have forgotten. With a stab of pain she noticed Laszlo's dinner jacket, hanging on the back of the kitchen door. He'd draped it over her shoulders when they'd left the party and she'd still been wearing it later when, dumb and still shivering from shock, she had let Janos get Gregor, the handyman and chauffeur, to escort her back to the cottage.

She lifted her chin. She would give it to him at lunchtime. Despite eating breakfast at the cottage, she'd resigned herself to the fact that seeing him one last time was inevitable. At least with Janos there there would be no risk of her losing control and throwing a bowl of soup in his face.

But at lunchtime Laszlo's seat was conspicuously empty.

Janos was apologetic. 'He didn't come down for breakfast either. He's probably with Mihaly,' he said, trying to sound encouraging as Prudence tried and failed to eat the delicious lunch Rosa had made especially for her. 'I'm sure he'll be here any moment.'

But he hadn't appeared.

Later, waiting at the airport, she felt almost sick with nerves, for part of her had stupidly hoped that he would come after her.

It was only when she was boarding the plane that she knew that it was really, finally over.

Glancing wearily out of the window, she watched the patchwork of green and brown fields disappear beneath the clouds. It was better that it had ended like this, with her on her own. There would be nothing to haunt her now, for that last evening in Janos's study seemed to have fled her memory.

Outside, everything had turned white, and she felt

something like peace slide over her. For even though it had been hard to leave, and it was going to be much, much harder to learn to live without him again, she didn't regret what had happened. Finally she could accept that she and Laszlo would never have a future together. And, more importantly, she'd learned that there was nothing to fear from the past: her mother's choices did not have to be hers.

She had the power to shape her life. Finally, she could face the future without fear or regret.

She shivered. Closing her eyes, she shrugged her coat over her body. But that was the future—right now she just wanted to get warm. Only, huddling into her jacket, she doubted she would ever feel warm again…

Staring at the museum's sprinklers longingly, Prudence sighed. If only she could set them off… But, even though it was her last day at work, she couldn't imagine herself ruining hundreds of priceless artefacts in exchange for one blissfully cool shower.

She scowled. London was in the grip of an Indian summer and she was sick of the heat. Tucking a strand of limp hair behind her ear, she took a breath of warm air and began to speak.

'And this is the cast of the Belvedere Apollo.' Gesturing to the statue in front of her, Prudence turned to the crowd of tourists gathered expectantly around her and smiled. 'It's a copy made for Lord Burlington in Italy, sometime around 1719. Before it came to the museum it was held at Chiswick House.'

She paused and glanced around at the faces staring up at her. Since leaving Seymour's she had been working part-time at the museum, and although she'd enjoyed it she was looking forward to leaving. These people were her last tour group. And after that—

She bit her lip. After that she'd take it one day at a time.

What was important was that Daisy and Edmund had been so understanding and so supportive. About everything. And, although she would of course like to get a place of her own, she had agreed to keep on living with them for the immediate future.

She looked up and took a breath. 'The Belvedere Apollo takes its name from the Belvedere Palace in the Vatican, where it has resided since the early fifteen-hundreds. The sculpture depicts the Greek god Apollo as an archer. He is nude except for his sandals and a robe slung over his shoulders.'

Pausing, she took another breath. It felt hotter than Greece in the museum, and suddenly she remembered the crisp, cold mornings in Hungary. For a fraction of a second, her smile faltered but, gripping her clipboard tightly, she ploughed on.

'That concludes our tour this morning. If you have any questions, please don't hesitate to ask. I hope you enjoy the rest of your visit to the museum and your stay in London. Thank you.'

Picking up her handbag from behind the desk, she walked towards the hallway, where the air conditioning greeted her like a fridge door opening. Fanning her face, she sat down and closed her eyes.

'Excuse me?'

For a moment, her brain was in free fall and then her eyes flew open as she thought she recognised his voice. But it couldn't be him, could it? Why would Laszlo be in London? He hadn't even bothered to say goodbye.

The sun was in her eyes. At first she could make out only a blurred dark shape. But then she saw his outline, and the breath seemed to freeze in her throat.

He stepped out of the light and she felt her legs slide away from under her.

He caught her as she fell.

'Here…'

She felt his hands, warm and firm, guide her into a seat. Her head was spinning.

'Drink this.'

Water from the water cooler. So cold and fresh it might have come from one of the streams that criss-crossed the fields around his castle.

She moaned and Laszlo crouched down by her side, holding a glass to her lips.

'Just sip it.'

The noise of traffic surged into the room as downstairs a door was opened.

'Are you okay, Miss Elliot?' Now Joe, the doorman, was leaning over her. 'Do you want me to get a doctor?'

She shook her head. 'No. Thank you.'

And then Laszlo stood up, his body screening her from Joe's anxious face. 'I've got it from here.'

He spoke pleasantly, but some alarm must have shown on her face, for Joe stood his ground. 'And you are, sir...?'

'I'm her husband!'

There was a tense silence, and then she heard Joe's feet retreating across the tiled floor.

She was suddenly furious. 'What are you doing here?'

He ignored her question. 'Finish your water.'

'Answer my question!' She glared at him.

He studied her impassively. 'I will. After you've finished the water.'

Swallowing her anger first, she drained the cup and handed it to him. 'Now answer my question!'

'Surely you should be answering *my* questions? After all, you *do* work here.'

She stared at him in disbelief and then, reaching up, pulled her name badge off her shirt and dropped it in the bin. 'Not any more!' She glared at him and then abruptly stood up. 'Goodbye, Laszlo!' she said quietly. 'I hope you enjoy the rest of your visit to the museum and your stay in London.'

He regarded her calmly and then, as she took a step forward, moved in front of her.

She shot him a frustrated glance. 'Could you move, please?'

He stood silently in front of her and she shook her head and looked away from him. 'You can stand there all day if you want. I'm used to silent men made of stone.' Her hands clenched at her sides. 'But it won't change anything. I have nothing left to say to you.'

He waited until finally, reluctantly, she turned to face him. 'Quite a lot to write, though, it would appear,' he said. 'About ending our marriage.'

She watched wordlessly as he reached into his pocket and pulled out an envelope. Her skin was suddenly tight across her face and she felt cornered. And then she met his gaze, for she wasn't going to let him intimidate her.

'What about it?' she said shortly. 'I told you in Hungary that I wanted a divorce. I still do. There's no point leaving things as they are.'

'And how *are* things?' His voice was hoarse. 'You see, I thought you were happy.'

She shook her head in exasperation. 'I was. I *am*. But when did my happiness matter to you, Laszlo? You only care about yourself, and you didn't look too happy when your grandfather asked me to stay on as curator. Or when he called me one of the family.'

She felt a stab of pain at the memory and suddenly could barely see his face through her tears.

'In fact, you were so happy you walked off.'

His face tightened. Running his hand through his hair, he said slowly, 'I didn't want you to—'

'Didn't want me to stay. I know—'

'No.' He cut her off. 'I didn't want my grandfather to

rush you. You seemed unsure, and he was so desperate for you to agree. I thought he'd just keep on pushing and—'

'And you thought I'd say yes?' Her voice rose and she shook her head. 'So you decided to talk it over with me and your grandfather.' She paused, her lip curling contemptuously. 'Oh, no. You *didn't*. You walked out.'

Laszlo looked at her, his expression bleak. Finally he nodded. 'Yes. I walked away. I didn't know what else to do. So much had happened between us, but so much still wasn't resolved. Like us being married. I knew if you agreed to take the job then you'd come back. And not just for a couple of weeks this time.'

Prudence felt like throwing up. 'Imagine that,' she said flatly. 'No *wonder* you couldn't wait to get away.'

She took a painful breath as he shook his head.

'I wasn't thinking about me. I knew *you'd* have a problem with that.'

Staring at him incredulously, she gave a humourless laugh. 'Not as big a problem as you.' Pausing, she gritted her teeth. 'I don't really understand what you're trying to say, Laszlo. But you know what? I don't care any more.'

'I do!'

He practically shouted the words and she took a step back from him.

'I care. And I cared in Hungary. You *hated* lying to my grandfather about us. And I knew it would be a problem doing it again. And for so long. I thought if he pushed you, you'd panic and say no—'

His voice cracked and she stared at him in shock.

'And I didn't want you to.'

For a moment she thought she must have misheard him. She opened her mouth and then closed it again. Her breath was burning her throat. 'Why?' she said shakily. 'Why didn't you want me to say no?'

He stared at her and then bowed his head. 'Because I love you.'

Her heart twisted inside her. 'Don't say that, Laszlo.'

Tears sprang to her eyes as he reached out and, taking her hands, raised them to his lips.

'I *will* say it.'

He looked up and she saw that his face was wet with tears.

'I will say it. And I'll keep on saying it until you believe me. I love you. I only worked it out when we talked about my parents and their marriage, and I realised that I'd only believed in *their* love and not mine.' He grimaced. 'I should have just come right out and told you, but...' He smiled weakly. 'I'm so bad at this stuff.'

He shook his head.

'I have trouble explaining it to myself. Let alone to the person I'm so scared of losing.'

She stared at him in exasperation. 'So you thought it would be a good idea to make me believe that our relationship was only about sex?'

'I'm an idiot.'

'So it wasn't?'

He screwed up his face. 'Maybe a little bit—at the beginning. When I was angry and mean.' He let out a ragged sigh. 'But I'm only flesh and blood, and I don't think you have any idea how sexy you looked in that blouse and skirt and those heels.'

He bit his lip.

'But it changed. *I* changed. I wanted more. I wanted my wife back! I was going to tell you before the party but I bottled out.' Letting go of her hand, he sighed. 'If only I'd let you open the *putsi* when you wanted to,' he said sadly.

Prudence reached into her handbag and pulled out the small leather bag that she hadn't been able to face discarding.

He stared at it as though mesmerised. 'Open it!'

His voice was husky and she pulled clumsily at the cord. With shaking fingers she tipped the bag upside down and into her hand tumbled an acorn, a key and a beautiful diamond ring.

She felt suddenly faint again. But this time with happiness. 'Oh, Laszlo!' she whispered.

'Prudence—' He reached out hesitantly and, taking the ring from her hand, slid it onto her finger.

'I thought you didn't want me,' she said, tears rolling over her cheeks.

He stepped close to her and took her hands in his. 'And I thought you didn't want *me*.' His voice cracked. 'After the party I went to Mihaly and I told him everything.' He clenched his teeth. 'He told me to stop being such an idiot and tell you how I felt.' He smiled ruefully. 'Actually, he didn't quite use those words. They were slightly more colourful.'

Prudence laughed.

His smile faded. 'But when I got back to the castle you'd gone.' He took a breath. 'Then I lost it and I told my grandfather everything as well.'

Prudence bit her lip. 'And…?'

Frowning, Laszlo pulled her closer. 'He told me I was an idiot too.'

She pulled away slightly and smiled. 'I wish I'd stayed after all,' she said teasingly. There was a brief silence, and then she said hesitantly, 'Were they angry?'

Laszlo shook his head. 'No. They were delighted. In fact, I think they thought I was quite lucky to catch you. And they love you already. Almost as much as I do.' His face tightened, grew suddenly strained. 'I just wish my grandmother was here. She so wanted to see me married and with a family of my own.'

He gave her an unsteady smile.

'I'm warning you now. You think my grandfather was pushy about you taking the curator's job? Just wait until my aunts hear that I'm married!'

'Never mind your aunts. What about *you*? Do you want children?'

He grinned. 'Yeah, I do. Loads. At least seven.'

'Seven?' she squeaked.

He nodded, suddenly serious. 'One for every year we were apart,' he murmured, tightening his grip around her waist.

She smiled. 'I see. I suppose we should get started, then?'

He grinned. 'Definitely! I'd like to be a father as soon as possible. Like in about nine months. Do you think that's possible?'

She kissed him gently on the lips. 'I can do it in seven.'

He looked at her blankly. 'Seven? You mean nine.'

In reply, she took his hand and put it gently on her stomach. 'No. I mean seven.'

He stared down at the slight bump of her belly. 'Really?'

She nodded. 'Really!'

Pulling her gently into his arms, he closed his eyes, too choked to speak. 'Only another six to go,' he whispered against her cheek—and then abruptly, he released her and took a step back, his face clouding over.

'What is it?' She stared at him anxiously.

He let out a long breath. 'Everything moved pretty fast after you left. Papi and Rosa have moved into the cottage, but…' He frowned. 'As of tomorrow I'm going to be homeless.'

'Oh,' she said slowly. 'Actually, this really is my last day at work. So, as of now, I'm unemployed.'

They stared at each other in silence, and then both of them burst out laughing.

'For better for worse,' he said softly.

She felt his gaze drift over her face. 'For richer for poorer!' she murmured.

He grinned, and then his smile faded. 'Don't worry. I'm not going to make you live in a trailer.'

'I don't mind—' she began, but he shook his head, grimacing.

'No. But I do.' A faint flush coloured his cheeks. 'I know I shouldn't really say it, but I don't really like living in trailers.' He shivered. 'They're even draughtier than the castle!'

Prudence giggled.

Reaching down, he picked up her hand and fiddled with the ring on her finger. 'I guess, with the pregnancy and everything, you'd like to live near your family?'

Frowning, she nodded slowly. 'Actually, I *am* living with them. They wanted to be there to help me when the baby comes.'

He stared at her anxiously. 'And that's what you still want, is it?'

Smiling weakly, Prudence leant against him and rubbed her cheek against his. 'No. I want to live with my husband. But I *do* want to be near them.' She sighed. 'It's such a shame. The cottage next door came up for sale and that would have been perfect. But it never even went on the open market. Apparently the buyer offered twice the asking price. I'm not sure why…'

Laszlo gazed at her steadily. 'Maybe he liked the location.' His hand tightened around hers and their eyes met.

She stared at him, confused. And then she realised that he was waiting—waiting for her to understand. '*You* bought it?'

He nodded, his face creasing into a smile. 'Yes. I think your neighbour thought I was insane.' He groaned. 'It's probably the first time ever that a Romany has paid more than the asking price!' His smile tightened. 'But I had to have it. You see, I wasn't sure you'd even speak to me—'

'So you thought you'd stalk me?' Prudence shook off his hand. But her eyes were dancing.

'I thought if I lived next door you wouldn't be able to avoid me,' he said softly. 'Then all I'd have to do was wear down your resistance.'

'Is that right? And how, exactly, were you going to do that?'

She felt her stomach flutter as his eyes narrowed.

'Let me show you,' he murmured, and then he pulled her into his arms and kissed her until, for the third time that afternoon, she thought she'd faint.

* * * * *

**Don't miss Sarah Morgan's
next Puffin Island story**

*Some Kind
of Wonderful*

Brittany Forrest has stayed away from Puffin Island
since her relationship with Zach Flynn went bad.
They were married for ten days and only just
managed not to kill each other by the
end of the honeymoon.

But, when a broken arm means she must return,
Brittany moves back to her Puffin Island home.
Only to discover that Zac is there as well.

Will a summer together help two lovers reunite or
will their stormy relationship crash on to the
rocks of Puffin Island?

Some Kind of Wonderful
COMING JULY 2015
Pre-order your copy today